Enemy Self

Enemy Self

By

Suzanne Kovitz

Enemy Self

Copyright © 2016

Third Edition 2025

Second Edition 2024

by Suzanne Kovitz

ISBN: 979-886933620-0

ASIN: B011P2U97K

ACKNOWLEGEMENT

I wish to thank everyone who helped me edit this long-awaited novel. Without their continued professional efforts and support, I would not have been able to bring my work to a successful completion: Kori Chaney, Proofreader, Tanya Y. Stokes, Proofreader, Tonya Blust, Copyeditor; and last but, not least, Rosemary Lawton, Copyeditor for second edition.

In memory of Terri Kane who organized the BJWG, for her excellence of service at heading the writers' group, offering support and motivation each, and every month.

Special thanks to my amazingly witty friend Arlene Friedland for her technical support in the exhaustive creation of the first paperback version. As a team, we learned the process of mastering self-publishing together from editing to Photoshop manipulation. And, of course, my recent husband, Dan Sherr for his thorough review and edits.

Second edition cover art was produced by GetCovers based in Ukraine. I highly recommend them as they are affordable and work diligently and patiently to suite customer needs.

The third edition cover design was designed by Qurat Z. from Quratz Creative in Pakistan. Qurat has higher level skills in Photoshop manipulation.

A NOTE FROM SUZANNE

I've always been enamored by creative "outside the box" thinking such as in the "Twilight Zone". Enemy Self is a mystery/thriller based on a dream I experienced shortly after graduating college.

There is little to no reference within the plot regarding my personal life. I merely stepped outside of myself to depict a wild boisterous character. It was the biggest challenge for me as a writer. However, I highlighted a few social issues such as bullying, rape, incest, prostitution, and dope.

An important message that I wish to emphasize: no matter how hard life may seem, never, never, never give up. Try to learn from your harrowing experiences.

This work of fiction is a cross-genre piece. The story takes place in the 1970s in a self-created world in which I, the author, wish to escape. A world apart in imagination and yet so eerily close to home.

WARNING: This work contains strong language and adult subject matter.

Table of Contents

THE NIGHTMARE

Confused, I'm standing here waiting. I don't know why. I'm holding a popped notebook binder cluttered with loose papers, while clinging onto the remnants of a broken pencil in my right hand. I'm in the middle of a crowded corridor at Eastwood Middle School. The white institutional walls are lined with lockers. At the end of the aisle stands a glass enclosure filled with framed yearbook photos, award certificates, and trophies. Updated policies and procedures are posted throughout. Still, I haven't a clue as to why I'm here. I just wait.

Boisterous students shove past me, ignoring me. They hustle to their lockers for coats and books then slam the metal doors shut. Friends wave good-bye to one another, slapping high-fives, hugging, and shouting from across the hall. Excitement glows in the eyes of each student as they will be free from the constraints of the school system for the rest of the day. Teachers patrol the lobby while the crowd scurries to leave. However, I'm deeply saddened because I can't join them.

Suddenly, all the students and teachers vanish into thin air. The corridor is now dim and silent, devoid of people and objects. The full moon gleams through the lobby door windows. I envision a coyote howling at the moon. Why is there a full moon? Why is there a moon at all? The school closes around 3:00 pm. According to my wristwatch, it is now 6:00 pm. This means that the school has been closed for three hours. Am I locked in the school building? I take a deep breath, fully aware that something is seriously wrong. I'm more apprehensive with each passing moment in the dead silence. How much longer must I wait?

As the answer comes to me, I squeeze my eyes shut, avoiding the dreadful thoughts. I should have known all along why I'm waiting. There is someone in this building with me.

Her shadow approaches me in the darkness. I step back, fearing her presence. She stands before me. She's about 5'6", with wavy dark brunette hair and blue eyes. As usual she's wearing her black leather jacket. Dangling chains hang fastened to the back pocket of her skin-tight jeans. Yep, that's her alright—Denise Bower, the unrelenting, crazed bully of ninth grade. Great, two non- negotiable enemies of adolescence in a boxing ring within the confines of a closed school building. What a raw deal!

She sneers at me. The silent tension builds between us. We enter into a mad staring contest. Just as I muster the strength to assert myself . . .

"I hate your guts!" She bares her teeth in my face.

"Why?" is all I can utter.

"You are such a fuckin' loser. I hate you," she articulates.

"W-what did I do?" I stutter, lowering my head like a coward, trying to avoid eye contact. At a time like this, I could use a bodyguard. "You pick on me all the time. You-you popped my notebook, shredded my papers, broke my pencil and took my lunch money . . ." I sigh, noticing the tremor in my hand. "You threatened to beat me up."

She bluntly replies, "That wasn't a threat. I meant it!" With raspy breathing and sadism in her eyes, she is ready for the kill. I'm about to get creamed. What was I thinking staying after school hours for this? Since I'm not a fighter, there's no way I can win this match. It's as if she'd willed me to stay after school.

She's not in the least bit impressed by my modest demonstration of courage. In fact, she's enraged. No, it's beyond rage—much more bizarre. Her head jerks around involuntarily. I watch in bewilderment, trying to stifle a scream. Her youthful olive skin reshapes into thick, dense flesh. She's growing massive in size with shaggy black fur penetrating through her pores. Oversized cat-shaped eyeballs pop out from her sockets. Her overbite protrudes outward like fangs of a wolf. She's foaming at the mouth! Globs of blood ooze from the cracks in her dry lips. Her face forms a muzzle on the wolf-like head. Whiskers spread across her cheeks. Docked ears pop out at the sides of her head. Her nails jet out into black claws. This is no seizure, Denise Bower is transforming from a middle school biker into a . . . werewolf!

Frozen in place, I'm in shock witnessing her metamorphosis. Hands over mouth, I can't avoid shrieking. It's as though my guts have jumped out and taken off without me.

Before I'm given the chance to escape, the thing grabs onto my collar and yanks me toward it! Its sharp claws dig into the fabric of my shirt as I jolt back in retreat; my collar is torn and severed as I free myself from the beast. I run like mad from hall to hall in search of a hiding place. Unfortunately, door after door is locked, forcing me to run into the unknown darkness.

My shadow follows me as I come full circle around the maze.

At each corner I poke my head out, but there is no sign of its presence anywhere.

Standing perfectly still, I listen for sounds, but the halls remain silent. I can only hear my own nervous pant.

The moment I turn down the wrong path, the werewolf approaches! I flinch, spin around, and yet another werewolf appears, coming at me from the opposite direction. What, more than one? I struggle to force a locked classroom door open. With no other options at hand, I slam my body weight against the door, trying to break it down. Too late, the werewolves have me cornered.

I cower in a fetal position, hiding my face, wishing them away. Their wicked snarls and growls close in on me. Claws force my hands away from my face, restraining them to the cold tile floor. Lying on my back, I squint at the dim ceiling light bulbs.

The werewolves are holding a syringe. "We've got you, my pretty!" Their wicked laughter echoes. I'm completely defenseless. "Please, no!" I beg. Regardless of my protest, I feel a stinging prick in my arm. My vision blurs. The walls appear to bounce around me faster, and, faster. The motion is making me dizzy. I see millions of eyeballs, fangs, claws, and light bulbs spin around in a fierce circle before me. Everything else is dark. My strength is instantly depleted. I feel sick and faint. Within seconds I shiver; chills spread though my body. All becomes darkness. All that I see are specks of light resembling stars of the nighttime sky. I'm paralyzed! Scared. What did they do to me?

Buzz-ring-snap. Pressure builds up in my inner ears as if I'm moving up great heights at warp speed. The specks have disappeared. Now there's nothing but darkness. No more ringing. I hear nothing. Not even my own breathing. I feel an enormous wave-like pressure on my body pulling on me, spinning me, sucking me into some sort of vacuum. Could this be a black hole where you get sucked up and then you disappear altogether? I'm in a state of total panic. Am I going someplace? What's happening? My screams are inaudible. In fact, I can't seem to feel anything anymore. No pain, no . . . nothing. Am I . . . dead?

TRAPPED

Bzzz . . . I was abruptly awakened by a buzzer. Reaching over to shut down the chatterbox, my fingers groped from button to button. A side switch silenced the alarm, finally. Once again, I was at peace, sighing contently. What an awful nightmare I had, I thought back, chuckling that I couldn't even remember the dream.

Taking a deep breath, I inhaled the unfamiliar scent of bacon. As I looked around the bedroom, I was completely disoriented. I mean, I didn't know where the hell I was. I couldn't focus either — blurry vision. Something just didn't feel right. I knew I wasn't in my own bed. I sank into the pillow, making myself comfortable under the stinky sheets. I needed to exit from dream hopping. Just as I got cozy, my stomach felt giddy, and my head throbbed. This was not the time or place to be getting sick, when I don't know where I was.

I sat up to stretch, rubbing my eyes. I saw someone off in the distance . . . a faceless man with an oversized circus hat and blue jacket. Blinking a few times, I tried to focus on him. He was looking right at me, motionless. Straining, I saw his stern, authoritative eyes as he pointed his index finger toward me. Fortunately, my vision cleared a bit more. I was staring at the old patriotic Uncle Sam poster. His white and blue hat was much larger than his head, and the big, black, bold phrase below, I WANT YOU TO VOTE, was hard to miss.

So, where was I? This ain't no motel chain. Appeared to be someone's bedroom. The morning sun piercing through the curtains shed some light on the fuzziness. This place was a mess. Various collages of male centerfolds, celebrity pin-ups, and rock' n roll posters decorated the walls and ceiling. Piles of clothes and junk were scattered about the floor. Clothes, belts, sports equipment, and board games bulged out through a crack in the closet door.

I was stumped. Whose bedroom could this possibly be? One suited for a teenager with a lot of unchanneled energy and a high sex drive. So why was I here? I jogged my memory for answers. Let's see . . . Monday . . . nothing. Tuesday . . . Science test. Wednesday . . . I spent the afternoon studying with Stephanie. Thursday . . . I don't remember . . . oh yes, that was the new unit on botany in science class. And I believe Friday I got together with Ann Millian after gym, which didn't explain a thing. Maybe I visited a relative on vacation or . . . or, I shuddered at the thought of being kidnapped and drugged.

My head throbbed again. Whatever the reason, I felt like I had a hangover. I badly needed aspirin. I had to get out of the bed to search for it. Carefully, one leg at a time, I set my feet to the floor. I was now standing upright. Progress. Something about standing was different. I think overnight I grew taller. As I took my first step, the carpet appeared to travel with me. I could not feel a thing under my bare feet. It was as if I were walking on air. A sudden wave of dizziness came over me . . .

Again, I awoke. But this time I was lying on the carpet. I didn't know why I passed out. Though my vision improved, the headache worsened. Without wasting another moment, I got up off the floor, darted into the bathroom, the room directly across from the bedroom, locked the door, and flicked the light switch on.

The bathroom was awesomely decorated with ladies' pocketbooks wallpaper. Even the hand towels hanging over the towel bar had matching pocketbook prints of sorts. Light bulbs above the mirror offered a soft yellow glow. If I could only show Mom this cool bathroom with such character.

I only glanced at the mirrored cabinets when I noticed her reflection. I had to do a double take to be sure my eyes weren't deceiving me. Recoiling, I screamed! I covered my mouth hoping no one heard. I dared myself to look into that mirror again. I had to be sure I wasn't seeing things; after all, my vision wasn't very reliable. Looking a second time, I was mesmerized, standing barefoot and baffled. The mirror depicted me, Jessica Wheaton, as Denise Bower—one of the bullies of my high school.

It had to be some form of trickery. I needed to prove to myself that this was a practical joke brought on by illusion. I examined every angle of the mirror. The image copied my every move and expression precisely. It almost had me convinced that I wasn't me. I mean, I knew I was wearing the identical clothes in the identical bathroom but under the surface, flesh and bones, I was not her. For a moment I almost doubted my own existence. I stripped off the stinky oversized T-shirt I had apparently slept in to examine my bare body against the mirrored image.

As absurd as it may seem, I became paranoid that someone was watching me explore myself. I was almost certain that this was some sort of set-up, and the sponsor of such an ingenious joke would, at any moment, jump out at me.

I stood three inches taller. My face was plagued with zits and moles. Yuck! But the slanting eyebrows were nicely shaped, and my dark complexion was a plus. But the long pointy- tipped European nose wasn't so cool and that hair . . . what happened to the auburn?

It's brunette-beige and . . . slightly oily—no body. Yuck again. Oh-my-God! My ears were pierced. Momma would never permit me to get that done before graduation. And what about the developed chest? Definitely adds to a good figure. But the belly will have to go. I could do without the extra fat. Well, I guess it's a trade-off.

The headache pounded again. I opened the mirrored cabinet in search of a bottle of aspirin. In the process of ransacking, I found various medications—everything from liquid bottles to tissue-covered pills, cough drops, allergy remedies, hand cream, nasal sprays, prescriptions, and ooh—here's a bottle of Bayer Aspirin. After carefully reaching in for the weightless bottle out from behind the clutter of remedies, I hurriedly twisted it open only to find it empty. "DAMN IT!" I tossed it aside. Suddenly waves of nausea came over me. I vomited into the sink. It was very embarrassing throwing up in some stranger's sink but, I couldn't help it. The sick urges just kept coming. I was moaning, holding onto the sink ledge until I was exhausted. The headache had finally subsided.

"Dini?" a mature voice asked from behind the door. I gasped! She must have been Denise's mother. "Is everything alright in there? I thought I heard you scream."

"I'm fine." I cleared my throat, sounding like Denise. *Lovely*, I thought to myself. I snatched a bunch of toilet tissue to wipe my mouth, then rinsed the sink bowl clean with water.

"You'll be late for school if you don't hurry," she cautioned. "Breakfast is ready."

Dini? What a weird nickname. Then again, her friends called her by that name. "I'm not really hungry," I tried to brush the lady off. After throwing up, food was the last thing I wanted.

"I'm warning you. Don't play sick again. You must go to school today. You can't miss another day, Dini. You've missed too many days already this school year." She paused with a huff. "I think it's about time you changed your attitude toward school, young lady. Now I made something for you to eat, and I expect you to come down in a few minutes." Luckily, she walked away from the door.

I turned on the cold-water faucet to splash it against my burning face. SHE gazed into my eyes with horror. SHE was nervous. "You did this. This is your fault," I accused. "How did you do this?" I asked the reflection. "Answer me!" I demanded. "Why did I throw up?" I questioned her. "Don't you see I'm trapped? How am I supposed to appear in public like this and pretend that I am you? Had you given this any thought before you meddled with me?" I was talking to myself, waiting for an explanation from the reflection. I felt hopelessly dehumanized as if she did this to humiliate me. I wondered what I had done to deserve such punishment.

I tried to think clearly. How could this be? This wasn't scientifically possible. More importantly, what could I do about this? I had to go on living with two separate identities. This would definitely make an unprecedented case. Should I consult a witch doctor and explain to her that I got trapped in someone else's body—please use some sort of voodoo to switch me back?

Or should I see a clinical psychiatrist who would then admit me to a mental hospital for shock treatment? "Denise, you got me good this time." I held back tears of despair. What other curses did she plan to zap me with next? I felt like putting my fist through the damn mirror.

The lady knocked on the door again. She startled me. "C'mon Dini," she pestered. I couldn't just open the door and allow myself to be revealed. I mean . . . suppose in her eyes I'm Jessica? How could I explain my presence in her house? Worse, what if she thinks I'm her daughter, but I don't pull off the act?

Fortunately, she walked away. Feeling faint, I leaned against the wall, slid to the floor, and settled in a fetal position. I wished I could just hide in a paper bag. Unanswered questions kept pouring in. Why was I sick? Did this mean that Denise was walking around in my body, having breakfast with my folks? I hoped Mom kept precious Daphne away from her. Gosh, she'd better not find my allowance or jewelry. What if Denise located my diary? She'd tell everyone at school all my secrets. Bet she wouldn't find the buried key.

Tears came streaming down my cheeks. My finger touched a teardrop. This teardrop assured me that I wouldn't lose grip with my inner being. Perhaps all that really changed was my appearance. I had to have faith that somehow, I could escape this nightmare. I was feeling better, ready to open the bathroom door. Besides, I got tired of looking at the reflection of my worst enemy. I held my breath and opened the door cautiously. The coast was clear. I darted around the hallway toward the staircase to exit the Bower residence. This is how I would like my dream to end.

TRAPPED II

Not-so-fast. Denise's father caught me in my tracks. He approached me as he adjusted his tie. He must have been preparing for work. "What took you so long in there?" he motioned. "Did you oversleep again?" Waving his finger in my face, he warned, "You best skip breakfast, young lady. You're not missing another class."

Mr. Bower was livid. My lips were sealed. I was in no position to argue with the Gestapo. I nodded in compliance.

"Are you feeling alright?" he asked.

"Yeah, why?"

"Are you high?" he accused.

"No," I almost laughed at the thought. May have been intoxicated but never stoned. "Just a headache," I assured, grinning.

He grunted, "Then you better get your ass moving to school on time," pointing to the front door.

Turning toward the staircase, I bumped into Denise's mother. The lady tapped me on the shoulder. "Watch your step, dear." I stared at her for the longest time. She resembled Denise—I mean, Denise resembled her, except her mother was a much more attractive version than I pictured. Mrs. Bower had a rather youthful complexion, though her elegant exterior defined her personality.

"Denise?" She felt my head. "Are you feeling alright?"

"I'm fine . . . just a headache. I was searching for aspirin."

The couple looked at each other. They had a firm conviction that I was on something when I repeatedly told them I only had a headache.

The lady held my chin firmly, examining my eyes. "Denise, tell me the truth." She described to him, "Her pupils are dilated, and eyes are blood-shot, Ray!"

"I feel fine, really," I assured her, uselessly. What could I say or do to prove to the Bowers that I was telling the truth?

She insisted, "What are you on? Don't lie to me. I can tell you're on something." The couple grew impatient with my reluctance to cooperate. They wanted me to say what they wanted to hear, that I'd been doing dope when I hadn't. I never did. It was a futile dispute. I felt like crawling under a rock.

"Just tell me the truth," the lady insisted, shaking her hands in my face in frustration.

I didn't utter another word. I'm not their child, and I don't have to own up to them, I reasoned. Besides, they wouldn't believe me no matter what I'd say.

Abruptly, Ray darted into Denise's bedroom. At his discretion, he ransacked through her possessions. Moments later he cursed, "Goddamn, she took Ecstasy, again!"

That couldn't be—it must have been a set-up. I had to act fast. Wasting no time, I disappeared from the dark hallway, down the staircase, across the living room, and over to the front door. The couple remained distracted temporarily as they argued over my peculiar behavior, suspecting that I popped the Ecstasy pills in the bathroom.

"Dini, don't you dare leave the premises of this house," Ray yelled.

I encountered great difficulty getting the front door to open. The knob wouldn't give. This was no time for guesswork. After releasing the deadbolt, the door still refused to budge. I heard mad buffalo rush toward me. *Any second now!* I studied the damn lock. There were no key inserts or buttons to push. *C'mon!* I urged. It came to me a moment too late. The lock was broken so a little metal spring had to be pressed back.

Once the door opened, I inhaled the aroma of flowers and fresh-cut grass. The tailored landscaped property of trimmed topiary trees and green garden glistened against the morning sunshine. It was breathtakingly beautiful. Breathing in the fresh air was just what I needed.

Suddenly, a set of knuckles gripped me by the collar, jerking me away from the awesome view, choking me.

"Where do you think you're going?" He pushed me up against the wall. I was presented with an open bottle of pills. "Who gave you this?" he interrogated, ready to pop me. I remained silent, fearing his next move. "I'm speaking to you, and I want an answer," he demanded. After a pause he yelled, "*NOW!*"

I quivered. "I don't know," I timidly responded, avoiding eye contact as he hissed. He pushed me against a wooden picture frame; I winced.

I sank to the floor. His foot firmly pressed into my chest. "Liar! I know all your little secrets, fun, and games, and I know where you're off to after school. You think you're a sneak don'cha? You think I don't know the punks you hang out with? You think you can get away with it all, don'cha? Well guess what? I caught you in the act." The bottle of tablets emptied onto my face. A few chalky tablets clung onto my hair. "Kiss your pills good-bye." The Gestapo kicked me repeatedly at the side, followed by a swift blow to my stomach. "I dare you to pop another pill again," he warned. His foot rolled me over to give me a sharp kick to the backside. "You keep this shit up and I'll cripple you for life!" he bellowed. Hadn't he accomplished this already? He continued to kick me until I lay listlessly from his assaults. I was so sore, I couldn't move. I moaned. I wasn't beaten by the school bully; I was just beaten by the school bully's father.

What's more, his wife, who was only a few feet away, was just standing there watching me get slaughtered. After she could take no more, she coaxed him to go to work, reassuring him that she would see me off to school. I couldn't believe she had the nerve to send me to school in this condition. What I needed was a hospital.

"She's stubborn and stupid just like you," he insulted his wife in his bitterness.

"She doesn't take after me. I never got myself in trouble with drugs. It's all your fault for raising her to be irresponsible," she defended.

"Irresponsible? I've been working my ass off at the firm for fifteen years now. I can swear on a stack of bibles that she never followed my example. She would have been an honor student if she would have listened to me. I studied my ass off throughout school with no parental support, mind you. I took initiative and paid every cent for college. I fuckin' earned each, and every degree hanging in my goddamn office, and you know it," he argued his point.

She grabbed his jacket and threw it at him. "I'm not the one doing the dope—don't lecture me."

"I'm not lecturing you, Claudia, I just don't want you blaming me. I'm sick of hearing your bullshit."

"Drop it, Ray. Go to work." She raised her hands in cessation.

Ray left the house in a huff, slamming the front door, only to return moments later to pick up his briefcase. He said nothing in his fury, slamming the door once again on his way out.

Claudia sat at the kitchen table sobbing for some time. The both of us were relieved that he was gone. There was no excuse for his outrage, even if I had done drugs. There were laws against child abuse, and I wasn't even his child. I thought about calling the cops but figured it would do more harm than good since the Bowers thought I caused the scuffle. They could have me locked up, charging me for possession of illegal substances.

Gradually I pulled myself off the floor and limped over to the lady to hold her hand as I would do when my own mother was hurting. Claudia abruptly pulled her hand away. "Why can't you be a good child?" she cried. After blowing her nose, she grabbed her pocketbook and insisted that I get ready for school immediately. Had she no idea what it feels like to be kicked around?

I hobbled my way to the car. She handed me an apple while she held the car door open.

She blurted, "Grab a few bites." I refused the offer. You sort of lose your appetite after you throw up then get slugged in the stomach a few times. It was beyond belief how she, as a mother, could be so apathetic toward her own daughter. Was this how the Bowers treated their young? Boot camp style? Or did she truly despise her own daughter? Claudia drove on in silence, once in a while sniffling or clearing her throat.

The moment we arrived, the drop-off buses were leaving. Claudia pulled up along the curb and parked the car. She handed me a pink pad of slips, instructing me to have every teacher sign it at the end of each class session. She warned, "If you cut class again, you'll be punished. You won't get away with it. Your father's going to watch your every move. He's not going to take his eyes off you. And you know what that means. You'd best wait for me to pick you up promptly at the late afternoon bell. Did I make myself clear?"

I nodded, rolling my eyes. Was she my parole officer? "Is that a yes or a no?" Fuhrer raised her voice.

"Yeah," I mumbled, looking out the window, avoiding eye contact.

"What? I didn't hear you."

"Yeah," I repeated louder.

"What's yeah?" she asked belligerently. "Look at me when I'm talking to you," she demanded.

"Yes." I looked her in the eyes, wishing to smack her across the face as she was probably tempted to do to me.

"That's better," she consented. Claudia gathered my books and handed them over to me. "Now hurry. Don't be late for class," the Gestapo's wife chided.

EASTWOOD MIDDLE SCHOOL

As if waking up in Denise's bed wasn't appalling enough, I had to show my new face at Eastwood Middle School before mobs of students.

A rambunctious clan waved to me as they passed by. They looked dressed to kill. Blue jeans slashed at the knee, chains dangled from the back pocket, and shredded loose seams dragged along the floor. Unknown faces greeted me—faces I had no interest in. *Just be cool,* I said to myself. A black dude with an earring in one ear waved to me from a distance. "How you doin'?"

I waved back. *Welcome to middle school popularity.* It wasn't so bad—in fact, it was sort of nice.

A brunette with shades tapped me on the back. She looked familiar. "Hey Dini. Can you do me a real big favor?" She smiled pretty, crackling her chewing gum, flicking her mascara- thick eyelashes. "I left my homework over Ricky's. Can you lend me your notes? You'll be saving my ass big time."

Save your own ass! Loser! I felt like saying. My stomach sank when she called me "Dini." "I don't know," I uttered.

"Oh c'mon. Kevin told me you got good notes. He said he helped you. I have good notes too, but I left them over Ricky's. He and I studied all night," she eye-balled me with a sigh.

Yeah, I bet you did. Kevin? I wondered. *Who's he? I think he's Denise's boyfriend.* I excused myself, "I'm busy right now, maybe later."

"No—now," she whined in my face like a five-year-old. "Oh c'mon, ya want something for it? I'll give you some stash."

What? I was almost afraid to know. *Stash?* I had hoped it wasn't what I was thinking. *Look, I'm not who you think I am so go bother someone your own type.*

Fortunately, I was saved by a slim, nerdy guy with curly hair. He placed his arm around the pest thereby distracting her. *He must be Ricky,* I concluded. Well now that Ricky had arrived, Blondie could get her notes back.

I tore away from the couple in search of my locker . . . #208 popped into mind. I set foot on the second floor, keeping a close eye on the passing lockers. I spotted Ann Millian over by #202. She was reaching into her locker for textbooks. Boy, was I glad to see a friend. She and Stephanie were my best friends.

I greeted her, momentarily forgetting who I was. "Hey Ann! How are things going?" She was not at all receptive to me. In fact, she ignored me. "How are you doing?" I continued, imposing my friendly gesture on her. She avoided eye contact as if afraid of me. I couldn't believe that my best friend thought I was Denise. I lost it. I shook her. "Tell me that I'm Jessica," I demanded.

She pushed me away. "Are you on something?" she hissed like a nasty cat as she slammed her locker door shut. The bang of the metal locker echoed down the hall. She took off in a huff.

Beside me, a black kid adjusted his tennis shoes by his locker. He looked up at me, studying me. "Are you lost?"

"No, why?" I sneered at him.

"You act lost like you new 'round here," the kid justified. He was right. I was lost… I lost myself.

A hefty black man approached me, standing before me, too close for comfort, showing who's boss. Stern and serious, he wasn't one to be messed with. He must have been one of the teachers. "Denise, is there a problem? Did you get your locker changed?"

"No," I replied. He talked down to me like I was some kind of inmate.

"Then why are you up here?" he insisted. "Isn't your locker downstairs? Class starts in five minutes. I'm keeping an eye on you, young lady. You'll get detention if I catch you meddling with someone else's locker." He yelled, "You hear me?" Did Denise's parents put him up to this?

Great, I thought, *I used to be the teacher's pet, now I'm a teacher's pest. At least I remembered my original locker number. Mine is upstairs right beside Millian's locker. I'm not totally losing my mind!*

"Did you hear me!" the teacher raised his voice again. "I know your parents and I'm going to see your ass in court if you disappoint me," he threatened. I looked at him in disbelief.

I couldn't take it much longer. Over, and over, I repeated to myself, *this can't be.* I darted like a frightened chicken into the restroom. As I entered, two girls were looking at themselves in the mirror, smoking and fixing their hair. "Hi Denise. You got a lighter on ya?" asked the skimpy, frosted-hair chick with a revealing low-cut sweater and skin-tight jeans.

"No!" I cried.

"Geesh, sorry to bother ya. Didn't mean to be annoying," she apologized. I sat on the toilet seat, hiding away from everyone, even myself.

Why me? I cried. *Why did this have to happen to me of all the kids Denise bullied? Why was I targeted?* I sobbed.

I heard someone knock at my stall door. "Miss, are you okay in there?"

"A—yeah, I'm okay." I had just embarrassed the shit out of myself. I had to get a grip.

Just be cool, the three words echoed in my head. *Think positive. I can do this.*

1ST ENCOUNTER

The second bell rang; class was now in session. I had to see to it that the pink slip was signed by every teacher or be faced with detention, or worse, Mr. Bower's wrath.

I hurried through the vacant corridor. No teachers were on duty which I was indeed grateful for. I made a beeline into English class. Two dozen pairs of eyes pierced at me as I pulled a random chair out from under a desk in the back row, screeching it against the floor, then hopped onto the seat. Fortunately, Miss Pearson, my favorite English teacher, had her back to the class, facing the chalkboard to prepare a morning drill. Not long ago, I was acknowledged as one of her most prized honor students. Once Miss Pearson finished the drill, she waltzed over to my seat with a smirk on her face then slapped a test paper on the empty desk surface. A big black "F" mark smeared the page. The test was signed by Denise Bower. It would have been more interesting to see my own score.

"Maybe if you'd come to class on time, you'd take better notes," Miss Pearson advised then walked away.

I was so eager to know how I did. Without thinking, I called the teacher back to my desk. I whispered in her ear, "Could you do me a personal favor? I know this sounds crazy, but can you tell me what grade Jessica Wheaton got?"

Miss Pearson laughed in my face. "Why do you care what Jessica Wheaton got? A little jealous, aren't we, because Jessica is a better student than you?" Miss Pearson said aloud. I blushed, completely embarrassed, scorned by my favorite teacher I so respected. It never occurred to me that she'd enjoy humiliating her students in the middle of a class session. In disquiet, classmates giggled and whispered to one another about me. Miss Pearson seemed surprised to have upset me. She silenced the class before continuing with the lesson.

I spotted . . . in the front row . . . never would have thought it to be really possible. She— I mean me. I saw my clone at the far end of the first row. She glanced back at me momentarily, probably wondering why I asked about her grade. She sat beside my best friend, Stephanie. I was in shock, unable to comprehend what I saw before my very own eyes—I mean Denise's eyes. It's as if I had an evil twin sister I never met. I was very uneasy about the whole circumstance. She had everyone fooled, including Stephanie, into thinking she was me.

Meanwhile, she took all the credit for the work I toiled so hard for. I swore she would not get away with any of this. I would see to that. I clenched my fist, silently enraged. I was ready to confront the imposter but knew it would be no easy task.

Class was dismissed 50 minutes later. Jessica and Stephanie stayed behind to copy notes off each other. I waited at my desk for Miss Pearson to leave the classroom. I had totally forgotten about the pink slip. Jessica gathered her books while babbling to Stephanie. I watched with immense jealousy as the two joked and laughed with one another. Wasting no time, I marched right over to Jessica.

"Hi Jessy." I tapped her on the shoulder insisting on her undivided attention. She quivered at my touch, glancing at me surprised. There was a moment of silence as I examined her—how perfectly she molded into my image. Short and slender with an oval face, she was just as I remembered. I got the heebie-jeebies standing before myself. "I heard you did a good job on the test." I looked cross into her eyes, almost nervously.

Jessica stood silently, rolling her eyes. Stephanie spoke up for her, "What do you want?"

"I want to speak to Jessica in privacy," I insisted, almost too polite to be convincing.

"Without you," I made myself clear.

Stephanie remained loyally by her side. "The only way you're going to speak to Jessy is in front of me."

It was obvious Stephanie was trying to make a coward of me. Though she pissed me off, I couldn't harm my good old pal. Besides, standing at 5′ 11″ Stephanie would be my bodyguard whenever the bullies ganged up on me.

"What about the test?" The sound of Jessica's voice reminisced as a sweet memory, mild with a slight Boston accent.

"You wanna copy off her next time?" Stephanie's remark broke the momentary tranquility between me and my clone. The two laughed at me, making me look like a fool. I grew impatient with my old friend. I felt like giving Stephanie a punch right in the jaw line.

"Shut up!" I snapped. I wanted the girls to know I meant business; however, I was ineffective. They shrugged me off and started out the door. I snatched Jessica's purse.

"Hey! What's your problem?" Jessica protested.

"How many times do I have to tell you, I want to speak to you, ALONE. Tell Stephanie to get lost," I demanded.

"I dare you to touch her," Stephanie warned. "You don't scare me."

I knew better. Stephanie was scared shitless. She was always good at hiding it, but she couldn't hurt a fly. All in all, I just couldn't strike an old friend. I glanced at the wall clock, "You're gonna be late for class, smart ass."

"So will you, full-of-yourself," she reciprocated.

I decided to give Stephanie what she asked for. I simply pitted one against the other. I coerced Jessica to confront her dear friend with the truth.

To Stephanie I said, "Ya know, I don't know why you are so protective over this little shit after she turned on you a number of times. I mean, Jessica never invited you to her brother's wedding. Not because it was a small affair, but because she thought you were so homely she didn't want her relatives to think she hung out with such ugly people."

Stephanie looked at Jessica puzzled, then at me, "Ya know you're queer to be making up these lies." Stephanie paused in slight doubt, turning to Jessica again. "Wait, how does she know about your brother's wedding anyway?" she pointed out.

"Don't listen to her. She's making all this up just to get you mad," Jessica blurted, denying the whole thing.

"Yes, but how does she know, or that you even have a brother? And why wasn't I invited, Jessy? You told me that your mother-in-law didn't have enough invitations to go around. Was that really true?"

"Of course. You know what she's saying is only gossip," Jessica tried to console her.

I pressed further, undauntedly added, "What about the $25 Jessica borrowed from you to go to a rock concert and never paid you back?"

Jessica winced at me as if to say *shut up*.

Stephanie's eyes widened with increased agitation. "That's right! I forgot. You never did pay it back . . ." she recalled. Stephanie questioned Jessy, pointing at me, "Were you friends with her way back? 'Cause you never told me."

I could tell I was now on the winning edge. "Tell her, Jessica— tell her how I fit into the story," I pressured her, confidently folding my arms. *I got you pinned!*

Jessica remained silent as I continued to badger. "You see, I know everything about Jessy. Don't I, Jessica?" I sneered. "I've known Jessica since she was born. In fact, I know where she was born—Mt. Cross Hospital. I've attended all her birthday parties, even her eleventh party which was only a family feast because her friends cancelled out on her. I sat in on every class she attended; she flunked algebra in 7th grade. I can even account for every dream and secret she buries. I even remember you telling Jessica about your very first date. Yup— Chuck Simons, in the back seat of his blue Pinto. Boy was he a dork! I can't believe you fooled around with him."

"How . . . what's going on here? Tell me Jessy, how does this . . . this pothead know all that stuff?" Stephanie anxiously insisted, almost hysterically, just as I had planned.

"Gosh, get over it," Jessica pleaded. "It's all gossip. C'mon. Obviously, someone's been sticking her NOSE in someone else's business. Don't let her get to you," Jessica attempted to save a losing battle; in denial, refraining from any explanation.

I continued on a roll, "Yup, and I remember Stephanie sharing her first intimate secrets, like the time she got her first period at 13 and couldn't figure how to insert a tampon."

Stephanie froze in place, perplexed and embarrassed. As if she had seen a ghost, she asked me, "Who told you all this?" Stephanie gave Jessica an evil eye. "Have you been giving away all our secrets?" she surmised. "What's going on here?" She searched desperately for answers in Jessica's eyes, feeling betrayed. "You big blabbermouth, how could you? I thought you were my friend." She was all choked up, on the verge of tears. Taking a few steps, she backed away from her long-trusted friend. "Look, I don't know how this pothead knows all that shit, but I'm not a part of this." Stephanie grabbed her purse and knapsack and scurried out of the classroom thereby abandoning her friend. I heard her whimper.

With vengeance smoldering my eyes, I smiled sinisterly. I stood proudly before the clone; at last, alone with her in the classroom. Now I could have my way with her. I pierced into her eyes demanding that she undo whatever black magic spell she zapped on me.

"You're outta your fuckin' mind," she cursed me, backing away in fear. "You gotta be stoned or something." Her eyes trembled not knowing what to do next. My eyes were locked on hers in rage.

The devil in my voice spoke, "C'mon Denise, you know how I know about everything. But I don't know how you switched us. I don't want to hassle you. All I want is to be switched back to myself. Just undo the spell, that's all I'm asking," I pleaded.

"What are you talking about? You've freaked out!"

"You know what I'm talking about."

"No, I don't. And if you're asking me for dope, I don't have any. Now leave me alone, you sicko!"

I grew very impatient with her lack of cooperation. I grabbed "Jessica" by the collar and shook her silly. I tried so hard to make myself clear, but she refused to cooperate with me.

In the corner of my eye, I saw a permed dirty blonde enter the classroom. She must have overheard the entire conversation, including the part when I wrung the little shit's neck. "*Give me my body back. NOW! You're not Jessica. You're Denise, damn it!*" Jessica's bulging eyes wandered over to the blonde pleading as I held her in a headlock.

"Dini, you feelin' alright?" The hourglass figure approached.

I'd seen her before but couldn't remember the damn name. She was in Denise's circle of friends—very snobby . . . Oh yes, Susan—Susan Henler. I released Jessica from my grip, realizing that I had made a complete fool of myself in front of Susan.

"You tryin' to get yourself expelled?" Susan asked. Susan apologized to Jessica for my eccentric behavior; however, she threatened to beat her up if she dared report me to the authorities. I saw fear in Jessica's eyes as she swore not to tell anyone, then disappeared as fast as she could. Just as I thought I had convinced the imposter to switch me, Jessica had made a fool of me instead.

Susan walked with me to the cafeteria. "What'cha been trippin' out on?" she asked. I mumbled, "I wish I knew."

"Ya wanna talk about it? I'm all ears," she offered.

I couldn't fathom this insensitive, self-centered snob wanted to hear my problems.

HOOKIE AT CAFETERIA

For the remainder of the school day, I sat in the cafeteria "playing hookie" with my new- found friends. I'd ask Susan to introduce me to her friends, but under the circumstance, I was already supposed to know everyone. Listening carefully to the conversations, I learned the names of each player within the circle. Christina was the most talkative blondie, to the left of me, chopping her gum and popping the bubbles she blew into everyone's face. A bimbo whose only care was to get laid. Marie Castino, a South American chick, sat to the right of me. A true punk rocker decked with a myriad of pins to her jacket. Her friend Paula, seated on her right side, remained quiet except for a few subtle whispers to Maria's ear.

"Yes, Vicki was sober last night, but Todd wasn't, and he was driving," Christina pointed out to Susan.

"I'm not surprised 'cause he always takes chances," Susan remarked.

The name *Vicki* rang a bell, but I wasn't quite sure if the girls were talking about the same Vicki I knew years ago. I overheard that she was doing dope with her boyfriend Todd McKane. The Vicki I knew wasn't into drugs in elementary school. But that was then. Christina announced that "Vicki" will be having a party in her club basement tomorrow and we were all invited. Hmm . . . my old buddy Vicki had a club basement. In fact, I remember helping her father build the auxiliary unit. Could she possibly be the same person? Her father left her mother in the late grade school years and that's when Vicki and I went our separate ways.

Just then, I felt strong arms embrace me from behind. I noticed a tattoo on his wrist. I inhaled the faint scent of cigarette smoke. A curly-haired fellow, wearing a bandana with a slight mustache, came onto Christina, massaging her shoulders, then kissed her. He briefly sat beside her, smooching on and off before taking off with the tattooed guy.

Susan whispered in Christina's ear, pointing her finger at me, making me uneasy.

Christina asked me quietly, "Dini, you upset with Kevin?"

Who? I was caught off guard. "Huh?" I acted dumbfounded.

"I heard you slept over his place last night. Did the two of you get into a fight?" Christina inquired.

The boyfriend, of course. The tattooed guy must have been Kevin, Denise's boyfriend.

"Yeah—I mean no." I shook my head confused.

Christina smacked the table with the palm of her hand as if she had finally understood the reason for my deviant behavior. "Well, c'mon, tell us about it. No wonder you've been so quiet. How did it go last night?" Christina raised her voice in anticipation. There was a sudden cold silence as everyone's head bobbed toward me. I did not know what to say. Should I make up a story? I could not remember anything that happened yesterday let alone some sexual escapades I may have had with that smelly scum ball who looked as if he were scraped up from an alley dumpster.

Susan tried to cover for me as she explained away my erratic behavior, "Don't mind Dini, she's been stoned."

Marie seized the moment as she really believed Susan, "Whatcha on, Dini? Can I have some?"

The girls laughed.

"I'm not on anything," I corrected Susan as she put me on the spotlight in front of the vultures. I wanted to disappear.

"She thinks she's in Jessica Wheaton's body," Susan disclosed my secret as she sneered at me for denying her accusation. "One of those out-of-body experiences."

After that final blow, I wanted to slide under the table and hide. "Wow!" Marie exclaimed. "How much pot you take?"

"I said, I'm not on anything." I reiterated, "Nothing." I defended myself against Susan's big mouth, regretting that she caught me in the first place.

Christina pulled on my sleeve. "I still want to know what you and Kevin did last night," she insisted as she cracked her chewing gum.

I was almost grateful she got off the current topic. But I could only stutter, "I . . . I don't remember."

Paula laughed, "I guess she slept through the whole thing." The girls laughed aloud.

"Are you alright?" Marie raised an eyebrow in concern.

"I'm fine," I gritted my teeth at her.

Marie's eyes wandered over to Christina, bounced off Susan, then finally met with Paula before suppressing a mocking chuckle. "Let me get this straight. You spent the night with your boyfriend, don't remember a damn thing that happened, and you didn't snort a particle? How should I put this? Let's get real, you are LYING," Marie emphasized.

The girls laughed at me, again.

Susan rubbed her hand across my back, "C'mon Dini, we're all buddies. If you have a problem, we're all ears," she attempted to appease the anger I felt toward her.

"Has this something to do with Jessica Wheaton?" Marie wondered. *She had to bring that up again.* "Of all people, why would you choose to trip as Jessica Wheaton—Ms. Prima Donna? Quite frankly, I'd rather have an out-of-body experience as Morgan Fairchild. At least she's a better makeover." The girls laughed in agreement.

Susan snapped her fingers as if she solved the mystery, "I know what's bothering you."

And Susan figured it out all by herself. "Your father's been giving you a hard time again."

"How did you know?" I was indeed surprised by her power of intuition.

"Dini, I know you better than Kevin knows you. Vicki tells me everything. Besides, you're so predictable. I mean remember last summer after the pool party your dad beat the shit out of you cuz you didn't dry your feet off when you came into the house," Susan recalled.

Christina sighed, "Darn, the way your dad treats you, I don't know why you don't just run away."

"That's why you do drugs," Marie added. "It helps ya cope with life."

"I don't know how it happened," I expressed openly, lowering my head in sorrow.

"And none of it's your fault," Marie rubbed my back trying to comfort me.

I wasn't sure she was referring to the abuse. "You're right." I agreed.

"So do you still think you're Jessica Wheaton?" Susan interrupted, refusing to change the topic.

"Susan," Marie tried to shut her up. "Don't be ridiculous."

"No really, you don't know what I saw in that classroom. Dini had that poor kid almost mauled over a desk. She was yelling at her, 'Give me my body back. NOW! You're not Jessica. You're Denise, damn it!' She was wringing her neck. She has a really sick hold on that girl. It ain't no joke."

The girls were disquieted over Susan's testimony. My face was flushed with embarrassment. I felt like wringing Susan's neck.

"Is that true, Dini?" Marie wasn't sure who to believe.

I remained silent. *Now they think I'm crazy and they'll commit me for sure.*

"She's under one of her spells again," Christina again came to my rescue. "Remember about five months ago Dini and Kevin came over Todd's apartment and acted really freaky? I mean they freaked everyone out. Dini thought she was Jesus Christ and was about to jump a twelve-story window; Kevin tried to burn himself with matches, thinking he was the Devil. Gee, they gave everyone such a scare."

"Yeah, you could be right," Susan recalled.

Marie retrieved a pill bottle from her purse and handed one over to me. "I have the perfect remedy. Vicki gave me this. Here, this is your antidote. Take one of these and you'll feel like yourself again."

Faint yellowish round tablets lay in the palm of my hand. "What is this?" I examined the tiny pellets. They reminded me of the pills that Mr. Bower threw on my face before he kicked the crap out of me.

"It'll relax your nerves and make you feel better." Marie sensed that I was skeptical. "Just trust me. I know what I'm talking about. Vicki and I tried them before, and they work excellent. You know I wouldn't harm you." She held my hand trying to reassure me. "Look, whatever you were on wasn't doing you any justice so maybe you just haven't tried the right stuff," she suggested. "Drugs are supposed to make you feel better about being you, not worse. You're not supposed to wanna be someone else, silly."

FALSE HOPES

I sat along the curb of the school parking lot waiting for Mrs. Bower to pick me up. *'Are you crazy?'* an inner voice asked me. I had only one reason to justify my decision to return to the madness. If I lay in that very bed I awoke in, I would possibly exit this nightmare.

Denise's bed may very well be the portal. It was a chance I had to take. However, I sure wasn't looking forward to seeing Mrs. Bower again. In fact, I began to feel sorry for Denise.

The white Ford pulled up along the curb in front of me, splattering my pants with mud.

The moment I opened the car door, the witch greeted me with an abrupt request for the pink slip, which I had long forgotten. I felt butterflies in my stomach. Though I went through the motion of searching my coat and pants pocket for the lost passport, I had no sound excuse and no pink slip. "I . . . I must have left it . . . somewhere," I finally resorted to say.

"Don't lie to me, young lady. You never had any intention of getting it signed in the first place. And you know perfectly well what you did to that slip. You tore it up and threw it in a wastebasket like you always do. You must think your parents are really stupid." She frowned with disappointment. "I'll have to call your teachers to find out if you attended your classes."

Mrs. Bower drove off in a huff. The veins in her neck protruded. I wondered what she had in mind as my punishment. I'm sure she had something malicious in store for my negligence. Maybe I'll get the belt. Or, better yet, she'll have Mr. Bower handle me. I repeated to myself that I was doing the right thing. This was the only way out.

After traveling for some time in utter silence, she remarked, "You received another deficiency notice in the mail today. This one is regarding your English class. It stated that you are in danger of failing." She added, "That's no surprise to you, of course?"

I did not reply, knowing that Mrs. Bower would be further appalled by the test results from English class today. I wished I could tell her that I'm really smart and I could prove it.

"Your behavior has been particularly disturbing to me lately," she added. I thought she was referring to my peculiar behavior. "And if you don't change your ways, your father will pull you out of school and into juvenile detention." She paused. I took a deep breath and cleared my throat in relief, as not to take this personally. The lady continued, "Can't you see you're ruining your life, hanging out with those bums? When are you going to wake up and realize that you're hurting yourself and the family? When?" She insisted on an answer.

Now that she mentioned it, I was curious to understand why Denise's folks were so dysfunctional. "How am I hurting the family?" I asked softly.

"How are you hurting the family?" She was appalled as if I had asked the most absurd question. "Your poor grades have disappointed both your father and I, not to mention that your disgraceful behavior is an embarrassment to the whole entire family. Goodness, we have a legacy to uphold. You have got to grow up even if it means putting you into a halfway home. You need to learn discipline. That means studying long and hard without a social life until your grades improve, young lady." Mrs. Bower pointed her finger at me.

"But it's hard to concentrate. I mean, I can't study with all that tension at home." I played along.

"Tension? If there's any tension, you created it," she clarified.

"You saw Dad beat me," I charged.

"I should smack you for saying that. Don't you EVER blame your behavior on your father. You're a spoiled rotten brat, you know that? You got YOURSELF into this mess. Your father has worked very hard to raise you and your brothers, and you've done nothing to deserve his love. You're a truly rotten child," she asserted.

That was the biggest blow to self-esteem I'd ever heard spoken from a parent. I could not believe what she just said. If I hadn't known better, I'd feel suicidal right about now. I took another deep breath, *round two in this boxing match.* "So, Dad hit me because he was mad about my grades?" I concluded.

"Because of grades? We caught you high, AGAIN!" she raised her voice defending her husband's actions. "Is that not enough? Doing dope is no shame to you? What kind of future are you paving for yourself, Missy?" Mrs. Bower counted with her fingers, "Uncle Tom, a professor at Yale; Cousin Steve, a computer engineer at seventeen; Timothy, of course, a Chemist at the Brookman's Institute of Cancer Research; not to mention your father, a top-notch lawyer; and John, working on his doctorate degree. But what kind of future do you hold? You couldn't even get an entry-level job with the kind of grades you average, let alone an undergraduate degree.

Start thinking about your future for a change. You're in your junior year for Pete's-sake. Did it ever occur to you that to make even $20,000 a year you need to pass elementary algebra... and English?"

"There's a lot of jobs that don't require . . ."

"Don't be foolish. You need a good education to be on your own. Now I don't want to hear another excuse as to why you can't improve, understand? And don't you dare blame your father, hear me? Put more effort into your study habits and you'll be sure to pass high school." Mrs. Bower wrapped up the conversation, "I want you to study until the material is DEAD in your brain," she emphasized.

"Dead in my brain, Mother?"

"You heard me—dead in your brain," she articulated.

You mean, brain dead. Her expectations seemed rather extreme and harsh. "What if I try my best and I still can't make top grades? Will a 'C' do?"

"I said no excuses, Dini. You have the ability to be a top achiever in everything you do. Now that's final and this discussion has ended."

"But . . ."

"No 'but's,' Denise. You want to get slapped?"

Mrs. Bower pulled into the garage and parked the car. I was ordered to go straight to my room and study. I obeyed, with another intention in mind. The moment I entered the house; I had flashbacks of Mr. Bower beating on me. In fact, the framed picture he pushed me into still hung crooked on the wall.

Upon entering the bedroom, I reached into my pocket and pulled out the pills Marie passed onto me. I lay in the bed comfortably. The two tiny yellowish pellets settled on the palm of my hand. Though I didn't know a thing about these pills, the miniatures seemed harmless.

The coating slid through my fingertips as I dropped them onto my tongue. I really wanted to believe Marie. *"This is your antidote. Take one of these and you'll feel like yourself again."*

Christina's voice echoed in my mind, *"Darn, the way your dad treats you, I don't know why you don't just run away."* Thoughts of Susan surfaced. *"No really, you don't know what I saw in that classroom. Dini had that poor kid almost mauled over a desk. She was yelling at her saying, 'Give me my body back. NOW! You're not Jessica. You're Denise, damn it!' . . ."* She was wringing her neck. She has a really sick hold on that girl. It ain't no joke," Susan insisted.

I swallowed the pills whole. Marie again came to mind. *"It'll relax your nerves and make you feel better."* I cleared my throat remembering Marie's last words, *"Just trust me. I know what I'm talking about . . . you know I wouldn't harm you. Drugs are supposed to make you feel better about being you, not worse. You're not supposed to wanna be someone else, silly."*

I tried to make sense of everything that's happened and then it came together all at once: I awoke at dawn into this strange nightmare. I remembered having a bad headache—it must have been a hangover. It felt like a hangover—a drug-related hangover. Evidently, Denise Bower poisoned me with some sort of spellbinding drug which caused the body switch. But is this the antidote? As I became more relaxed, I lay there waiting for something to happen. Minutes went by and nothing changed. I grew impatient waiting. Minutes turned into hours. I studied my hands, hoping to see some sort of reformation, but all that I had gained was a peaceful nap.

SALVATION DREAM

The soft sheet cuddled me in its warmth. A gentle evening breeze from the open window rattled the blinds. I heard the sounds of night settling in. Crickets chirped away, moths snapped their wings against the light post, and lightning bugs danced before the open window screen. Slowly, I drifted into a dream-like state . . .

A lightning bug works its way through the tiny holes in the screen to pay me a visit. Most annoyed, I brush it away with the back of my hand. Suddenly, flying light explodes in front of my face!

I stand in darkness, looking up at an illuminated doorway of a SPACESHIP. Out comes a little human-like creature. It resembles an embryo. It communicates to me that it means no harm. It informs me that it has read my thoughts throughout my suffering and wants to help me. I am grateful. It tells me that if I willingly enter the space vehicle, it could transform me into my original being, permanently and painlessly. I am anxious and excited. "Permanently?" I doubt. The little alien nods. It extends its little webbed claws toward me.

"Is it really true?" I wonder. I cautiously approach the entrance of THE WORLD OF LIGHT. The closer I draw, the more content I feel. My eyes peer into the huge mystic ship. I step aboard. I feel privileged, for I am singled out from all mankind to share in the secrets of an alien life force. I am mesmerized by the ingenuity of design. Everything glows. The mirrored walls of the spherical ship reflect my image as Jennifer Wheaton. I smile brightly. Colors are more rich, and vibrant than any compared on

Earth. Little lightning bugs fly around the spherical platform. The alien shares with me that the lights in the bugs are the energy forces of their being. Nothing is born or dies in this alien life force; the aliens simply convert to light energy at any given time, re-energizing themselves. Their purpose, as the alien explains, is to make humans SUFFER to seek truth and find meaning.

"Suffer?" I repeat the little creature's word, hoping that it was only joking with me. I hear an upheaval of outcries beneath me. The alien insists that I not look back into the world of evil. It encourages me to move on through the space vehicle for new enrichment. But I can't ignore the screams and cries.

Has the air thickened? I have trouble breathing for some reason. Am I getting nervous or am I running out of oxygen? The alien assures me that I will eventually adjust to the new atmospheric pressure. I want the alien to explain what it meant by "suffer" but I am distracted by a violent rippling turbulence in the background. It sounds like explosive fireworks! While the spaceship door slowly closes, I am compelled to turn my head if only to get a glimpse. What I see horrifies me. Down below, raging fires uproot into a mushroom of smoke, forming a nuclear cloud at the horizon. Skeletal figures cry out to me from the midst of hell. I feel as if I have abandoned my people. They are suffering and at my mercy. The forces pull me downward past the door into the darkness.

"No!" I resist the forces. "That's not fair!" I am separated from the vehicle as the door closes. I cry out in the darkness asking for another chance.

SINKING

I shot up from the mattress startled by a violent—BANG! The bedroom door flew open, and Mr. Bower yelled, "Where's the goddamn pink slip?" He snatched the pill bottle from my side and threw it into the Uncle Sam poster, whereby putting a dent in it. His fist dug into my collar. "You cut class again, didn't ya?" I thought he was going to strangle me. "I don't want to see your face ever again," he growled. "You're grounded. Get the hell out of bed!"

Before I was given a chance to get up on my own, he pulled on my wrist, yanking me out of bed. Unfortunately, I was too drowsy to fight back. As he tugged on my arm, I clumsily fell to the floor. He dragged me like a mop along the carpet, giving me rug burn. I struggled along the way, trying to withstand the crane's great force. I winced as I reached the top of the staircase. He wasn't about to . . . I shut my eyes. I always had a fear of heights. Now I knew why. In seconds, I tumbled down a flight of twelve steps. I screamed the whole way down! Everything spun around me. Once I recovered from slight vertigo, Mrs. Bower stood beside me at the bottom of the steps, just watching, as she had done before. "Mrs. Bower, do something!" I called out to her for mercy before thinking, then corrected, "I mean . . . Mom, help me!" She didn't respond. She just watched, empty of expression.

I was sure the Gestapo had come to finish me off. However, this time Mr. Bower didn't kick me around; instead, he dragged me along the tile surface. This time it was down into the cellar, another flight of steps. It was a darn good thing that I was on heavy-duty sedatives. I didn't feel the burns and battery until long after it was over. Again, I rolled and tumbled passively like a rag doll until my body lay flat on a cold hard surface. I heard the door slam shut. I felt as if I were a trash bag being tossed into the dumpster.

The dumpster was a very dark, cold, and quiet place. I got up off the cold damp floor and carefully climbed to the top of the staircase. I was bruised and bleeding. The door was locked. I rattled the handle and banged at the door, but no one answered. I yelled repeatedly for Mrs. Bower to open the door, but she did not respond. At first, I thought of kicking the door open but why bother? It wasn't worth the abuse. I sat by the steps waiting for her to open the door and rescue me. This time no one attended me. I concluded that this was their way of punishing me—more like solitary confinement. Where's the straitjacket? Seriously now, how long do I have stay down here? It's cold and creepy here. There are probably nasty water bugs and leeches down here.

I spent my "time-out" on the bottom step of the cellar staircase. There, I gathered my thoughts, trying to make sense of the situation. Now I'm sorry that I didn't take Christina's advice. I regretted coming back home. As I sat in deep thought, I grew agitated. I needed another hit. I reached into both pockets. Oh no! The pill bottle was missing! Bower threw the bottle at the poster. What was I to do? Would Prince Charming with shining armor come rescue me? I waited endlessly for some supernatural event to take place. "Please," I moaned in prayer.

I felt a chill above my shoulders, but no windows or doors were open. I heard a noise behind me. "Who's there?" I jumped. No answer. I heard footsteps in the background. "Hello?" This was getting creepy. "Who's that?" I listened more intently. I heard the faint sound of someone breathing. I panicked. I suspected some lunatic was down here hiding somewhere waiting to murder me. Perhaps Mr. Bower secretly came down to finish me off. I felt a tickle on my shoulder. "Go away!" I snapped, scratching fiercely. Once I came to my senses, I realized how foolish I was. It was just the silence of the darkness that was haunting. My mind was playing tricks on me.

"This . . . this . . . this… is your antidote . . . dote . . . dote . . . You'll feel like yourself again . . . gain . . . gain . . ." The words of Marie's advice echoed as if she were right beside me.

"Darn, the way your dad treats you . . . you . . . you… I don't know why you don't just run away . . . way . . . way . . ."

"Dini had that poor kid . . . kid . . . kid . . . mauled over a desk. She was yelling at her saying, 'Give me my body back. . . back . . . back NOW! You're not Jessica. You're Denise, damn it. . . it . . . it!' She was wringing her neck . . . neck . . . neck . . ."

"Look, whatever you were on . . . on . . . on . . . wasn't doing you any justice, so maybe you just haven't tried the right stuff . . . stuff . . . stuff . . ."

Those damn girls screwed me over, I contested. Marie flat-out lied to me. The pills were merely a sleeping aid, not an antidote. As if that wasn't bad enough, I was trapped in a cold dusty cellar. How could things possibly get worse?

I heard a knock right before me—in the empty void. What's going on? I felt something crawl around in my hair. I shook my head wildly, trying to brush it out. Something tickled my backside. Not before long, I was scratching all over, rubbing my back abrasively against the cement floor. I tried to convince myself that if there were any nasty critters on me, they'd all be squashed to pieces by now. I lay still in meditation. I had to believe that I was just paranoid and there was absolutely nothing to fear. However, when I made an effort to get up off the floor, my arms and legs were restrained to the surface by chains! I struggled fiercely but I could not set myself free.

"Help!" I shrieked.

Within the darkness of the cellar, a bluish dome forms around me, encasing me.

What's happening? Suddenly, the hard floor gives way from under me. I fall through the opening in the floor. "Am I going to hell?" I shriek. My hands reach out from their restraint to grasp at anything possible, but my fingertips remain suspended within the vast abyss. I can hear my screams echo through the chamber. I feel as if I am falling through several stories. I come to a halt. I must have hit the bottom of the pit. I look up to darkness. How long am I going to be stranded down here? Just as I think the ride is over, the surface caves in once more. Is there no bottom to this pit? How far must I fall before I smash? I'm very dizzy and cold. I have trouble breathing. I need air. Finally, I see the bottom of the pit. A swamp of crocodiles chomp their jaws, ready to devour me! There's nothing I can do to stop. I land instantly, smacking the surface.

Once I lifted my head, I realized that I had not fallen at all. I took a deep breath and sighed. *Thank God!* I couldn't handle another hallucination. I was exhausted.

I wrestle with the chains, trying to set myself free from them but they unrelentingly tighten their grip on my wrists, cutting into the flesh. "Ouch!" I cry. I must believe that everything is just an illusion. I repeat the words silently over and over again. And each time I recite the phrase, the walls appear to move in on me. No! This can't be real. But it's happening, I argue. The four walls draw in too close. I fear they will squash me. They inch over toward my hands and feet. The cellar is now about the size of a tiny closet. The back wall hits my head, and the front wall presses against my feet. "NO!" I cry, insisting that it's not real.

My feet felt gritty. The enclosure disappeared. My hands and feet were spread apart on the dusty cement floor, but I was free from restraint. The gritty texture rubbing up against my feet was nothing more than a stack of bricks. At last, the effects of the pill wore off. I had never experienced such a frightening delusion before. It was alarming to think this experience was induced by a tiny little yellowish sleeping pill.

EXILE

I couldn't bear to stay in this dungeon much longer. I was going stir crazy. There were two small windows about six feet above. Oddly, the windows were covered with plastic wrap.

Denise must have managed prior escapes. I was surprised that the windows were left broken. I guess Mr. Bower got tired of repairing them. I wondered how Denise managed to reach them. I came up with the perfect solution. I carried the bricks over to the windows, one at a time, constructing layers of steps. I trusted the clumsy steps I fashioned to raise myself just high enough to reach the window ledge. As I tore through the plastic, a fresh breeze blew into my face. I couldn't express how good that felt compared to the musty cellar. Carefully, I supported myself as I pulled myself over the ledge. The escape was almost too easy. Was Mr. Bower waiting outside with a rifle?

To avoid being sighted and captured, I ran for the shady forest. It was as though I were some kind of fugitive seeking a hideout. Following a trail, I dodged swinging branches, got my shoes and socks soaked crossing a stream, fell into a ditch after jumping over a huge log, then climbed a steep hill in total exhaustion. I wondered where the trail would take me. The sun lowered against the trees as dusk approached. I pushed along the trail into the darkness. I had no idea that the trail would be this long. How much time had passed? An hour? Two?

I rested under a tree beside a huge rock. I shivered. I did not come prepared with a jacket. I guess I was now considered a runaway. Night came and the cold air nipped my face and hands. Feeling miserable, I regretted running away. At least the cellar was warm.

I was awakened by humming birds in the treetops. They whistled away as if to say, *hang in there.* I looked up into the cloudy morning sky with wary eyes, searching for the heat of the hidden sun. I knew I had to keep moving if I wanted to stay warm, but where was I headed?

Home? Where was home? Which way? I felt like a stranger in my own hometown.

It was not the maze of the forest that baffled me so much as my lost sense of identity. I just couldn't remember the details anymore. The past seemed to have short-circuited. I knew I was once Jessica, but all the clues of her past were slowly diminishing. It was almost ridiculous to think that I had a former identity. I was so confused I didn't even know where I belonged, if I ever belonged. I wasn't Jessica anymore and Denise's life was in ruins. Could I possibly begin a new life in Denise's image? Did I have a choice? Depression swept over me. With no place to turn, I felt scared. Scared of who I was. Terrible thoughts came over me. Thoughts of self- destruction. I cried. Why not? No one knows where I am, not that they'd stop me if they knew. I had my eyes locked on a sharp stick in the dirt. I pulled it out and rubbed my finger along the edge. Tears rolled down my dirty cheeks.

Suddenly, I felt warmth as the sun poked out from the clouds and lit up the forest. I glanced up at the rays of light hitting the trees. I saw a neighborhood through the rays, a distant vague image—an apparition. It was Mom! She waved to me from the distance then disappeared as the sun went back in. I cried, "Please don't go." I raced over in the direction of the apparition. I sighted a housing development in its path. Not only was I relieved to see civilization, but I knew this had to be of significance on my journey and I was about to find out.

VICKI

Icrossed over a stream, climbed a fence in the direction of the apparition, only to set foot in someone's backyard. There was nothing majestic about this property. Only a big black whiny Labrador leashed to a tree. The friendly tail-wagging canine jumped around in merriment egging me on to play. As soon as I knelt down to pet the pooch, it jumped on me, greeting me with its paws, whimpers, and wet kisses. We hugged. It was the first warm body I'd felt in a while.

This place looked familiar. I heard faint music of a piano. A shade was lifted slightly. The music stopped. Was I trespassing on someone's property? I was ready to make a run for it. The basement screen door opened, and a young blonde stepped out.

Fortunately, she didn't appear to be upset and was not armed. She knew me. In fact, she acted as if she had expected me. "Denise? Is that you?" She turned on the porch light with uncertainty. It blinded me. She stood a little taller than I, with a medium build, fair skin, brown eyes, and uncombed matted frosted hair. A pack of cigarettes stuck out from her shirt pocket, a penknife in her back denim pocket, and a lighter in her denim jacket pocket. Her tennis shoes were aged and worn, no worse than mine. She looked badass. She pulled the playful dog back while unraveling the leash.

I recognized her. I'd seen her before. I bumped into her in the school hall. She was hiding behind shades then. At the time she was whining about needing my notes. Flashbacks traced her to elementary school about six years ago. We used to play hopscotch together. I remembered Vicki showing off on the monkey bars. We'd bounce around on the see-saw and dig earth to make clay models. Definitely the same person—Vicki Norris, my old friend whose father had been long divorced, and the most talked about at the gossip bench.

Was it not a mere coincidence that she just happened to live on the other side of the forest?

She examined me, brushing off dirt and thorns from my clothes. "What happened to you? You're a mess." She invited me into her club basement. "And why are you limping?"

"I fell," I fibbed.

"You're shaking."

"It's cold out."

"So why aren't you wearing a jacket?" She glanced at her watch. "And why are you so late?" she bombarded me with questions.

Late? Late for what?

"You're really not prepared, are you?" Vicki closed the piano. "What did you do? Roll around in the dirt? You can't be this filthy. Go wash up—hurry!"

When I returned, Vicki was sitting on her couch munching away on potato chips. I thought she would have been impatiently waiting by the door. I sat down beside her, hesitating whether or not to ask her about the special occasion. I figured maybe I was late for a birthday or some other type of surprise party. Vicki lit a cigarette. The fumes got me coughing.

"Want a chip?" she offered, ignoring my cough.

"No thanks." I wasn't hungry. I stuttered, "D—don't we have some place to go?"

"Yeah, but what's a few more minutes when you're already late. You need some fresh clothes, huh?" she offered.

I consented, "It would be nice."

She got off the couch and handed me a sweater from her laundry basket. Changing into fresh-smelling clothes was definitely rejuvenating. I felt alive again. Though the sleeves were a bit too long. She watched me change. "What he beat ya for this time?" she asked as if she knew.

How did she know? She hardly seemed alarmed by the bruises all over me. "I cut class," I mumbled, wishing to change the subject.

Vicki nodded in a comforting way. She put her arm around me. "Hey sport, ya ready to dig up some green?" She changed her tone, though I didn't know what she was referring to.

Green what? Vicki raised her eyebrows. "Are we all set to go now?"

"Ah well, I forgot what you had in mind."

"Bustin' for dope, Dini. Remember our little routine—hit and run—or did your dad knock your brains out, too?" Vicki giggled at first then turned solemn, observing my reaction. "You aren't on anything, are ya?"

Did she say dope? The word bounced around in my mind.

She handed me an encased penknife. "Ya gotta be on the ball, kiddo."

"We're not going to kill anyone, are we?" I had a worried look sealed to my face. "Only if they give us a hard time," she clarified as she grabbed her leather jacket. She tossed her cigarette to the floor, squashing the burning ashes with the sole of her shoe.

I think she meant it. I had to find an excuse to back out. "I don't think I'm really up to it."

"You'll do fine," she assured. "As many times as we've done this, I don't know what's bothering you now," Vicki remarked as we left the house to return to the woods. "Are the cops after ya or something?"

"Oh no . . . I'm just . . . a little apprehensive. It's been a long morning," I replied, trying to behave like Denise.

"Then take a chill. Everything'll go fine if you don't mess up. Just remember not to breathe hard and keep your cool even if you hear a creak in the floor."

I didn't understand what Vicki was talking about. I must have had a dumb look on my face.

She signaled me to be very quiet. I followed as she snuck into someone's yard and hid behind the bushes. Vicki checked for clearance. "No one in sight. No cars in the driveway. It's very quiet." She paused. "I'd say the coast is clear. Are you ready, Dini?"

We're breaking and entering, aren't we? I was about to break the law. "Are you sure we should be doing this?" I tried to talk her out of it.

"Why? Do you see anyone around? Everything's quiet to me. I say we head in now while the going's good." Vicki misunderstood what I meant.

I insisted, "They might have a burglar alarm installed, or some kinda mean watch dog, or a booby trap, ya never know."

"You're so funny," she snarled. "I thought you were a sport. You're acting like a sissy. I don't hang with whiners." She gave me no ultimatum. "We're going to race down that stairwell as fast as we can. You understand?" she instructed. I nodded reluctantly to her bossiness. She hadn't changed a bit. "Ready—go!" she signaled. I felt as if I were in boot camp.

Once we reached the bottom of the stairwell, Vicki used her penknife to toy the lock. In seconds, the door gave. Apparently, Vicki was well adept at breaking and entering. What a valuable skill. I was afraid the owner was standing on the other side of the door with a shotgun. We were groping around in the dark. Only a few morning sunrays came in through the window to aid us. Vicki, of course, came prepared with a flashlight. I remained outside. "I'll guard," I volunteered, trying to cop out.

She got pissed. "No, you're not, I need your help. I didn't bring you along to look stupid. Ya know this is a joint effort and if you don't help, you won't get a piece of the profit."

She and I stood in a well-furnished basement. Vicki handed me her flashlight, instructing me to guide her up the stairway. *Me? You're the leader.* However, I obeyed without protest.

Each step creaked on the way up. I could feel my legs and hands tremble as if I were walking through a haunted house.

2ND CONFRONTATION

"Are you positive no one's home?" I whispered to Vicki, nervously.

"Just be careful," she cautioned. "There's a door at the top of the steps. I don't think it's locked."

"Who lives here anyway?" I was thinking how cruel it would be to rob an old lady or some poor folks.

"The people with the BMW," Vicki informed to the contrary.

Once we landed on the second level, Vicki instructed me to split up with her. I was to grab a pillowcase from a bed and throw in all the valuables. "And don't take too long. We should be out of here in no more than ten minutes." Captain Vicki warned, "And don't be so noisy—tiptoe!" she articulated in a whisper, taking the flashlight away from me.

Now on my own, having never robbed before and with no criminal record, I had no idea of what I was searching for. I wanted to jump out of a window and run away. But where would I go this time, back home? I groped around in the darkness until my eyes adjusted to the faint light coming in through the windows. I came to a bedroom. So far, so good. I pulled the pillowcase off a pillow. That part was easy. The bed was made, and stuffed animals lay on the spread. I wondered where the family had gone who lives here. Were they on vacation? I wanted to turn the light switch on to see what I was doing but I knew it would alert the neighbors so I turned the TV set on to create a mild glow. As I looked around, a feeling of deja vu came over me. The bedroom looked so familiar. Funny how I guessed where the jewelry box and the money was stored.

My foot accidentally got caught in a cord, and a radio fell to the floor. I shuddered with trepidation. NOISE! I'm not supposed to make any noise. I froze. Vicki may race over and scold me. Did I wake up a sleeping dog or set off an alarm? Moments later, another sound followed, one that I did not cause—footsteps.

"Vicki?" I called out to her softly. No answer. I repeated a little louder. Still no answer. I felt a little uneasy about this. Someone was in the next room. Maybe it was a house pet. I had hoped it was a cat; I didn't want to be attacked by a dog. Why wasn't Vicki saying anything?

Was someone in the house with us? Couldn't be—Vicki said there were no cars in the driveway and the coast was clear. She would know these things, she's the expert. My mind was simply playing tricks on me; it had happened before. I ignored the sound and went on with my scavenger hunt. When I was done, I placed the heavy sack on the floor. Again, I heard footsteps. I listened intently. The sound was coming from another bedroom. I called out to Vicki again, nervously awaiting a response. For sure, Vicki would have answered my calls by now. Had someone killed her? My skepticism grew. I paced back and forth, debating whether I should investigate, hide, or jump out the window. I was afraid to leave the bedroom. I'd rather lock the door and hide. No, that'd just drag out the suspense. I clutched onto the penknife inside my pocket. I pulled it out. The blade shined against the morning sun. What was I afraid of? No one can hurt me unless they have a gun. What if they have a gun? Do I have a choice?

I boldly launched across the hall toward the noise. I heard a tapping, clicking sound as I approached the suspect. I rigidly held the pointed penknife. I had really hoped it was just a stupid house pet making all that racket, but then, to my surprise . . . I discovered her . . . Jessica! She was making a phone call. At first, I thought this was another delusion. But then I came to my senses that this was my own house I was robbing. I lived here! I mean, this was Jessica's home. It was Dad's BMW missing in the driveway, and I stole my own possessions. How could this be?

What was she doing here anyway? Never mind the questions, the imposter was phoning the police! The instant she noticed me she screamed while holding the receiver as if it were a weapon. "Go away!" she cried, backing herself against the wall. "Hello? Hello?" a voice called out to her from the receiver. I raced over to her, attempting to grab the phone from her but she pushed me away. I slashed the phone cord with my blade before she had a chance to give away any information. Once she realized the line went dead, she threw the disconnected receiver at me. As I dodged it, I accidentally dropped the knife to the floor. She dove in quickly to grab for the knife, but I stepped on the back of her hand, smashing her knuckles. She let go of the knife, but in turn, she tripped me. We wrestled each other for the knife, strangling and scratching. This went on for some time. Only after I banged her head against furniture did she surrender. I quickly grabbed the penknife and held it out in defense. We were both exhausted, huffing away. She fought well. It was a tough match. The shiny blade was pointed on target. She slowly backed away from me, massaging the back of her head. "Please don't hurt me," she begged.

"Why not? You hurt me. Besides, I want to make you suffer the way you made me suffer," I reasoned. With my ammunition, I backed her into the corner of the wall and a chest of drawers. I stood before her too close for comfort. She stood still. Eyes locked on the blade. The knife landed on her throat.

"Don't!" she cried.

"Then tell me what you did to me. What's the antidote, Denise?" I pressured her.

"I don't know what you're talking about," she swallowed.

"No, no sweetie, that got you by in class with Stephanie at your side, but that won't go over well with just you and me."

"I don't know what you're on, but please snap out of it."

I lost my patience with her. I knew she had to be lying. I didn't know why she refused to cooperate. The blade lay sharp against her pulsating vein. I wanted her to know how grave I was. I'd been waiting for this moment for some time. She was trembling nervously but remained perfectly still for she knew I had every intention of following through. "You're on death row, you know. I'd love to slice you . . ." I pierced haughtily into her eyes. "See all the blood splatter all over the furniture and walls," I envisioned with madness.

She shut her eyes to avoid mine, muttering under her breath over, and over, "Please don't hurt me, please," and prayed silently in a cold sweat.

"It was a drug, wasn't it? Which one? Tell me which one. I'm sure it wasn't over-the- counter." I laughed sinisterly.

She did not reply, despite my intention. Did she not believe me? Gradually pressing downward, I was ready to pop her vein.

"No . . ." she cried, again.

"You only get one life," I threatened, clenching my teeth together.

"Um . . . Cocaine," she swallowed in a big lump.

"Cocaine. Why cocaine? It's got to be something more potent. You lied, didn't you?"

"No, it was cocaine, I swear."

I didn't believe her. Even if she told the truth I wouldn't believe her. That's how much I despised her. Though she answered me, I still pressed the blade into her flesh and slit it. It wasn't a deep cut, but I bled her, just to show her I meant business. She was surprised at me after submitting to my demands. Though she needed first aid, I still refused to let her go. The blood oozed out gradually from her cut down her neck.

"You lied," I insisted.

"I feel faint," she pleaded in a cold sweat.

"Are you going to tell anyone?" I threatened.

"No. I promise I won't—not a soul." She shook wildly in fear.

"Good. Then let's keep this little squabble just between ourselves, understand?"

"Yes," she nodded assent obediently.

Within the remaining moments, I used my merciless anger to slug her hard in the face, still feeling unfulfilled in my triumph. She fell back from the blow. "And by the way," I paused, "if you're lying, I will find you again and finish you off."

Once I let her go, she dropped to the floor and fainted. When I turned, I noticed Vicki standing by the doorway. Had she witnessed it all? I was somehow more embarrassed now than when Susan caught me making a scene. Where was Vicki when I needed her?

CONFESSION

"**W**hy didn't you tell me you planned to rob Jessica Wheaton's house?" I yelled at Vicki, raising my hands in disgust.

She argued, "I thought you knew. How was I supposed to know you have a vendetta against her? I had no clue she was home from school. We've been planning this scheme for weeks."

I pulled myself together then collapsed on Vicki's couch, picking dog fur off my pants. "Really Vicki, you expect me to come to you and say, 'Hey, I think I'm Jessica Wheaton, isn't that odd.' "

Vicki offered a cigarette. I refused. "You quit smokin'?" she asked.

"I'm not in the mood," I fibbed.

"Ain'tcha jittery after all that mess?" she questioned.

"No, I'm over it." I pet the dog. "But one thing I can't figure: where were you when I called for you?"

Vicki took a few puffs. "I was downstairs. I heard something drop upstairs, but I had to move carefully to make sure I wouldn't get caught. I'm not stupid, ya know. Then I heard the screams in the master bedroom . . . well, it sure explains why you've been acting so strange lately. You've been very annoying," she exhaled. "You know, you really screwed up. She called the cops. I'm sure they traced the call, and the place is combed with sirens. She's a witness to the robbery, and I know she'll charge you with assault."

"I had to hurt her," I sighed. "I had to get important information out of her. It's more important to me than anything."

Vicki sensed my obsession. "How long have you been like this?"

"What do you mean, as if I have some kind of disease? Can't you just accept that I'm not Denise, your partner in crime?"

"Fuck you!" Vicki seethed. "I'd rather have a partner in crime than a fuckin' wench who picks her nose and wears coke bottle lenses. Jessica's a fuckin' loser."

"Oh, like a dope is a winner," I inserted bitterly.

Vicki raised her fist at me, restraining herself. "I can't believe . . . I can't believe you're talkin' like this. You talk just like her. Some kinda out-of-body experience?"

"I wouldn't call it that," I shook my head.

"Okay Miss Psychiatrist, what would you call it, altered states?" She tapped her ashes in an already overflowing ash tray several times. "It's kinda hard to categorize something you can't prove."

"That's just it, you don't believe me. You think it's some kinda ploy."

"No, I think you're delirious," she snapped.

"Oh, then how do you account for the memories at the school playground—on the see-saw and the monkey bars? We used to dig for clay and then have them kilned."

Vicki looked quite astonished. "How did you . . ."

"You see, I really am Jessica, or I wouldn't know about that stuff, would I?" I pointed out.

"I forgot all about those days. Wow!" She studied me as if I were some kinda freak. I could tell that Vicki was trying to understand, piecing the puzzle together. She broke the long silent stare, "So I'm really talking to Jessica?"

"Yes," I nodded, almost winning over her faith in my convictions.

"This is really strange," Vicki remarked, shaking her head.

"Yes, I know. Don't you think it's just as hard for me?"

Vicki snapped her fingers as if she had me figured out. "Jessica told you all that stuff, didn't she?"

"Vicki, think. How did I know exactly where to find the money and jewelry in the bedroom without ransacking the house first?"

"You've probably been over her house before."

"Denise was never invited over. The two were never friends. Unfortunately, I met Denise as an adversary when you and I drifted apart many years later; you paired up with her and her friends."

"I see." Vicki thought it over then shook her head. "This is just too bizarre. What if what you're saying is true? I can't believe I'm talking to dorky Jessica right now. I mean, how could this be?"

"I don't know. I just know it is. And 'dorky' Jessica is slowly forgetting who she is. Jessica's memories are disappearing, and Denise's mind is taking over. I think I'm going through some kind of metamorphosis. I'm losing my identity. It's very frightening," I said dramatically.

"And you think this has something to do with cocaine?" Vicki added, indicating she overheard Jessica's submission.

"That or some kinda really exotic drug," I suggested.

"But why do you think it was caused by a drug at all? Why not something supernatural?" she insinuated.

"Like what?"

"Ya know, hocus-pocus . . . witchcraft . . ."

"What?"

"Well, it's a lot more interesting to think about than just plain old dope."

"Vicki, I'm not going on some live talk show as a freak or a guinea pig."

"So how would you describe it?"

"I don't know. My soul left my body and it's now with Denise's body. Call it what you want, out-of-body experience or altered states, but it's vital to me to find the cure. Please, I need your support because I'm alone in this. I need to find answers. I miss my folks back home; but of course, I can't return like this. I feel like I'm slowly fading. I wish I could see a doctor, but I'm afraid they'll put me away. It must be kept a secret, you understand," I begged of her.

"Don't be so dramatic," she protested.

"I'm sorry."

She continued, "So why do you think this is drug related? Do you know for sure?"

"Yes, because when I woke up yesterday in Denise's bed with a hangover, Mr. Bower found pills in my bedroom. That's why he beat me. He caught me in possession of Ecstasy."

"Good point." She thought it over, "Ya know, if this is some kinda ailment you got, I hope you pull through real soon 'cause I feel funny pretending you're Jessica Wheaton."

"But you won't tell anyone?" I urged.

"Your word is safe with me, whoever you are," Vicki granted, "but I ain't comfortable with the idea. I . . . think you'd better get a grip on yourself." Vicki watched my every gesture with uncertainty.

I cleared my throat. "You want to just forget about this whole thing? I really didn't want to cause any trouble," I assured, feeling a bit insecure about disclosing the truth.

"Yeah, but can I still call you Denise?" Vicki asked uneasily.

"I wouldn't have it any other way. Besides, I'm so used to the name now, I probably wouldn't respond to anything but Denise," I smiled reassuringly.

Meanwhile, Vicki prepared for a party. I assisted her as she moved the couch against the wall and unrolled the area rug toward the center of the floor. She pretended as if nothing had happened, but I knew she was uncomfortable. I figured she just needed time to digest it all.

What worried me more was that Vicki had a big mouth. She had trouble keeping secrets.

THE PARTY

This "party" Vicki arranged was not what I had in mind. I figured she'd invite the few girls from the gossip bench, but I underestimated her circle of acquaintances. The clubroom was packed with "clubbers." The guests were boisterous and classless. "Chicks" were dressed to seduce, flaunting their figures with body-tight tank tops and above-the-thigh minis. The "bikers" came dressed as rebels with cowboy boots, mo-hawks, and earring studs. Chains dangled from back pockets. Tattoos covered sleeveless shoulders and arms. Collars folded upright. Their statement was indisputable: they were "bad to the bone." Motorcycles lined the front lawn. Cartons of six-packs came strolling in. Conveniently, Vicki's father was away on a business trip.

In came Todd with Denise's boyfriend . . . if only I could remember his name . . . Kevin. Vicki flew into Todd's arms. The two kissed passionately. There was a suspicion that Todd had been cheating on her. But then again, she'd been two-timing with some Ricky guy. I offered Todd the courtesy of a handshake. He, in turn, kissed me firmly on the lips. At the same time, a hand from behind squeezed my butt. Who else? When I turned myself around, Kevin slobbered over my lips with intense lust. Bad breath! I pushed him away. That was a BAD move.

"Ay, what's wrong, babe?" His bloodshot eyes were saddened by my rejection. *What's wrong?* He had the most repugnant body odor and dressed like a homeless drunk with razor-slashed blue jeans. And OMG, he's armed! There was a switchblade dangling from a chain in his back pocket. I didn't dare mess with him. What did Denise ever see in him? The thought of having sex with this guy made me want to puke.

The gossip girls stood in the background watching me. *Shit, they caught me!* I grinned. I knew I was in trouble. I put my arms around Kevin, holding my nose away from him. "I'm glad to see you," I said to him.

Abruptly, Marie pulled me aside. "Did it help?" she whispered in my ear.

"What?" I asked.

"The pills I lent you. Did it help?"

Now that she mentioned it, I recalled Mr. Bower throwing a pill bottle against the Uncle Sam poster, and the delusions of paranoia, falling, and claustrophobia. I wanted to thank Marie for the practical joke she played on me. It was just what I needed. I really wanted to strangle her. Instead, I just smiled and nodded, "Oh yes, thanks."

"So, you're feeling better?" she prodded. I nodded restraining my fist.

"Great!" she exclaimed, "I knew you just needed some rest." She finally admitted that she really offered me a sedative.

Susan snuck her busy nose in on the little scuffle. "You alright?" She poked in my face.

"I'm fine." I wanted to change the subject, but . . .

"Were you sick?" Kevin asked me, overhearing all the chatter.

I looked up at him, glanced at the girls, then at Vicki. All eyes were pinned on me, awaiting a reply as if I were on trial and they were the jurors.

"Ah . . . no, just a bit depressed. But I'm over it now."

"Are you sure you don't want to talk about it?" Kevin pressed.

Though it was most thoughtful of the junky to offer me his support, what intelligent advice could he possibly have to offer? I'm sure he would be very entertained by my problems, but there didn't seem to be any substantial nerve activity processing in his wasted mind.

"Really, I'm okay. I just had a bad trip."

Susan accepted my explanation. But, Christina mouthed, *does he know*, while rolling her eyes in Kevin's direction. I nodded to quiet her.

"Well baby, let's do it together tonight so you won't have to be alone," he laughed, putting his arm around me. Trying to retain my composure, I was soaked in perspiration.

Vicki must have sensed my discomfort. She cleared her throat then cheered, "Let's party! Todd, c'mon," she signaled. Todd clapped to get everyone's attention. "Let's get the show on the road. What are we waiting for?"

The guests gathered in a circle along the area rug, at the center of the floor. Kevin and I joined the group arm-in-arm. I just wished Denise had been a bit more selective when choosing a boyfriend. Either she had very poor taste in guys, or I overlooked some well-hidden attributes.

A clump of instruments lay at the center of the circle including bottles, syringes, and brown particles in plastic baggies. The guests indulged in their entree. Vicki turned on the stereo, raising the volume. Either we weren't supposed to hear one another, or she didn't want the neighbors to get any ideas. Some folks popped pills, swallowing them down with beer, while others passed around cigarettes. A few used syringes.

I felt a little queasy watching Slim, across from me, torture his bruised arm. He affixed a rubber band at the joint of his elbow until the skin buckled underneath. Squinting, he injected the serum as his hand shook. This had to be some sort of masochistic way to seek pleasure.

When he was finished, he passed the used needle to the next player for the same satanic practice, who refilled the tube with fluid from a medicine bottle. That same used needle was passed around the circle for anyone's disposal. I was aghast at the purply marks on some of the users' veins.

The raunchy guests soon quieted as they became heavily intoxicated.

Kevin's dilated pupils stared at me. "Ya wanna joint, babe?" he hollered over the volume. "A joint?" I asked, paying little attention to him.

He nodded as his head pivoted. "Yeah, pot," he offered me his black cigarette pressed between his finger and thumb.

Pot? Marijuana? Could that be the mystery drug I've been searching for? No, no, Jessica said it was cocaine. So, I asked for cocaine. Kevin yelled over to the black host for coke.

"We ain't got no coke, ches' pot," the host slurred.

"What?" Kevin yelled.

"No coke" the black dude raised his voice.

"No, no," I articulated to Kevin, "I'm not thirsty, I just want cocaine."

Kevin smirked at me with weary eyes. "Not that kinda coke, silly. He ain't got the stuff that make you turn loose."

"Oh," I felt stupid. I had to learn these things if I was going to conceal my true identity.

A marijuana cigarette was passed over to me. I refused, "No thanks. I only want cocaine."

The host bickered, "Well shit, that's your loss. This ain't no fuckin' restaurant."

Moments ago, I wanted nothing to do with this circle, but I began to see things differently.

The junk was doing something exciting for the guests. With glazed-over eyes, the "groupies" were smiling contently. Oddly, they began to laugh and giggle for no apparent reason. Each participant was enjoying a private fantasy, an inner joy. I wondered why everyone gathered in a group just to be in solitude. Some lay back on the floor, grinning off into space, while others had the tolerance to take another shot. Behind me, a big-busted blonde paused after snorting her particles. Her brows rose as she exclaimed, "Wow!" *Was it better than sex?*

"Babe, what's the matter wichoo? You been die'n fer dis stuff. You earned it. C'mon," Kevin coaxed me to try his joint

I finally gave it a whirl. I held it, examined it. The crust of Kevin's rolled lightweight black paper was already withered. Ashes eroded the tip, casting off fumes of a foul bitter odor. I just couldn't imagine how this . . . plant could offer me such a pleasure.

"It's sooo cool . . . it's sooo . . . FLUIDY!" The blonde stared off into space, elbowing me.

That did it. At first inhale, I felt an irritating tickle pass down my throat. I coughed. Kevin seemed surprised that smoking bothered me. "Easy babe, don't inhale so quickly. I guess it been a while for ya."

I tried again, and again. Inhale. Hold. Exhale. With practice, I got the hang of it. I was already creating little smoke rings. It did indeed feel good, and it was relaxing. I felt . . . content. I could see how these addictions get started.

The host asked if I was enjoying myself. Before I had a chance to say anything, the blonde crawled over him and kissed him. "Oh baby, yeah," she answered for me.

I gazed at the guests as they swayed from side to side, uttering total nonsense. Not before long, the group sang and danced obscure routines. Once the mood hit me, I chimed in. My awareness as being separate from everyone was just an illusion. We were all one universal being, undivided. One magnificent force of energy.

Everything has a majestic glow about it. As if animated, objects tell me that they love me, and I know that it is true. They cast genuine smiles. The piano plays love tunes. The sofa bounces about in place. The television spins around on its built-in wall unit. All is merry. Voices sing in harmony. I cannot discern the words, but the sound flows like orchestrated melody, smooth like the flight of an eagle to shore. Laughter jingles like bells and chimes; I sing along and dance in place, loud and proud, with glory and passion. The room is filled with peace and joy. We all sway together as one complete, inseparable family, loving each other and ourselves. I lead, they follow. Pleasure bestows upon us.

THE ORGY

It only took one horny individual to ignite a game of Simon Says. The flame spread like wildfire. The dude with the long ponytail kissed the chick with the spiked purple hair sitting beside him in the circle. In turn, the chick passed a passionate kiss to the next player, male or female. It didn't matter. The chain reaction broke midway around the circle when a kiss became more than a kiss. Tongues were in action. Giggles preceded intense lust. The next overt display in progress came from a young lad who took her top off while kissing. This led to nipple sucking. And, like a chain reaction, each player around the circle did exactly as "Simon" said.

Vicki got up off the floor and walked away. I had hoped she was going to put an end to the blatant inhibitions. Much to my surprise, she returned with a finger paint palette for anyone's disposal. In addition to touching skin and licking, we now had the creative option to paint each other's skin as if on a canvas. And, of course, once painted, the delicious sweet edible colors delightfully licked off. It brought out the wild canines in us.

I drifted into fantasy . . .

I am one among the many on an exotic nude beach. My metallic gold fingers and toes dig into the cool, moist, red sand. As pastel violet tides rush to shore, the cool refreshing saltwater soaks my feet. The sun rays blind my eyes shut.

A light, gentle warmth touches my shoulder, slowly gliding down the length of my arm. Who could it be? Venturing around the hills of my chest, it moves about in an elliptical fashion, aimlessly, provoked by desire. Mysterious long fingers softly fondle my hardened nipples, caressing, stroking, then squeezing as they move on. Changing their course, they slowly meander past my belly, tickling my sides, then journeying steadily toward but not overlooking the contour of my outer shape and curves. They appear to have a mind of their own, traveling wherever they please. They are in control. I hear heavy breathing, not my own.

The hand slides downward in conquest of the treasure. The lock is tampered with. The finger unlocks the forbidden treasure chest. As an irresistible desire engulfs me, I ooze and moan in excitement. I know who the intruder is: the seductive violator, the masseur, the arouser, the fondler. IT makes me crave for more. THE HUNGER! I have no intention of stopping Kevin's hand from its ambition. I anchor my pelvis anxiously, allowing him.

The physical warmth abruptly abandons me! I feel cold and dissatisfied. I yearn like thirst to be finished, completed.

Fortunately, I am touched once more. My flesh begs for pleasure. His lusting fingertips are an instrument of that pleasure. I again give him the rights to my treasure. What used to be mine is now his. I totally surrender myself.

Oddly, the hand hesitates. I wonder what's stopping it. I open my eyes in my customized paradise. Metallic silver hands reach out for Kevin, pulling him away from me. They are masculine intruders! Barbaric! I am appalled. My arms reach out in despair, begging him to return. Silver nudes mount over him as he faces down on the red sands. I am disappointed that he has abandoned me for masculine rebels and that he may never return to complete me.

I tried to break away from my self-created fantasy, but it was too late. What . . . what was she doing? This was embarrassing. A glob of royal blue paint sealed her fingers together. Blue paint was stroked across my chest. Her face drew downward; lips latched onto my nipple. I felt her teeth gently nibble on the hardened tenderness as she sucked. Her warm wet tongue licked me like a dog, slobbering over my breasts. She momentarily gazed into my eyes, winking at me. I looked away in disgust. Her strong perfume saturated my sinuses. Meanwhile, Slim with the shoulder tattoo rolled over beside me as if he wanted my body, but instead, french-kissed the black lesbian lying on top of me. Another male nude climbed aboard behind the dike, groping for her tote bags, weighing me down, caking me in further. I was short of breath. I felt his sack swing against my privates, but it was not me he was trying to enter.

The stinky, sticky, slimy sweat of bodies around me had me branded in captivity. This was clearly not the neon beach fantasy I had in mind. Faces, buttocks, breasts, and genitals were splattered and smeared with primary colors. There weren't any metallic figures to be found here. The air was filled with the scent of sex.

Was this some kind of whorehouse? What had I gotten myself into? I wanted the lesbian intruder off me, but my arms and feet were caught under the bodies of others.

Somehow, I had to wiggle myself out from under her. I squirmed, pushed, and shoved. Once I managed to raise myself above sea level, I saw past the dike. Christina was sandwiched between two guys. One dude mounted her from behind, thrusting in her, while she gave head to the other moaning john. Milky cum escaped her mouth, dribbling down her chin, bouncing off her pink-painted nipples. Snake, over there, received a rather nice mouthful blowjob from Marie while he Picasso painted her ass. How fortunate for Vicki and Susan to be privy to one nice ménage-a-trois with a huge bulging dick in the middle. In this game, no one is exclusive with any one partner. Everyone shares.

As for me, I was the most blessed of all to have a "bi" on top of me with a dog humping her from behind while her tongue locked with Slim. Her patterned nails dug into my tits as she squeezed them during her arousal. I'd had enough of this obscenity. I was at war with the nudes, trying whatever it took to escape, including shoving and clawing. As I cried out, I heard the whimpers and groans of others. I fought my way out from under the dogs in heat. Tongues were flapping for my genitals. Hands were grasping for my ass—wouldn't let go of my ankles. I was caught in a giant colorful cobweb.

Once I finally shook off all the begging, hungry dogs, I was set free. I darted into the bathroom and quickly locked the door behind me. My bare buttocks, full of colored fingerprint stains, leaned against the locked bathroom door as I sighed in relief.

My wet body was shivering from the absence of body heat. I was a bit stunned that I had just participated in a gang-banging orgy.

THE WATER

I studied the reflection in the mirror. She remained an enigma to me. She looked a mess—hair matted, love bites saturating her neck, lipstick stains on her breast, blue splattered paint across her chest. All were vivid evidence that an orgy had indeed taken place. Sticky and smelly, I needed a bath. I drew the blinds. Beyond the blinds stood a Jacuzzi. "All the better," I exclaimed. It was effortless to operate. Power switch on—automatic high-pressure beams shot off hot sudsy, bubbling bathwater from various vents. I gradually set foot into the depths of the hot water. Hastily, I scrubbed myself, trying to wash away all the impurities.

Soon after I turn the faucet off, I notice that the water level continues to rise. I check the drain; it is sealed in place. Instantly, the water level ascends over the edge, overflowing onto the floor! The power is dead! Darkness and silence overcome me. I yell for help. No response. Are my buddies too busy seeking pleasure to save my life? A sudden surge of sudsy warm water squirts into my face! The water comes in waves as it splashes over me. I hold my breath. I fight to stay afloat in what appears to be a sea of monstrous tidal waves. The unrelenting currents spin around like a tornado as it swats about aimlessly . . .

It lassos over my head, whipping at me with great fury. There is a hand behind it, instructing its brutality. A leather belt lashes at my behind, engraving the pain I endure, long overdue. "I promise I won't do it anymore, please Daddy," I beg, shielding myself with my baby elbows, flattened over his knee.

The water is the killer. Daddy is innocent. A high-pressure jet stream of icy water shoots into my eyes, blinding me. "No!" I cry. I squirm away from it. It races around like a rattlesnake, chasing after me. It catches me, shooting venom down my throat. I can't breathe. I choke. "Please put the hose down," I plea as I cough.

A soft touch to my forehead awoke me. I heard whispers. They were talking amongst themselves. "She's comin' around." I looked up and saw Kevin's lazy eyeballs gazing down on me. I was lying on the couch in Vicki's clubroom with Kevin by my side, pressing an ice pack against my head. I was pleased that my buddies had their clothes on. I tried to sit up, but Kevin pushed me back down on the couch, insisting that I lie still. He explained, "You had an accident, hit your head on the Jacuzzi. You gotta deep gash, but I think you stopped bleeding."

Vicki asked, "What happened to ya?"

I couldn't remember. All that came to mind was the flood, a memory I didn't wish to share. "Where is everyone?" I changed the subject, rubbing my sore head.

"You mean the guests?" Vicki snickered, "Everyone left early this morning. Did you have a good time?" She raised her eyebrows as her eyes opened wide.

"Aw! My head hurts," I whined, refraining from answering her.

"Why did you run off to the washroom during the party?" Vicki persisted. "Kevin had to bust the door open cuz he heard you scream. He found you lying on the rim of the Jacuzzi. I guess you lost your balance and bumped your head. Were you shooting up in there? 'Cause you could'a drowned or somethin'," she surmised.

I did not reply.

"How could you run off to the Jacuzzi without me?" Kevin pouted. "You know I would'a joined ya. You could'a told me." He pointed out, "You've been doing a lot of things without me, lately. Are you mad at me?"

I shook my head at the idiot when I really wanted to nod.

Vicki added, "You gave us a real scare, ya know. When we heard you scream, we thought you were being attacked," she asserted. They each agreed. Vicki whispered into my ear, "Were you trying to kill yourself? You can tell me. You know I won't tell anyone," She comforted me, holding my hand.

"No." I almost laughed at the silly thought that I once contemplated.

"She'd better not, I'd be a widower before my years," Kevin remarked then smooched me on the lips. I silently said to myself, *over my dead body would I marry you—you dirty, filthy, wet, slimy, scuz-bag.*

Vicki insisted I rest for a while. She hinted around that Kevin and Todd were going for a *drag* later on. I wasn't quite sure what a "drag" was, though I hoped it wasn't boring.

I laid on the couch for some time thinking about the visions and searching within the deep recesses of my mind for some sort of explanation. The water. The belt. The hose. What did it all mean? It had to be some sort of symbolism. The visions had to be a part of Denise's troubled mind since they were too realistic to be just a bad dream. I was certain that it really happened. I played it over, and over in my head. *The water is the killer. Daddy is innocent . . .* Yeah, I bet. That bastard abused Denise in her early years. He hadn't changed at all. It was rather sad to learn about this hidden secret, especially about someone I despised. I almost felt sorry for her. That's scary.

SHOPLIFTING

otorcycles were revving up in the garage. Vicki grabbed her jacket. "The guys are hittin' the road, c'mon!"

"Not again. This better not be a robbery," I refused.

Vicki tugged on my arm. "No silly, we're going to drag race. C'mon, this'll be fun. There's no way you can screw this up."

Kevin had me hop on the back of his vibrating seat. I was to place my arms around his waist as he geared up for the journey. The motor was so loud, I couldn't hear a thing. Vicki sat behind Todd on his cycle. At first the ride was mild. A light breeze brushed my hair aside. But once we accelerated, my breath went against the wind. "Aren't we supposed to wear helmets?" I hollered.

"Fuck no. That ain't no fun," Kevin snarled.

"Slow down," I yelled. "You're going too fast."

"This ain't nothin' babe. Wait till ya see some real action."

The two Harley partners raced each other across town. The needle on the speedometer jumped from 30 to 70 mph.

"Let me off here then you can do whatever you'd like," I panicked.

"Hey baby, what's wrong? Don't forget you're with the champion," Kevin assured. And he went to great lengths to prove his sportsmanship, at my expense, as I clung onto him for dear life.

The opponents sped across the barren fields exceeding 80 miles an hour. Kevin's passion for drag racing had exceeded his ability to reason. He and Todd started off at the same point, but Kevin was undeniably in the lead. Todd soon caught up to him and surpassed him. But Kevin was not to be underestimated. He pushed himself beyond limit, determined to beat Todd. The Harley shook wildly as it buzzed up the speedometer. Ten yards before the finish line, near a magnolia tree, Kevin surpassed Todd. We cheered him on. At the finish line Kevin had trouble breaking; hence, he rammed right into Todd's fender, putting Todd's front tire out of alignment. Todd was outraged, cursing at Kevin, ready to slug him, but the two buddies broke from anger into hysterical laughter. I didn't see what was so funny. My whole life was on the line.

Kevin put his arm around me, trying to loosen me up. "What's wrong, babe? Aren't ya havin' fun?"

"I'd rather be drunk," I said sarcastically for this was not my idea of fun in the least.

Of course they took such a remark literally. Todd heard the magic word. "Yeah, Dini's right. Let's stop off somewhere. I could use a six pack."

"There's a convenience store up ahead," Vicki pointed out.

"Yeah, let's go shopping," Kevin cackled. Todd consented, giving him a high five. "I could use a pack of Marlboros," Vicki giggled.

I couldn't figure why they were so amused about going shopping. We came up to a small-town convenience store. Todd circled the store with his bike a few times then gave the *okay* signal. "No cops or guards—coast clear." Kevin peaked inside the store window. The two Indian chiefs whispered amongst each other then came to an agreement and alerted us chicks, "We'll do the five-minute stand-by, okay?"

"What if something goes wrong?" Vicki asked.

"Do whatcha gotta do," Todd advised. He kissed her goodbye. Kevin and Todd casually waltzed into the convenience store while Vicki and I sat by the parked motorcycles waiting for them. I wasn't sure what was about to happen, but I had a bad feeling about it. After a few customers left the store, Todd gave us another okay signal from the store window.

Vicki glanced at her watch. "Are you ready?" she asked me anxiously.

Me? Ready? My nerves rattled as I wondered what I was getting into. *What? Not again. All you guys do is rob places. You need to get a job. This isn't someone's home, this is a public place. What if we get caught? We could be arrested this time and if I'm lucky I will be sentenced to life in prison instead of waiting on death row to be executed.*

"Dini," Vicki waved her hands in my face, trying to get my attention as I was in a trance. She grunted, "What's wrong with you? You've got to stay alert. Don't buzz out on me now. Just let me do the talkin', okay?"

"Why don't you go by yourself. You know this is not for me," I hinted cowardly.

"No way. C'mon, we're in this together," Vicki insisted, undermining my point.

The moment we entered the store; I spotted the clerk at the counter. He wasn't very friendly or welcoming. I suppose he already had suspicions. There were no visible cameras or mirrors.

The clerk cleared his throat, "May I help you?"

"Don't act lost," Vicki whispered to me. She walked over to the counter. "Yeah, I'd like a pack of Marlboros and two sticks of that red chewing gum over there," she pointed to her choice. The clerk reached over to the shelf to fill her order.

"Anything else, Ma'am?" the clerk asked before ringing her up.

"No, that's it," Vicki replied. Meanwhile, she spotted Todd over by the exit door with his pockets full. He signaled that he was ready to sneak out. Vicki immediately asked for another pack of cigarettes to keep the clerk distracted. Without question the clerk turned around to the cigarette stand, behind him. Vicki winked at Todd, giving him the go.

"And I'd like this too," Vicki tossed a roll of sweet tarts onto the counter.

Just as Todd darted out, Kevin scurried around the aisle with a six-pack of beer. He inadvertently brushed against the magazine rack, drawing attention as the loose magazines plummeted to the floor. I held my breath as my heart pounded. The clerk bounced over the counter catching Kevin in the act of shoplifting.

"Oh fuck!" Vicki fretted under her breath.

I wanted to say, *don't say I didn't warn you*. Nevertheless, Kevin darted out the door. "Hey boy, get back here!" the clerk yelled over at Kevin, making no attempt to chase him.

The clerk turned to us. "You girls with them?" he questioned. He looked me in the eyes. I shook my head and remained silent as Vicki instructed.

Vicki seemed offended that the clerk would even think of accusing us, "Are you kidding? With them? Who'd wanna be with those creeps?" She remarked to me, "They coulda snatched our purses or better yet, held us hostage." Vicki asserted to the clerk,

"Who knows, they might be armed!" She feigned a worried look. "I don't think it would be safe for us to leave the store, sir?"

"Ladies, excuse me for a moment." The clerk hurried over to the store phone. Both of us knew what he was up to—the police. My eyes were locked on Vicki. *Now what?* Vicki's eyes were quickly searching. She located a phone cord dangling within the separation of the counter. As soon as the clerk picked up the receiver, Vicki pulled her penknife out. My heart throbbed.

Oh shit, she's not going to . . . She stooped down under the counter, reached for the cord, then slashed it. The clerk couldn't figure out why the phone went dead. "Strange, the phone isn't working," he muttered. Vicki stood up waiting to see how long it would take for the clerk to figure out the problem.

I couldn't bear another moment. I snatched the unpaid merchandise from the counter and darted off. As I pushed the exit door open, I heard the clerk yell for me to come back and accuse me of shoplifting. Only after I flew out of the store did I realize I had left Vicki behind, vulnerable to the hands of the clerk. Fortunately, not a moment later did I feel a push on my back side, as Vicki had run into me.

"We did it!" Waving and shaking her fists in the air, Vicki danced. The Harleys were revved up. Vicki and I hopped on as the bikes darted off with a tremendous burst of power, kicking dirt behind.

Miles away, the guys stopped along a rural county road to open their stolen six-pack. Vicki reiterated what happened. "The clerk tried to phone the cops, but I cut the phone cord. When he figured it out, I showed him my knife. Well, he had no choice but to back off. You could tell he was pissed having to let us go." Vicki cackled, retrieving a pack of cigarettes from my back pocket. "And thanks for being a good sport." She grinned at me, messing with my hair.

I had trouble convincing myself that I was completely off the hook. I was certain at any moment a police car would turn up out of nowhere or I'd hear sirens. But nothing happened.

Absolutely nothing. And the craziest part of it all was that I felt no shame or regrets, but rather a feeling of invincibility. The slight smile on my face was vain.

THE SECRET REVEALED

Audible cheers and boos from a nearby school could be heard a mile away. The gang was eager to check it out. Exploring the school grounds, we spotted a Little League softball game in session. The bikers settled themselves by a shaded area on the field's hilltop to watch a game in progress. The fresh cut grass was quickly littered with cigarette butts and smashed beer cans were tossed aside.

"So," Vicki sighed, stretching her jacket out on the open grass to shape a blanket. "Ya havin' a good time?" she asked me.

"I guess," I answered unenthusiastically.

"What do ya mean, you guess?" She studied me with uncertainty.

"It's just a bit much," I lowered my head, picking at the blades of grass.

"You wanna smoke?" she offered.

"Not really, I'd rather just chill out," I said despondently.

"You okay?"

"I'm fine. I'm just not used to . . ."

"What happened in the Jacuzzi?" Vicki interrupted. She began to scrutinize me again. I knew something was up.

"You told me I slipped," I reminded her.

She raised her voice, "Is that why you were crying in there? We thought someone attacked you. Why were you screaming? Were you doing dope? Be honest."

The guys momentarily glanced over at us as they were chatting amongst themselves about the game.

I sighed. "No," I whispered, trying to keep the conversation quiet. "I was not doing dope, but I did have the strangest hallucination. It's really a private matter," I cautioned her.

Vicki smirked, rolling her eyes as if to say, *that again*. "Does this have anything to do with the OBE we discussed earlier?" She acknowledged that she did, in fact, remember.

"It may," I admitted.

Vicki remarked, "I want to really forget about that but you're really acting peculiar. I don't know about you, man. I mean first you harass Jessica Wheaton when we broke into her place, then you spaz out in the Jacuzzi. I think you're losin' it. Kevin told me he thinks you're shooting up too much."

"So, you think I'm crazy," I asked belligerently.

"C'mon Dini, we've been friends for years. Is there something you're hiding from me?"

"Are you sure I'm Denise? I could very well be Jessica," I placed doubt in her head, making her very uneasy.

Vicki's eyes were enraged with distrust. "You think you're funny, don'tcha? 'Cause I know you hate her guts. I mean, you've told me so many times that she's a total loser, a nerd, and incredibly wimpy. You love tormenting her."

"Do you agree?" I challenged her.

"Well, she is a teacher's pet, ya know what I mean? So old school. Very wormy, totally unpopular, and so uncool. Yeah, I think she's a geek. She dresses sooo outdated with God awful grandma clothes, with those ugly coke-bottle lenses, and no makeup at all. Sickening." She paused. "I don't know. I used to like her way back but don't like the crazy person she is now."

"Why did you pick on her?" I wondered.

Vicki seethed. "Why are you asking me all these silly questions? I really don't care to give Jessica the time of day. I have better things to think about." She raised her voice, again. "Besides, I don't even know who I'm talking to!" She turned away from me disconcertedly and lit another cigarette.

I changed the topic. "I'm sorry. I just need to figure out a few things I'm confused about. Please bear with me."

Vicki took a few puffs.

"Tell me, what do you think of my father?" I asked her.

"Do we have to get into that again?" Vicki whined.

"Please, just tell me," I urged.

"I don't like him, okay?" she said reluctantly.

"Why not?"

"'Cause he's an asshole—he's not nice to you. Why are you asking me?"

"Don't tell anyone, okay, but I had visions in the Jacuzzi of Mr. Bower beating me with a hose and then with a belt on two separate occasions. Had I ever told you about these instances before?"

Vicki looked bewildered, almost speechless. "No."

"But you know he beats me, right?" I questioned her, eyeballing her.

She nodded. "But you never told me the details. Gee, I'm really sorry, that's terrible. Did you ever tell anyone else?"

"No—just you. But I wonder if anyone had ever reported him to the police. I mean, you've known all these years that he beats me, right?"

"So, was I supposed to report him to the police for you?" Vicki looked at me as if I were placing blame on her.

"Why didn't you?" I insisted. We looked at each other cross in the eyes.

"Well, you never wanted anyone to know about that. I guess you were ashamed of it. It was a secret," Vicki explained, justifying herself.

"Maybe I was afraid he'd find out," I whispered, "and maybe —kill me."

"Denise, stop that—stop that now." Vicki slapped my leg as she became quite agitated. "You're trying to blame me, aren't you? I remember you secretly told the girls that he beats you now and then, but it never really bothered you. You never complained about this before. And I can assure you that if you report your dad to the police, the cops will book you, not your dad, cuz you have a criminal record. So just forget about it and keep it to yourself like you always have," Vicki warned. "Just shut up . . ."

Todd crawled over to Vicki, placing his head on her lap, whereby abruptly terminating our little chit-chat. I wished I could have asked so many more questions, but perhaps it was out-of-character for me. I was supposed to be the loud, rambunctious, detached, unemotional kind, not a sensitive do-gooder type. Behaving like Jessica with Denise's façade was not at all cool. I had merely scratched the surface of unraveling the great mysteries of Denise's dark past.

VICTIMS OF HUMILITY

The softball game was over soon enough. The winning team was surrounded by cheering fans. The losing side, however, had to clean up afterward. Eventually the fans disbanded.

Two players from the losing team remained. The little juniors began their own game of catch for practice.

After a few beers, Kevin and Todd grew restless. Agitated by the novice action on the softball field, they booed, insisting the losers get off the field and go home. Unfortunately, the youngsters ignored their insults. The two innocent boys, alone at play, would soon regret their decision.

Todd threw his used cigarette butt toward the boys. I could see ashes fly. "Where's the fuckin' game?" he grumbled, "I want to see some bad-ass performance." He continued to insult the youngsters with vulgarities. His remarks even offended me.

Vicki played along, laughing at the cruelty. To think she'd be concerned about a friend's child abuse allegations would now appear totally absurd.

Vicki and I were smoking the leftover joints from the party. After a few drags, the weed tranquilized my nerves. Everything went dull as though it was all just a movie.

Kevin whistled. "Hey Sonny, where did you learn to catch like that?" he called out. The boys snubbed him. "Which mental institution?"

Todd added, snickering, "Great throws."

Kevin whistled again, as he tossed a pebble at the players. "You ought to go to war for our country. Knock the dicks off every enemy."

Todd snapped, "Hey, you in the blue jacket." The kid momentarily turned his head but then diverted his attention. Todd mimicked in an infantile manner, "Who buys your clothes for ya? Your mommy? What store does she buy them from?"

Vicki giggled, "Save-A-Lot. Mommy always gets the best discounts in town."

Kevin grew increasingly agitated as he gulped down his fourth beer. He called out to the taller kid, wiping his mouth with the sleeve of his shirt, "How old are you, boy?" The kid ignored him. Kevin called out again. He demanded an answer. "Hey, I'm talking to you, boy." He was getting seriously pissed. "I said, how old are you?" Still no answer. Kevin grew outraged from the silent treatment. He charged down the hill, ran right into the boy, knocking the kid over. "Are you deaf, boy? Didn't you hear me ask you a question?"

Kevin tried to intimidate the child, but the boy got right back up off the ground and protested, "Leave us alone." The kid was trying to be brave standing up to the bully but didn't know what was in store for him.

Kevin grabbed the boy by the collar and shouted, "What did you say to me?" He shook the kid silly.

The boy's friend whined, "C'mon, leave him alone."

Kevin turned around to the friend and shouted, "Then tell your fuckin' friend to answer me!"

"Rob, ya better listen to him," his friend urged. "Alright, what do you want?" Rob yielded.

"I already told you, I want to know how old you are, ROB," Kevin articulated as if the boy was deaf.

"I'm 13, okay. Are you satisfied?" the boy answered rather reluctantly with a nervous swallow.

"Speak up, I can't hear you."

"I said 13," the boy raised his voice in compliance.

Kevin folded his arms. "Uh-ha, you think you're a tough guy, don't ya? What's Rob stand for? Robin Hood?" Kevin badgered him.

"Robert," the kid clarified.

"Nice cap, Robert," Kevin snatched the cap right off the kid's head. Rob chased after it. Kevin taunted him, "You really want it back, huh? Well, let's see just how tough you really are." Kevin passed the cap to Todd, who joined in on the harassment. Just as the kid ran over to retrieve the cap from Todd, it was tossed back to Kevin. The boy foolishly jumped after the cap several times as it was volley-balled back and forth. It became clear that a game of Frisbee had begun and Rob had no chance of getting his cap back.

Rob cried, "Give it back!"

Todd pushed the boy into the mud. "Get lost kid."

"You didn't say please," Kevin vexed the boy.

"Please, please give it back." At this point Rob was willing to say just about anything as he was at their mercy.

Todd winked at Kevin. "Alright, if you really want it . . ." Todd slapped the cap through a mud puddle then forced it back on Rob's head. Kevin cackled as the mud dripped down the sad kid's face.

"Man, that's brand new," Rob grieved.

Rob's friend grew tired of the derisive behavior. He courageously snuck up behind Todd, who was almost double his height, jumped him, and grabbed Todd by the collar, attempting to strangle him. Rob was about to aid his buddy when Kevin pulled Rob's friend off Todd and pinned the kid down to the ground. "So, you think you're a tough guy too?" Kevin punched him in the face.

Rob ran away. Todd started to chase after the kid, but Kevin insisted Todd forget about the wimp.

Meanwhile, the friend cried, "Let me go!" as he kicked and squirmed from under Kevin. "Ya know, I like you better than Rob cuz you play tough. And I really want to be proud of you, but first ya have to prove that'cher cool." Kevin retrieved a pack of cigarettes from his pocket while sitting on the five footer's chest. "Would you like one, Pal?" he offered to the youngster.

"No."

"Oh c'mon. You have to try just one before I letcha go."

"It'll make me cough," the kid refused.

"Don't be a sissy like your friend. If you don't give it a try, I'll have to beat you up," Kevin warned.

"Okay, okay," the kid submitted.

"Good sport," Kevin praised. "That's being cool—real cool." Kevin placed a cigarette in the boy's mouth and ignited the tip with a lighter. "What's your name, big boy?"

"Garris."

"Garris. I like that. It's different. Garris, I don't like your buddy Rob but I do like you," Kevin sweet-talked him.

In only moments, Garris started coughing wildly. The boy spit the cigarette out. Kevin and Todd laughed hysterically in amusement. Todd insisted, "You'll have to get used to it." Garris's eyes widened in disbelief as he was trying to clear his irritated throat from the toxic fumes. Kevin forced the used muddy cigarette back into the boy's mouth against resistance.

FLASHBACKS

Vicki and I were totally stoned out of our mind at this point. She lay in the tall grass talking gibberish. I lay in the sky looking down at the school baseball field . . . I saw everything in reverse. I mean, I was viewing the field from the sky. A plane flew right past me—scared the shit out of me. Abruptly, flashbacks came over . . .

I'm a toddler held in the arms of a husky bearded young man with hair combed back. I cry; he pacifies me. He is my half-brother— Timothy Bowers. He's twenty years older than I. He just got married. I'm sad that Timothy is moving away from home. I don't want him to leave.

A tall, thin, dirty blond with glasses pats Tim on the back then hugs him. He's the younger half-brother, middle child, named John. He's about fifteen years older. John resembles Father. John, too, is leaving home. He's off to Penn State University for a doctorate degree. I'm afraid to be left alone with Father because of his terrible temper.

I always look forward to visits with Uncle Joe and Aunt Mary over the summer months while Mom and Dad go away on vacation. Auntie plays with me and spoils me with lots of gifts. Big Joe and Auntie teach me to swim, skate, and bicycle. We go on long hikes and camping trips. They're so much fun. I wish I could have lived with them. They really made me feel loved. Unfortunately, Big Joe dies from cancer years later.

Things are never the same thereafter.

Years pass. I'm much older. I find myself in bed with another John. He's my first boyfriend. John appears to be only about fifteen years of age. He has a bad temper, like Dad, and beats on me when he's pissed. I'm always afraid to deny him of sex. He's very pushy and hostile about making out.

Vicki comes into the picture. She always did love to throw parties. She informs me at a barbecue that she, too, had a relationship with John but they broke up due to sexual issues. She urges me to leave him. Vicki and I soon become best friends.

"Oooh!" Vicki moaned. I snapped out of my trance. I had no idea what Vicki was experiencing, but it had to be better than what I envisioned.

My eyes wander down into the field. I imagine the boys fighting to be like guppies playing on the bottom of a pond. The two guppies, in the depths of shallow water, swim off in different directions. There are many other beautiful fish as well. Nature has designed them so splendidly. The pond appears as one harmless and perfect world, full of enchantment. I'm particularly captivated by the baby bluefish swimming in circles. They're so cute and irresistible that I reach my hand in the water for one.

Just as I touch the guppy, I feel something slimy and massive hit me. It startles me! I jump back. The pond becomes an ocean of darkness. The tiny bluefish turn into a huge man-eating white shark! I yell hysterically. The shark jumps out of the water to devour me whole. Its huge jaws open wide, ready to swallow! My fierce screams echo within its mouth. Its razor-blade teeth close in on me. Am I being eaten alive?

Instantaneous visions flash before me: I am bound to a bed by rope—gagged, stripped naked, and raped by a black man. I grin and bear the pain. Denise's spirit is possessed by an evil, malicious laughter; a black woman is sleeping with Todd. She is a prostitute.

Vicki is pregnant with Todd's child! Again, a wicked laugh. I'm behind bars in a jail cell craving dope. I throw up—the hunger—the desire. The shrieking laughter terrorizes me. I try to jump from a high-rise building . . .

Cold hands shook my face. I heard the sweetness of human voices. "Dini, Dini?" Once again, with gratitude, I awoke finding myself in the hands of friends. I was able to move all my limbs and, by god, they were still attached. Not a cut, bite, or scratch. Fortunately, I had only fatal visions and nothing more. I sighed.

Vicki smirked. "Another bad trip, huh?" She knelt before me holding my hand. Kevin, on my other side, caressed my head. Todd remained standing as if on surveillance. Unlike the horrors I envisioned just moments ago, Vicki was not pregnant. In fact, the two lovers were still happily together. From this moment on, I kept my secret insights to myself. I really didn't understand the visions, but I knew they were hidden clues to my mystery.

"You smoke too many reefers," Vicki concluded about my erratic behavior.

"Man." Todd frowned. "We was havin' so much fun with them kids before you went nuts on us. We had to let' em go cuz we thought the cops was comin'." He may have been waiting for me to apologize, but I wouldn't give him the satisfaction.

Kevin nodded in agreement. "We gotta get outta here now. Them kids on the loose most definitely be callin' the cops," he cautioned. "You okay, babe?" he asked, concerned. I wasn't sure. He kissed me softly on the lips then rubbed his nose against mine, mumbling under his alcoholic breath, "I love you, babe. No more freakin' out, okay. I want you around, hear?"

At the same time, the late school bell sounded. Its loud echoing ring annoyed me like hands striking tambourines together. My head exploded. As Kevin was gearing up, I pulled a large stone from the dirt and threw it into the school window. Kevin nearly ran his cycle into a tree when he heard glass shatter. "Woman, you crazy? You just set the fuckin' alarm off!" he shouted at me.

Fortunately, Todd was a little more cool about it. "Ooh, good aim, nice throw Dini!" he applauded.

Kevin was really uptight, "Fuck! Get your ass over here right now!" he ordered me.

As I hopped on, he drove off, flooring the gas pedal. "I couldn't deal with it. It gave me a nasty headache," I whined.

Kevin insisted, "You need a fuckin' drink. I'll take you to a bar but don't do nothin' stupid no more, okay?"

A bar wasn't exactly what I had in mind. I was thinking more along the lines of aspirin.

THE BAR

In the heart of the city, the motorcycles sped right past the police headquarters before making a sharp right turn into a tavern off the beaten path. It was a piano bar. In the corner of this tavern, a pianist performed a variety of Broadway hits. Though I didn't mind it in the least, I couldn't imagine Denise agreeing to such a quiet, relaxing atmosphere. We were seated at a booth overlooking the bar counter. Kevin, sitting across from me, stared into my eyes, holding my hands. "Feeling better, babe?" he asked with his bedroom eyes. I nodded.

Unfortunately, the tranquility died promptly on the hour. The pianist packed his apparatus and a DJ took over. Dim, mellow lighting brightened into blinding flashing colors. A disco ball lowered from the ceiling above the dance floor. Video screens came alive, sounding off at high volume. Scores of people stormed into the bar until it was filled beyond capacity. Cigarette smoke polluted the air, burning my eyes and saturating my clothes with its putrid scent. Now I understood what drew Denise to this tavern. It was much more than a piano bar.

Of course, my buddies felt right at home and were as crude as ever. They joked about the store clerk they hassled and the youngsters they harassed at the school grounds. I could barely hear them over the loudspeakers, not that I was missing anything.

My head pounded again. I felt as if an electric drill had sawed its way through my skull. I did not feel well.

Provocative dancers entertained on the bar counter. I couldn't help but to do a double take at the lovers necking and undressing each other over at the corner by the crowded pool table. "Let's go," I urged Kevin.

He argued, "We just got here." He glanced at the time. "It's only been a half hour." An erotic waitress in a hot pink bikini top wiggled her way over to our booth. She leaned over the table, shining her boobs against the light. I knew there was no leaving now. "Ooh, Momma!" Kevin's eyes undressed her. He was so tempted to reach over and pinch her ass. Why couldn't he just dump me for her? She was much more his type. Four alcoholic beverages were neatly placed over a folded napkin set on the table. "Take some," Kevin offered me his drink, trying to loosen me up. I could smell the noxious booze on his breath.

Vicki and Todd got in on the bandwagon. "Yeah Dini, where's the party animal in you? Take a sip," Vicki pushed.

"It'll make you feel better," Todd added.

I shook my head and whined, "I don't think so."

Vicki hassled me, "C'mon . . . take a sip. Be a sport."

I gave in. I took one sip.

All eyes were locked on me, waiting for a reaction. One sip, two sips, three sips . . . not bad. It had a limey sweet and sour taste to it. "Are you going to burp?" Vicki teased. They had me drink the whole glass of margarita then ordered a second helping. I didn't appreciate their intentions. Oddly, the alcohol didn't me. In fact, I shot it down like water. I lost count after the second shot. My headache calmed. Golly, I felt like a goofy kid again. Maybe they did know what was best for me. The fizzing of Kevin's beer and other little silly distractions began to fascinate me.

A fatso uncorked a bottle of champagne, and the fizz overflowed onto the floor. After his first gulp, the fatso let out a long-winded burp. I laughed so hard that I could hardly hold the booze down.

Vicki momentarily gazed at my drink then lowered her head, squinting her eyes at level with mine. In a low whispering tone she asked, "Have we corrupted you, Jessica?" She sneered. Out of resentment, I spit the booze right on her white lacy tank top. Todd and Kevin rolled with laughter. Vicki pouted, "Ooh gross, look what she did!" Instead of wiping off the spit, she pulled her top off, sitting there exposing her revealing bra. Needless to say, she was entertaining the guys. She knew she had offended me. I resented her. She had better not betray our little secret. I shouldn't have trusted her in the first place. I'm sure she knew, under all the alcohol, how disenchanted I was with her.

"I gotta go to the restroom," I raised my voice to Kevin over the loud speakers.

"Gotta piss?" he asked with such class.

"Yeah," I replied, giving her a nasty glare. The instant I got up off the bench I stumbled to the floor. I was weightless, bouncing around as if I were walking on the moon. Clumsily, I made my way to the restroom. I rammed into a waiter carrying a serving tray full of wine glasses. Oops! The glasses shattered across the floor. Instead of apologizing, I laughed at the young waiter. I could tell he was pissed.

"Watch where you're going, lady." He knew I was tipsy so why didn't he look out for me?

The urge to throw up overcame me. I raced into the restroom. Darting into the first available stall, I knelt over the toilet and vomited all the margarita I drank into the darkness of the bowl. When done, I flushed the toilet and collapsed to the tile floor in exhaustion.

I reach over the bowl to spit up a little more phlegm, and . . . and . . . something isn't right. The toilet shakes violently as if it's going to explode! Red STUFF is splattering upward along the sides of the bowl. Boiling red liquid gushes over the toilet seat. Vapor fumes rise above the toilet. The stall steams. I attempt to evacuate the stall, but the metal strip lock has melted in place! I scream for help, pounding at the door with my fist. Burning liquid oozes toward my feet! I jump around, dodging the spits of splattered lava. The only other way is up, but I can't put my feet on the toilet seat and climb over the partition without getting attacked by the hot molten spits. I whimper at the slightest tingle on my ankle.

Suddenly, the door opened. A black hand pushed it open. I was so eternally grateful that my valiant savior arrived not a moment too late. I wanted to hug her. "Oh, excuse me!" The embarrassed lady glanced at me. "I didn't know anyone was in here." She blushed and took off.

I hurried out while I still had the chance. I wanted to alert her about the emergency, but when . . . I looked back . . . it was gone! Couldn't be . . . where did the molten splatters and vapor go?

Everything was back to normal. I knew it really happened—I was caught right in it. I felt the spits against my ankle. It was NOT another hallucination. I was positive.

Moments later, the next potential victim, flashing a grin at me, waltzed right into that little booby-trapped stall and locked the door. I stood there watching, waiting . . . After flushing, she opened that door with the same pleasant smile. I was baffled. Nothing happened. Perhaps a breath of fresh air would do me some good.

As I left the restroom, I spotted my so-called buddies sitting at that booth giving a waitress a hard time. They were too busy laughing and drinking to notice me. I was so pissed at Vicki, I couldn't face her again. This was the perfect opportunity to make a clean getaway.

Besides, I never really fit in with those thieves from the get-go. I snuck outside to escape from my nightmare but this time no one stopped me. It was refreshing.

RICHARD DUNN

Apronounced sunset lit up the sky. I plopped myself down on the garden chair outside the tavern's backyard patio to watch the sun as it lowered. I was free at last, on my own, with a chance to start over. I inhaled the fresh cool outdoor air.

A tall, professionally dressed man in a burgundy sports jacket and black suede shoes approached me. "May I?" he asked to join me. Was he also enamored by the vibrant coral and violet streaks across the evening sky? I was delighted to be accompanied by such a handsome gentleman.

"Sure," I accepted.

He pulled a spare chair over by me and sat himself down. Moments later he asked, "Are you with anyone?"

I glanced into his deep blue eyes. "No, why?" What an improvement over Kevin. It couldn't have been made more obvious that I was drooling over him.

"'Cause I've seen you hang out here from time to time with some guy," he explained.

"Oh, you must come around here pretty often." *And just how often does Denise swing by here?* I fibbed, "He and I are just friends."

"I see." He offered his hand to shake. "My name is Richard Dunn. And yours?"

"Denise," I greeted him. We quietly shared the remainder of the sunset together. How romantic.

"You know, you remind me of an old friend of mine. Isn't that funny?" he laughed.

I giggled, "Yeah, I guess. Is that good or bad?"

"Oh, it's definitely a compliment. She was as beautiful as you and very special to me. I'd do anything for her because she was the love of my life. But . . ." Richard sighed. "If you're anything like her . . . I don't mean to intrude if you're unavailable . . ."

I assured him, "No, that's okay. I'm not taken."

He seemed rather anxious about me. I felt the same for him. We sat silently again, unsure of what to say. "Would you care for a drink?" he asked.

I replied, "No thanks. I've already had one too many."

He appeared to be surprised. "Really? You seem sober to me. I wouldn't have guessed."

I insinuated, "Well, I got really sick from it, if ya know what I mean."

He changed the subject. "So, you're here alone, huh?" he flirted.

"Yeah."

"Would you care to spend some time . . ." he insinuated. "Sure."

He pointed. "I live about three blocks past the school grounds. Would you care to join me? I have a nice cozy apartment," he invited.

"I don't think so," I muttered under my breath, though I had no place to stay. I didn't even know him. I mean, he was a total stranger. But he couldn't be much worse than Kevin.

He extended his hand, smiling patiently. "C'mon," he persuaded, "don't worry about a thing."

How could I refuse that smile?

"Alright," I agreed, "But I don't want to be an inconvenience."

He helped me up from the garden chair. "No inconvenience at all. It's my pleasure."

We strolled arm-in-arm toward his red Fiero sports car. Then, as a gentleman should, he opened the car door for me. Within the brief time we spent in his car, he informed me that he was 25 years old, and he spoke highly of his car and his successful car dealership. Frequently, he would ask me about "the guy" I hung out with, but I would change the subject. I figured he was jealous.

He introduced me to his second-level penthouse. His place was quite lavish, more than I'd expect of a young bachelor. I asked if he had a roommate. He assured me that his "male" roommate was out for the evening as if he had prearranged an intimate evening with me. It disturbed me to know quite obviously what his intentions were. "Please make yourself comfortable on the couch. Would you like a cup of coffee?" he offered.

I declined, "No thanks." I wanted to ask him how much the Renoir paintings on his wall went for and the price range of the chandelier fixture over his dining room table, but I felt it was none of my business. I quietly retreated to the soft-padded couch. I sank so low, I melted in the seat. There had to be something we could talk about which would be safe conversation. "How long have you lived here?" I asked as he hung his jacket in the closet.

"Oh, a while—about three or four years. I really love it here. I have peace and privacy, stores are only minutes away, and my neighbors are hospitable and friendly. This is where I want to start a family," he insinuated, winking at me, then stared into my eyes for the longest time. He broke from his trance. "Would you care for some music? I have a four-speaker stereo cassette player . . ." He tried to impress me with his technologies.

Again, I declined.

"Hmm . . . how about a Bud Lite, really a light beer," he offered.

"No, really nothing please," was followed by a really uncomfortable moment of silence. "Does that work?" I pointed to the television, figuring it would be harmless entertainment.

"Oh, yes. I nearly forgot. Would you like me to turn it on? It's brand new." He anxiously picked up the remote, searched the keypad, then pressed the power button to demonstrate his many cable TV channels. "What would you like to watch? It has over 50 stations and . . ."

"What you put on is fine, really," I interrupted him. We were watching a commercial. He sat down beside me, crossing his legs, relaxing before the tube. Gradually, he inched his way over to me until he had his arms around me. We were nestled together, quietly looking at the tube though not watching a thing. I sensed that he was a bit agitated. I didn't want him to think I wasn't interested in him, so I placed my hand on his leg. He gazed into my eyes. "You know you have beautiful eyes." He paused. "And a lovely figure. You're more attractive than I remember." *How did he know what I used to look like if he had just met me?* He continued, "I can't believe I'm with you right here in my own living room, tonight. I must be dreaming."

"What do you mean?" I wondered.

He pouted in disappointment, "You really don't remember, do you?" He removed his arm from my side. "Way back when we were dating, your parents didn't approve of me and forbade you to see me again. They thought I corrupted you. That isn't true. I'm the best thing that ever came along. I was the only man who ever cared about you. You never knew love before you met me."

I was baffled. I had no idea he knew me prior to meeting me at the tavern. He had only mentioned that I reminded him of an old girlfriend. He didn't explain that I was her. Besides, I had no memory of him, only of John. I was disturbed about his story but accepted it. "Sounds like my parents would do something like that," I agreed. "They're really nasty. I mean I love them but not the way they treat me. It's weird but lately I can't even accept who I am anymore." I sort of felt closer to him, as if we were old friends. I was hoping he might explain why my parents behaved the way they did, since he knew them. However, he only said, "I understand.

You've had it tough." He paused. "Ya know, you're always welcome to stay here with me. I still love you very much. We can start a family now that we are together again." He wrapped his arms around me and kissed me on the lips, softly. "If you only knew how much I miss you." He adored me with his puppy dog eyes then charged me with kisses again.

I backed off. "But I really don't remember you. I mean, it's been so many years," I insisted in a huff.

Richard seemed very insulted. "C'mon, you must be kidding. You told me you weren't attached to that other guy. Or do you have another man in your life you haven't told me about?"

I snapped, "I really don't think it's any of your concern."

As I attempted to get up off the couch, Richard tugged on my arm, pressing me down. "Everything you do, honey, is my concern. I love you."

"So, you were forever infatuated with someone you could never have," I stated bluntly.

He said adamantly, "That's not true. I have you now."

He threw himself at me, kissing me wildly in the mouth and all over my neck. I tried to push him off, but I couldn't. My shirt was hastily unbuttoned. Though it did feel good to be touched and kissed by the handsome stranger, he scared me for some reason. With great struggle, I finally got him off me. "Please, not now," I insisted. "I just want to rest, okay. I'm . . . I'm just confused. I need some time to sort it all out. I'm confused. I need to be alone."

He apologized, "I'm sorry, forgive me. I got carried away. You do look tired. I will help you to bed." He lifted me from the couch and carried me into his bedroom, repeating over, and over, "I love you so much."

RAPE

Richard gently tucked me in his bed. I let out a long-winded sigh. Peace at last. After a peck on my quiet lips he left the bedroom, closing the door behind. Richard's stories troubled me because I had no recollection of him—only of John, the first boyfriend.

Though my eyes were shut, I felt his presence once more, beside me, staring at my tired face. He shook the bed. I lifted a brow and gasped! He joined me in bed, stark naked! I feigned sleep. His fingers combed through my hair; his lips touched mine. My eyes opened wide, *stop*. He just couldn't leave me alone. He rubbed his nose against mine. "Tell me you love me," he whispered in my ear.

"Let me sleep," I pouted.

"No, no," he insisted, "I need to hear you say it."

I bargained, "If I say it, will you leave me alone?"

"We will both rest in peace, once you express your yearning to fill my heart's void."

"So poetic, aren't you? Are you preparing for a eulogy?" I stated cynically.

"Now, I want this moment to be truly romantic, for this is the first time in years that we're together, in bed. So, please tell me to comfort my fragile heart."

"Alright, dear Romeo, if it'll mend your wounded soul, I shall say, 'Oh Romeo, oh Romeo, I do love thee.'"

"Do you mean it with all your heart and soul or are you just being cute?" he asked solemnly.

"Richard!" I snapped. He tried my patience.

"You really do, don't you?" he concluded. Somehow that gave him permission to crawl on top of me, charging me with kisses and heavy petting. It was clear that he had no intension of letting me rest. "Your lips are so tender, so juicy, so luscious," he muttered, slobbering along my neck. I could feel his growing excitement. His tongue plunged into my mouth. I tried to push him off, but he became an overbearing dog. I turned my face away as he feverishly unbuttoned my shirt then snipped off my bra to suckle my nipples. I lay passively as he tossed his flippant wet tongue about my tits, licking and stroking. He continued on, not caring that I showed total disinterest in his passion.

"Tastes so good, so delicious," he groaned. I did not reply.

"Wouldn't you like me to screw you dry?" His mind leaped into fantasy as he huffed away, drooling over my chest.

"I'd like you to get off! I'm not in the mood," I protested.

He chuckled, "You're just saying that 'cause you want more. A-huh, you tease." I would slap him across the face if he hadn't restrained my hands.

He forcefully undid my belt, nearly tearing at the seams of my pants, unzipping me in a hurry. Momentarily, he got up to yank my pants off. He spread my legs apart. I closed them. He tried again. I kicked him. I couldn't help it, he asked for it. "Behave yourself," he grumbled. "You do it again and I'll knock the shit out of you," he threatened. And this was the same guy who claimed to be madly in love with me. Was he bipolar or just mentally unstable? What had I gotten myself into?

I felt him poke his hard flesh inside me. I quivered. I told him repeatedly to stop. Now he was going to rape me. "Please not now," I begged. *Am I a virgin? If I am, will it hurt?* I cringed.

He pointed his finger at me in anger. "I want you to shut up." He aligned himself again then thrusted in.

I jumped back in shock.

"I thought you were good at this. Why is your pussy so dry and tight?" he whined. "I know what'll make you horny for me."

He got off me. For a moment I thought I was spared. No such luck. He pulled my legs to the edge of the bed and lowered himself to perform oral sex on my dry spot. His fingers eased in, stroking my pubic area. I felt his moist flopping tongue lick at my clit, lubricating it. "Good, you're not so stiff anymore. You know you taste so sweet. "His warm tongue slid back into my slit and suckled at the juices. I felt his finger worm its way in. He had me moaning. His finger appeared to grow in size and strength as it pumped into my canal. My walls expanded to encompass him. I felt the dagger hard inside me. Pleasure surfaced. I anchored my pelvis to allow easy access. I wanted more, though I wanted none. I wanted to scream with pleasure, though I didn't want to give him the satisfaction.

Then came a release of pressure like the world was tearing away from me:

I see Mr. Bower's face over me. He scolds, "Shut up and stay still." Tears wet my face, "But Daddy, it hurts."

"You must learn how to do this right to please your daddy," he grunts. My nose is stuffed and runny, eyes watery. "But I can't."

"You can't do anything right, can you? You'll never satisfy any man."

John, my first boyfriend, the alcoholic, appears over me, mounting me. He's disappointed with me. "You're not a virgin, are you? Who you been foolin' around with? I thought you told me you saved yourself for me? If I find that you cheated, I'll make you pay." He smacks me around. I fake an orgasm to please him.

I lie under monstrous glaring arm-lamps, feet clasped to clamps, in the delivery ward at Sun Valley Hospital. Though I'm dressed in a light, flimsy hospital gown, I perspire under the sheet. A man in a white uniform questions me, "Do you have insurance to cover this procedure? Do your parents know you've decided to have an abortion?"

Mr. Bower's face appears before me. He's enraged. "You took a life. That's murder! Why didn't you use protection?" He embarrasses me in front of the nurse.

I gasped, "You better be using a condom!" Richard did not answer. He was too caught up in the act. I panicked—pregnancy! No, I did not want to have his child, nor did I want an abortion, I demanded to myself.

"I don't want to get pregnant!" I cried. He ignored me, nonetheless, pursuing after me like a dog in heat. He had me pinned down, devouring all my strength, leaving me passive to his wishes. I felt myself surrendering to the chops of a wild and hungry beast. His thrust burned hard inside me, biting its way into dry meat. The pressure ate away at my genitals. I mustered up enough strength for just one last revolt. I threw my head upward, hitting him in the face.

Like a wild cat, I tossed and turned, scratched and dug my nails into his skin. He screeched but retaliated, throwing several punches at me. He got his way.

Finally, he got off me after he came. He lay quietly in bed, shifting the remote about, as if nothing had happened. The television flicked on. I retreated to the foot of the bed in anguish, sore, swallowing my tears, confused. "You hurt me," I cried.

Totally unresponsive, he rested contently, as if he didn't care. "You hurt me, you fuckin' bastard!" I threw a pillow at him.

After he paid no attention to my outrage, I jumped on him, throwing punches, ready to kill.

"Hey—hey, stop that!" He was finally compelled to listen.

"You motherfucker, you hurt me!" I repeated, determined to get through to him.

"I thought you like to play dirty," he argued. "You chicks play hard to get."

"Look at me. Do I look like I was having fun, you asshole?"

"I was a little rough," he admitted. "Ya want something to eat?" He changed the subject.

"You told me you loved me, but I can see now that it was all a big lie to get what you wanted," I insisted.

Richard adjusted the pillow back in its place against the headboard. "What do ya want from me? An apology? I thought you wanted to play rough. You used to like it. You've changed." He paused to reach for the remote. "All you damn broads are the same." Again, he ignored me, resuming his channel surfing.

"You raped me, you fool!" I yelled with tears of fury.

Richard was appalled by my accusation. "I did no such thing. I was just playing around with you," he defended.

"Playing? You call that playing? If that's what you call 'playing,' I wonder what your angry side is like. Tell me, did I act like I was enjoying it?"

"C'mon, give me a break. Just cuz you couldn't get off, you're pissed. Stop complaining."

"It was YOU who got off at my expense. The only thing I got out of it was suffering and bruises. Go examine the evidence, Your Honor. Do not fear to witness the truth."

He sighed. "I'm sorry, okay. I was a little rough. I guess I got carried away. I mean, after not having sex in so long, don't you think it's hard to hold back? Come over here and lay beside me. I'll prove to you how gentle I can be."

"Oh, 'sex in so long.' I'm sure you've had other 'broads' fill in for my absence and babysit you all those years."

He smacked me across my face.

I got off the bed and gathered my belongings in a hurry. "I think it's time for me to leave."

Richard jumped into his trousers, following me over to the front door. "Oh, c'mon. Stop being this way. You know I love you. I understand if you're upset with me but we can work things out. Just forget it, okay." He changed his attitude as I darted out the door. "Hey, you're not really leaving, are you?" Richard watched as I opened the front door. "You can't go," Richard sulked, "I said I was sorry. I really didn't mean to hurt you. I guess I just lost it."

"You lost it alright. Hasta la vista, baby," I saluted, slamming the door in his face.

GUILTY CONSCIENCE

I left Richard's apartment in anger with no place to go in the nippy, bone-chilling dark evening. With no money and no transportation, I could only go on foot. I wouldn't dare call Vicki for a ride after she pulled that stunt on me at the bar, nor could I remember her number.

I thought about the visions I had during sex. *"You can't do anything right, can you. You can't even satisfy your own father."* The old man had me feeling sexually inadequate. Maybe he was right. Maybe I was lousy in bed. Besides, Richard was only being playful like Dad would. It was rather selfish of me not to consider Richard's needs simply because I wasn't in the mood.

Every relationship has a give and take. Richard hurt me because I was being selfish and insensitive to his needs. I mean, suppose I wanted sex, and he didn't. He said he loved me. He wouldn't intentionally hurt someone he loved. If I could be more understanding, I'd possibly make a better bed partner and maybe I'd feel better about myself. With that in mind, I returned. I felt it was big of me to do so. Richard seemed rather surprised that I returned. "I'm sorry," I apologized. "I'm not very good in bed, am I?" I hugged him. "But I'll work on it. I won't disappoint you again, I promise."

I cuddled beside him in bed for the duration of the night, kissing and hugging him as if he were a helpless infant. He was long asleep while I lay beside him thinking things over. I learned that my superior father beat on me and molested me frequently as a child. John got me pregnant. I had an abortion. Father was never content with me. I guess I just wasn't good enough for any man, not my first boyfriend John, nor Kevin nor Richard. Was there any hope for me? Would I ever improve in the bedroom?

'You're not worthy of respect. You're nothing but a cheap slut,' an inner voice echoed.

An opposing voice interceded, *'Come to your senses. You're sleeping with a rapist. Get the hell out of there!'*

'You should be grateful that Richard let you in his apartment in the first place. Where else would you stay? Out on the streets like some bag lady?'

'You must go back to Kevin. There's no future for you here!' My head tossed and turned in agony. I wanted to scream.

The phone rang! It sure startled me. After it rang twice, I dared myself to reach over to Richard's night table and answer it. It was almost a quarter-to-three in the morning. I rested the receiver against my shoulder. I heard the utterance of a feminine voice speak with uncertainty, "Hello . . . Rich?"

I hesitantly replied, "No, this is his . . . ah, friend. Who's calling?"

The caller was silent for a moment. "Is Richard there?" She asked impudently.

"He's asleep at this hour, like the rest of the world," I remarked cynically.

"Who are you?" The caller ignored my attitude.

"I told you, his friend," I snapped. "Can I take a message?"

The caller's black tongue was audible. "I recognize your voice," the black lady caller pointed out. "But I don't suppose you recognize mine."

"Ah, no. Should I?" I felt uneasy with the mind games.

"And I suppose you sleeping wit my boyfriend?" The caller accused. I was speechless. I felt trapped.

"What you tink, he's yours?" she scolded. "I live wit him. He's mine. Ya wanna fight over him—I'll beat the fuck out of you. And whatcha tink yous doin' under those sheets? You his part-time mistress?" the lady bickered at me.

I furiously slammed the phone down. I guess his so-called "male roommate" was really his "temporarily off-duty sleep-in girlfriend." What a fuckin' liar! And to think I felt guilty about leaving him. What an ass I made of myself. I guess his real girlfriend was the one who liked to play rough. I'd be gone long before he awoke. I'd teach him a lesson he'd never forget. I quietly got dressed and, without an ounce of guilt, stuck my hand in Richard's pants pocket, stealing his wallet, car keys, cash, and charge plate. *"Thank you, DICK!"* I thought to myself. *"That ought to keep him off the streets for a while."*

HITCHHIKER

Keys jingled. The door to the Fiero was unlocked. The ignition was started. "Neat!" I exclaimed as the dashboard display lit up in green neon like a spaceship. Everything was computerized. I adjusted the rearview mirror and set the gear in drive. I was now in motion—only going the wrong way. Silly me, I switched the gear in reverse to back out of the parking lot. It occurred to me that I had never been behind a wheel before. So how did I know how to operate this car? Flashbacks of Mr. Bower taking away Denise's car keys to ground her explained a few things. I was indeed impressed that she got her license at all. I'm sure it was the only constructive thing she accomplished.

I needed a destination. The only two places I had in mind were not an option: returning home or Vicki's club basement. I had to come up with something more creative. Now that I had a car, I could go anywhere in the world—Hawaii . . . Jamaica . . . Bahamas, I considered.

C'mon, let's be more realistic. I was driving around in a stolen vehicle with little cash. This was an opportune time for a JOY RIDE! I was the only one on the road at 3:30 am in the morning. I drove around town completely ignoring all road laws—running red lights, driving the wrong way on a one-way. What a blast! It was kinda fun to see how much I could get away with.

After driving recklessly for twenty minutes, I was seriously lost. The fun was over. Only a quarter of a tank left. I needed to settle somewhere before the morning rush hour. Eastwood Middle School was the only landmark that I could remember. That was the destination I decided on.

I stopped at a gas station to ask for directions. The attendant had never heard of the school. He looked it up in a phonebook, but it was unlisted. "Sorry, I can't help you," he apologized. I did not believe him. I grabbed the yellow pages from him and examined the cover. It was a phonebook for Cresten County. I had no clue as to how far I had driven in the wrong direction. "Do you have a listing for Philley County?" I asked him.

"No, ma'am. This is all we have," the attendant informed regretfully.

I pushed the phonebook over to him. "Do you have road maps at least?"

"Only of Cresten, ma'am"

"Which way to Philley County?" I asked desperately. The attendant estimated somewhere around 45 miles northeast. Though I had no sense of direction, I knew 45 miles was a lot of driving. I hit the road and drove off toward what I considered northeast. A half hour later, I saw a billboard ad for cigarettes. I couldn't believe my eyes when I passed the *Welcome to Fowlersville* sign. "Damn!" I cursed, banging on the steering wheel. Had the gas attendant lied to me or was I way off course? The tank was near empty. I had no choice but to buy gas with the stolen money. I had the next gas attendant fill the tank. After gas expenditures, I had only twenty dollars left. I asked this attendant if he knew where Philley County was, but he'd never heard of it. Was I in another world or did people out here not get out much?

Fowlersville had an old, rugged, run-down ghetto-like appearance. The streets were weather-beaten with potholes and cracks. The town was marked by row houses and widened sidewalks. I was sure I was within city limits.

Stopping for a red light, I noticed a hitchhiker standing by the curb, waving his hands, trying to flag me down. For a fleeting moment I glanced over at him, considering asking him for directions. He was a young white oval-faced dude with stubble. He had a gold stud in his right ear as well as a gold chain around his neck. His long straight chestnut brown hair was held in a bun. A stained white wrinkled t-shirt was covered by an unbuttoned heavy navy-blue lined jacket. His tight-fitted jeans were mud dirty. How long was it since his last shower? Na, not a good idea. I ignored him, though he continued to wave in desperate appeal. I had no intention of offering him a ride. I shouldn't have looked over at him in the first place. He became a nuisance. He tried so eagerly to get my attention for the fleeting seconds the light remained red he made me nervous. Just then, I noticed that my car doors weren't even locked! "Fuck!"

Where was the lock button? How do I lock them? I studied the door controls for the appropriate switch. I prayed that the light would turn green. He rapped on my window. I tossed my head repeatedly, refusing him, *I'm sorry.*

I was startled by a swift pull of the car door! He leaned in the passenger side door. I screamed!

"Lady, I need a lift. It's urgent," the kid insisted. "Please . . . I'll pay ya if you want me to. My ride stood me up."

"Then catch a goddamn cab," I yelled at him, wishing a cop would be nearby. My heart skipped a beat at the thought of him being armed. He momentarily glanced around the traffic in search of a cab, while still leaning against the car.

"Awe, c'mon lady, I ain't gonna do nothin', I just want a darn ride."

The light finally turned green. The foot that impatiently held down the brake floored the gas pedal in hopes of blowing away the intruder. Unfortunately, he dove into the car, struggling to close the door. "I ain't got no time to wait for a fuckin' cab." He bounced around in the seat.

I instantly slammed my foot down on the brake, bringing the vehicle to a whiplashing halt. Cars were honking at me from behind. "Get out of my car!" I demanded.

"You're holding up the traffic," the kid pointed out.

I sat there, in total disbelief, stunned by his carefree intrusion. The debilitated bum imposed on me, nevertheless. Was he insane? I wondered what his next intention would be—car rape?

"Sorry lady, I didn't mean to barge in like this, but I really do need a lift. I couldn't stand out there much longer before my feet would give way. You just don't know how tough hitching rides is," he whined.

I had a hard time feeling sorry for him.

"Could you please take me to 34 South Koppler St.?" He emphasized "please" in his request. Without any reply, the guy thanked me profusely. Of course, he presumed that I knew my way around this uncharted town, and I had nothing better to do. Needless to say, I was very suspicious of him. He was the most aggressive hitchhiker I had ever come across. I had totally forgotten where I was headed in the first place.

"Missed your school bus?" I started to grill him, allowing him plenty of room for a good explanation, but apparently, I touched a nerve.

He looked cross at me. "Look, don't go there. I don't do no fuckin' school, okay lady," he snapped.

"Get out of my car, NOW!" I shouted.

"Fuck lady, I said I'd pay you. C'mon."

"How much?"

"How much ya want?"

"How much ya got?"

"Uh . . . how much, lady? Name a price."

"Fifty bucks."

"Deal." The kid shook my hand while all the cars from behind had passed me. I started off.

He looked around in the direction we were headed. "Ya know where ya going, don't ya?"

"No," I replied.

"Where you from anyway?"

"Never mind. If you'd be so kind to give me directions."

"You school age too, ain't ya? Why ain't you in school?" The kid fired back at me.

"That's really none of your business. Now, if you would kindly direct me," I most discreetly requested, trying to keep whatever sanity I had intact.

"Make a right after this light, then go up two blocks, make another right, then after five miles make a left at the church, got it?" He hurried through the directions trying to make it hard on me.

I didn't quite catch on but said nothing. I felt like punching him in the nose, or better yet, pushing him out the door. I snarled at him instead, thinking *I ain't no taxi caber.* "Does your mother know that you hitchhike?" I belittled him.

The kid suddenly grabbed me by the wrist and squeezed it firmly while I was driving! "What's it to ya? Hey lady, you don't mess with me, and I won't mess with you, ya got it?" he warned.

"Sure," I answered, feeling corns in my stomach.

He realized that he could have caused an accident. "Sorry," he apologized. After that little panic episode, there was an icy silence between us.

"I'm Brad, what's your name?" The kid began a fresh unadulterated conversation. "Denise," I answered.

We each came to a silence again. "This your car, Denise?"

"Umm . . . yeah, why?" I stuttered, baffled as to why he asked.

"Then what are you doing with a Penthouse in the glove compartment? You like women?"

"What?" I glanced over, catching Brad snooping through Richard's glove compartment.

Just when I thought he and I understood one another, there he went again violating my privacy. I hollered at him, "Hey, put that back! Stay out of there. That's none of your business." Despite my disapproval, he searched and found other magazines, a cigarette lighter, and a package of condoms.

"I said stay out of there or I'll drop you off right here," I threatened.

He totally ignored me, chuckling, "You like lots of sex, huh?" He waved the condoms in my face. It came as a surprise to me, too.

I had no idea Richard kept all those sex items in his glove compartment. I guess he fucked in the backseat with his black mistress.

"Do you do acid?" he asked.

"What?" I was getting really tired of his nosiness.

"Have you ever done dope?" he restated.

I snapped at him, "Do you ever shut up? Do you always stick your nose in other people's businesses?" I huffed, "Am I going the right way?"

He looked out the window. "No," he snickered at my inability to follow his directions. "I ain't gonna pay you if I have to show you how to get there."

"Don't do me any favors; besides, you probably haven't got a cent on you anyway. Look, I'm not your taxi. So, if you don't like my service, just get the fuck out." I was on the verge of losing my temper.

Suddenly, Brad lowered his head to his lap, ducking. "Are they gone yet?"

"Who?"

"Woman, didn't you see a cop pass?"

"So?"

"Are they gone?" he insisted.

"Yeah—yeah, so?"

"Are you sure?"

"Are you in some kind of trouble?"

"Just answer me," he yelled from his ducked position, losing his temper.

"Yes, I'm sure—I'm positive!" I affirmed.

He tilted his head above slightly to see for himself, still in disbelief. Then he relaxed.

"You have some explaining to do. Did you rob a bank or murder someone?" I asked with uneasiness, wishing I hadn't said that as I bit my tongue.

"Just . . . stay out of it, okay?" Brad avoided me, trying to calm himself down.

"No, no, you better tell me if you want me to take you where you want to go, cuz I'm about to drive right up to the police headquarters."

"Okay . . . ah . . . Denise, right?" he took a good guess at my name, demonstrating his inattentiveness. He sighed. "I'll level with ya. I'm in hiding."

"What a surprise," I replied sarcastically. "And for what?"

This time he conveyed a more serious side of himself. He warned, "If you tell anyone, you're dead . . . understand?"

Oh, you really scare me. How would you like me to let go of the steering wheel—ha, ha.

I must remember from now on to proof lock all car doors.

He began to explain, "I'm sorta involved with street drugs. I have connections with people who sell dope and if I get them leads, they pay me 15% of the profit . . ."

A RAW DEAL

A light bulb went off in my head. *He's a dope dealer!* There's a good chance he might have the antidote. Was this destined to happen or what? I ventured, "Hey, ah . . . Brad, I ah . . ." I didn't know quite how to put it. "Could I . . . buy some stuff?"

"Shit no, so you can show the cops the evidence? Why not just stroll up to the goddamn station and spill your beans that I'm loaded? Spare me the grief."

"Na, I'd rather stay alive. Besides, once you're obtained in police custody, you'd be out on probation in no time, pursuing after me. Don't you think the justice system really sucks?"

"What you trying to get at?"

I admitted, "First of all, I wouldn't even know where to find a police station, let alone a gas station. I'm from Philley County, wherever that is on the map. I'm trying to say I'm lost. And as to your other question, yes, I've done dope before. I'm looking for the right fix."

"So, you want to buy some, huh? How much you want to spend?" Brad asked abruptly, trying to cut to the chase to cut a fast buck. He couldn't care less that I wasn't a local or that I was lost.

"Well, that can be a problem. I don't have much money on me."

"What about your boyfriend, how much cash he got?" Brad found Robert's registration in an adult magazine.

I felt cornered. "He's not my boyfriend."

"Your brother, cousin, boss, whatever. He's got money." "Look Brad, that's personal. Please."

"Oh, so you want a quick fix, but you ain't gonna give me nothing in exchange."

"I'm driving you to your destination. What more do you want?"

Burying his nose in the magazine, Brad requested, "Sleep with me."

"What?" I was in shock.

"Here's the deal, you sleep with me, and I'll give you the dope for free."

"Are you insane?"

"Call it a deal or forget it. How badly you want the stuff? You don't have at least $50 on ya, right?"

"Forget it." The idea sickened me.

"Got pure freebase coke in my inventory."

"Cocaine?" My eyes widened. That's the drug I'd been long searching for. Yes! That's what my imposter said she was on. This may be the opportunity I'd been waiting for! I'd do anything for— well, on second thought, almost anything. "Why can't I be of some other service to you, like cooking or cleaning?"

"I just need a good lay." He grinned. "Yes, or no?"

"You're not giving me much of a choice," I argued.

Brad directed me to an old dilapidated little barn in the middle of a cornfield. This was his emergency destination that he was in such a hurry for? He couldn't spare another moment to flag down a cabby? This was the hiding place of his stash?

He opened the wooden barn door for me. Wow, such a gentleman. I walked into the darkness of the barn. Fear immediately overcame me. Was I afraid of the dark?

"It's really dark and spooky in here," I remarked. The door shut from behind. He locked me in! I banged against the wooden door. "C'mon, this isn't funny." I waited in the dark, ready to kick the door open. I was sure the rotted, weathered wooden door couldn't take more than a rap on the hinges. "Brad, I'm serious—open it. It's disgusting in here, smells like manure." I put my ear against the door. I heard heavy breathing. "Brad, what are you up to?" I banged on the wooden hinges. The door finally opened. The light of day blinded me. Once my eyes focused, I saw Brad standing before me, butt naked and holding a Penthouse magazine photo in his right hand. I backed away into the darkness. This wasn't what I signed up for.

"Take your clothes off and pose for me like the model in the picture," he insisted. As his shadow approached, his audible breathing grew more rapid with desire. He left the door open.

"No, you give me the stash first then I'll undress. You play fair. We had an agreement, now stick to it." I refused to yield to his male ego. Brad was a pathetic, self-indulging, low-life loser and I wouldn't allow myself to be intimidated by him or any other man.

He huffed like rabid dog. "I don't give a fuck what you want, take it off NOW," he shouted.

What happened to Mr. Pretty-Desperate Hitchhiker? I guess that was how he solicited business. I backed away from him until my head hit something, then I fell sideways. I landed on something soft. "Is this a bed?" I asked nervously, trying to remain calm. "What's a bed doing in a barn?"

"Kiss me," he demanded. I felt his body heat next to mine. I crawled away from his smelly body, disappearing into the darkness. He chased after my shadow, but he could not see me.

"C'mon now. Don't play games," he whined. He was just like Richard. How did I find'em? I groped around on the dusty damp wooden floor for a place to hide. I came upon an object which appeared to be a furniture leg. I was surprised that the barn had been furnished like a motel room.

The barn was lit at once by two lamps across on each side of the bed. Brad spotted me under a table. He walked over to me then stooped before me. He put out his fist. I thought he was about to punch me. Instead, he opened his palm to show me a tiny plastic bag of white powder. With a conniving grin on his face, he said, "This is cocaine. You believe me now?" I wanted to touch and smell it to see that it was real, but he pulled it away too fast. "Now take your clothes off," he ordered. I had to obey to get the reward.

'*Don't do it. It's not worth it. He's deceiving,*' my inner voice argued.

'*You want to be normal again, don't cha? Your imposter said she used cocaine. This is the cure you've been waiting for,*' another voice interceded.

'*He could be a murderer!*' the opposing voice warned. '*Kick 'em where it counts.*'

I got out from under the table and removed only my top. He grabbed me forcefully, pushing me onto the bed, then slid over me sucking on my lips and neck. Déjà vu. I had to come up with an exit plan. "This is not a good idea, really. You know I've slept around. I have a disease," I cautioned.

His only reply was, "Hold still." He undid my pants.

"I'm really not good in bed."

"Look, if you have an attitude, you're not getting dessert," he threatened.

I needed to come up with a more repulsive idea. "I have my period!"

"All the better," he groaned.

I warned him, "You better have a condom."

"Fuck you."

Once he adamantly refused, I kicked him in the balls. He fell to the floor, cussing and shrieking in pain. Half naked, I rolled out of the bed and scurried outside to the car. I opened the car door and jumped in only to realize that the car keys were missing. "That lousy bastard!" I cursed under my breath, banging against the steering wheel in frustration.

He lay on top of me under the sheets. Sex with Brad was worse, if possible, than with Richard. I couldn't bear the pressure I felt inside. It was hardly worth the compromise for a contaminated drug package. He was so rough with me, five minutes seemed endless. I had to lay there and subject myself to humiliation and brutality, waiting for the asshole to cum. Faking orgasm was the only way to get out. He got off me and dressed. Abruptly, without a word, he left the barn. I heard the car start. He took off with Richard's Fiero. "Great!" I said to myself. "Now what do I do?"

I waited a long time, but he never returned. The hitchhiker used me then abandoned me in the middle of a cornfield. As soon as I got my sticky self out of the bed, I noticed the tiny baggie of powder still lay unattended on the table I hid under. "YES!" I cheered in excitement about the reward left behind. I shook all the magical crystals into an ashtray then inserted a used straw to snort.

Each inhale was absolutely incredible. I continued snorting despite a light-headed dizziness. Every last particle shot straight up my nose. Once finished, I sat there in total confusion. I forgot why I bothered to snort at all. My thoughts became jumbled and distorted. I drifted away where there was, no right or wrong, just soothing sensations. *It looked fuzzy or funny or furry. I smelled long and short, and, felt loud and bouncy. When I spoke, I could see the words fly away from my mouth. They flew around me before they laughed. My thickness crushed a fish then fell slimy through pithlets. Seven ears screamed lemonade before shaving solo. . .*

THE AFTER-LIFE EXPERIENCE

After great pleasure came great pain. My sinuses stung after inhaling too many particles too quickly. Gasping for air, I flew out of that barn like I was on fire. Once the throbbing subsided, I found myself alone in the middle of a cornfield. Inadvertently, I fell into a ditch. I lay there passively. My eyeballs bounced around at the clouds in the sky then gazed at the tall stalks of corn. Not a single thought or feeling came to mind. Nothing.

My spirit rises from my body. Weightlessly above ground, I levitate over my physical self. Looking down upon the battered cadaver lying in the depths of the cornfield, I study the new and fascinating perspective. I fully accept this reality without any attachment. I acknowledge my present state as death. Neither asleep, nor awake, I exist in a unique state, without form or emotion. Is this what it's like to be a ghost? Not in the least concerned about this new circumstance, I am peacefully content.

I envision a car driving along a country road. The car is the stolen red Fiero. Brad is behind the wheel driving me to a destination. He is drunk and speeding. He recklessly drives the vehicle into a telephone pole. The car blows up in flames. I'm instantly killed. He escapes alive; evades the scene.

A glistening sphere of light surrounds me. It's more beautiful than I can describe using the limits of human language. It's as if water from the sea has risen upward and wraps around me like the wind. I'm cradled like an embryo in a warm and cozy womb, fully protected and cushioned from danger.

I'm "sucked" with amazing force into a sort of vacuum, instantly pulled into a narrow vessel. Zapped through this long, spiral-like, twisted transport, my translucent environment has no platform, no gravity, and for that matter, no direction. I can't figure whether I'm facing up or down, but I know I've been set afloat through this fascinating dimension with incredible speed. I see waves and flashes of light pass me. The waves are colorless but full of energy and beautiful. Globs of mist, somewhat like clouds of dust, periodically pass me. At the end of this journey, I learn that the vessel is merely a transport vehicle from the physical world to a spiritual realm. I bypass other beings toward the end of the ride. I'm informed that the beings are newcomers who are uncertain about their entrance into the portal. I "read" these spirits with concern. They want very much to complete the transition, but they're ambivalent — in a state of limbo.

Spirits from across the uncharted stretch of the vessel catch my attention. They are very loving and friendly. They welcome me with open arms into the new frontier. I'm at the threshold of experiencing the beauty of the new realm when a gatekeeper stops me from entering. It questions my certainty. I inform the gatekeeper that I'm ready and eager. I peak through the portal, pushing my way past the gatekeeper. "Wow!" I exclaim. It's the most brilliant encounter I've ever experienced. It feels like . . . paradise. Though not at all a physical place of beauty, it's a spiritual sanctuary, one that only dreams can nearly depict: a place for recovering souls to rejoin loved ones, rest and rejuvenate then reassign for the next journey. Unfortunately, the destination of the forthcoming journey is not disclosed within this utopian city. The city is fertile with every positive thought including pleasure, joy, giving, serving, contentment, fulfillment, gratitude, satisfaction, peace, love, learning, wisdom, and truth.

The gatekeeper persists in holding me back. It asks me who I am, catching me off-guard without an answer. It asks me if I'm a suicide victim, one whose soul has been deeply tormented, in a state of disrepair and emptiness. It responds to me, "YOU ARE."

It informs me that I shall not enter the portal until I resolve my inner conflict. I insist that I did not kill myself and therefore I do not wish to go back into the physical. The gatekeeper explains that I'm a lost soul on the brink of suicide.

The gatekeeper sends me back to find myself. I'm disappointed. My wish is abandoned. I obey without protest. I understand and accept that nothing I've learned or witnessed will be retained upon passing through to the other side. My mission is to find myself. I will not be privy to the utopian city until I complete my mission in the physical world.

The gatekeeper sings a song of prayer for me, which echoes through my soul . . . "Thou shalt dance merrily amongst thy castled skies until thy moonlight cometh thou return . . ."

BARCINOCA

I was awoken by the tapping of glass. I was in the barn lying naked under the bed sheets. Brad was present. He was sitting on a chair guzzling down booze. I didn't know where he took off to after he abandoned me, but I did remember how he mistreated me before he left.

He looked a wreck: his dirty white shirt hung loose, hair unruly, and a beard formed along his sideburns.

Funny how he appeared to have been seated outside the barn in some distant space. Despite the distance between us, I smelled booze on his breath and heard his swallowing as though he were only a couple feet away. He seemed too preoccupied with his drinking to notice me.

The cracked mirror across the bed appeared to have expanded beyond the capacity of the barn. The realization of distorted space hit me as I attempted to get out of bed. I reached over, looked downward, and gasped! There was no . . . bottom . . . I mean the floorboards were gone! There was nothing down there. To be sure, I knocked an empty smashed-in beer can over the edge of the side table. It rattled at the bottom. The exaggerated distance was an illusion.

Unfortunately, I caught Brad's attention. He was almost gazing through me with his tired, glazed-over eyes. After he released a long-winded belch, he held me down firmly. "Stay still." I wondered what he was up to. I thought he was going to violate me again. Instead, he left the barn. I knew he was up to no good.

This was my chance to escape. But I couldn't. I was too drowsy. What was with the distortion? My eyes wandered over by the side table. I noticed a medicine bottle at a great distance. Squinting, I saw a syringe beside it. I strained to read the fine print on the bottle. Barcinoca? What was that? I doubted it was cough syrup. I concluded it was something really potent, and I thought he used it on me. I noticed a puffy vein on my wrist. "NO!" I cried. "What did he do to me?" I feared a slow and painful death. I closed my eyes and prayed.

The barn door slammed open! Brad raced in, huffing. "Get out of bed, NOW!" he yelled.

I stood up and rubbed my eyes, trying to shake off the drowsiness. The space around me bounced as if on a boat. When I took a step, the surface waved over. I tripped and fell on my third try.

"Whatcha do wif my stash?" Brad jumbled his words, searching the barn, totally ignoring my situation.

Stash? Couldn't he see that I had fallen, or didn't he care?

"I said, whatcha do wif my stash?" he repeated, growing hostile.

"What stash?" I pulled myself up onto the bed. I saw anger in his eyes. "You mean that powdery stuff you left on the table?" My mouth dropped. I assumed the powders were left for me as part of our agreement, but I think I made a huge mistake. I bit my tongue because I knew I was in big trouble.

"That's right. You took 'em, didn't ya," he accused.

"What if I did?" I tested.

Brad knew that I did. He shook me silly. "You stole it!" he repeated, outraged.

His head spun around me. "Stop it! I thought we had a deal. You know, cocaine in exchange for sex. Right?" I reminded him.

He backed off only for a passing moment. He reached for the bottle, guzzled down more booze, then re-approached me in a more subtle manner—to pursue a gentle kiss on my dry lips. His gesture confused me. I quickly learned that his kiss was merely a lure. "I need mur green. Jus a little more," he asked with such endearment as if I were his mistress. "Tell me where you keep the green." His childish eyes bobbed at mine.

I was wondering what he was up to. "Why do you need more money?" I asked.

"I need crack," he burped again. "Give me whatcha got."

Crack. This came as no surprise to me. I opened Richard's wallet to discover all the cash was gone! "How much money did you take?" I asked him, implying that he stole it.

"Shit, I took it all." He threw his arms in frustration as if I asked a stupid question. He didn't seem to mind the accusation against himself.

"What did you buy with the cash?" I insisted suspiciously. He just laughed.

"You purchased booze and that what-ever-it-is medicine you drugged me with, didn't ya?" I affirmed, not that it made him feel any smaller.

"Barcinoca," he burped then giggled.

"What's it do?" I was almost afraid to know.

He cackled for some time, making me more uncomfortable. Maybe I would be better off not knowing. "It makes you easy," he winked. "Calms ya down. I got you back for kickin' me in the nuts." His mood shifted from teasing to grim. He looked cross into my eyes as he leaned over the bed. "You do that again and I'll dig your grave." The booze on his breath was enough to kill me.

"Well, I guess Barcinoca doesn't work real well cuz I'm rather agitated right now," I blurted, letting him know that I wasn't afraid of him.

"Ah, shut up, bitch. Just give me some cash," he ordered.

I looked at him in disbelief. Did he not understand that there was no more money? That he spent it all? That he left me penniless?

"Give it to me NOW!" he shouted, startling me.

"Don't you have savings from all the profit you made on your drug deals?" I got smart with him.

He turned his back away from me momentarily. Next thing I knew, he knocked me off the bed onto the floorboards. Vulgarly, he accused me not only of stealing his "stash," but of robbing him of MY cash. He slugged me several times. Déjà vu, he reminded me of Mr. Bower with the brass knuckles. He pulled me off the floor by my hair and shook me. I saw stars before my eyes. My ears rang. I knew I was in grave danger and had to do something before he'd knock me out cold. For some crazy reason, I felt as if I had deserved the beating. I blamed myself for exacerbating his violent tendency.

I inched away, reaching for Richard's wallet. "There ain't nothin' in 'er, 'member," he reminded.

I pulled out a credit card from the cardholder and presented it to him. "What good would that do?" he argued.

"Charge it," I insisted in tears.

"You think I'm stupid? I ain't dealin' with no department store." Brad snatched it from me, tossing it aside.

"Here." I did not give up. "Use this checkbook. Make out a check payable for the amount you owe, and the guy can cash it to Richard's bank account." I studied the balance inside the book.

Brad grabbed it from me. "It's in Richard's name, you dumb bimbo," he pointed out. "What kinda fool do you think I am?"

"I thought you were a pro. I thought you knew every trick in the book, Mr. Suave—forge it," I insulted him. "You got his license, charge plate, and checkbook, too. What more do you want?" I threw the wallet at him. "You sort of look like him. Wear some shades."

He threw the wallet right back at me. Pointing his finger at me he snapped, "You better watch yourself. You think yer smart, don't ya? Ya know, I'd like to finish you off right here, but I need you for sometin'. You gonna take me to my stop."

"What stop?" My eyes widened.

ON THE ROAD

Brad shoved me out the barn door with a set of car keys in my hand. "Stop asking so many questions," he blurted.

I saw double of the keys. *DRIVE?* I was in no condition to operate a car. Didn't he remember that he drugged me? Then again, I guess I was the more capable of the two since he was cold drunk.

He wrote out a check payable to Marko Gonzolas, some Spanish dude. It wouldn't surprise me if the dude was an illegal alien. "We have to be at Crescent Gardens in 20 minutes so don't do anything stupid," he warned. "Just follow these directions and everything will work out just fine." He handed me a piece of scrap paper with scribble on it. *Right. Sure.*

I tried to place the key in the ignition, but I couldn't find the key slot anywhere along the steering wheel. Had the slot been removed or relocated? Brad yanked the keys from me impatiently and inserted them himself. "I said no games," he snapped. He started the engine for me. Now to find the brake release and gearshift. I searched all over. The gear appeared suspended in midair. Brad grew agitated. "Look, I need you to drive so I can hide from the cops. Otherwise, I woulda got rid of you a while ago." *Well, thanks for keeping me alive. I'm forever indebted to you.* I drove. I don't know how I did it, but the car was running down the road in gear. Though I had no idea where Crescent Gardens was, I drove on as if the car was somehow going to direct me there.

I fought to keep my eyes on the road. I relied on the yellow marker, in the middle of the road, to guide me safely in my lane. The delusions kicked in, again. The marker disappeared then the two opposing lanes merged together. It appeared as though oncoming cars were coming straight at me. I skidded to the right, trying to avoid a collision. Close call! A motorist in the right lane honked. Brad gave them the finger while cussing me out. I bit my tongue; I nearly sideswiped an innocent passing car.

I was determined not to be fooled by any more delusions. It was far too dangerous. The patch of grass along the curb distracted me. It spread across the road. I was driving on grass, but I didn't let that bother me.

To avoid an accident, I turned onto a side street. I turned the steering wheel to the right after braking but . . . the car slid sideways to the right. It did not turn—it slid. And it was about to hit the curb. I pressed down on the brake but that did little good. The brake, pedal, and steering wheel had all lost power! The car appeared to have a mind of its own. It hit the curb but did not stop moving. The vehicle drifted sideways over the curb and onto the stretch of grass as if it were some kind of amusement ride. It was headed toward a fence! Brad's glazed eyes reacted. He grabbed the steering wheel, yelling at me, "What the fuck you doing? Stay on the road, woman. Jesus Christ, keep your eyes on the road!" I envisioned Brad as Superman, wrestling with the wild beast. The car's tires screeched, and the horn sounded. Finally, things were back on track. I continued my forward course, driving down the mysterious path. I wanted to relax with some easy listening music, but I couldn't find a single button on the dashboard, let alone a radio. I settled for a soothing breeze. Again, I would roll down the window if I could find the knob. When I looked at the window, there was no glass!

An oncoming car approached from down the road. It vanished then reappeared in my rearview mirror. That's funny, I didn't see it whiz by. Instantaneously, as if on fast-speed film, the vehicles and pedestrians were darting around, making me dizzy. It was challenging to drive defensively when everyone was racing around me at warp speed.

I came to a halt at a traffic light. Brad opened the car door to spit on the street. I paid little attention to him. Instead, I glanced over at the blue car in the left lane. As the light turned green, the blue car proceeded forward but I was sliding . . . backward! The car behind me honked. I was surprised I didn't hit him. "What's yer fuckin' problem—GO!" Brad yelled pointing ahead. Couldn't Brad see that the car was sliding backward? The gear was set in drive, so I knew it had to be another delusion. I pressed the pedal down and floored it. The car whiplashed forward. "Where the fuck did you learn to drive?" Brad grunted. I rolled my eyes at him.

Lightening bolted across the angry dark skies, followed by a loud roaring thunder. The earth trembled. Raindrops bounced off my windshield. But there was something unusual about this rain shower. The raindrops shot upward from the land, flying away into the sky. It was in reverse. *Neat!* I exclaimed. Brad insisted I turn on my windshield wipers.

The puddles along the road lit up as I raced over them. They glowed in the dark. It was a true spectacle. The puddles became animated. They glided around, forming bigger pools of water. The tires pushed through the water as if the car was a steamboat crossing a great riverbank.

Then came a rather haunting traffic light. It sort of had eyes— wicked evil ones, like a witch leering down at me. The green light spitefully turned yellow as I approached. It lowered its eyeballs at me, threatening me with its ominous intention, daring me to drive through it. I challenged the beast, I floored it. But the streetlight did not yield to me. It turned fire red, jumped right out of its wired encasement, and landed on my windshield! The tires screeched into the curb! Brad blew a gasket, "What the fuck is wrong with you? You're fuckin' nuts. You fuckin' better not get no fuckin' cops on our goddamn tail." He was outraged.

Nevertheless, the nightmarish fairyland continued: A parked van drifted toward me. Trying to avoid it, I swerved to the left. A yield sign took a leaping hop over to my car, chasing after me like a loose playful dog. I tooted the horn, scaring it away. A stop sign jumped right in front of my car, hopped on the hood, denting it with its metal base. As soon as it hopped off, I ran the mother over.

The trees were watching with pleasure. They swayed their massive trunks back and forth, whistling, "We are so tall; we can see very far away. We see cops headed your way." The trees teased me because they knew I was paranoid. It wasn't funny.

I turned off on a country road where I could be free of cops and animated objects. Night fog settled in after the brief rain shower, leaving me little visibility on the dark narrow path.

There were no streetlights. In mid-evening, this country road was dismal and dreary. The high-beam headlights glared against the after-rain mist. I raced around curbs and up hills, frazzled by all the animated encounters and talking trees who allegedly saw cops that weren't there.

Intoxicated, Brad slurred over, and over, "What the fuck you doin?"

Suddenly, came a steep hill I could not see past. Nevertheless, I flew over it and the last sound I heard was a loud "BOOM!"

BAD GIRL

I moaned . . .

White-jacketed aids rush back and forth, taking orders and preparing. My right leg is bound in a cast. An IV bag drips liquid from a cord to the tube in the back of my hand. Beside the IV, a respirator monitors my heart. Okay, so what's going on? My eyes widen in horror! Rubber gloves maneuver a shiny-bladed butcher knife. The surgeon draws the blade toward the cast. He's about to make an incision! Where's the anesthesia? Pleazz put me to sleep first! Without a voice, I can only toss my head in protest. I feel the vibrations of the blade sawing into my leg. They're amputating! I cry as spits of blood squirt into my face . . .

A bolt of thunder shook the car. With eyes shut, I wiped my face on a warm stinky cloth carrying Brad's scent. I opened my eyes and examined it. It was stained with blood! My god, it was the backside of Brad's sweaty T-shirt. I was lying behind Brad's back along the vinyl car seat in a very uncomfortable position. My right leg was throbbing. I struggled to lift myself up. I called out to Brad. When he did not respond, I panicked. I cocked my head up. *Dear God,* I gasped! Brad's head was stuck in the shattered windshield! His body leaned against the dashboard, entrapped, hopelessly dead. To be sure, I felt for a pulse. There was none. *Maybe he was shot*, I insisted to myself, in denial that I just had a fatal car accident, smashing into a huge tree trunk. This had to be another delusion, couldn't be real. I cried, not knowing what to do.

Smoke rose from the bent-in hood. Was the car going to explode with me in it? I came to my senses—think fast! Looking for a means to escape, I tried to exit either side of the car but both doors were busted. It wasn't even possible to lower the windows. The keys were jammed in the creases of the dashboard. I sat there scared shitless, with one eye on the cadaver, as if it were going to attack me, and the other eye on the fumes. I guess I'd seen too many scary movies.

Suddenly Brad fell backward, landing on my lap! I screamed so loud that someone somewhere should have heard me by now but not a soul in sight. It was the most gruesome face I'd ever seen. His eyes . . . slit, blood oozed from his eye sockets, nose, and mouth. His left shoulder was torn out of its socket. He had fragments of glass in his face. I was hyperventilating hysterically. Where were the police? The firemen? Where in hell was I? In the middle of farmland? I couldn't endure another moment in the company of a dead body. I had to lift his heavy head and torso to place him in his seat.

There had to be a way out. The driver's side window—I had to break the glass. I took off my tennis shoe and banged it against the cracked glass until it gave way. The fragments flew around everywhere. The rain poured in. Feet first, I climbed out of the narrow opening. I was soon free! Yes, this was truly a miracle.

Drenched by heavy downpours, I hurtled down the narrowly paved country road in the misty rain. I was tempted to look back at the accident site, but I could not. Still in shock, I wanted to wish it away, as if it never happened.

The cold damp rain had me shivering. Though I had just survived a fatal car accident virtually unharmed, I was in no condition for a stroll through the country barrens in a heavy downpour. I had no idea where I was going nor when I'd find shelter. I strode through slabs of mud and floods of cold dirty water that soaked my socks and swooshed in my shoes. My overworked legs grew weary. All I could think about was shelter and warmth.

Father drives me home from church. I'm seven. It's stormy outside. I turn the car radio on to break the icy silence. Father instructs me to turn off the radio. I don't listen.

Father always drives in silence. I am in the mood for some cheerful music. Again, he demands that I turn the radio off, or I will be punished. I don't want Father to think I'm a coward, so I ignore him. He pulls the vehicle over to the curb, coming to a screeching halt. Father raises his voice, ordering me to get out of the car and shut the door behind me. I'm all choked up, in tears. I obey, unsure of his intention. The rain sprinkles in. I never meant to get him that upset. I apologize. Father takes off with the car, leaving me stranded in the rain. I've little doubt that he will not return to pick me up. I shiver. I remind myself that I'm a bad girl, that I had just come from the Holy Sanctuary to atone and here I go again, sinning. I ask for forgiveness. Would Jesus forgive me for being bad?

"That bastard," I shouted. "I hate you!" But was I referring to Mr. Bower or myself?

Was I any better than he? I just had Brad killed. It should have been me lying there dead in the passenger seat, waiting for the car to explode while the murderer abandoned me. Besides, who would've cared if I died? Would the Bowers have mourned my death and prepared a funeral with unconditional love? Would Vicki or Kevin have noticed my disappearance from the bar and put out a search for me? I doubted it. I was sure the world could go on quite fine without me.

Besides, I was probably wanted under several charges, including murder. It didn't matter that I just killed a deviant sex offender, a thief, and a strung-out drug dealer. In the public's eye, I took the life of another human. I could just imagine a police officer whipping out handcuffs from his back pocket and shoving me into his vehicle. If the cops ever caught me now, I'd surely get the death penalty. I was officially a fugitive of the law, following in Brad's footsteps.

I must have staggered on foot for what seemed like hours, on a country path that led to nowhere. Fortunately, the rain let up. I passed through acres of farmland. Finally, the sun's rays beamed through the grey sky. Disbelieving my eyes, I spotted a gas station across the rows of trees. It looked promising but was it just another hallucination? Blocking the sun's glare, I saw customers pumping gas. It was real! I heard pumps rattle and inhaled the scent of gas. *Yes!*

People. At last! I felt invigorated.

As I approached the service desk, the town folks were staring at me like I was from another planet. The clerk cleared his throat. "Can I help you, ma'am?"

"Yeah, I'd like the key to the restroom."

He studied me. "Ma'am, you're soaked. Are you alright? You're limping. Are you hurt? Should I call paramedics?" he asked, genuinely concerned.

The first image that came to mind when he spoke of "paramedics" was bandages, stitches, and ointment. That felt soothing. But then I envisioned authorities questioning me, and soon enough, cops popped into mind—NO WAY! I had to keep a low profile no matter what. "I'm fine," I said. "I jus' need keys."

The clerk handed over a set, each labeled accordingly. Hastily, I snatched the keys from his hand and darted out of the station. The town folks surrounded me, staring at me. Realizing how rude I was to the clerk when I should have been grateful, I briefly turned and uttered a quick "thanks." The folks followed me as I walked toward the restroom, gawking at me from head to toe as if I was some kind of freak. What was with these people? Was I that despicable? I backed away from the curious crowd and disappeared into the restroom.

I was soaked and shivering; my hair was dripping wet. With great apprehension, I looked into the restroom mirror. I could barely distinguish my reflection in the old, tarnished, tiny, square footer full of black spots, fingerprints, and stains. But what I could see was indeed sad. It was the pale face of a very frightened child with old and new scars, cuts, and bruises. Her long brown hair formed a matted drape along the curve of her worn face as if it were hiding disgrace. I reminded myself that I was not looking at me but a deeply troubled stranger.

I turned the hot water faucet on and plugged the drain, letting the sink fill. I splashed my face with the water. The steam fogged up the mirror. I continued to splatter the water against my face, trying to burn it. "It isn't working," I cried. It wasn't making the pain go away. I felt the pressure surface . . .

I hear Father call for me. I know better than to lock the bathroom door. Father would beat me if I locked any door in the house. He never trusted me behind a closed door. Hurry—what can I do? I panic! I have Mother's lipstick and blush all over my face. Father will be angry if he catches me this way. I quickly sweep all Mommy's cosmetics back into her vanity drawer. Father pokes his head into the bathroom, noticing my reflection in the mirror. I can tell he is upset. "No Daddy," I toss my head in denial. "I wasn't playing with Mommy's makeup; it's my own."

Deservingly, Father accuses me of lying. "You had better wash every particle of your mother's makeup off, you hear me!" He scorns me. "I never want to catch you wearing makeup again, little one. I told you before, makeup is only for pretty women like your mother." He fills the sink with hot water before immersing my face into it! Once he frees me, my skin is scorched. I cry.

Steam coated the mirror with vapor. I lifted my face out of the sink. A headful of dripping hot water ran down my cold damp clothes. Grotesque images of the accident flashed before me: the slit in Brad's eye, blood oozing from his socket, smoke rising from the bent-in- hood, Brad's severed shoulder and the key stuck in the ignition. I hid my face in shame. A wave of sadness overcame me. *'Daddy's right—I am an ugly person. I need to burn in hell for murdering Brad. The evil in me permeates outward. I am darkness. I am sin.'*

'But Brad was mean to you,' a voice in my head interjected.

'I killed Brad,' I corrected.

'Brad drugged you,' the voice argued.

'It doesn't matter, the accident was my doing,' I insisted. *'I caused it.'*

'You could be locked up in the slammer,' the voice agreed. 'So just don't tell anyone,' The voice advised.

S.O.S.

I'm a survivor, I reinforced to myself with a proud smile across my face. So, where did I go from here? I needed a place to stay. Without a car I hadn't many options and hitchhiking was not one of them. Fortunately, Richard's wallet was in my pants pocket. I found a Dunn & Phillips Auto Dealer business card. Richard's home number was printed on the upper right corner. Though I was tempted to call, I had to come up with a really good explanation for the loss of his stolen car. I was sure he reported the incident and was awaiting my capture.

I could explain that I betrayed him for cheating on me with his mistress. I'd say, "After getting away for a while and thinking things through, I forgave him and miss him very much. BUT . . . I had a . . . well, a minor accident. Yes, one of those fender-benders—nothing serious. Yes . . . dropped it off at a shop overnight. So, if you'd kindly do me a favor and pick me up . . ." I rehearsed my lines. After Richard would pick me up and take me back to his place, I'd then be able to trace Vicki and have her rescue me from the cunning sex offender. I thought it over and it sounded feasible—a shot in the dark, but I had to chance it.

Upon returning to the service desk, customers were still standing around, staring at me, again. I stared them back. "Don't you have something better to do?" The town folks had a look of shock on their face then averted their attention. Why were they so nosey? The thought of being posted on "MOST WANTED" fliers entered my mind.

I asked the clerk if I could use his desk phone. He was more than generous and did not ask any questions. I made a long-distance call to Richard's apartment in Philley County. The phone rang several times. I was really distressed about the whole idea. I mean, what if he answered? After the phone rang five times, it occurred to me that he may not be home. Just as I was about to hang up on the sixth ring . . .

"Hello," a feminine voice answered.

"Hel . . . Hello?" I stumbled as a lady's voice had caught me off-guard. My mind drew a blank.

"Who's this?" the voice asked.

"Ah . . . a friend of Richard's. Is he there?"

"No, he ain't back yet. Can I have' um call ya?"

"No, that's okay," I said, about to hang up. "Thanks anyway."
"Wait—can I tell him who called?"

I drew silent. I recognized that once-indignant voice. I knew she also recognized mine; we had spoken yesterday.

"Are you Denise?" she conjectured.

I was in shock! How did she know my name? I replied with a shaky voice, "Yes."

"Denise, what can I do for ya?"

That's funny. The same lady, a day ago, accused me of sleeping with her lover. What provoked her to be so friendly now? I didn't trust this. My train of thought came back as I recalled the scheme. "Ah, tell Richard that I'm okay and everything's fine . . . but ah, I had a minor fender-bender—nothing serious though. Tell him his car is in a shop, okay," I added, "And . . . a . . . if you could, I'd like a lift," I muttered.

"Where are ya, honey?" she whispered as if a close friend. "I'll come and getcha," she granted.

I didn't believe what I was hearing. This was too good to be true. "But where's Richard?"

"Rich ain't gettin' in till dark. I'll take my BMW and getcha as soon as ya gimme good directions." She paused. "Don't worry, hun, Richard told me everything boutchas."

"What did he tell you?" I asked but didn't really care to know.

"He told me yous his cousin from outta town, and yous got into a squabble wif him ova family matters but he's chillin', girl. He say he forgive ya," she explained.

"Is that what Richard told you?" I asked in disbelief. *Now who's puttin' on who?*

"You bet. Look, he only meant well. He ain't out ta harm nobody. He jus get carried away sometime." She paused. "Now you tell me where to pick you up at and I'll surely be there soon." She silenced, waiting for my directions. After moments of reluctance, she tried to clarify things. "Look, if you's in any kinda trouble, I ain't gonna call no cops or nothing . . . and I knows you can use some extra cash," she implied. Had she read my mind? I was hesitant, but I really didn't have much of a choice. It felt too incredulous to believe that Richard told her that I was his cousin. Besides, she mentioned nothing about the disappearance of his Fiero.

I tested her knowledge by telling her where I was, assuming she wouldn't have the slightest clue; after all, I'm in another far away city. But I underestimated her. She knew exactly where I was—the junction between Waterside and Maywood. As I hung the phone up, I felt flip-flops in my gut. Though I couldn't quite pinpoint what was troubling me, there was a deception in that voice. I mean, after all, she was the mistress. I was sure she had evil intentions. Nonetheless, without anywhere else to turn, I stuck around and waited for her.

SUGAR

An hour later a passing motorist honked at me. The vehicle turned into the filling station and stopped before me. The windows of this white BMW were darkened so I could not see through them. The passenger side window was lowered. A light-skinned Afro-American youth, around my age, waved me over. She was a natural beauty, a familiar face I had seen before but couldn't place. With the push of a button, the passenger door was automatically opened for me. This deluxe model had a very luxurious interior: plush seats, dashboard combed with fancy control buttons, and seat gadgets on the armrest. First class taxi service, indeed, but at what price? No doubt the mistress hadn't spent a cent on the car. She probably borrowed it from Richard's dealership. Mistresses were big on borrowing. Her low-cut V-neck sweater revealed what appeared to me as artificial implants, face caked in makeup, with long, thick eyelashes and Botox thick lips. Strong perfume had me wonder why she came out of her way to pick me up. Was I going to be a third wheel on a hot date with Richard? I mean, I was grateful that she showed up at all, but . . .

She was smoking. She offered me one as she took off on the country path. I declined. She lifted an eyebrow. "Ya do smoke, don't ya?" She nearly sneered at me in disapproval.

"Sometimes," I fibbed.

There was a tension between us. Perhaps it was my initial impression of her from the middle-of-the-night phone call. All-in-all, she was rough around the edges. After a while I timidly asked, "Ah . . . where you taking me?" I had to prepare myself for the worst.

She tossed the question back at me, "Where ya wanta go?" indicating that my options were open. Unfortunately, I had no place to go. Was I to humiliate myself by telling her so?

"Where you live, sweetie?" she reiterated.

I had to confess the uncomfortable truth. "I don't have a place to go, okay? I don't have any money or nothing," I sighed. "I thought you were taking me back to Richard's."

She puckered up. "There's ain't no fuckin' way you goin' back to my man Rich. No way!" she made herself clear, pointing her finger in my face.

"Really? I'm surprised. I thought that's what you had set out to do all along."

"I neva said nothin' of the nature. Donchoo go puttin' words in my mouth," she snapped again. "I'll see to it that you ain't never mess wif him no more."

I studied her. "You made up the story, didn't you? You know he and I aren't cousins."

She grinned. "That bit I made up to get you ta tell me where you is." She paused to take a drag. "And ain't I dirty smooth about it." She tapped her cigarette ashes against the edge of a built-in dashboard ashtray.

I changed the subject. "He never mentioned you," I expressed regretfully. "He told me that I was his only lover. If I would have known . . ."

"Girl, you fall for that shit? He ain't nobody's lover. He mess wit you. He say anything that make you want him. C'mon, he's a player. Tell me what he say. Did he promise you pearls, diamonds, furs, a beach house, Porsche, real nice evening wear? Or he say he love you and take you away with him to the Bahamas or Hawaiian Islands 'cause you special. Or better yet, maybe he got a bit more imagination and mess witcher mind. He say you a real special girlfriend from way past and—ya know, it funny 'cause he recognize your face but you ain't know him from nowheres. So, he sweettalk bullshit about bein' yours ex-lover. Before ya know it, he's makin' up some phony story and he get you roll'n. Shit, he a trip!"

My mouth dropped and eyeballs nearly popped out in surprise. How could she have known? She confirmed Richard's stories of flattery were nothing more than cheap thrills he used to prey on many other naive young girls. "Well, if that's true, then you're not his either," I argued.

"Right, I ain't."

"So why are you seeing him?"

"He's a trick. Ya dig?"

"Huh?" I was completely baffled.

"He's my regular customer." She paused to take a drag. "I make up to $300 a night by him, alone. Honey, he got MONEY, and I make sure he don't get no free lunches, ya understand?"

"No, not really." I knew she had to be running some kind of business and selling to him.

"Child, you ever get let out?"

"What?"

"I'm a hooker," she clarified. "Ya know what that is?" She turned toward me with a grave look. "Yeah, I'm a street hooker," she repeated in a haughty way.

"You mean you're a prostitute?" I restated. *And to think I gave her the benefit of the doubt that she was just a mistress.*

"You ain't too dumb, ain't ya," she replied sarcastically.

"But—but why?" I was sitting in the presence of this beautiful . . . low life.

"That's the best way to survive out here on the streets," she defended herself. "The way you's goin, you be down under in no time," she emphasized. "But I can't figure why you be hangin' out in this neck of the woods if you ain't workin'. This ain't no place for homeless. I knows about this area 'cause I got some rich customers livin' north here. It's miles from main town," she danced around for an explanation.

"I took a drive out here, that's all. And some idiot hit me." I explained in accordance to my scheme, careful to dodge the truth.

"You mean you's been leisure drivin' for hours? Is that how you ended up with a battered face?" She tried to put me on the spot.

I got indignant with her. "Look, I don't know what you're trying to get at but I'd appreciate if you'd stick your nose out of my business. I mean, I appreciate you picking me up but if you're not comfortable with me, just lend me some cash and I'll get outta your hair." I paused, feeling resentment. "You can drop me off right here and I'll catch a cab." I couldn't believe I just said that.

"You stupid, ain't ya? You think you's gonna catch a cab out here? The only vehicle you gonna find is a train. And it ain't no public transport."

"Can we change the subject," I urged.

"Call me Sugar," the testy, fast-mouthed bitch finally introduced herself, trying to start over on a better note.

"Is that your nickname?" I asked.

"Street name. That's the name everyone uses." She puffed away. "I'lls take you to my place down here since you ain't got no place to go, alright?"

"Are you sure? I don't want to be an inconvenience." I was more apprehensive than gracious.

"No, I don't mind. It'll just be a temporary arrangement till ya's get yourself back on your feet again."

"But do you really have space for me?"

"We'll make do. I sleep out at night anyways," Sugar added. "You're really a pros . . . prost . . . prostitute?"

"That a hard word for you to pronounce?"

"No, it's just . . . it's like a profanity to me. I mean why would you want to be . . . that?"

"I didn't choose to be a hooker," Sugar explained. "I wanted to be a model actually. But I got wit this boyfriend and he got me pregnant so I quit high school and then my life completely changed. My boyfriend made me his hooker and that's how I got started. I got used to it after a while, makin' lots of money got me hooked." She winked at the pun.

"You left home?"

"My momma and me neva got along. She left ma' dad when I was small so she had to work. I pretty much always been on my own. I have five other younger brothers and sisters. I'm the first, all under one roof so Momma kicked me out when I got pregnant 'cause she didn't have no money to raise my baby, Tia. She wanted me to abort it, but I fought hard to keep it. So, I moved in wit my boyfriend in this town and that's when I met my landlady, Shirell. She been workin' in a beauty shop on South Way when she got me workin' sometimes for her on the side and we's best of friends since. She and I both single moms so she offered me her place to stay after the fallout wit my boyfriend. That's my story. What's yours?" Sugar asked, creating miniature smoke rings with her lips.

I still felt uneasy about her, though she was trying to break down the barrier between us. "There's no story. I ran away from home and fell for Richard. That's it."

"Did he get you pregnant?" She looked at me.

"I sure hope not," I sighed.

"Then why you run away?"

"My dad beat me, okay?"

"Why he do that?"

"Why did you have a fallout with your boyfriend?" I snapped.

HER SECRET

Someone making up to $300 a night and driving around in a BMW would most likely live very lavishly in an upscale neighborhood. Again, I was wrong.

Pollution permeated through the thin walls of the apartment. There were noticeable paint strippings on the walls and ceiling. Some rooms looked like the remains of a fire. Most windows were boarded up or covered with plastic wrap, therefore there was no cross-ventilation. The bathroom reeked of urine. The floors needed a mopping. The tub was corroded with mildew and the sink faucet dripped. The toilet flusher was worn so waste backed up now and then. They had a plumber, I was told, but he was always too busy. And, last but not least, little pussy ants—drawn to the old spills and little cookie crumbs—lived in the kitchen cupboard, on the counter, and by the sink. Cleaning the kitchen, I guessed, was not a priority either. I was sure rats and roaches were also dwellers here.

Needless to say, the construction was in desperate need of repair. The apartment should have been condemned. While the entire apartment rotted away, Sugar's pretentious bedroom was fit for a princess. The master bedroom was the only room in the apartment that was meticulously decorated and maintained. A king-sized waterbed stood over a huge black and white striped zebra area rug. Huge mirrors surrounded the vanity. Two adjacent walls opposite the bed displayed a mural of nudes at the beach. The remaining two walls were a vivid red.

Sugar introduced me to her landlady friend, Shirell, and Shirell's son, Shawn. The older, stocky caretaker stood at 5'3" with jet-black tapered hair. Shirell didn't greet me with a smile or a handshake. She made me feel rather unwelcome. Perhaps she disliked white people. Shirell held Tia, Sugar's baby. The older woman of about 55 years worked part-time in the shop in addition to raising the baby, while Sugar and Shawn teamed up in their corrupt lifestyle. Shirell had three sources of income: rent money, part-time work, and welfare. She was bitten by poverty for eleven years after her husband, a Spanish native from Brazil, walked out on her, leaving her with a toddler. Shawn, her only child of 12 years, was precisely of mixed breed.

These children were being raised in a dilapidated shack. The boy probably knew nothing other than crime.

I joined Sugar in the kitchen for a cup of coffee. Sugar winked as she poured the cream in. "Ain't my baby cute wit that smile?"

I nodded, "How old is she now?"

"Oh, 'bout six months," Sugar estimated with delight.

"Does your boyfriend have visitation rights?" I asked.

Sugar had a malicious look on her face as if I had betrayed her. I didn't mean to offend her.

"Why you ask?" She got testy with me.

"I didn't mean to upset you. I'm just curious. I mean, is it a problem?"

"What's it to you," she sneered.

"Nothing, really nothing. If you don't want to discuss it, you don't have to. I just wanted to find out more about your situation, ya know, like you wondered about mine," I explained, feeling very uneasy.

She hesitantly nodded, understanding that she had no need to be defensive. "Can you keep a secret?" she lowered her voice.

"Well, it depends . . ."

She intervened, "I'm gonna tell you my story and you better NEVER speak a word of it to anyone as long as you alive, understand?" She emphasized the seriousness of the nature. I nodded, listening intently, waiting for her to reveal her secret. My heart was pounding with anticipation.

"You remember what I told you about my boyfriend?" she began.

"Yes."

"I told you he made me prostitute for him, right?" Sugar paused to sip her coffee.

"Yes," I recalled.

"He's a pimp," she clarified. "That mean he made me turn my wages over to him," she explained. "Ya see, I's working for him. I's paid to sleep wit other men but had to give him every penny I earned. But I didn't mind at the time 'cause I thought he was savin' up for ours future together but then I caught him spendin' my hard-earned dollars on his other lady dates for dine'in and gifts and shit. That's when I left him and moved in wit Shirell. I knew I was safe here 'cause he didn't know nothin' 'bout Shirell. So now I'm in hidin' from 'um."

"You mean he still wants you to work for him?"

"It ain't me no more that he want. He want my baby. He say he has rights to the child 'cause he the daddy. He want me to give up my little girl so he can sell the baby to the black market and make a handsome fortune for himself."

"He wants to sell your baby?" I was alarmed. "But she's his baby too."

"He don't care. Child, he fathers so many babies, he can sell 'um wholesale. He only in it for the money. He don't care about nobody's child," she lamented.

The boyfriend was obviously a sadistic con man. He traced Sugar's disappearance to Shirell's apartment not too long ago and had been calling periodically to harass Shirell into giving him information on the whereabouts of the baby. He was trying to get Shirell to surrender the baby from its hiding place in exchange for big cash. Sugar told me he had already tried blackmail. Now he was threatening to kidnap someone for ransom. "I have to watch Shawn closely." Sugar swallowed. "Who knows." A worried look painted her young, pretty face.

"Has he made an appearance yet?" My eyes were glued to hers, thinking that my problems were nothing compared to hers.

"No, he wouldn't dare come over here 'cause Shirell got a loaded automatic weapon hidden away and wouldn't hesitate to blow his brains out. No, he too slick. He'll wait for the right moment. He probably too busy hasslin' his other pregnant women down. I ain't the only one, ya know. But Lord have mercy, you best protect us all, you hear," Sugar cautioned.

I had no idea of the magnitude of her situation. She couldn't let the cops in on the matter since she was illicit as well. Besides, the black-market interactions would be his word against hers.

"Sometimes you have to be your own policeman," she sighed. She said she couldn't trust anyone on the outside. I figured that meant she trusted me. I promised not to tell a soul.

There was also a story attached to Shawn, Shirell's son. Shawn was a street kid. He placed his life in danger every day. He was suspended from school several times to become a prominent drug dealer, working every street corner. After selling dope, he handed some of his profit over to Sugar. Sugar admitted that the cops gave him a hard time, but there was nothing lawfully they could do to restrain him since he was underage. Sugar treated the matter favorably as if she'd been coaching him for her own selfish gain.

PROCUREMENT

Immediately after our little chat, which began our female bonding, Sugar had me sit on the edge of her waterbed while she threw me a fashion show. She indeed owned the finest clothes money could buy. She had on fine silk lingerie made in Paris and Italy, glittery sequins dangled from evening wear, not to mention the hand-crafted, leather, five-inch pumps. After modeling her satin white evening gown, she insisted I try it on.

"No, that's okay," I declined the glamour of material wealth. Besides, I didn't like the idea of wearing a hooker's clothes, custom altered to fit every curve of her figure. But she insisted. She had me strip off all my garments, including panties and bra, to parade around in her pink-padded laced bra, silk bikini underwear, and white silk gown. The cup was way too large on me, accentuating my figure.

She stood back and evaluated my outfit. "No, it's missin' sometin'." She snapped her fingers. She handed me a see-through baby-blue velour bathrobe to complete the attire. At last, she was pleased. "Now doncha feel sexy?" she asked rather pretentiously.

"Not really," I chuckled, feeling a slight draft. I was not comfortable wearing Sugar's nightwear. "Could I take it off now?"

She ignored my request. She sat me down at her vanity desk then set out to paint my face with the various colored creams, pencils, and powders. Next, she selected ruby earrings and a 14K gold necklace from her six-drawer jewelry box for final touches. Not finished yet. My hair had to be briskly brushed and combed with professional sprays for a more manageable bouncy, soft, and sassy look. She pulled my hair back with clips, sprayed it in place, then turned me to face the mirror.

"Now ya feel sexy!" Sugar leaned over my shoulder in excitement. A complete makeover gleamed in the huge vanity mirror. She had, indeed, done a professional job considering I had just had a car accident and was weather worn. Foundation and makeup hid the bruises and scuff marks. I smiled brightly for it was the first time I didn't mind looking like Denise. Alright, enough playing beauty school, what was the meaning of all this?

"Well Denise, whatcha say for yourself?"

"I look really good. You're quite a makeup artist. I think you should quit your day job," I joked.

She laughed. "Think so? Well, you know what I think you be good for?" She gave me that suggestive look. "I make you one of me," she grinned.

"What?" I huffed. "No way!" I adamantly declined. It was so clear what she was up to. She was trying to procure me.

"Listen to me. I make you real rich, real fast. You's can meet the nicest and richest of all the men in the world—and hunks—uh! Top picks," she exclaimed. Again, I tossed my head *no*. Intolerantly, she babbled on and on like a sales lady on commission, "You neva have ta work days no more and it be the biggest night life you ever imagined. You make new friends and . . . and get lots a passion, and oh God, once ya start ya can't stop." She paused. "It's really not what you hear on the news. It's a profession. And it's easy to learn. But the best part, girl, it's tax free! That mean no deductions, child." She fixed her sparkly eyes and long lashes on my face. "I said tax free, under the table, cold hard cash," she emphasized. "You set your own price. You can swindle a single trick for $100 easy," she boasted.

I did not fall prey to her persuasion.

"C'mon, whatcha scared a? Give it a shot. Just one shot is all I ask, one night," she pleaded, grasping onto my shoulder firmly. "You gotta."

"Why do I have to? Tell me why I can't find legit work. Do you think so little of me that I'm not capable of securing an honest position?"

She clenched her teeth together. "Just say you is." She twisted my wrist. I pushed her off in defense. I didn't understand why she was so upset that I didn't wish to be a hooker. What was it to her? We got into a catfight by the vanity area. She overpowered me, pinning me to the zebra rug. A switchblade was flicked open and pointed to my throat! "Gimme your dope," she demanded, assuming I was in possession.

I was in shock, confused by her sudden behavior change. After she picked me up from the station, offered me a place to stay, and revealed a deep secret to me, she turned on me. "What? What's all this about anyway?" My gut knew all along that she was deceiving me.

"You know very well. You don't fool me, gimme your dope or I'll beat the shit out of ya."

"Search me," I pleaded. "I swear I don't have any."

She did. She searched my street clothes only to clear me of the charge. "Okay, so you ain't got none on ya. But I want to make you understand that nobody messes wit me."

"Okay, I understand. You don't have to beat me into submission to make it register. Really, I'm not that dense."

She sat on her waterbed contemplating an explanation for her behavior. "I know everything," she stated bluntly.

"Everything about what?" I felt goose bumps forming.

"You know, the stolen car and the accident," she acknowledged. I felt knots in my stomach. "You knew all along?"

She nodded, "I drove past the site of the accident on the way to pickin' you up. It was all up in smoke and fire. The cops and fire trucks all there puttin' it out. I was in shock, so I called Richard on my car phone. Well, he was pissed. He told me to make you pay for all the damages right up front in cash. That's in addition to stealing his wallet and money. That mean that you owe me $25,000 in green cash and you payin' up before you leave here."

My face must have turned pale. I felt faint. "You can't be serious. $25,000—how?"

"If you don't pay up within the next month, Richard will report you to the cops. And I know you don't want that kinda trouble, do ya?"

"Why didn't you tell me you knew all this before? Why are you bringing it up now?"

"Gotcha, didn't I," Sugar snapped, snickering. "I's a sneaky nigga, ain't I?"

I felt trapped. She was no better than Richard or Brad. "That's not fair. You can't do this to me. I'm leaving,"

"What?" Sugar laughed. "You don't think I'd letcha off the hook after all that, do ya?"

"Sugar, there's no way I can pay him back in a month. That's insane," I pointed out.

"You ain't got no choice."

"You don't scare me." I gathered my clothes and scurried over to the bedroom door. I placed my hand on the door handle. "Thanks for offering me a place to stay but I can do just fine without your help." I was about to walk out and slam the door shut, with her gown on, when the gown caught on the door hinge. I bent over to unsnag it. When I looked up, Sugar had the switchblade pointed in my face, again.

"You ain't goin' nowheres," she threatened.

I drew back, startled. "Wait . . . I thought we were a team." I chuckled, trying to remain calm about this.

"I ain't never said nothin' of the nature. I only offered you a place to stay until you pay up. Then I'm gonna throw your white ass outta my cabin."

"I get it. This is just a big scheme to get me to work for you just as your boyfriend had done to you. You never called Richard, did you? And you also made up the story about the black market just to get me to support your drug habit. Let's be honest about it for a change," I asserted courageously before the blade.

In anger, Sugar showed her teeth, again as if she were about to bite me. She grabbed me by the collar while drawing the blade near my eye. "You better watch your mouth, Whitey, or you'll lose a precious organ. Don't ever accuse me of nothin', ya understand. I told you I don't like people messin' wit me. I like you as far as I can poke this blade into yours thin white honky flesh. If you ever betray me, I's slit the last livin', beatin' pulse outta ya. And don't try me even once. Now I ain't no murderer until you make me one. I'd love to throw you out into the streets of hungry beasts but let me give you one last piece of advice based on experience. If you want to survive, you best behave yourself cuz you ain't got no frail chance out here in this town alone. So, if you's smart, you cooperate wit me. You work real hard out there and bring me your wages." The knife drew closer to my eye. I held perfectly still, trying not to flinch. I was afraid of losing an eye, but I wouldn't give her the satisfaction of making me humble.

"I'd rather rob a bank than work for you," I sneered, sickened by the aroma of her perfumed neck.

"You tellin' me you ain't gonna listen to me and I'm pointin' a raw blade against your thin eyelid? You think you's tough, don't cha? Well then you need to learn a lesson the hard way." Sugar raised her eyebrows with malicious intent. She temporarily blinded me, not by the blade, but with her bare knuckles.

I didn't wish to submit to a prostitute—an uneducated, mean-spirited, self-indulging prostitute. I was framed. She forced me to sell my body to strangers against my will to pay Richard back and there was nothing I could do about it. Putting it in perspective, after being abused by Richard and Brad, this time, at least, I would receive money for it, not that I would get to keep any of it. Besides, how hard could prostituting be? Nothing that I hadn't already experienced. Little did I know what it took to be a prostitute.

THE STREETS OF FOWLERSVILLE

Not in my wildest dreams would I have imagined myself procured into prostitution. How low could I go? I couldn't believe I was actually going to do this. Besides, out here on the streets I had a perfect opportunity to escape from Sugar's wrath but where was I to go? A runaway. Penniless. Delinquent. Without a car. The only possessions I had along this tumultuous journey were the torn shirt on my back and the soggy shoes on my feet. Who was I kidding? Too young to legally work without consent of a parent. Without a permit, people could get suspicious since I wasn't in school. Sugar was right, how else could I survive?

Philley was predominantly a white-collar upscale community. In contrast, Fowlersville was a city battered by social decay. The lowest element lived in this ghetto, spreading misery like an epidemic.

In three-inch heels, I tapped from block to block along the widened city sidewalk. To my left, a barbed-wire fence and guardrail surrounded the city jail. To my right, ditto row houses lined the street. The residents could be spotted sitting outside on their porch chair or steps, gazing into meaningless empty space. There didn't seem to be much hope in their mindless, lazy eyes, saturated with despair and injustices. After all, their row houses faced the city jail across the street. Nothing scenic or desirable in that, not that they cared. They lived off food stamps, soup kitchens, and handouts. Some went without gas and electric in their one-room efficiency, supporting more than five children. They accepted that the rats or roaches in their pantry might be breeding at this very moment. For all they knew, their school-aged children were out on the streets armed, on drugs, or endangered; viruses or sexually transmitted diseases may go untreated simply because they couldn't afford medicine or healthcare. And . . . when they would get their next welfare check, they could try again for that lottery ticket or buy some more dope to keep from going insane.

I strayed onto a path leading to a schoolyard. The side of the school building appeared as one huge doodle pad. There were writings, colorful paintings, and sketches along the brick wall. They call this graffiti.

Noise pollution from horns to sirens to music pounded the streets with confusion and excitement. One hostile driver yelled profanities at a jaywalker, showed another driver his finger, and honked his horn at the standing traffic as if he were shooting a firearm. The pedestrians were no better than the intolerant motorists. A group of teens knelt in a circle smoking joints right in front of a liquor store in broad daylight. Their rap music, in stereo, at top volume, shook the sidewalk.

The terror of crime was apparent everywhere, though the city folks pretended not to see. But there was no way the blatant acts could be ignored or kept in secrecy when store windows were barred, when shattered glass left impressions of bullet holes, when security guards were posted at night to stomp out looters, when it would seem almost fashionable to carry a handgun or penknife on a belt loop or mace spray in one's purse, and when arson or bomb threats forced abled parents to pull their children out of public school systems. No, the paranoia of crime could not be concealed.

My heart raced as the eerie feeling of danger enveloped me from block to block.

The 25th block of Maison Avenue was cluttered with trash—in the gutters, on the sidewalks, and in the allies. Stray dogs and the homeless toppled trashcans onto the sidewalk in search of food. Exhaustively, they picked through smashed soda cans, chewing gum, candy wrappers, matches, and cigarettes infested with flies and bees before they found potato peelings, bread crusts, and leftovers from McDonald's.

As I was passing though Mernick Avenue, I spotted an unshaven, filthy, stinky drunkard slouched against the corner step of a stairwell leading to a bar cellar. He momentarily paused from his booze to get a glimpse of my legs then burped before returning to his solitude. *How disgusting,* I thought. At the corner of my eye, I spotted two kids wrestling over in the alley. I intentionally ignored the racket.

PROSTITUTION FOR BEGINNERS

Break dancers were entertaining at a street corner. An audience had formed. I had to check it out. As I approached, I drew attention. Eyeballs were bouncing up and down on me as if I were on display in a store. Two black dudes in shades strolled past me as they bobbed their heads back and forth to the tune playing on their headset. They raised their eyebrows and winked at me. Moments later they slapped each other a high-five, exclaiming, "Awhoo!" They thought I was HOT. I couldn't believe it. Me? I turned them on? I never knew I had it in me. I mean, I was flattered but I didn't think I could really make it out here on the streets. I thought Sugar was joking when she said it was easy. I'd been feeling so awkward until those dudes were looking me over. I grinned back at them, flicking my mascara sticky-thick eyelashes, thinking, "What in hell am I supposed to do now?"

I gazed into a store window, observing my reflection. I wasn't her, but she was me. She was half naked, revealing cleavage through her pink tight-fitted tank top. Though she had a cute belly button, her tattooed Cupid's arrow through a red heart distracted from it. Weather-beaten raw hands secured themselves to her hips as if posing for a Playboy centerfold. She stood well postured in the high-heel lizard pumps. A black leather skirt draped her waist down to her thighs. Her long, silky blonde treated hair had plum streaks. I didn't recognize myself at first. I mean, Sugar did a real professional job on my face. She covered up all the blemishes with foundation, including the black eye she gave me. She told me over, and over, "It's all in the way you look." So, I asked her if I looked like one. She smiled back at me, cracking her gum, feigning a haughty, streetwise tough guy. I never knew her to be anything other. She taught me well. Sugar knew which dates to approach and the ones to steer clear from. She instructed me on how to negotiate price, how to please a customer, and how to avoid pimps and madams. She was quite skilled on how to earn a pretty dollar performing safe sex that would gratify a man every time. The prostitute in the mirror was my mentor. She was the shadow that would guide me through this risky business. I just had to pretend to be her.

A white limo pulled up along the curb right behind me. I noticed a few teen chicks dressed seductively, mingling with one another across the street. They noticed me. I was sure they were prostitutes too. I could tell they were talking about me, pointing fingers, giggling, and whispering. A sharp-dressed black man stepped out of the limo. The black chick with the over-sized, ring-shaped earrings approached the parked limo. She charged over to the prospect, anxious to proposition him. I watched as she put her seductive arms around him, caressing his back and shoulders, then pinching him on the buttocks. To my surprise, he brushed her off. She persisted to win his affections aggressively until he got firm with her. She finally yielded to his wishes, "Okay—okay," backing off, steering her hands clear from him.

She faced me, signaling me over. "Hey you, he wants ya," she conveyed his message, pointing to him.

I just stood there baffled, in shock.

"Yeah, you. This fella wants ya," she confirmed. Disappointed that she lost the prospect, she walked away, returning to her circle of friends.

I did not budge, almost hoping that this was some sort of joke. The man waved me over.

Still, I did not move an inch. I was afraid. Unfortunately, the man closed his car door and walked over to me.

I wanted to run in the other direction, but I was . . . possessed. With a soft-spoken voice, I greeted, "Hey handsome, what can I do for you tonight?" The words I spoke rolled off my tongue on their own. I placed my hand over my mouth in embarrassment. *He's a stranger! Have I no restraint? He could rape and murder me if I'm not careful.*

"You new around here. What's your name?" The tall black man dressed in a white business suit folded his arms, sizing me up. He wasn't friendly at all. He was rather intimidating.

"Bambi." A smile stretched across my face as I recalled the name Sugar provided me.

"Nice name," he replied, nodding with a slight grin. "Bambi, would you be interested in going for a nice ride with me?" He extended his hand.

He had me cornered. All I needed to say was *no*. "What would ya like, sweetie? What turns ya on?" I said involuntarily. I was ashamed of myself. *Snap out of it, NOW!* I warned myself. I was putting my life in great danger.

"Humm . . . just give me some head."

I must have had a dumb look on my face. Head? Well, was I not supposed to ask what he meant?

He was annoyed, "All you dumb blondes are alike. Where do you come from? A farm?" If he didn't like blondes, I could help him there. But I didn't think his point was the color of my hair. Sugar had her reasons behind coloring it. She explained that more men were attracted to blondes than brunettes.

"I want some head. You understand or you new to this country? You blondes don't come with an interpreter, do you? I WANT YOU TO SUCK MY DICK. YA UNDERSTAND?" he raised his voice, speaking slowly to be clear.

"Shhh . . ." I put my finger to my lips. "I hear yer hungry, I'm just gearing up for the ride." I licked my finger salaciously. Indeed, SHE'S adept at handling these crisis situations."

"Ooh, yeah! Name your price?" The stud got excited.

I should have said, *I'm not for sale*, but instead I asked, "Ah . . . $50 for starts." Sugar advised to start offers with a minimum of $50 then raise in increments with experience.

He declined indignantly, "Fuck no! I bet you ain't ever done no fuckin' blow job in your life," he raised his voice, embarrassing me further in front of the hustlers. "You must be a fuckin' virgin or somethin' but I think you're pretty. You're worth about $30."

Don't do me any favors, asshole. I wanted to smack him across the face but I refrained. I said humbly, "You won't be disappointed." I didn't have to accept the offer so why did I? I had a high minimum to meet each night. Should I consider this my practice trick?

He opened the back door and gestured *ladies first*. I noticed an older man with salt and pepper hair in the driver's seat. He must have been the chauffeur. The hustlers across the street were watching. Though I was nervous, I had to relax, or I would be jeopardizing everything.

This was my first time in a limo. The interior was more lavish than Sugar's BMW. "Wow!" I exclaimed under my breath. *This guy is rich!* I thought to myself.

The black dude made himself comfortable on the soft blue velvet upholstered seat, lit only by a backseat spotlight. He quickly lowered his fly, whipped his dick out, then lay there waiting for me. I just sat there. I was thinking, *How could she give him a . . . blowjob with another man in the car? Didn't she need privacy?* He was getting impatient. "Fuck lady, you want your money or not. I ain't payin' you to look dumb, ya know." He paused. "You've seen a black dick before, haven't you?"

"Many . . . but it's making me sooo wet."

"You want it?" he repeated several times.

SHE fingered his pet. "Hard inside me . . . I wanna feel it all over me," she muttered with heavy breathing as she unbuttoned her top.

"Oh yeah baby, do it."

His shirt was unbuttoned. Fingers ran through his hairy chest. My shadow was at work. Her breasts were pressed against his sweaty chest, mouths kissing passionately and tongues locking as he thrusted his tongue into hers. The windows were fogging up. She pretended she was in the mood even though she was totally turned off. Sugar taught me it was one big act. *"Ya have ta imagine having sex with an incredible hunk and that's how you get 'round the disgust."* She lowered herself to his crotch and stroked his pet with her silky fingers. She held the rod firmly in her palm. Each rhythmic stroke and squeeze on the sensitive little organ triggered a moan. *"That's how you win the game,"* the shadow pointed out, *"gettin' him moanin' is what it's all 'bout."* The penis grew in size as it rose upward, yearning for her moist, warm mouth. She placed the dark hotdog between her lips and drew it in whole. After bobbing vigorously for some time, sticky-salty fluid oozed out the sides of her mouth onto him. She refused to swallow. I heard him moan in pleasure, "Oh Bambi."

He reached up, attempting to put his arms around her. She pushed him down. "I think it's time for me to go," she said.

"Oh, c'mon babe," he persisted breathlessly.

"I don't want to hurt you, I just want my money," she threatened valiantly.

"Then fuck you, you bimbo." He was pissed but he had his escort pay her anyway. The chauffeur was given permission to release the back door. As she quickly lifted to put her tank top back on, she saw in the rearview mirror the reflection of the driver jerking off. She got out of the car with little hassle, wiping the cum off her chin. The green was stashed away in her bra.

Once I finished this initial assignment, I knew the shadow had left me because I felt a huge wave of nausea come over me. I think I lost my sexual appetite for the rest of my life. I could smell his body odor all over me. I hurried into an alley and threw up. How could I continue to do this hour after hour, night after night, week after week? How could Sugar expect this of me? I'd go insane for sure. Not only was it hard to walk gracefully in high heel shoes while my feet blistered, but the filth was unrelenting. I couldn't take another trick. I called it quits for the night and decided I would just hand over the 30 lousy bucks. I knew Sugar would be displeased with me but even she told me that some nights she went home empty handed.

I was so thankful to have lived through my first trick. I felt that this was more than enough punishment for totaling Richard's car. For Christ's sake, he owned a car dealership. I was sure he could get a nice cut on a brand-new car replacement. I was putting my life on the line for a piece of metal. Fuck it. It wasn't worth it.

STEVE GETTS

I was sure pedestrians could overhear me curse under my breath while waiting at the crosswalk of Lincoln and 2nd Street. I was headed back to Sugar's apartment.

Someone tapped me on the shoulder from behind, startling me. "I didn't mean to scare you." A tall slim in a black leather jacket stood before me. My eyes widened with an instant fixation on his gorgeous deep blue eyes. For a fleeting moment, I had forgotten who I was and why I was so upset. I was in total bliss. He spoke, though I did not hear his words, only his eyes. He repeated, "Would you know which way to Woodhaven Boulevard, ma'am?" I shook my head, still dazzled. My chance to cross the street had come and gone and I had not a twitch. He tried to place me. "Do I know you? Are you a model or something?"

Still gazing into his eyes, I stammered, "Ah . . . no."

"Well, it's nice meeting you . . ." He offered a handshake. "I'm Steve Getts."

I reciprocated, "Denise—I mean Bambi," I stumbled.

"Are you sure you're not a model, getting mixed up with all your aliases?" he joked. "I'm a freelance photographer," he politely introduced himself.

"Nice to meet you, Steve." I was ecstatic to have won over the affections of this real and alive gorgeous hunk. After our initial chat, we resumed to our silent staring contest. There was a strong magnetism between us. Neither of us wanted to depart. "Ah, you're not in any hurry, are you?" Steve finally made his pass.

"Not at all," I assured, trying to ignore the prickling dollar bills against my chest.

"Great." He gestured. "I was just heading toward Woodhaven Boulevard to pick up a part for my camera but that can wait. Would you care to join me for a drink? I know of a cozy pub just up the street?"

I was more than thrilled about the offer though fully aware that I would be violating the rules of the street by accepting. I was prohibited from making any social calls or contacts on business hours. I knew it was my responsibility to inform him that I was the new hooker on the block, but down deep inside I desired a genuine romantic relationship and wished to forget this whole mess I got myself into. I was so eager to start over, again.

We shared taco chips, salsa, and fajitas. He went on to tell me about his business as a photographer, the beautiful models he worked with, and how I resembled a lady named Bonnie. He showed me some stock photos for *The Clip Magazine* and *Penthouse*. Very impressive portfolio. Even as we chatted, we stared off into each other's eyes. I had no reason to doubt his marital status since he had no ring on his finger and was highly flirtatious. I fantasized that he was the guy in the limo I gave a blowjob to. He placed his hand gently over mine. "I want you to know that I find you very attractive," he whispered. "Do you have plans tonight?"

My heart fluttered as I said, "Thanks." I was falling in love for the first time. "Why, what do you have in mind?"

"Just to be with you."

Steve paid for our tickets at the metro to take me to his place. I felt so comfortable with him, as if I had known him for years. Had I discovered the sole purpose of my fate as a hooker?

But reality check—I knew I had to tell him the truth about myself, or he'd eventually find out the wrong way. I mean he would eventually ask where I lived, what I did for a living, or why I wasn't in school. Should I lie or tell the truth? He came into my life with such perfect timing.

But Mamma would always say, *if it seems too good to be true, it usually is.* I wanted him to be a part of my new life. What could possibly go wrong with me and Mr. Right?

In bed, he informed me that he was married. My enamored heart suddenly shriveled up and melted. In defense, I mustered up the courage to tell him that I liked him very much, but I was a paid hooker. He was initially shocked, as he should be, but then he thought it over. "Does that mean you're good in bed?" he teased.

I laughed. "No, I'm serious. I really am. In fact, this is my first night on the job."

He raised his eyebrows as if surprised. His hand reached over and held mine. "Well, if it would make you feel any better, I'll pay you $300 so you won't get in trouble."

My mouth fell open. *$300!* I cleared my throat. "Are you rich?"
"No, I wish," he chuckled. "I just think you're worth it."

I was destined to meet Steve. My cries had been answered. I was now actually being paid to sleep with one of the most handsome men who ever lived.

We never had sex. He only wanted a sounding board to vent off his marital problems.

See, if he wouldn't have had marital problems, he wouldn't have given me the time of day. I was sure his wife was out there hunting me down with a rifle. I asked if there was any hope of him leaving her. He told me he wished he could but said she wouldn't agree to it. She said it wouldn't be a good idea for the baby. So, not only was he married, he had a newborn. He assured me that he hadn't had sex with his spouse for at least a year so I should feel much more at ease, which I didn't. I was curious to know where he got IT from within the past year. His wife, Maggie, was a buyer for a cosmetic company, which required extensive international travel. After two years of marriage, she got involved with a few clients on the job and slept with them. After three years, one of her clients' girlfriends disclosed the secret to Steve. Needless to say, Steve was very upset over the news. In spite, he cheated on her. But it was only when he asked Maggie for a divorce that she announced she was pregnant with his baby.

"How do you know the kid is yours?" I asked.

"We'd have relations on weekends and vacations. I mean, I always had a hunch she had affairs behind my back, but I guess I didn't want to believe it. I thought the ring on her finger would chase them all away."

"You must be heartbroken."

"I figured if I'd confess to Maggie, she'd confess to me. But no, she just laughed in my face and said she didn't believe any other women would desire me, less be attracted to me."

"She's nuts. She doesn't know what she's losing. I mean you're a fox." I kissed him, patting his hairy chest.

"You really know how to build a man's ego, don't you?"

"Everything'll be okay. Don't worry. I'm here. I won't let you down," I insinuated that I wanted to be his future wife. He held me in his arms as we drifted asleep, naked.

THE SCHEME

I was so excited to break the good news to Sugar about my new boyfriend that I danced into her apartment. I called for her. No answer. "Is anyone home?"

Shirell cracked the baby's door open slightly. "She ain't back yet. She spent the night with Rich." She closed the door.

I remembered Sugar mentioning Richard was her best customer. The stud who got me where I was today — deeper in doo-doo. I knocked at the door. "When is she coming back?" I asked.

"I don't know," Shirell answered quietly.

I heard a baby's cry. I cracked the door open to peek in. Shirell was bottle feeding Tia.

Shirell was definitely a more fit mother. I wanted to get acquainted with Shirell but she was aloof and unfriendly. I mean, she wouldn't even look in my direction let alone look me in the eye. I knew it had to be a race thing so I shouldn't take it so personally.

I waited in the kitchen for Sugar to come home, nearly in a trance, I had so many unresolved, conflicting thoughts and feeling regarding Steve. Though he and I had a strong chemistry, it was unfortunate that Steve couldn't offer me his flat due to his renter's agreement with his landlord requiring only single occupancy for his efficiency apartment. However, I couldn't deny that I was infatuated with him.

Later that evening I heard the front door open. Sugar did not hesitate to approach me with greed in her eyes. "How much ya got?" she asked abruptly.

"$330. How much did you make?"

"None-a-ya business. Gimme' the green."

I retrieved the bills from my bra, attempting to recount the green, but Sugar snatched them from me.

"This everything? You best gimme everything," she demanded.

"It's all there, I swear."

I saw the expression on her face as she counted the bills. She could not believe that I had made so much on my first night. She grew real skeptical. She questioned me, accusing me of stealing. "You pick-pocketed, didn't ya?"

"I earned it, honestly. I did two johns."

"Did ya really?" she wanted to believe me. I nodded.

"Did you enjoy it?" she asked curiously almost snickering.

"The second date was amazing," I admitted.

Sugar was overjoyed by my instant success. "Just think, if you do that good on the very first night, how good you be in a week. Yes!" she exclaimed. "Hot damn!" She danced, hopped, and jumped as if she hit the jackpot on the number's game.

Cash changed hand, from Sugar to Shawn. In exchange, a packet was covertly passed from Shawn to Sugar. The money I placed my life on the line for was now in the possession of a street kid.

Sugar yanked me into her bedroom, shutting the door behind us. I demanded, "What's going on?" She instructed me to sit on the bed and shut up. I wasn't sure if I'd get a lecture on the profit I earned or if she'd frisk me again; after all, she was most unpredictable. I was prepared to tell her about Steve. Sugar asked me if I had any dope in my possession, again. The answer had not changed.

"I ain't want you spendin' no money on dope, ya understand?" she snapped at me.

"You think I'm some kinda pothead?" I wondered. "Is that what this is all about?

Sugar paced back and forth on her creaky bedroom floor like a nervous, agitated smoker. She was making me nervous. "You 'member what I told ya yesterday, right?"

I nodded. "Yes, you told me I was in debt to you for totaling Richard's car," I answered promptly.

Sugar paused momentarily from her nervous pace to look me in the eye. I knew then that she was holding back something BIG. I felt uneasy. "You don't rememba, do ya?" She studied me.

"Remember what?" I asked, feeling knots in my stomach.

Her eyes locked with mine. "Tell me, do ya remember way back when you was in a wild party at Vicki Norris' place?"

I nodded.

Sugar continued, "Y'all was doin' dope and gettin' horny on each 'ova . . . You remember a big black busted women on top 'a ya?"

I didn't wish to; but nevertheless, I acknowledged.

Sugar clarified, "She was Nina Jones."

So . . . what's the connection here? Wait, how does Sugar know about that? Suddenly, I broke out in a cold sweat as I compared the resemblance between the two—Nina/Sugar. I wanted so badly to deny what I pieced together, but I had to admit to her that I understood what she was trying to say. It seemed as if the party had only been days ago. I had run away from that circle only to have it follow me like a phantom.

"But you listen up now, cuz I ain't got no feelin's fer you. You got dat? I only do dat sort of shit when I get high or I'm paid. The only real reason I offered you my place is cuz I knows you got what I need—Vicki Norris. Her boyfriend got connections with the best dealers in this town. So, I figured she lent you some stash." She paused. "I do crack," she said emphatically. "I was thinkin' I could split a deal with ya if ya give me some infa'mation."

"No more deals, Sugar—I mean Nina. I don't want any more commitments with you. I'm tired of your games. First, it's the debt from the car accident and now it's this drug scheme. One scheme after another. I just want out," I pleaded. "In fact, I'm sorry I ever met you in the first place . . ." I snapped boldly.

"I knows you killed Brad Spears in that car accident," Nina disclosed the secret she had been withholding to blackmail me.

I was in shock. "How did you . . . I didn't kill him," I clarified. "Believe me, I would have rather died in his place. He drugged me," I insisted.

"You okay. You ain't gotta go fendin' for yourself as long as you behave," she reassured. "You just gotta get the connections I need." She sighed, tossing her head. "He was one of the best drug leads in town. Shit, that stuff nasty hard to get."

Sadly, Nina revealed to me her ulterior motive. She had pursued me not because I wrecked Richard's car but to acquire dope. She saw something in it for herself. This should not have come as a surprise. "Are there any other secrets you're withholding from me?" I asked humbly.

"No," Nina shook her head.

"Then can I ask of you just one favor," I tried to reason with her. "You know, we have something in common here. So can we work together as a team instead of crippling one another?"

"I treat you nice, I said, as long as you listen to me," she repeated. "As long as you listen to me." Nina didn't know the first thing about diplomacy. She reached over to the phone by her night table. "I want'cha to call Vicki and invite her over wit her boyfriend."

"I can't do that," I protested. "Why can't you get your boy Shawn to buy you all the shit you need?" I grew intolerant of her demands.

She raised her voice in anger, pointing her index finger at me. "I don't want no flack outta you!"

"I—I can't . . . I don't know her number!" I came up with a lame excuse. It didn't fly.

"Dat's why they invented phonebooks." Nina threw the flimsy heavyweight at me.

"I'm afraid you'll need the Philley County edition," I argued.

She searched. "I got all the fuckin' counties in the state. Philley's buried down here somewheres." She pulled out a thick One Book. "No more excuses," she warned with a sharp tone, raising her eyebrows. I sighed. Nothing I would say could stop her. She'd break my arms if she had to.

I combed the listing under Norris. There were many pages, and I didn't know Vicki's father's first name. However, there was a listing under Todd McKane in Philley County. Nina was delighted that I located the boyfriend's phone number. She explained to me what her intentions were. Another scheme. She planned to deceive Todd into sleeping with her to acquire free dope from him. It did not bother her that she would be sleeping with Vicki's boyfriend for Nina had no conscience. But the most appalling aspect of this scheme was that I was coerced to be an accomplice to it.

Nina placed the phone on my lap. I felt as if I were handcuffed to it. I lifted the receiver and dialed. What was I to say to Vicki as to my disappearance? I felt like a traitor.

Unfortunately, after many rings the phone was answered by none other than Vicki. I was ashamed of myself for what I was about to do. I wished she would hang up on me or, better yet, the line would go dead. Reflecting back, was I to tell her that I chose prostitution over the sweet paradise she offered?

Nevertheless, my long-time friend sounded overjoyed to hear from me. Her initial concern was for my safety. After I assured her that I was fine, she asked me where I was. I told her about Fowlersville. She remarked, "All the way out there? I wish you would have told me you were moving out of town. Were you running from the cops?" She listened for a response. I fell silent. She continued, "Well anyway, it's real good to hear from you after all these years."

Years? Vicki hadn't seen me in years? I was certain it had only been a week ago. I was rattled momentarily, trying to process it all so quickly. In any event, she had good news to share with me. She told me she was five months pregnant. Todd and she had been engaged for a year and planning for a wedding in May. She listened for my reaction. I fell into deep silence, again. "Aren't you happy for me?" she asked. There was a huge lump in my throat. Vicki asked if I was alright. Nina signaled me to stop babbling and get to the point.

I gathered my composure and abruptly invited Vicki to Fowlersville to meet at a local bar so that we could discuss "the good old times." This time Vicki drew silent.

"Hello," I checked.

"I'm here. Gosh you haven't given me much notice. I mean, I'd love to see you again but why can't you come up to Philley? Ya know, travel can be a strain when you're pregnant."

"I'm sure you won't have any difficulty making this trip. Besides, you'll love the nightlife. There's so much more to do here."

"I'll discuss it with Todd, but tell me, who have you shacked up with?"

"Well . . ." I stalled, glancing at Nina. "I have a new boyfriend but, for now, I'm sharing an apartment with another gal," I grinned at Nina. She looked puzzled.

"You do? Wow! Is he rich and good looking?" I piqued Vicki's interest.

"He's well off. He's a photographer, and might I add, gorgeous," I emphasized.

Again, Vicki wowed. I could almost hear her smile. She thought it over. "I'd really love to meet him, but I think it's a better idea if you'd come this way. Besides, I could show off our new apartment and all the knits I've stitched for the newbie," Vicki persuaded.

"Tell me, is Todd still in the business?" I hinted.

"You mean drugs?"

"Yeah," I bit my tongue.

"Why, you need some? He'd love to get rid of it all before the baby is born. He quit some time ago. He's in therapy once a week."

"That's not a bad idea. Say, come down here, drop the leftovers off, and I'll take you to some popular shows, entertainment spots, and dine in some fine restaurants."

That offer sounded more appealing to her. "Do they have Mel Rottino's comedy hour there?"

"Every Saturday night," I fibbed.

"He is so funny. I think he went national."

"So, what do you say?"

"You just don't quit, do ya?" Vicki laughed. "I guess it would be alright. But you must come up here when I'm due. I really want you to be a part of it all, okay?"

I cleared my throat again, *if we're still talking,* "Sure."

Vicki asserted, "I'd like to meet your boyfriend, the photographer. If he's good, I'll use him for my wedding."

"So, when are you coming?" I persisted.

"Mmm . . . by the way, I meant to ask before, what happened with Kevin? You two broke up?"

"Ya, he wasn't my type. Once you meet Steve, you'll understand."

Vicki and I finalized plans and wrapped things up. Right as I hung up, Sugar hassled me,

"She comin', right?"

"Yes," I frowned. "Just leave things alone, will 'ya."

"You not shittin' me?" Nina warned, ready to punch me out.

"You heard the conversation. Unless we used Morse code, she bought into it."

"Don't get smart with me." She looked sore at me.

CHASE FUME

Nina paraded around her bedroom humming gospel as she had done when I handed her the $330. She wasted no time alerting Shawn of her conniving plans. They slapped one another a high-five. Only then did she present me with the packet that she purchased with MY money. Within this packet was a new drug hip on the streets called CHASE FUME. The acronym stood for "Chemical Hallucinogen Additive Stimulant of Euphoria, For Ultimate Mind Elevation." CHASE FUME was a multi-compound chemical derivative of the PCP leaves—a very dangerous substance. The drug's popularity was primarily due to its catchy name and low price.

Nina placed a white porcelain plate on her mattress then opened the miniature clear plastic baggy, dumping the contents onto the plate. Curiously, I placed my finger on the compressed yellowish powders. An orange-like residue rubbed off on my fingertips. I handed over all my hard-earned cash so she could spend it on dope and lie about me owing her for Richard's wrecked car. "Why did you make me call Vicki if you have this?" I asked bitterly. I must have really pissed her off because abruptly she forced my face down onto the plate. I struggled as she wrestled me, holding my head down firmly, tilting the powders toward my nose. I gasped from the inhaled powders. My nose stung. Once she released me, I nearly went into shock. I felt ablaze! My nose bled! I panicked! I tried to whimper, "Why?" but it was inaudible. I gazed at Sugar then at Shawn.

I think she said, ". . . all the girls do it." *What girls?* My burning eyes filled with tears, begging for mercy—lips dry—pulse raced. I felt as if a ticking bomb was bubbling though my veins. Was I going to explode?

A platform lifts me up to the ceiling. This vehicle of transport is somewhat like a flying carpet. I'm in a funnel-shaped environment, pointy-end down. My captors I cannot see. All that is visible is a window at eye level and tiny dime-sized objects below. This unique perspective may seem amusing, but I have a fear of heights. I shield myself as the mindless platform repeatedly swings against the sides of the funnel. I don't know how to control it.

Mystically, a hummingbird lands on the windowpane, taking a break from flight. It watches as I clumsily drift about. It chuckles. I ask in distress, "Are you laughing at my expense?" The bird looks down then cocks its head toward me. It offers support, humming away beautiful notes that I can understand. It teaches me that I can learn to fly gracefully if I flap my wings, concentrating on the direction of the wind currents. I don't even realize that I have wings because they are invisible. I try them. They are weightless. I fail. The bird instructs me to imagine the wings as a huge sail on a boat, and I am to push and pull them, opposing the wind, in the direction I wish to be guided. I try again, and again. Finally, I catch onto the magic—the secret of flight!

"Yes," the bird praises. "You've got it! It's how you flap your wings that controls the direction and speed. You must learn to be attentive. Listen to the sounds of nature," the bird directs.

I take flight gracefully around the room without the need for the mechanically flawed magic carpet. I fly at different elevations: diagonal, in loops, backward, and idle. I have now ventured the joy of flight. I feel so free and in control like never before.

The bird signals me over to the window. This window is my exit from captivity, from Sugar's wrath. I shift toward the bird, following it as it guides the way. I never question the bird; after all, this is the bird's world. The bird holds my hand firmly as we fly through the window, the gate between heaven and hell, the entrance to paradise. I view the splendors of the great outdoors: beautiful budding flowers encircle a Chinese garden path; colorful polka-dotted butterflies on green lilies; ducks lined in a row in a crystal-clear pond, casting off a reflection; and the most breathtaking view of a rainbow in the horizon. I breathe in the aroma of a blossomed valley of flowers, and at great distance, a mother horse nurses its fawn.

Something abruptly grabs me from behind and will not let go! I cry for the bird's rescue. My captor holds me back! The bird tugs at my hand, trying to free me. Between the bird's grip on my hand and the captor's pull on my feet, I feel my limbs stretching apart from all sides in this endless tug-of-war. Terror sustains as my fingers are pulling apart like silly putty, tearing away at the fibers of my joints. They snap! The bird holds my hand in its beak! My feet—they too have been severed. "Set me free!" I cry as I am caught in the window between heaven and hell. Suddenly, the bird, who I trust with great reverence, turns on me. It pecks at the filaments of my wrist! "What are you doing?" I cry. The bird would rather devour me than surrender me to the hands of hell. Its beak pokes me in the eye! I despondently scream!

"Shhh . . ." a voice quieted me as my eyelids were gently pulled open by cold fingertips. Fluid drops flung into my eyes. I jumped, blinking wildly. Hands pushed me back down. As my vision cleared, I recognized Shirell sitting beside me on the edge of the mattress. She pressed a cold dishcloth against my forehead. I couldn't believe she was nursing me, of all people. I thought she hated me. "You causin' too much trouble." She grimaced. "I ain't takin' responsibility for you too. I neva wanted no whitey in my place to begin with. But my dear baby insis' on it," she explained. "I don't know why you can't be livin' in the clubhouse with the others." I had no idea what she was talking about. *What clubhouse? What others?*

"Child, you freaked out from that damn CHASE shit. That shit so dangerous. You should thank the Lord Jesus you didn't go into no seizures. I wish . . ." Shirell paused, shaking her head.

"Wish what?" I insisted she finish.

She covered her face with her hands in shame. "It ain't right—none of it," she sobbed. She tried to gather herself for a while, taking a deep breath, then resumed, "You was gonna jump out that four-story window and Nina wasn't gonna do nothin' 'bout it. Ya know she was doin' it too. I wish she'd straighten up her act. Someday . . ." She shook her head then covered her face again. "So," she took another deep breath and cleared her throat, trying to avoid crying, "Shawn got my attention to save you from killin' yall's self cuz he know I don't want no cops 'round here. Ain't no cops better come lookin in my place for my baby. We do anything poss'ble to stay away from them. And you better behave yerself and do your shit somewhere's else, understand?"

I understood what she was trying to say. She was guarding Sugar's baby from the ex-pimp. Now that I'd come into the picture, she expected me to help protect the baby. I was eternally grateful to Shirell for saving my life and in turn, I promised to see to the infant's safety.

She grinned and whispered, "Thank you."

I rubbed my eyes. "Why are my eyes burning?" I asked her.

"CHASE FUME very irritatin'," she explained. "It make them swell. Sugar needed medication too," Shirell added. "They say Visine gets the red out." We both laughed.

Shirell pointed out that Sugar's way of celebrating good times was through using. I stood my ground, insisting that Sugar forced me into this mess. Shirell shut her teary eyes and nodded. "Promise me that you'll stay away from the cops and I'll have a word with her," she bargained.

THE SISTAS

Sugar was not bluffing about her intentions and I knew it. As planned, we arrived early at a bar called Trio Café. Since the "clubhouse girls" hung out at this joint, it was the agreed meeting spot for Vicki and Todd. Sugar introduced me to the "Sistas" while waiting on her "prey." The four chicks sitting by the bar looked quite familiar. After all, it was just yesterday when these girls "across the street" tempted the limo stud as he pulled up for my first trick. I thought I was in competition with these hookers but that was not the case at all. We were all one big team. That's why they called themselves "Sistas." I was sure they'd be cutthroat, like Sugar, but they were nothing of the kind. They were sweet, all four of them.

Ruby, Glenda, Margie, and Shashona each introduced themselves by their street name because it was a hazard to call the Sistas by their birth names.

Glenda was *Lace* by night as she revealed lace cleavage. At 25 years old, she was into S&M—both bondage and gang banging. Wild sex was her specialty. She was a call girl. She ran her own business, an escort service, and set her own hours. Lace was established so she didn't need to pound the pavement.

In contrast, 19-year-old Margie, referred to as *Pussycat*, had a demure disposition. She was in this business for fast cash due to a nasty break-up with her boyfriend which left her penniless.

Shashona, or *Baby*, was anything but a baby. At 21, she had developed a strong backbone and steadfast determination after being sexually abused by her stepfather, who got her pregnant. After dropping out of high school, she felt her only ticket out of poverty was the street profession.

I mentioned to Sugar that I met my boyfriend while turning a trick.

"So, you have a steady john?" Sugar deduced, delightedly.

"No, Sugar. He's really my boyfriend," I corrected.

She argued, "No, child. I told you before, no man in this profession want you for you. There ain't no true lovin' here. That don't happen. Don't be fooled. And rememba what I say, don't let them cheap talk you. Besides, socializin' is off duty."

I sighed, "Yes, I know. It was my fault for letting him take me out to dinner, but he and I are very compatible. I just happened to be on duty when we met. His name is Steve, and he's much more man than any stud I'd ever been with."

Sugar looked cross at me. She remembered me mentioning him to Vicki over the phone. She was curious as to what I was up to. She pointed her finger at me. "You best stay away from him, you hear."

"I'm falling in love. Believe it," I insisted just to piss her off. "Just because you can't settle down into a committed relationship doesn't mean I can't," I argued. I saw a mean fist form on her lap as her face turned red. Fortunately, Margie stole her attention to ask her about Richard.

Ruby spared me from my big mouth, introducing herself as *Tasty*. She was the youngest of the bunch. She couldn't have been more than 14 years. I asked her why she was doing this shit at her age. She explained that she ran away from home and got picked up by a pimp. She asked me the same question. I looked at Ruby, then at Sugar. Was I to tell Ruby the truth, that I was blackmailed into this, or should I lie?

Saved by the bell, a broad-shouldered black lady approached the bar, toying with her curls, whereby distracting me. She was a large, big-busted broad. She had me scoot over to make room for her. The lady smiled into my eyes, blinking her mascara wildly in my face, then kissed me on the cheek. The girls restrained themselves from giggling. "Hi darling, how are you today?" she greeted me with a rather deep voice. Her smile sickened me. What was she up to?

The lady retrieved a powder case from her purse then fluffed her cheeks. The powder case was then tossed aside as she smeared a gloss stick across her thick lips. Indeed, she seemed a little too preoccupied with her appearance. I caught her eyes wandering over to my boobs. Feeling totally uncomfortable with her, I got up from my barstool and moved over one. The girls chuckled. It didn't seem very funny to me. The big mama pulled herself off her stool and shifted one over to me. "Can I buy you a drink, sweetie?" She grinned at me. Her perfumed neck overpowered the stale cigarette smoke in the air.

"No thanks," I declined.

"You sure are mighty pretty."

"Thanks," I smirked.

"What's your name, sweetie?" Her face closed in on mine as if she was about to kiss me.

I glided over to the next stool. "You hit on all the women?" I asked.

"No, just the sexy ones. I have discriminating taste."

"Well, you're not my type," I brushed her off.

"What's your type?" She moved over one more toward me.

"For one, I prefer men over women," I stated boldly.

"So, you think I'm a woman?" She grabbed my hand and forced it against her crotch. My eyes widened as I felt something big bulge from her skirt. She—I mean he—laughed wildly.

I was embarrassed. "Don't you do that again!" I barked.

"I love to play games with people. It's so much fun," he exclaimed.

The girls were laughing so hard that the patrons were staring. "He's a transvestite," Glenda explained. "Just imagine the look of surprise on the faces of her male johns."

"You definitely had me fooled," I sighed.

"I been cross-dressing for years. I really love it. Someday, when I save enough money, I'm gonna get me a sex change operation." His eyes glowed with anticipation.

I looked at him as if he lost his mind.

PREGNANT VICKI

Ten at night, someone tapped me on the shoulder as I was talking to Margie. Beside me stood two old familiar faces smiling brightly at me. "Oh, I miss you," Vicki hugged me tight. Following her initial reaction, "Did you get your hair colored, 'cause I don't remember it being that light? You're all dolled up in Barbie clothes." Vicki studied me. I studied her back, noticing her pregnant belly and hair pulled back with a barrette. She looked so . . . so sophisticated—not the pothead I remembered.

"Glad you could make it." I ignored her abrupt remarks, feeling corns in my stomach.

Sugar stood by me waiting for the cue. I nodded. Todd put his arm around Vicki and kissed her. I wished he hadn't. "We had no trouble getting to Fowlersville, but once we arrived in town, it took us an hour to find the bar," Todd commented. "Not really what I expected." He looked around at the dive.

"Mel Rittino performs here?" Vicki questioned skeptically. "We thought it would be a bit more . . . classy," Vicki explained Todd's comment.

"Could I buy you a drink?" Sugar offered Todd with a slick wink of the eyelash.

Vicki leered into Sugar's face for the longest time. Instead of saying, *excuse me but he's my fiancé,* she asked, "Don't I know you from somewhere?"

My eyes yelled at her, *Yes Vicki, she's the hustler that participated in your orgy.* I had to distract Vicki. "Vicki, why don't we take a nice stroll through the park while Todd gets acquainted with my friends. After all, isn't that why you came down here in the first place?" I yanked her arm.

"But what about Todd?" she questioned.

I tugged on her. "Oh, we won't be gone for long. We have a lot of catching up to do, wouldn't you say?" I grinned pretty, baring my teeth at her. Vicki promised Todd she'd be back shortly. Todd didn't seem at all offended by Sugar's friendly persuasion, but he wondered what was bothering Vicki.

Vicki and I strolled through the turbulent streets, chatting about Todd and their wedding plans. Everything was going smoothly until we arrived at a park. We sat on a swing silently staring off into space. The pigeons bobbed around for food. Once the pigeons flew away there was nothing to do for distraction. It was as if we were strangers to one another. Soon the troubling thoughts surfaced in her. She asked me why I had abandoned everyone years ago in Philley. "You told us that you were going to the restroom. You didn't add that you weren't ever coming back."

I had to think up a quick story. I told her I moved out of town for Steve.

"Where did you meet him? In the restroom?" She sneered.

"No. Out here."

"I'm totally confused. Nothing you say makes sense."

"Alright, I went to the restroom then decided to step out for air, and it was at that moment I met Richard Dunn. Well, he took me to his place."

"So, you cheated on Kevin."

"So? I'm sure Kevin cheated on me too."

"Huh? How could you say . . . Kevin would never. What's gotten into you? He was so faithful," Vicki fended for him.

"Look, I wasn't happy with Kevin, okay? I'm much happier with Steve."

"I thought you told me Richard Dunn took you to his place."

"Yes, and I slept with him but then he cheated on me, so I left him."

"Serves you right. So why didn't you come home after you dumped him?"

"I was going to come home but . . . I got lost and ended up here. This is where I met Steve."

"You got lost?" she questioned. "Dini?" Vicki asked, using my nickname.

"What?"

"That girl that offered Todd a drink, she looks familiar," Vicki changed the subject as if she was content with my explanation for leaving town. But of the two topics, I'd prefer to stick with why I left town. It seemed relatively painless compared to the present issue. I felt a lump in my throat. Of all the things to discuss, why did she have to choose that one?

"You mean Sugar? Her real name is Nina. You remember her from a wild party you threw some years ago."

"That's right. She's a . . ." Vicki snapped her fingers.

"Hooker," I aided her.

"Right. So, what are you doing in her company?"

"I can ask you the same. Who invited her to your party?"

"Friends, Dini. I told my friends they could invite anyone they'd like. I didn't know her personally. I don't hang out with hookers like you do," she accused.

"So, you had friends that knew hookers," I snarled, determined to win this feud.

"Are you one too?" she surmised. "Is that what you were waiting to tell me?"

"Yes I am. Couldn't you have guessed by the way I dress? I'm in it for the money," I used the explanation the other hookers offered.

Vicki chastised me, "Why? Have you no decency? Why don't you go back home where you belong and where it's safe?"

"What? Decency? You should talk. You were dealin' dope and poppin' them every damn day before you got pregnant so don't preach to me about decency."

Vicki argued, "I never sold my body."

"No, you just fried your brain."

"And you didn't? Aren't you the one with the 'out-of-body experiences,' Ms. Wheaton?" Vicki disclosed our one-time secret I had totally forgotten about. I lost my train of thought, slipping into a daze. Vicki tried to get my attention repeatedly when I blacked out. I wanted to recall the out-of-body trauma far repressed in my subconscious that I'd been oblivious to.

I disregarded the troubling thoughts immediately. "I don't know what you're talking about but if you really want to know, yes I still use," I blurted out.

"Yeah, right. You remember our little discussion on the couch before 'that' party. You had me convinced. You made a damn fool out of me, didn't you? It was all a lie, wasn't it? It was a setup to make me think you were actually Jessica. And to think I bought into it. Someone must've told you about me and Jessica in our early school days." She paused to wipe her tears. "And I'd like to know who that was." She drew silent. After some time, "You know, I thought we were close friends who could really level with one another, but no, you're beyond that now. You're fucked up. I . . . I don't even know you anymore. I have nothing more to say."

That moment, a car pulled up along the curb and the passenger side door flew open. The driver pushed the youth out on the street. The car took off in a scurry, skidding around the corner. I raced over to the scene and found Ruby bent over on the asphalt in pain. "What happened?" I called to her. A curious crowd formed.

Ruby panted as she wiped the blood from her nose. "My trick and I got into a fight, and he kicked me out."

I saw blood oozing from her chin. "Oh dear, you need medical attention?"

Ruby looked up, "Who she?"

"An old friend," I explained.

Ruby blurted out in pain, "He cheated me, Bambi. He didn't pay up. That motherfucker didn't pay me. Now I ain't got no wages to bring home to my man. He'll blow my brains for sure."

Vicki stood there in total disbelief. "He can't get away with that. What's his name? We'll report him to the cops."

Ruby was outraged at Vicki. "Who the fuck does she think she is?"

"Calm down, Ruby," I pacified her, "just tell me what the john looks like. We won't call anyone, but we will be on the lookout."

"You gonna get in a lotta trouble if you interfere," Ruby cautioned.

"Too late for that," I mumbled. "What's his name?"

"Simmons. That's all I know. He's fat and ugly and owns that dark blue Mercedes."

"How much does he owe?"

"$60. Look, I gotta scram. I don't want my man come lookin' for me, ya know what I mean. I be alright. But thanks Bambi. You a good friend." She held my hands momentarily before taking off in the other direction.

Vicki's eyes were sore with disgust. "Bambi?"

"My street name," I clarified.

"What?"

"To work the streets, you have to change your entire identity. Protection, ya know."

"Whose idea was this anyway, your boyfriend's?"

"No, it was Sugar's. I don't work for my boyfriend."

A passing dude approached, quickly spanked me on the butt, then darted off. I winked back, "Hey cutie." Then I frowned. "What a loss."

"Are you nuts? He's . . . he's black," Vicki exclaimed. "How could you sleep around with every stud in town? God knows what kind of diseases they carry."

"Don't gimme that shit, you slept around too."

"That's different. I had relationships. I didn't sleep with total strangers, night after night."

"Look Mother, don't stick your butt up my ass. Maybe you're right, I've changed. But just because you're pregnant doesn't mean you have to be an asshole."

"I'd like to go now," Vicki zipped up her jacket in a huff. "I'm sorry but I can't stay overnight. I suppose you'll be with a 'trick' anyway."

"No, I don't work every evening."

Vicki lowered her head. "I don't know why you bothered to invite me in the first place."

I wish I hadn't, believe me, I felt like saying. I reminded, "The drugs. Todd came in to deliver the leftovers, remember?"

JEOPARDY

Vicki repeated, "The leftovers," mimicking me. "Of course, how could I have forgotten? The main reason I'm here," Vicki inserted cynically. "Come right this way," she waved me to Trio Café. Returning brought knots to my stomach, but I had run out of ways to stall.

Vicki searched the bar for Todd but there was no sign of him. I suggested to Vicki that he and Sugar probably headed for her apartment. Vicki asked why they would decide to do that. "We took longer than expected so they left," I explained. Escorting Vicki up to the complex, I forewarned her of the apartment's condition. She was not surprised. When we arrived, no one answered the door. Vicki presumed no one was home.

"So where is he?" she asked eagerly.

As I opened the front door, I pretended not to know, withholding the dark truth from Vicki. I rationalized, since I never cared for Todd in the first place, this would be the perfect opportunity to destroy their relationship. I wanted Vicki to know the truth but not through my words. Sugar had me promise to keep it a secret, so I let Vicki figure it out for herself. I instructed her to wait in the kitchenette while I searched the apartment for Shirell. I explained that Shirell didn't like strange whities walking around.

I slowly turned the knob to Nina's bedroom door. There, the two were going at it, making out as Sugar had planned.

Remarkable, I thought, how she could cunningly persuade any man she desired. But then reality hit. This was no soap opera. This was really happening. What should I say to Vicki to console her? I didn't know what to do. Vicki was in the kitchenette, only a few feet away from her future husband, who was having an affair with a prostitute in the bedroom. I wanted to bury my face in shame. While I poked through the crack in the bedroom door, Vicki approached. She had the most traumatized look in her eyes as if someone had died. I had never seen her so upset before. She, too, glimpsed the bedroom scene. Both she and I heard moaning.

"No, this can't be! It simply isn't possible. That's not Todd in bed with . . ." Vicki gawked at me as if she were about to have a nervous breakdown. "Dini, I'm talking to you! I'm serious!" Her baby blue eyes turned swollen red as she held back her angry tears.

"Your eyes are as good as mine," I remarked apathetically, almost speechless.

"This has to be a dream." Vicki shook her head in disbelief. "It can't be true. Todd would never—never be disloyal to me. He never once cheated on me—not once. He's been hurt by other women. That's how I know. You and I both know that."

Abruptly, Vicki marched off into the kitchenette. She opened each drawer in pursuit of a knife.

"Vicki, don't you think you're being a bit irrational?" I stood by the swinging doors of the kitchenette watching Vicki's every move.

"Irrational?" She threw her hands in the air. "I'm going to kill him. I mean it—I'm going to slash his dick to pieces!" As soon as she found the type of instrument she was searching for, she bolted out of the kitchenette, clenching a butcher knife in her fist, ready for the stabbing.

I firmly grabbed her arm. "Look, Vicki. If you want to hurt someone, hurt me," I sighed. "It's all my fault. I'm part of this whole conspiracy."

She peered into my eyes as if to ask, *'Why?'* She swallowed. "I thought you were my friend."

I yanked the knife from her hand. "I had no choice, Vicki. She made me do it." We heard more moans and groans in the background. Vicki's eyes widened.

"No," I insisted, blocking the swinging doors with my arms.

Vicki pushed me, trying to get me out of her way. I pushed her back then tripped her.

She got on her knees and cried to me, "Then kill ME with the knife." She shook my leg. "There's no need for me to go on any longer. Kill me now!" pregnant Vicki insisted frantically.

"Calm down, I'm sure he doesn't mean to hurt you," I tried to appease her bleeding heart.

"What did she do to him to make him so . . . vulnerable? That's really what I want to know." Vicki struggled up off her knees, standing before me, arms locked as if to wait for Todd to finish.

I sighed, "She's a prostitute, Vicki."

"So? I'm his fiancé and wife to be, and for God sakes I'm pregnant with his son." Vicki again attempted to push me aside.

"It doesn't matter," I argued. "This is her profession. She's trained to seduce."

"What's wrong with my body?" Vicki pouted.

"Nothing—nothing. It's just business," I tried to make her understand.

"He has no business with her. He's mine," she cried.

"Yes, but for now she's with him."

Vicki's eyes were teary and inflamed. "I don't care. She has no right. He's mine!" she yelled. I placed my hand over her mouth to quiet her down. She was hyperventilating. She urged me to save him from Nina's wrath, but I made no attempt to rescue her future nor had I any mercy for her. I was selfishly absorbed in my own survival. The hard truth was that I never cared about Vicki in the first place. Besides, I needed to break away from her world to find my own.

Vicki gave one last revolt. She grasped for the knife I hid behind my back. I pushed her away. She finally gave in and surrendered her hopes. She grabbed her purse and, without a word, left the apartment never to be heard from again.

I sat alone in the kitchenette listening to the moans and groans of the two lovers in the heat of passion. Tender thoughts of Steve Getts entered my daydreams. Vicki could have driven me to drink after all that drama. But what I really hungered for was a little action with Steve. Besides, I was free from Sugar's constraints for the evening. It was my turn to be satisfied!

MISTAKE

Around two in the morning I knocked on Steve's apartment door, totally oblivious to the hour. Fortunately, he was in the kitchen sipping on a cup of coffee, watching a late-night show. Though I popped in on him without notice, he was delighted to see me. He held me tight. "Is everything alright, sweetheart?" he wondered. "What brings you here so late?"

Why did he even have to ask? I stared into his baby-blue eyes. "I'm longing for you." I gave him a powerful kiss.

His face beamed. "I couldn't think of a better reason myself. Come sit down. Would you like a hot cup of chocolate latte?" he offered.

"No baby," I declined, "I'd rather go to sleep." I added, "Had a rough evening."

"It's late, isn't it," he yawned. "But boy am I glad to see you again. I wasn't sure what kind of impression I left with you. There were some things I wanted to discuss but you never gave me your number. I guess you don't have a phone, huh?"

"Of course I do. You never asked. What did you want to talk about?" I held his hand, listening attentively.

His attention faded. "Well, it's a little late to talk now. Why don't we get some sleep and talk about it in the morning?" he suggested.

Though I didn't care for the prolonged suspense, I agreed. I stripped my clothes off and landed in bed beside him, cuddling. I found a comfortable spot right against Steve's chest. I whispered in his ear, "I love you."

No response. Had he drifted off into deep sleep so quickly?

The morning sun beamed against the silver bedpost. Steve stretched his tired body. "What time is it?" he asked with a groggy voice.

I checked his watch. "Seven," I replied.

He rolled over, landing on top of me. In his zombie state, he suckled and fondled my breasts. I gazed into his blue eyes. "Did you hear me say 'I love you,' last night?" I asked as I kissed him.

"I love you too," he responded, empty of expression, kissing me back.

Deep in my gut I felt something was horribly wrong, but I couldn't put my finger on it. "What is it that you wanted to talk about last night, honey?" I asked with much anticipation.

"Oh yeah, I have good news. Maggie signed the divorce decree yesterday," he announced without a grin.

I was thrilled to hear this news. "That's great! That means we can marry now, right?"

He didn't share the same enthusiasm I had hoped for. He only mumbled, "Yeah, how about that," then French kissed me. These mixed signals were giving me belly flops.

Nevertheless, our lips suckled each other's. His tongue penetrated deep into my mouth, bobbing back and forth. Before long we were racing like mad dogs into each other's skin—heavily necking, stroking, petting, and squeezing. The fire was so hot and steamy. The urge so strong. We became rabid animals wrestling in the joy of pleasure. Oddly, once he came, he hopped off me and immediately jumped into his trousers. As he zipped his pants, he unexpectedly asked, "How much do I owe you for this?"

I gawked. "What?"

"Ah, c'mon, you know what I mean. What's your price?"

"Steve!" Almost speechless, I had to unscramble the jarred messages I'd been receiving all along. "I'm in love with you. That's priceless. I wasn't working last night. I'm with you on my off hours. I chose to sleep with you because I want to be in your life. I thought that was understood."

"But you're a hooker," he argued.

"Is that how you see me after all that's been said and done? You really have no feelings for me, do you? You just see me as a sex object, don't you? Then why did you tell me about the divorce papers?"

"Denise, I can't love a hooker. I'm a monogamous man," he explained.

I was utterly perplexed. "I can't believe . . ." I waved my hands in the air. "I thought we both wanted a future together if you'd separate with your wife. And you did."

"I need stability in my life," he restated.

"I do too. You think I sell my body for the fun of it? You think I enjoy getting raped and used by men? Then apparently you don't understand me at all, do you?" I was irate. "If you want me to quit hooking, just say so, rather than treating me like some low-life cattle meat." I promptly gathered my belongings and dressed hastily.

"I thought you came over for a fuck. Didn't ya?" He blushed.

I couldn't believe his words. "Wrong," I corrected. "You damn fool, I came over to be with you. How many times must I make that clear?"

"But hookers don't know the first thing about love," he insisted.

Utterly appalled by his remark, I actually regretted the entire sexual encounter I had been longing for. "Well, I can't speak for all hookers, but apparently I know a lot more about love than you do." I marched out of his apartment, slamming the front door behind me.

Alone, I permitted myself to shed a tear remembering Sugar's words of wisdom: *"No, child. I told you before, no man in this profession want you for you. There ain't no true lovin' here. That don't happen. Don't be fooled. And rememba what I say, don't let them cheap talk you. Besides, socializin' is off-duty time."* It wasn't so much the wisdom that saddened me inasmuch as the source of this wisdom. I despised Sugar and everything that she stood for, especially for making a fool out of me when, each time, she was right on target. Nina might have been the bitch from hell, but I must not underscore her experience and street smarts.

REBOUND

I'd had enough! The lying. The cheating. The manipulating. Not to mention, the deceiving, spiting, and abusing. And above all, the USING. I wasn't in the mood to be messed with. I was ready to take out the scissors and castrate the next man who crossed me.

Upon leaving Steve's complex, I noticed the all-too-familiar dark blue Mercedes parked on the side of the bank building. I was loaded with ammunition. In tight pants and an open blouse, I trotted over to his parked vehicle. Fat and ugly, exactly as Ruby described Simmons. He was reading the stock market section of the newspaper with a wide-open window. Perfect target.

I put on my actress and grinned. "Hey sexy, care for some lunch?"

He ignored me. My arm reached into his car, pressing down on the newspaper until his crotch was within reach. I squeezed it. He looked up at me in shock. He didn't expect me to be so aggressive. With heavy groans, I whined, "I want to suck your cock so bad."

"Who are you?" Simmons seemed intrigued, not in the least turned off.

"Bambi—the hottest ass on the street." My tongue moistened my lips seductively. "I'm burning for you."

"Why me? I didn't pick you up," he questioned.

"I'm just so horny, I could fuck a car."

"How much are you asking?"

"Oh, what's it to ya?" My fingertips wandered down his tie. "I want to do it right here. Right now. I can't wait."

"I'm married," he objected.

I didn't believe him. "Then you have the kind of experience I'm looking for to relieve my achy tension," I moaned. I had him framed. Before he could say another word, I kissed him in the mouth. I tasted tobacco on his breath, just as stinky and filthy as Ruby depicted.

"Alright—alright," he huffed. "Hop in. I'll take you to an inn."

I saw to it that we'd never make it to an inn. I had him so aroused that he couldn't focus on the road. He put it in park, I might add, in a no parking zone. In a heaving rush, he undressed me, nearly popping the bra snaps off to suck away at the plump fruit. His heavy weight leaned up against me. It was no easy task pretending to crave him. In retrospect, I think the black limo date was a better experience. Once Simmons got on top of me, I suffocated under his weight. I must have turned blue. He nearly crushed my ribcage. "Ya want it, you really want it," he asked excitedly, whipping out his well-hung cucumber. My Jesus, it was the biggest dick I'd ever seen! I mean it was as if two dicks merged into one jumbo pumping machine. If he was married as he claimed, then I was sure he had a hard time getting it from his wife at that size.

Was I hurting due to its enormous size or simply because I really didn't dig him? I promised myself never to play this trick again. I'd rather give birth. I was afraid he'd get stuck inside me. After he came, he got off of me. I gasped for my first breath.

The only good thing about having sex in the car is a fast escape. I scurried to get dressed as fast as I could with his wallet in my possession. Unfortunately, he pressed the automatic door lock, demanding his wallet back. I guess I didn't acquire Sugar's slick finesse. I pulled my switchblade on him and poked him in the nose. "Ruby says hello," I hissed. I pressed the automatic open, darting out of the car before he could play with that damn lock again. He struggled out of his vehicle with a tissue pressed against his bloody nose. He yelled for the cops, claiming that he had just been assaulted. The pitiful fat loser couldn't even chase after me.

The double-doors to Trio Café swung open. Right before Ruby, Simmons' wallet was tossed onto the table. She studied the contents of the wallet in disbelief. "How did ya . . .?" She had a look of bewilderment. "Sista, you gonna get in big trouble for this. I don't know what to say." The child had an ice pack over her bruised eye.

I beamed, feeling mighty proud. "I'm only getting pure satisfaction. Dickheads don't scare me. The next time a john fucks you over, you come to me, hear?"

Ruby began to cry. "You are so gutsy. Thank you so much. I owe you one." She got up and hugged me. Ruby whispered in my ear, "Your keeper is here." She pointed over to a booth.

Sugar signaled me over, smiling brightly. She was in a surprisingly pleasant mood. "I's got it!" she whispered, folding her arms haughtily.

"Got what?" I asked.

"Got the dope off Todd."

"How did you do it?" I pretended not to know. *How long did you fuck him before he gave in.*

"We got drunk, and he handed it all over to me. I got him so bad drunk he probably still ain't sober."

I frowned. "This isn't a game, Sugar. You really messed his life up."

"What you talkin' about?"

"Vicki left him. In fact, she left town because she saw you and him going at it. She was a friend of mine."

"So?" Sugar failed to see my point.

"I betrayed her," I explained. "Don't you understand?"

"Shit, which would you rather have, the friend or the dope?" As she put it, I didn't respond. She pointed out, "Look, I's got the acid and dat's the main thing."

I thought it over for a moment and concluded that Sugar was not capable of offering sympathy. She only cared about two things in her life: her baby and dope. Everything else was a means to an end. But she was, indeed, an ingenious con artist to have pulled off the scheme so smoothly. "You think Vicki will report us?" I wondered, gazing off into space.

Sugar chuckled, "Shit, I don't care. You say she's all fucked up anyways. She find someone else to screw." Sugar noticed my complacency. "Whatchoo you grinnin' about?"

"Ah nothing. Some fatso swindled Ruby so I short-changed him for it. It really made my day," I admitted. An eerie feeling of turning into Sugar crossed my mind. I was careful though not to mention a word about Steve.

"It a good day, ain't it? Do me a favor. Go down to Silkside Avenue and hound down Shawn. Give him this plastic bag. He be rollin' when he see what I got." She handed me the miniature baggie of brownish-green crushed leaves.

"Is this what Todd gave you?" I examined the packet. She nodded. I questioned, "Why are you giving this to Shawn? He'll just sell it. I thought you wanted it for yourself?"

"I got a whole bunch set aside. I ain't stupid," she intimated.

As I was told, I searched for Shawn along Silkside Avenue. I spotted him sitting by the curb with another street kid. My foot stood at his heel but he did not notice me, so I tapped him on the shoulder. Startled, he pulled out a switchblade and was about to strike. He remained guarded even after he recognized me. His friend darted off without a word.

"Hey," I greeted, keeping my distance.

The street kid wore his cap backward, had a dirty black leather jacket with a poison symbol on the backside, and carried a penknife attached to his denim belt loop along with a pager. He never said much. "What you want?" he sneered.

I slowly pulled the packet out from my jacket pocket. "Sugar had me deliver this stuff." The boy quickly pushed the packet back into my pocket. "You stupid or sometin'? People can see this." He signaled me to follow him into a dark alley. Dark alleys weren't really a haven for me. The 12-year-old could have killed me in this dark desolate place if I didn't know better. He made sure the coast was clear and then permitted me to hand over the packet. He opened the bag and examined the substance. "Wow," he exclaimed.

"What?" I was curious.

His eyes widened in amazement. "Where'd you get this? Shit's hard to find."

"So, I was told. That's a long story. Let's just say Sugar got it from a friend of mine. I'm just delivering it."

He placed the packet in his pants pocket. For the first time he looked me in the eye with a slight grin. "This motherfucker will sell like hotcakes!" The young man took off in a scamper without thanking me, not that I expected anything more.

I remained in the dark alley, standing by a large dumpster, a pile of dirt, and other debris, smelling a stench in this vacant narrow alcove. Was it the odor of decay or the body odor of Simmons I smelled on myself?

THE PHONE CALLER

This was my second evening off duty. It felt so great not to be pedaling the streets. After cleansing away all the impurities with a hot bubble bath, I crawled onto the Majesty's king-sized waterbed throne, pulling silk and satin layers over me. Though very cozy, I lay in unrest. It wasn't the mirrored background, the murals of nudity, or the water in the bed that bothered me. What troubled me was that this was the very bedroom Sugar frisked me, where I tried to jump out of the window on CHASE FUME, and where Sugar slept with Todd. I let out a deep sigh, closing my eyes. For the first time, this would be the bedroom where I would find total peace. I grinned contently, rolling over on my stomach. I thought about the male cross-dresser. I couldn't help but laugh. In fact, I couldn't stop laughing. Oh, for goodness-sake, I took things way too seriously.

The phone awoke me as I dozed off. I figured it was Sugar checking to see that I delivered the packet to Shawn. With eyes closed, I reached over to the night table, felt for the receiver, and positioned it against my resting ear, "'Lo," I answered. I heard heavy breathing. At first, I was suspicious but figured it was some kid playing games after school hours.

As I was about to hang up, a deep black male voice articulated, "Do you know who I am?"

I asked inquisitively, "No, should I?"

"Tell me who you are," he inquired.

He got me perturbed. "Wait, you called me, right? Then you need to introduce yourself."

"You're a new resident," he surmised confidently, ignoring me. "What's your name?"

"I was about to ask you the same," I jested.

"You know what I want," he inserted then paused, breathing heavily into the phone again.

"You are going to cooperate, aren't you?"

He had to be some horny john calling for sadistic phone sex. "How much is it worth to ya?" I negotiated, reluctantly discussing work offers on an off-duty night.

He yelled into the receiver, "Cut the shit, lady. Where's the kid?"

He just gave the password to send chills down my spine. I remembered what Nina told me about her ex-pimp, the father of her child Tia and how he wanted to sell the baby off to the black market. I promised both Shirell and Nina that I would help protect the baby. After all, Shirell saved me from a foolish death. Unfortunately, the ex-pimp caught me off guard, unprepared. I didn't know what to do. "W . . . What are you talking about? I . . . I think you have the wrong number," I stuttered.

"I have your address. If you hang up, I'll pay you a visit very shortly," he threatened.

"You're crazy. What are you . . ."

He raised his voice, interrupting me, "Answer me, I said. I want a straight answer—no lies. Only the truth—absolute truth." He paused. "Or I'll fuckin' kill you," he emphasized.

There was a moment of silence. "Look, I don't know which prison you escaped from but you're not going to threaten me. So take your psychotic episodes somewhere else." I slammed the phone down, hanging up on him. I was pleased with myself for being so resolute. However, seconds later the phone rang again. My palms turned sweaty, legs shook, and heart raced. *Don't let him get to you,* I said to myself. I let it ring. The angry ring did not cease. I peeped out the window to see if he was standing at a phone booth, as if I knew who I was looking for. The phone drew silent. *Gosh,* I thought, *I never would have believed for a moment that he'd harass me. It's not even my problem.*

The phone rang again. I froze. What had gotten into me? I'd been harassed by a number of men, and Sugar, not to mention raped by many and up through this moment, I'd been unrelentingly bold and dauntless, but I'd let a prank phone caller scare me half to death. *Snap out of it!* Perhaps I should just leave the receiver off the hook. No, someone important may try to call. Like who? This time, I picked the receiver up and silently listened. I heard the mad breathing, again. He said, "I'm waiting for you. You've left me no choice." The tone went dead. I yanked the phone cord right out of the wall jack in a nervous huff. I went through the apartment locking every door I could think of and every window that had a working lock.

Paranoia got the better of me. I was afraid to leave the apartment but, at the same time, afraid to stay put and do nothing. I couldn't call the cops—against Shirell's wishes. I needed to run but to where? I wished I was still with Steve. The ex-pimp would never find me there.

I snuck out to Trio Café in search of Sugar. She was the only answer. I cautiously entered the bar. I spotted her with some date.

I interrupted her, "Excuse me, Sugar, I have something urgent to tell you. I gotta see you privately."

She sneered at me, "What you doin'? Can't you see I'm in the middle of somethin'?"

My eyes lit with fire. "I said urgent!"

Sugar rolled her eyes. She told her date she would be right back. She warned me that it better be good, or she'd burn my ass. She was clearly pissed off, accusing me of costing her a night's pay. I took her into the ladies' room where we could be safe.

"What's wit you?" she said indignantly.

"He called the apartment," I whispered in her ear.

"Who, Todd?" she surmised.

"No, your ex-pimp." The fear in my eyes was animated.

"What he want?" Sugar listened attentively.

"He's after me. He insisted I tell him where the baby is. I think my life is in jeopardy."

For the first time Nina held my hands, comforting me. "Look, don't be scared, child. He want to scare you so you listen 'um. You gotta be stronger than this. Don't give a shit. Hun, he cause any trouble, you call me right here at Trio. Just keep your blade concealed." She pointed her finger. "You can't be actin' like no sissy. Those motherfuckers take advantage of shallow types. They like bees—if ya run away from 'um they chase after ya; if you swat 'um, they sting ya; but if you ignore 'um, they find another victim to prey on." Sugar jotted down the number to the Trio Café.

"Is he all talk?" I wanted to be reassured.

She handed me the number. "He hassled me before, but I keep a gun in my place." She patted me on the back. "You just gotta be tougher." She didn't tell me what I wanted to hear.

ARRESTED

In fear of the ex-pimp, I was surveying the pub windows to see that it was safe outside. Sugar was right. I was behaving like a coward. I took a deep breath then courageously opened the exit door to Trio Café. I kept an eye out for the sisters—they would protect me. However, when I searched the street corners for the girlfriends, they weren't at their usual posts.

A clean-cut white guy dressed in a business suit approached me with a subtle grin on his olive-skinned face. "Hey sexy," he flirted. Though I was hardly in the mood for a date, I figured this would be an opportune time to make some money instead of wandering the streets alone, a nice diversion.

"Ya wanna good time, handsome?" I offered, winking at him. "How much, foxy lady?" he asked anxiously.

I brushed my hair aside. "I'm Bambi," I said, advertising my boobs. I placed my arms around him, whispering seductively into his ear, "One hour of AROUSING, MOANING, PULSATING, SALACIOUS SEX is a couple hundred." I paused, extending my palm. "Ya got it?"

He pulled out his wallet and flicked through the cardholder. "Yeah, I think I do. Let me see. Gosh, can't turn this down."

I thought he was joking, "Sorry, I don't take credit cards," I laughed.

He flipped out a City Police I.D. badge! "Ma'am, you're under arrest for illegal solicitation and indecent exposure." An Undercover police officer.

Son-of-a-bitch caught me off guard. This time I was not laughing. I was in shock. Well, that explained why the sisters weren't at their usual spots. The officer read my rights then ordered me to raise my hands and face the brick wall behind me. I raised my arms in submission. I couldn't believe this was happening. "Officer, I . . . can explain. The girl in charge is inside that bar," I pointed. The cop ignored me. I was handcuffed. "Look, I can explain, I said . . ." I insisted as I was frisked. I pulled away from the officer in a fit.

The officer warned, "Do you also want to be charged for resisting arrest?" He confiscated my penknife then directed me to the unmarked police car. "Please step inside the vehicle, ma'am," he instructed as he opened the rear door.

The door was shut, and I was secured in the back seat. It was only then that I realized that this was actually a blessing since there was no way the pimp could attack me here. But—oh no, my criminal record—the car theft and the accident—they'd trace it, throw away the key, and lock me up for life! Haunting thoughts flashed through me: prison sentence, death row, electric chair! The Miranda rights echoed, "You have the right . . . right . . . right to remain silent . . . silent . . . silent. Anything you say . . . say . . . say can and will be used against . . . gainst . . . gainst you. You have the right . . . right . . . right to a lawyer."

 At police headquarters I was placed in a long line with the other low-lives. I felt like a real loser since I got caught. The main objective on the streets was to avoid the cops. Hostile-looking creeps sat around like they hadn't shaved or bathed in weeks, ready to spit at me. They probably played a big role in the drug trade. I overheard them bad mouth the legal system and cuss people out. I saw white men in business attire mingling amongst themselves, probably lawyers.

When my turn finally came up in line, the handcuffs were removed. I massaged my aching wrists. I had to undergo a long grueling process of getting fingerprinted, mug shots, charges recorded, and other legal paperwork. A plastic ID bracelet was fitted and snapped to my wrist.

The only number I had to offer for release contact, or, in other words, bail was the folded piece of scrap paper Sugar noted at Trio Café, so I handed it to the desk clerk. She seemed surprised that I had no other information to provide.

The guide rolled each forefinger in black ink then pressed them onto chemically treated paper. Another line awaited me. This time around, I was waiting to get my mug shots. The cameraman took three quick shots of me in different positions. So far, painless. I guess I had expected to be beheaded, hanged, or burned at a stake. Ya know, cruel and unusual punishment.

After all that, I was escorted to the shower room by an ugly, fat-bottomed, hairy, oversized, black woman. They called her the Custody Officer; I called her Sasquatch. She instructed me to take off all my clothes and wash in the shower stall. After an automated brief lukewarm spray, I was handed a towel and a white oversized sheet with strings dangling down the sides. I was to wear this. Sasquatch led me into a private room that kinda resembled a gyno's examining room, which included stirrups with a padded bench. I was told to remain seated until further instruction. I waited endlessly in the paper-thin gown. A nasty breeze from the ceiling fan had me shivering.

A petite white lady in a doctor's uniform entered the examining room with a clipboard. She greeted me, shook my hand, and apologized for the wait. She informed me that she was going to examine me, a routine procedure for all sexually related crimes—*in other words, prostitution*. She retrieved a form to proceed with some preliminary questions.

"Your name, hun?"

"Bambi."

"Is that your birth name?" she asked for clarity.

"No, it's Denise Bower."

After clearing her throat, she resumed, "Place of birth?"
"Philley County."

"Age?"

"Seventeen," popped into my mind.

She asked if I had any sexually transmitted diseases. I shook my head. She continued to ask personal questions, such as if I had used any form of contraceptives. I told her sometimes my johns used condoms, but I never tried the pill. She nodded. The doctor explained the procedure for the physical exam. I was about to experience my first pap smear and rectal exam. Now *that* sounded painful.

She inserted a cold instrument into my genitals. She hurried through this uncomfortable exam. Repeatedly she insisted, "Just relax. Denise, you'll have to relax." I was resisting the internal pressure of the pap smear. I noticed an agitated look on her face as she checked around inside me. When she was finished, she snapped off her gloves and jotted down some additional notes to her chart. "How long have you been out on the streets?" she asked.

"A while."

"A month, six months, a year?" the doctor fished around for accuracy, leaning against the bench frame.

"I . . . I don't know. I don't keep track of things like that. What's the difference?"

"The difference is," the doctor raised her eyebrows and lowered her tone, "you have scar tissue in your genitals. I don't know what kind of sexual activities you engage in, but you need to put an end to this sort of practice."

"What the fuck are you talking about?" I raised my voice. She scared me. I was thinking of venereal diseases.

"Have you ever had an abortion?" she suggested. I thought about it.

The image of a man in a white gown comes into focus. He stands before me with a grim expression asking me if I'm covered for the procedure. He means if I have insurance. My legs are held in place by stirrups . . . I notice the bloody fetus in the doctor's hands as he wraps it . . . Father's face appears before me. He's enraged. "You took a life! Are you proud of yourself now? Why didn't you use protection?"

"Denise?" the young doctor called for my attention. "Are you alright?"

"I . . . I had an abortion," I cried.

She handed me a tissue. "It's okay, you don't have to worry. I just want to advise you to put off sexual activities for a while. You shouldn't aggravate those old scars."

"And what if I do?" I tested her. The doctor didn't reply.

JAIL

The Sasquatch walked me down a dimly lit path, rattling keys, focusing her flashlight ahead. I was placed in a vacant dark enclosure only lit by a single bulb. Was this what they referred to as jail? The holding cell was small and narrow, about the size of a walk- in closet, housing a cot, toilet, and a water fountain. It was a cage.

I sat on the padded cot, staring off into space. So now what? I needed to make a call to Sugar to have her send bail. She had to get me out of here.

My mind drifted. I thought about the examination. Scar tissue on genitals. How did I get the scars? Could the abortion have left scars? No, it had to be some kind of violent sex as the doctor insinuated. Who was responsible for this? I thought back — John. He was my first lover. Had he done this to me? I envisioned him over me . . .

"You're not a virgin, are you? Who did you fool around with? I thought you told me you saved yourself for me. If I find that you cheated on me, I'll make you pay." He smacks me about . . .

No, he might have been a pushy, controlling little bastard but not the culprit. Then came the answer . . .

I shrieked, "NO!" covering my head in sorrow. I could not bear much more. Another vision came into focus. I was so choked up, trying to avoid a breakdown. It was like being a part of a violent movie I couldn't shut off . . .

I was lying in a cradle position within the same claustrophobic cell. I acknowledged the deeply buried truth: Father was responsible for scarring me. I kept this nightmarish secret hushed for too long. The horror manifested like a cancer growth, chipping away at the core of my being. I had to strike at something, anything, so I kicked and punched the iron bars that rattled back. It left me bruised and in severe pain. *Damn him!*

I had to get a grip, or I'd eventually maul myself.

I needed . . . somethin'. It was . . . it was calling. I could feel pangs eating away at my gut. It was dope. Daydreams of snorting heroin or smoking pot preoccupied my thoughts. As the minutes rolled by, the urges grew. Shawn crossed my mind. That kid had a pager. FUCK! I banged against the iron bars, again. If only I could get to a phone booth. I studied the cell for escape routes.

I felt giddy. Drinking fountain water worsened my sore stomach. I threw up in the toilet. I thought I was coming down with a bug of sorts: sweaty palms, racing pulse, and nausea.

I had reoccurring visions of killing Mr. Bower. I wanted to strangle the bastard for ruining my life—for conceiving me—for allowing me to live. I banged and shook against the iron bars yelling for someone to release me. No one responded. Unrelentingly I shook, kicked, and threw my body weight against the bars, trying to break through. The bars rattled back each time, but I had exhausted my strength wastefully.

The giddiness returned. My cravings went unsatisfied. I vomited several more times in the toilet. What was happening to me? "I need some acid," I cried out loud. I vomited dry heaves. Each time I vomited, I grew weaker. Hopelessly, I sat on the cot, moaning time away. "Please save me, oh Jesus," I prayed. A sudden wave of dizziness came over me, forcing me to take ill. Was it that the Sasquatch never heard my cries or that no one cared?

Finally, I figured out what was happening. They knew I was hooked on drugs. They had arranged for me to suffer through withdrawal. That's what all this was about. This was my punishment. They had it in for me. I couldn't take it much longer. I had trouble breathing. I wondered where Sugar was. Did I call her yet? I didn't remember. Not that she cared, not that anyone cared.

I heard footsteps approach my cell and a set of keys rattle. The lock was opened. I swore it to be a delusion until I heard Sasquatch's voice. My adrenaline must have propped me up from the cot to glimpse into the darkness. The custody officer stepped in with a flashlight and asked me if I was ready to leave. I didn't believe her.

She said bail was posted for me and it was my choice. If I wasn't so weak, I'd try to kill her. Instead, I laughed, "You think I'll fall for your fuckin' bullshit?" I snapped, "Can't you see I'm fuckin' sick? I threw up all over. I need a fuckin' doctor, asshole!" I threw my shoe at her.

"Would you like me to deny you bail for giving me a hard time?" Sasquatch warned. "Someone by the name of Shirell Davis is here to take you home."

"Did you say Shirell?"

"Yes, ma'am."

"But I never called her."

"We called her for you when we tagged you. This is the correct number, isn't it?" She showed me the form with her flashlight pointed at it.

I consented, "Yeah—yeah." I peered straight into her eyes, shielding my sensitive eyes with my hand from the blinding flashlight. "Are you serious? Am I really free to go?" *But if you let me back on the streets, I'll go right back into drugs and prostitution, you fool.*

CLUB FANTASY

Shirell was handed a receipt for the posted bail amount at the main office cashier desk. Delighted to see her, I almost smiled but knew better to act ashamed. I remembered how she warned me to stay away from cops. I really blew it this time. She might evict me. I studied her with uncertainty. "I want to thank you," I said humbly. Feeling uneasy about it, I hugged her.

"Child, you look pale," she remarked.

"I've had a stomachache," I fibbed.

Shirell, ignoring me, took time to thank the officers for calling her and promised that I wouldn't cause any more trouble. It was only when we left the police station that she spoke to me. She scolded, "Didn't I tell you I wanted no trouble out of you?"

"Look, I didn't do anything wrong, I swear. It must have been some kinda setup."

"Setup huh?" Shirell rolled her eyes. She must have heard it all before.

I told her what had happened. "I thought the guy was a date, but he turned out to be an undercover cop."

Shirell shook her head pretending not to hear me. She unlocked the passenger side of her old, dilapidated car. After a few uncomfortable silent moments of driving, Shirell mentioned, "Sugar told me you answered the phone when her pimp called, and he threatened to get you."

I nodded, recalling how afraid I was at the time.

"So why were you loose on the streets?" Shirell tried to figure. "I was too afraid to be alone in the apartment," I justified.

Shirell ignored my answer. "So, you think the setup has somethin' to do wit the phone call?"

"I'm not saying that. That might have been a routine bust for some rookie."

"No, cops don't go around arrestin' young girls unless they drug traffickin' in the area. You know anyone who wanna spite you?"

I thought about it. "Yeah, my ex-lover, Steve. He resented me for being a hooker."

"Then stay 'way from him. Ya have ta be careful wit who you meddle wit," she advised.

The stomach pangs and urges returned as I set foot in the apartment. I charged into the bathroom just in time to throw up in the toilet. "I need . . ." I cried to myself. "I can't go on this way." I had to find . . . and fast. Shawn popped into mind. He had everything.

I was now possessed by the devil. It left the bathroom. It came down the hallway into an open doorway, the baby's room. It noticed the crib and bassinet were unoccupied. It almost stumbled over a mattress sprawled over the floor covered with a blue blanket. Loose dirty laundry lay on the other side of the mattress along with a clutter of mechanical toys, batteries, and cigarette butts. The devil shut the door quietly to rummage through Shawn's sleeping quarters. Within the back pocket of his denim blue jeans was a tiny baggy full of pills. In addition, a stash of rolled pot was buried under the mattress. And, of all places, tightly rolled green legal tender was found folded neatly inside the battery compartment of a mechanical toy.

Shawn's sleeping quarters were, indeed, a treasure hunt. It heard footsteps approach. Shirell was passing through the hallway. She paused then opened the door to the baby's room. She looked at me suspiciously as she caught me in the act.

I asked nervously, "Ah, where's the baby? She's not in here . . ." as if I cared.

"What you hidin' there?" She noticed my arms behind my back.

"Nothing. I just wanted to see the baby." I raised my arms in the clear after the baggy was quickly inserted into my back pocket.

"Baby Tia is somewheres else for protection. I can't tell nobody," Shirell explained.

I slowly backed away from her as I left the room into the hallway. "Well, I guess that was a smart move." I took off in the other direction, hoping she wouldn't follow me. She didn't.

Without a word, I left the apartment with Shawn's stolen dope and money.

With a few sips of fountain water, I swallowed a pill. I had no idea what type of pill it was but knew it had to have value if Shawn hid it away. I was in the heart of the city watching a few pedestrians wait at the crosswalk while others gathered at a local pub or liquor store. For someone who was once uneasy about city culture, I was now parading freely in all its confusion and excitement. Fowlersville city became a fascination to me.

I approached an artisan center. Various vendors promoted their artwork in aisles of booths full of handcrafted merchandise. My eyes were drawn to a huge, framed Disney illustration of Mickey and Minnie Mouse holding hands. In the background, the iconic Disney castle was centered in a beautiful rose garden. "Wow," I thought to myself, enamored by the piece. It was painted so meticulously.

Mickey Mouse motions me to join them. I can't resist. I take a leap right into the frame and become a part of the 2-D world. I'm now in the Magic Kingdom, colored in like the rest of my animated friends. I look around the lovely Kingdom. Everything is created with a spectrum of watercolors and line thicknesses. The world is a place of circles, squares, rectangles, and odd shapes where colors overlap the contours of shapes. Amazing. We are each created by the swift brush stroke of an artist's steady hand and can be just as easily deleted by the swift stroke of an eraser. But no worry in this existence. We're a completed and polished masterpiece. Everyone and everything is merry.

Other faces appear. Alice in Wonderland, Snow White, Sleeping Beauty, and Cinderella all join in to form a big circle, holding hands and dancing merrily. We have so much fun, laughing and singing, "It's a small world after all." Minnie and Mickey approach me when the circle breaks up. Mickey introduces Alice in Wonderland as Ruby, Margie is Snow White, of course Shashona is Sleeping Beauty, and last, but not least, Cinderella is represented by Glenda. Wow, the girls from the "clubhouse" are in this 2-D world with me disguised as Disney characters. Ruby asks me if I want to visit the "clubhouse." I'm sort of curious. She tells me that all I must do is follow the yellow-brick road. And so, we go skipping down the mysterious path.

This bright yellow path is depicted with sun-lit green trees plus a yellow and rose flower garden.

"Ah-oh!" I say as we come to a dead-end cliff.

"Not a worry," Ruby assures. "Close your eyes and hold my hand." All the sisters hold hands with each other. One by one, each of the sisters flies off the cliff, over the endless abyss of mountainous rock and swamp, onto a beautiful valley of rich green land. At the horizon stands a huge, gorgeous crystal castle. This castle casts a bluish light against the nighttime sky. Within this four-story castle are ten bedrooms, two balconies, a marbled spiral staircase, an entertainment center with a theatre-sized movie screen, a huge ballroom, three-leaf clover indoor swimming pool and servants . . . happily ever after . . .

The sisters smile brightly, eyeballing each other while raising eyebrows. "What?" I ask curiously.

The sisters wonder why I can't stay with them in this magical castle. I don't know. "I think I know what you should do." Glenda's face lights up. "Why don't you ask the witch for permission?" She winks.

"The Wicked Witch of the East?" I quiver, visualizing her black-pointed cone hat, dirty black kinky hair, long two-inch black nails, and crystal ball. A witch with evil intentions.

Glenda folds her arms. "No, silly. I'm referring to Sugar."

Someone knocks on the 2-D door. I answer it. The door opens and in flies the 3-D world.

"Hey lady, can you spare some change?" a black homeless guy appeared out of nowhere, interfering with my fantasy.

"You scared the fuck out of me." I jumped. I found myself reclining on a frayed wooden step. I was surprised I didn't get splintered.

"Sorry—real sorry," he insisted. "I just need a little somethin'-somethin' change—a dollar kindly, God bless," he begged.

I reached into my pocket, distraught and confused. "Here, take these quarters and leave me the hell alone."

"God bless." He bowed before me, repeating his grace profusely, then took off in a scamper before I had a change of heart. The homeless beggar left behind a stench that stagnated in the air.

Examining my surroundings, I was sitting outside the ruins of a rejected, perhaps arson-related, burned-down row house. A collapsed roof hung within the structure and some two-by-fours were missing. This was the "clubhouse?" I stepped inside, walking carefully over the creaky floorboards. The rotted interior was clearly used as a drug hideout. An old dusty bong lay beside a filthy toilet bowl. Inside the bowl, besides stool, a bloodstained tampon, a used needle, and a cap floated about. The flusher was broken. I concluded that the sisters couldn't possibly live here. Perhaps this "clubhouse" was just that. A condemned, nobody-would-think row-house for clubbing purposes. It was a shame that fantasy was not reality.

REVENGE

I had the biggest smile on my face upon returning to the apartment, because I had the most amazing hallucination ever, thanks to the magic pills I stole from Shawn. I wished I could stay in that 2-D kingdom forever where everything was so innocent and filled with happy endings.

As I approached the stairwell, I recognized a familiar face leaning against the foot of the staircase. He lowered his head as he was smoking. I was sure it was him as he drew closer. I had completely forgotten about him . . . and them. Disheveled and slovenly, Todd McKane immediately noticed me, as if he had been waiting for this moment for some time. Whiskers formed along the curve of his face. His eyes were drawn and hair unkempt. I figured after his affair with Sugar, he would have been satisfied and made into a regular, but I underestimated him. He was truly in love with Vicki. He had a rather livid expression sealed to his rough face. He tossed his cigarette to the ground, smashing it to shreds with sole of his shoe.

I backed away a few steps. His breathing was labored as he questioned me, "Where's Vicki?" He closed in on me, cornering me against the brick wall. I did not know how to safely answer without upsetting him. How ironic—I kinda wished a police officer was nearby. Where were they when you really needed them? Too close for comfort, Todd pressed up against me, strapping me to the wall.

"Did you hear me? I want an answer," he huffed in my face. I could smell the booze on his breath.

"I don't know," I replied. I did not know how to comfort him, but I knew that I was in great danger. And I knew I was partly to blame. "She just took off," I said.

"Where did she go?" Todd emphatically insisted.

"I don't know."

He clenched my collar! "Tell me," He shouted. He jerked me away from the wall then spun me around to face it, twisting my wrists firmly behind my back. "I'm gonna hurt you if you don't," he threatened.

I swallowed at the uncomfortable premonition of becoming a statistic. "She went back to Philley County. That's all I know. Please," I pleaded. The increasing pressure exerted against my wrists had me throbbing in pain.

"Why did she go back without me?" He was forcing me into confession. I moaned, "Todd, you're hurting me."

"You should be grateful I'm not killing you. Now answer me!" he shouted.

"Ask Nina. She knows," I insisted.

"Where is she? If I find her, I'll strangle her with my bare hands."

I was in so much pain, it felt like he was disjointing the tendons in my wrist. "Aw!" I cried, "Alright—alright." I surrendered the truth. "Vicki caught you in bed with Nina, got real upset, and skipped town."

He let me go. "You fuckin' whore," Todd raged on. "I never thought you would betray your best friend. It was all a setup, wasn't it? You're really sick, you know that?" he shouted.

I massaged my sore wrists. "Please, you don't understand. It wasn't my intention. I had no choice but to do as she told me. She turned me into a prostitute . . ."

He slammed me into the brick wall. The right side of my face was abrasively scraped before I dropped to the cement pavement.

"You lousy whore—you fuckin' bitch. I ought to fuckin' kill you, you no-good cheap slut." He grabbed onto my hair.

I wrestled him off. "Leave me alone!" I cried. Clearly now, he was beating on me. A case of assault and battery. I screamed for help. His hand pressed over my mouth when he spotted a pedestrian walking by.

Quickly he dragged me into the corner of the complex doorway where we could not be spotted in the shade. "Who let you out of jail?" Todd questioned, shaking me incessantly.

I was stunned that he knew at all. I had figured out the anonymous tattler. "You did it," my weak voice quivered.

"Your fucked-up happy hooker roommate got me drunk, but when I got sober, I found myself in that black wench's bedroom. And to top it off, my drugs were fuckin' gone, not to mention my fiancée. You damned straight I reported you and that fuckin' nigger to the cops for soliciting. I want your asses permanently kicked," he pointed emphatically.

"Wait." I realized he had me locked up when he, in fact, sold dope. He was a hypocrite. I couldn't let him win on this battle. "You dirty bastard," I fretted. "I'll have you charged in possession of crack."

"Shit, there ain't no crack on me. Your fuckin' hooker snatched it, remember." He grabbed me by the ear and pulled on it firmly, "But I'd like to see you try real hard to book me." I gazed up at him with only one eyelid open. He drew his face almost kissing close to mine and whispered with his thick boozed breath, "If I ever see you again, I'll whip your ass for good, comprende?" I nodded, swallowing my tears.

Todd took off into the darkness and disappeared. I stuck my head out from the dark corner, spotting several neighbors watching from afar.

I treated my facial wounds in the bathroom with a washcloth and cold running water. In the mirror, I saw a battered Denise who was just assaulted by her best friend's boyfriend. *Was it all worth it?* I thought to myself. Plotting against Vicki so Nina wouldn't beat me up? If one didn't attack me, the other one did. I'd become a human punching bag. Was this how I'd been rewarded for cooperating fully with Nina? And what gracious words of thanks did she have in store for me?

While bandaging my sore bloody cheek, I saw Nina's reflection in the mirror. "It's amazin' what you do for dope, ain't it," she remarked, standing behind me, ready to attack. "But ya end up losin' anyways."

"What are you talking about?" I sneered, fed up with her crap and everyone else's games.

"Don't act like you don't know." She pointed her finger at me. "You stole from Shawn."

"Oh, I must have forgotten after Todd McKane took a few swings at me."

"He was chasing after his stash?" Nina guessed.

"Wrong again. He's chasing after you. He already revenged me. It's your turn. And since you're such a good schemer, try to get out of this one: He wants to kill you."

"I don't like your tone of voice," Nina snapped.

"Well, I don't like being used as a guinea pig or being taken advantage of," I disputed, sick and tired of her treatment. Nina slapped me across the face. It burned. I backed away with angry tears. "Look, I'm not your property and I don't want to be treated . . ." She slapped me again. She shook me and I shook her. I cried, "Leave me alone, damn you!"

"You nothin' but trouble since the day I picked you up." She pushed me against the sink. "Todd shoulda finished you off."

We heard the cries of her baby. Shirell stood by the bathroom door holding Tia. The little girl was adorable. Her little fingers reached out to us. We could see her eyes were filled with tears and fear. She cried for Momma. Nina had to swallow her anger and gather herself to pacify the infant. It made a lasting impression on me.

It was at that moment that quiet Shirell suddenly lashed out at the both of us like never before. "Both you girls are diggin' your own graves fightin' over drugs. And I don't cares what your reasons or purposes is. You should be ashamed of yourselves for all the fussin' you cause. I's tired of protectin' ya'll and givin' you's a roof over your head and all you's do is cause more trouble. Now, if you wants to go on fightin', take it outside so all yours enemies can laugh with pleasure watchin' you's killin' each other."

A sad silence quieted the bathroom. Nina hid her face in shame behind the baby. She mumbled to me, "I'm sorry," and I forgave her.

We continued on with our daily business like nothing had happened. Later that evening I asked Nina once more if we could make peace with each other—become partners or friends.

Nina seemed rather puzzled. Real friendship was a foreign concept to her. She did not have the background and experience to fully understand what it was I wanted. She was not cultured and led a very guarded, closed life. But, for the first time, I saw through her rough exterior into her vulnerability. I saw tears in her eyes. She cleared her throat. After a long silence she just said, "I mean well."

As time passed, I had a greater understanding of what Nina was made of and it was bittersweet.

KIDNAPPED

Three weeks later I became an official member of the "clubhouse" circle. I moved out of Nina's apartment and into a shared townhouse. The townhouse, just a block down the street, was well furnished, clean, and maintained respectably. The "sisters" and I got along splendidly. Things were looking up.

I was assigned to hustle Harrington Blvd. Harrington was an especially rough section with open drug dealing. Having worked Harrington before, I was well aware of the competition. Johns would fight and shoot over hookers.

I'd been working the block for a few minutes when, in the corner of my eye, a van pulled up along the street curb. In the midst of a noisy busy evening, a tall black guy called out my name from behind me. The instant I turned to glance, he sprayed mace right into my face! I shrieked as I was overwhelmed with fear. My entire body was paralyzed in fright. My eyes burned. I could no longer see. Strong, forceful hands sealed my mouth, pulling my head backward. My arms were restrained behind me. A paper bag was thrown over my head, crackling around me. I was afraid he was going to smother me. I was lifted and dragged off somewhere. I felt completely helpless, fearing death. I fought the menacing captors endlessly, though my efforts were futile. I bit on a clump of hair caught in my mouth. My eyes were swollen shut. I was tearing profusely. All I could do was kick and scream as best I could against the duct tape.

I was placed onto a vinyl surface. They turned me over on my stomach to have my wrists and ankles tied by rope. The bag was lifted only to be replaced by blindfolds. I heard grunts, vulgarities, and arguing in the background, but couldn't understand any of it. Once the tension calmed, I heard one guy say to the other, "Are you sure she's the right one?" He paused, "You'd better be 'cuz if she's not, it gonna be your ass." I concluded from his remark that I was being held captive by some street gang—thug. I told myself that they simply captured the wrong one. They'd release me once they discover this.

I was set in motion, still lying on my stomach. My mind raced around trying to make sense of it all. I must have been placed in the van I noticed as I was walking by. I needed an accurate description of the van for a police report. It was a black van . . . no, I couldn't say for sure since it was dark outside and dark colors blend in well. Were there words or some kind of description on the van? I tried to play back the image in my mind but all I could remember was a dark van and a tall black man approaching me dressed in business attire. Didn't anyone see the racket going on or hear me cry? Why didn't someone stop him? I was working in the middle of a crowded city street. Pedestrians were all around. Weren't there witnesses? Had to be.

Something told me that I was alone in this crime. I groped around for a window to bang my head against, only to have my cheeks rub up against walls of fabric.

I considered a connection with Todd. After all, he had me arrested and threatened my life. Was it he who arranged this scheme against me? He might have hired a hit man. No, this had to be an organized gang effort. During the travel, the back stereo speaker blared off in my ears. I knew it was turned up intentionally to drown out the voices in the front of the van.

When the motion ceased, I was again lifted and carried. At first, I heard sounds of pedestrians and motorists, then of a bell and squeaky door hinges. I was relieved to be inside a building and not thrown into some dumpster like I heard about in the news. I was eventually lowered onto a bouncy surface. The blindfold, gag, and restraints were removed. I had never appreciated the ability to see as I did now. Once my sore eyes adjusted to the dimly lit room, I found myself lying on a bed before three well-dressed black thugs in a hotel room. Two of the three thugs stood by the door pointing their handguns in my direction while the taller bearded slim stood above me. I presumed he was going to rape me while the others guarded the door. I knew from here on out, it would be put out or die. So where did Todd fit into the story?

"Do you know who I am?" the bearded slim greeted me with a rhetorical question. Though the voice sounded vaguely familiar, I could not place him. Perhaps he was one of my tricks. I did not reply. He answered grimly, "I don't expect you to know who I am because we never met. But I know all about you." He folded his hands rather arrogantly. "I'm Mr. Ruxton, the father of Nina Taylor's child," he explained, standing tall. The connection startled me. I remembered how he harassed me over the phone. I quivered. My irritated eyes widened in surprise. He knew I knew where he was coming from. Funny how I blamed Todd for this one. I couldn't decide which scenario would have been more threatening. Sadly, I acknowledged that they caught the right bait.

"Now you have a choice." He paced the floors, contemplating with fingers to his chin. "You can make this a very painful experience for yourself, or you can make it easy by cooperating with me." He grinned. "I only ask you to tell me the truth and then I'll let you go. It's that simple. Alright?" I nodded with increasing skepticism and distrust, recalling his cold-blooded revenge on Nina. I knew what he was after before he made his demands, only I was not willing to assist him.

"I want you to tell me where the child is hidden."

"Why? What are you going to do her?" I questioned accusingly.

"Hey, that's none of your business," Mr. Ruxton snapped. "Let's get the procedure straight here. I ask the questions, and you answer them, got it?"

"But . . . but why do you care? She's alive and well. That's all that should matter," I inserted, trying to get him to speak the truth.

"I see you'll require a little patience," he sighed. "Let's get the facts straight, shall we?" He knelt over the bed beside me. "The kid is my daughter Nina stole and hid from me. You think that's fair? She's withholding my child illegally. You can't do that under the law. Haven't you heard of custody and visitation? We haven't even had a court hearing to allow the judge to determine who's a better-fit parent. I know I'll win because she's a fuckin' prostitute and they don't make fit parents. Besides, she doesn't even care about the kid. She lives day-by-day on dope in a substandard apartment in the city ghetto. That's not being a responsible parent, is it? Ya see where I'm comin' from? I'm a lot brighter than that. So, if I were you, I'd look out for the child's best interest and turn the helpless kid over to her more mature father," he stated with conceit.

I snickered. "What do you know about the law? You're a pimp," I defended Nina's position as courageously as ever. I must have totally forgotten that I was under the gun. The words flew out of my mouth indiscreetly.

He smacked me across the face. "Shut the fuck up right now. You ain't gonna play smart with me. I'll beat the shit out of you the next time you sound off your mouth, you understand? I'm warning you," he raised his voice, pointing his finger near my swollen eye. He pulled himself back to composure, adjusting his tie.

I slowly crawled away from him in fear, anticipating more lashes from his temperamental disposition. He pulled out a pack of cigarettes from his jacket pocket and lit one. "Where do you think you're goin'?" He lifted an eyebrow, snickering at me, watching me timidly crawl to the other end of the bed. The gunmen chuckled as well. "You set foot on the floor, and I'll have you tied to the post," his face straightened as he threatened. I froze in place at the far corner of the mattress, lowering my head in submission.

"I want you to look at me," he demanded, closing in on me. "Please leave me alone," I begged.

He said in an almost soothing voice, "If you behave," then paused. Abruptly he yelled, "Now stop stalling and tell me where the goddamn kid is!" he hissed.

He startled me. "I don't know." I swallowed, shielding my face.

"Damn you! Why are you being so fuckin' difficult? I know you know. Why are you fuckin' protectin' a hooker when I'm threatening your life? Do you not think I'll kill you?" He sighed out of frustration, tapping his cigarette against an ashtray. "What's it to you anyway? It's not your baby." I remained silent. "Talk!" he yelled.

"I said I don't know. She never told me," I cried.

"Don't give me that shit. You told me the baby is alive and well. You do know. She did tell you." He waved his hands about like an Italian Mafia leader. "Do you understand English? I'm thinkin' of blowin' your fuckin' brains out." He paused. "Oh, I see, you think I'm playing with you, don't ya? You don't think I'm serious, do ya?" He punched me in the jaw. "Now where is the kid?" he demanded.

I massaged my sore, achy chin. "She didn't tell me," I insisted. I was ready to dodge the next blow.

He drew himself before me, close to my face. "I don't like liars." He shook his head before puffing cigarette smoke into my face. "I punish them."

I coughed. "I'm not lying," I cried.

"She's with Nina, isn't she?" He looked me steadily cross in the eye as if it were a form of mental telepathy.

"No," I protested. I let out a shriek as he burned my arm with the butt of his cigarette!

"Liar! You're a goddamn liar," he huffed. "The next time you lie I'm going to poke a hole in your eyeball with this butt, understand?" he threatened me with the burning tobacco paper. I nodded nervously, holding back the tears of fright, blowing and soothing my burnt flesh.

"Ah, see you're scared. Are you now willing to tell me where the baby is? I'll tell ya what, I'll make it easier for you." He signaled the two gunmen to leave. "If you can't say so, just tell me where Nina lives, okay. I know where she lives but I want you to tell me. Easy, right?"

My swollen eyes gazed into the foul-scented fumes ascending the cigarette butt then at the burnt flesh on my arm. I coughed and sniffled. I had flashbacks of little Tia crying and reaching out for

Nina during our last skirmish in the bathroom. It seemed only moments ago. *Is it all really worth it?* I asked myself. *The money and hassles Nina had put me through. No. I'm not doing this for Nina. She does not deserve a martyr. It's Shirell I'm sticking it out for. She not only saved me from foolishly jumping out a five-story window, but she also bailed me out of jail. But this doesn't change the fact that I truly don't know where baby Tia is hidden. Shirell wouldn't tell me. The only thing I know is that Shirell knows.* To preserve my last hours, I made up a story. It was the only thing I could think to do, "She's with Nina's friend, Lacy. She's hidden in a torn-down warehouse." I could tell he was pleased with my answer. *Thank God.*

"Aw, now that wasn't so hard, was it?" But then he pulled me over to him and crawled on top of me. Somehow, I knew all along that he wouldn't live up to his promise. He placed his wide wet lips on my mouth. I turned my head, avoiding him, keeping my lips sealed. He was displeased that I rejected him. "Woman, you kiss me back—kiss me, I said." I refused to yield to such disgust. I could only make love to venom when I was doped up. He forcefully positioned my lips then kissed me hard, piercing deep within. I bit him. He recoiled momentarily. "Damn you! You're the meanest bitch I ever had and you're going to pay for it right now!"

He raped me! The butcher grabbed the seams of my shirt and tore it. All the buttons popped off, including the bra hook. Teeth and tongue sucked, squeezed, and bit at my nipple until I turned blue. I tossed and squirmed. In no time he was aroused, tearing into my pants to rip through me. "You're going to enjoy making love to me or I'm goin' to beat your fuckin' brains out till you behave." He grunted over, and over, "I'm gonna make you enjoy it." I felt a torpedo hit inside me. I gasped, shutting my eyes tightly. "Say you love it," he demanded countless times. "Say it!"

I was too consumed in pain, unable to respond. I prayed to stay alive through the torture. I thought to myself, *C'mon, I've been raped before, why should this be any worse? Maybe because I really thought he'd finish me off after he was done.* He bounced over me like a mechanical drill pounding its way through the surface of pavement. I had thoughts of castrating him. I wanted to tear him to pieces. All the hatred inside buried itself under tears. I felt faint, slipping in and out of consciousness. "Say it!" the echoes rang inside my head. I had to find the inner strength to stop him. I envisioned the father, Ray Bower, over me. Then it seemed so familiar and normal. My lips came alive, and my tongue lisped the magic words. I didn't hear myself say it in utter exhaustion, but I knew it must have been spoken because when I awoke, my naked body was chilled from a draft. Mr. Ruxton was no longer on top of me.

SEX SLAVE

Mr. Ruxton sat at his desk arranging appointments by phone for sex services. He announced to each client that he had a hot and sexy nymph ready and willing to do anything for rugged, mean sex. He set a fee for various services, jotting down numbers on his clipboard. As soon as he noticed that I had awakened, he hung the phone up. "You worth a lot, aincha?" he asked curtly, raising an eyebrow at me. I said nothing. "How much you get a trick?" he probed. I remained silent. "A hundred? Two hundred? Five hundred?" he estimated. "And just think, I got it for free," he laughed sinisterly. "I gonna make some big-time green off you yet." He got up from his chair. "I'm sure you heard the phone conversations and know exactly what I'm up to."

"Why?" I asked mercifully.

He answered briefly, "Supply and demand." He began to pace the floor. "Cuz hungry men need it. I'm providing a service just as you did."

"I told you what you wanted to hear. You promised . . ."

"Oh, go fuck off. You're my mistress now and that's the way it's going to be. That's your punishment for giving me a hard time. I did warn you." He gave me that sorry look.

"What are you up to?" I meant, *are you going to kill me?*

He rolled his eyes. "You know very well. I'm sure Nina told you all the nitty-gritty details."

"Yes, she told me you run a black market on babies."

He pointed to me. "Yes, and you are going to be my baby maker. I can't afford to lose another one. You will not desert me like Nina did. I will see to that with my tight security force. I've planned to get at least three healthy little ones out of you. Of course, if you miscarry any of them, I'll have to dispose of you. I'd prefer at least one female from you for future breeding before you expire. And I should emphasize, if you disappoint me, you can easily be replaced," Mr. Ruxton made himself clear.

"You're sick," I protested.

I had to escape. I looked around for possibilities. There were no windows or anything to hit him with. The only movable objects were the phone, the guest chair, the office chair, the desk, and my pillow. If I could make a mad dash for the door, I could probably find a way to hide and flee. I needed to distract him. It was all in the timing. I was sure Mr. Ruxton would never let me go. He'd have a watchman guard the room when he wasn't present. I came up with the only option. I waited for him to sit quietly at his desk. I watched as he grew tired after working endless hours arranging phone contacts. It felt like twilight hours. I cautiously threw the sheets off and tiptoed over to the door. It would have been a smooth escape if only the door would open. Apparently, it was locked from the other side, which I did not figure into the plan.

"What in hell do you think you're doing?" he asked, rubbing his tired eyes.

"Umm . . . I need to use the restroom," I explained as my heart skipped a beat.

He sneered at me. "That's what the bed pan is for. You thought you were going to get away, didn't you, you sneak." He got off his chair, grabbed me with his murderous hands, and tossed me back into that bed. "I can't trust you with anything," he grumbled. I noticed a syringe in his hand. I quivered, thinking about the torment I went through with Brad under the influence of Barcinoca. Mr. Ruxton called his two guards in to assist him. My wrists and ankles were tied and chained to all four poles of the bedpost. The guards held my left arm in position, snapped a rubber band in place, and injected me. This wouldn't be the last time they'd drug me.

"If you try to escape once more or do anything to disappoint me or my clients, I'll have you mauled for life. Is that clear?" Mr. Ruxton threatened, then, unexpectedly, kissed me. I was now Mr. Ruxton's sex slave and there was nothing I could do about it. I was to call him Master and treat him like a Royal Highness.

Being penetrated by wild animals, coupled with drowsiness, made sex more of a nightmare than madness. The animals ranged from short, fat, stinky slobs to skinny, tall, lizard dicks. Having sex with multiple partners and acting excited about it was nothing new in my profession. The only disturbing difference here was that I didn't have protection and I wasn't getting rewarded at the end. Fortunately, I didn't show any signs of pregnancy. The Master himself, Mr. Ruxton, would rattle me night after night, trying to impregnate me. My vaginal wounds began to irritate me. I remembered that the gynecologist warned me against having rough intercourse. Should she have written an excuse note for abstinence?

I couldn't comprehend how sex-hungry animals could find me attractive when I was chained to a bed, bruised and filthy. I didn't really think it would've made much difference if I were lying dead and they were penetrating a cadaver. There were, though, a few professionals among the clients that required I be cleaned. These requests presented an opportunity to be freed from the shackles, get out of bed to stretch, and be bathed by the guards in the shower room.

They, of course, carefully drugged me so that I wouldn't remember where the shower room was. The important key to survival was to please the clientele no matter how I suffered.

However, a sex slave did have a few advantages. Upon request, there were the few times I was free from restraint. Sometimes I had the privilege of abusing the customer. It's really therapeutic to whip a guy's butt with his own belt until he cums. One encounter urged me to urinate in his mouth and gently nibble on his penis. I wished one of them would've given me permission to mutilate them. It would have been my highest honor.

I couldn't estimate how long this ritual went on. It felt like years. The measure of time quickly diminished during my captivity. There just wasn't any way of telling time; no windows to reflect sun or moonlight, no birds to tweet the coming of dawn or crickets to chirp the dusk.

I was slowly losing all hope of survival. The Master would provide nourishment only as a reward for my good behavior. My joints ached and stiffened, and dreams turned bizarre. I needed a thought to hold onto—a wish. But I couldn't even come up with one. I had totally abandoned memories of Nina, Shirell, and the sisters. I had no parents, no friends, no destination in life, and most unfortunately, no love. I wanted to escape the torment of captivity but for what in its place? Frequently in a groggy state, my only mental outlet was delirium. I had no choice but to make myself believe that this was what I wanted to live for. I was slowly dying:

my hair was unruly, the insulted veins on my arms turned blue and purple, my eyes were bruised and swollen, I couldn't see straight much less think straight, my buttocks ached from bed sores, anal penetration, multiple beatings, not to mention a sore pussy. The sheets were stained with blood and semen. But this was all I had to look forward to, day in, day out. The days seemed to grow longer and longer and eternal.

I think I must have had a nervous breakdown because I would dream and fantasize about making love to the Master. He wanted me to believe that he was the ruler of the universe and all- powerful. He had me worship him. He told me that I was lucky to have the privilege of loving him. When he beat me, it was to whip the devil out of my spirit. It was for my own good. I would also have delusions of Ray hurting me, and I yearned for this pleasure. It was as if . . . as if I had been brainwashed.

One time a really heavy-set client laid me. I remember how he nearly suffocated me. I couldn't breathe. My face must have turned blue because I saw stars. I suggested to the client that it would be more pleasurable if I were on top of him, but he adamantly insisted on his position. He filed a complaint with Mr. Ruxton after the service, informing the Master that I didn't satisfy him therefore he refused to pay for the service. The next thing I knew, the Master came storming in and banged my head repeatedly against the headboard, trying to give me a brain concussion.

The most memorable of all experiences was the day the Master bled me up with a belt to my butt after I had to seduce an impotent married man who just wanted to cause trouble. I felt sorry for the client and tried to arouse him, but he was hopeless. I begged him to tell Mr. Ruxton that I had fully satisfied him. He agreed only to betray me. Oddly, just as Mr. Ruxton was beating on me, he suddenly dropped the belt to the floor and disappeared. I waited for his return, lying in position with my knees buckled under me, gritting my teeth. When I turned my head to the door, I noticed a middle-aged Latino woman dressed in a white smock, holding the doorknob open with uncertainty, gazing at me. She acted as if she'd seen a ghost. Her mouth quivered for some time. She finally said, "I . . . excuse me." She could hardly gather her thoughts. The lady vanished. Moments later I saw a glimpse of a white man's face looking at me through the door then whispering to someone out of view. I assumed he was just another john waiting to pass a deal with the Master. But something was different this time. Mr. Ruxton never returned. The hallway was silent, void of guards.

This same young man approached me at my bedside. His chin was combed with visible whisker stubbles. Was he the next client? No, something set him apart from the rest of the clientele. He was nice. He expressed sorrow and seemed dismayed by my appearance. He smiled briefly. His genuine grin brightened my spirit. I felt comfortable in his presence. I knew he was non-threatening. He noticed my wrists were tied as I attempted to cover my bare breasts. My bone-dry cheeks cracked a smile. He asked me if I was here against my will. *Will?* I thought about the meaning of that word. Did I have the ability to have a will? Did I have the power of choice, thought, or conviction? Was I human or just a piece of meat? Why did he ask? What did he care? Why should he help me? What did I mean to him? I had no reason to believe I should even want to be saved.

Fortunately, refusing the pleasant thoughts bothered my conscience. I nodded. He studied my eyes momentarily then winked. I saw a penknife in his hand but knew he was harmless. I didn't believe he would get away with it. My eyes searched the hallway entrance for Mr. Ruxton, but he was nowhere in sight. The gentle one told me to relax but not to say a word. He said help was on the way. I didn't know exactly what he meant by the word "help." He offered me a sip from his water bottle and instructed me to swallow a sleeping pill. I obeyed him without question. I went out like a light.

KEVIN

I awoke in a very different world. For one, this place had a window. The sunlight alone lit the room. I was dressed in a cotton rose-pink floral patterned pajama set. I also must have bathed because I smelled like a rose. But above all, my wrists and ankles were free of shackles. Mystery man, the one who had me swallow a sleeping pill, waltzed into the bedroom holding a glass of lemonade. Brown-eyed with a goatee, Mr. Wonderful stood at about 5′8″, medium-build with slightly spiked light-brown hair. He wore a baseball cap. Not a bit shabby. The obvious bachelor had to be within five years my age. "How you doing?" He stood at the foot of the bed, keeping his distance.

I studied him, convincing myself that his benevolence was either deceptive or that he was simply not real. "Alright, I guess." I spoke like a bashful child. "Who are you?"

"Kevin O'Connor," he answered with pride, shaking my hand. "I rescued you."

Ignoring his self-indulgence, I questioned, "Why am I here?"

"This is my place. I figured it would be a safe haven for you, for now," he granted.

"Safe from what?" I snarled.

"Don't you remember you were in bondage?" He raised a brow.

"Yeah, I try not to think about that nightmare. He turned me into his sex slave. Is that what you mean?"

Kevin confirmed, "Mr. Ruxton, you're referring to?"

"Of course. I had to call him Master. You know him?"

"For a few months. I've been working as a bartender there, at the Hilltop Refinery. He'd come down to the bar every so often — a regular." Kevin lowered his long face. "I know all about the things he's done. He's a real thief," he added, taking a sip of his drink.

"You said you know all about the things he's done. What do you mean?" I tested.

"He's like a whole lotta other assholes in this crazy town." Kevin shook his head. "He's in the business to make under-the-table cash. Those types never get enough. They're really greedy."

"So how did you get me outta there?"

"That's a long story. I'd give the new cleaning lady all the credit though. She was assigned to clean rooms but made a mistake and went off to the wrong wing of the building. She went to a very restricted area past the 'Do Not Enter' sign. She's a Philippino, can't read English too well. Fortunately, both guards happened to have been absent at that moment. She went hysterical when she witnessed Mr. Ruxton belting you butt naked." Kevin paused to finish his drink. "So anyway, she came running down to the bar to confront me with the news. She knew she could confide in me after getting to know me during training. I really didn't want to get my nose dirty, but I could tell the lady wanted me to do something about it and wouldn't let me off the hook. I knew Mr. Ruxton had that room sealed off for business purposes, and there were always guards by it. But I was kinda curious about what was going on. Besides, I felt responsible to at least check into it.

So, while Mr. Ruxton and his guards were missing, I stole the chance. I stuck my head in there and saw you lying in a daze. Well, I wasted no time. I grabbed a knife from the kitchenette and had the cleaning lady guard the area for me. She was really uneasy about me rescuing you, but I was up for the challenge."

"Why did you do it?" I asked instead of thanking him.

He looked baffled. "You mean, why did I rescue you?" he asked. I nodded. "Because you needed . . . help. You . . . you were battered." He acted as if I asked an absurd question.

"You felt sorry for me?" I concluded bluntly.

"Yes—I mean no—I mean—I, I spared your life, what difference does it make?"

"Because I want to know why you saved me."

"Because . . . because I wanted to." Kevin grew infuriated. "Didn't you want to be rescued?"

"No. I was just fine. I was really content there. I loved 'umm . . . Mr. Ruxton."

Kevin was stunned. "You can't be serious. I asked you if you wanted to be set free and you nodded 'yes'. Are you off your mind?"

"But he loved me."

"He tortured you. He would've eventually murdered you."

"No—no, he beat me when I was bad. But when I was good, he loved me."

"Beat you? He tied you to a bed and whipped you with a belt. For one, that's illegal. Secondly, is that the kinda relationship you find rewarding? Tell me," He let out a little steam.

"So?" I replied. "There's no such thing as love. It's a myth. You're all alike. The only thing all of you male dogs want is a good fuck," I said emphatically.

"What are you trying to say—I rescued you because I want to rape you?" Kevin shook his head trying to understand my twisted logic.

"Well, isn't that what I'm here for?"

"No," he raised his voice. "Your assumptions aren't even close." He waved his hands. "For one, I'm not a pimp. I'm just a nice guy trying to make this world a better place. In fact, the only thoughts that entered my mind when I saw your wrists tied in that dark stuffy room was that you were helpless and I thought I could save you. I wanted to give you a second chance. I had no desire to jump your bones or anything of the sort," he insisted.

"You mean you don't want me to work for you? And I'm not obligated to you in any way to repay you for this?" I didn't believe him.

"Yes, Cinderella. I think you're leveling. You understand where I'm coming from?"

I pulled off my pajama top just to test him, legs wide open. "What are you waiting for?"

Kevin shook his head in disbelief. "Look, I think you have a great body, but right now I'd just like to get to know you, okay. Is that alright with you?"

"Why?" I asked.

"'Cause . . . I can use the company. I get lonely. I mean you can leave whenever you wish, but I'd like you to stick around for a while. It's a nice place and I won't charge you rent. Besides, I think you'll be safe here," he asserted with a smile.

I returned a smile without an answer. *I guess I could give him a chance to prove himself.* As soon as I tried to get up, he held me back down. "The doctor said you need to relax," he cautioned.

"What doctor?"

"I took you to the emergency room at Central Hospital. You were really bad off. Malnourished and dehydrated with lots of sores. By the way, the doc asked questions about you that I couldn't answer. He wanted to contact your parents, but I told him I didn't know you. So please introduce yourself. What's your name and where are you from?"

"Denise Bower. I'm originally from Philley County," I answered.

"Really? That's about a two-hour drive?" he estimated. "What brings you here?" Kevin wondered.

I had to think up a story. "A college buddy of mine got a good deal out here so I moved away from home and roomed with her. Then I got kidnapped." I steered clear from the truth, thinking that this gracious stranger would disapprove of me if he knew the truth. "Can I ask you a question?" I studied his brown eyes with doubt.

He said, "Sure."

"Are you clean?" I asked. "I take showers."

"No, I mean lawfully. Had you ever done anything wrong?"

"Shit yeah. I earned dozens of speeding tickets, got busted once for a bar fight, and evicted for not paying rent."

"That's cool but did you ever get trashed?"

"Trashed?" he asked.

"Strung-out?" I reiterated.

"Strung-out?" he was merely repeating my words at this point.

"High. Did you ever get high?" I searched for a word he would hopefully understand in his sheltered language.

He shook his head as he still wasn't following.

"Never mind." I could tell I was treading in uncharted territory. I guess he was a farmer boy.

"No really, I want to know."

"It's not important."

"Yes, it is. Please tell me."

"Okay. Have you ever tried illegal substances, ya know, like pot or coke?"

"Oh, I steer clear from that. I tried marijuana once in grade school but other than that I'm clean. You don't have to worry about any of that. I don't do drugs or smoke, and I'm not an alcoholic. I've never committed a crime or hurt anyone. I really do have a good record," he reassured me, as if he was trying to impress a blind date. He didn't get it. I was afraid he and I were completely incompatible for each other. "You want some lemonade?" he offered as he was about to prepare himself seconds.

"No, but I'll take a can of beer," I hinted at him.

He expressed regretfully, "Sorry, I just threw out the last one." Little did he know that I was under the drinking age. He returned to the bedside with more lemonade. "Listen, umm, you think you'll be alright alone for a few hours? 'Cause I gotta go into work tonight and I'd like you to hold down the fort for me, okay."

I was in shock. "How could you go back there after you swindled Mr. Ruxton?"

"It's my job, Denise. I'm not scared of him."

It took less than ten minutes after he left for me to get into trouble. Out of boredom, I explored the apartment, looking for paraphernalia. Of all Kevin's possessions that would define him, I thought I'd find the all-too-familiar Playboy magazines, handcuffs, condoms, and centerfold posters mounted on the walls. But I found nothing of the sort. He was into books, maps, and money. He was a simple guy—not home much. In fact, it appeared that he was never at any one place for very long. But what about a sex life? There were no photographs on his dresser, not a hint of sexual interest in the whole apartment. Now what kind of guy leaves no mark of sexual appetite lying around his habitat? He sure didn't act gay.

I found a whole lot of cash stashed away in his kitchen cookie jar under prepackaged, individually wrapped cookies. Not a smart idea. I shoved the paper money into my bra. I could always use it for a quick get-away.

Kevin returned sooner than expected, cussing as he threw his jacket onto the sofa. "Something wrong?" I asked, scratching at my bra.

"I've been fired," he grunted. "Somehow they traced me. The boss yelled at me for meddling in Mr. Ruxton's business. Ruxton hassled the bar manager to give information on my whereabouts. He threatened he would hound me down and reclaim his lover. You were right. I shouldn't have returned to work so soon."

"So, what are we going to do now?" I asked, feeling guilty about stealing his cookie jar money.

The phone was in his hand. He dialed. "We'll need police protection."

I grabbed the phone from him. "Don't," I pleaded. "The cops won't do a thing, trust me. You like to travel, don't you?"

Kevin eyeballed me as if I were up to something. "Why?" he asked, baffled.

"We have to leave town. It's the only safe thing to do," I insisted.

"Run away?" he raised his eyebrows curiously as if he was sincerely considering the option. "To where?"

"To . . . ah . . . to Philley County. They'll never find us there."
"Where you used to live, huh? Can I get a quick job there?"

"I'm sure there are possibilities," I encouraged.

"Okay, but I still think I should contact the police to put Mr. Ruxton on the record."

"N—no. They have better things to do than to worry about our petty problems. Their priorities are homicides and genocides," I discouraged.

The receiver slipped from his hand back onto the hook. I let out a deep sigh of relief. Kevin gazed into my eyes with incredible suspicion but said nothing. He saw fear in my eyes but made no attempt to question it. "You know how to get to Philley from here?" he said after staring at me for some time.

I thought about it. I remembered taking off with Richard's car in the early morning, straying off course, but I didn't remember the name of the highways I took. "You have travel maps, don't you?" I intimated.

YOU CAN LEAVE FOWLERSVILLE
BUT FOWLERSVILLE CAN'T LEAVE YOU

We had no time to spare. Kevin and I packed the luggage bags as fast as we could. There was no way of knowing how long it would take Mr. Ruxton to track down Kevin's address and be on his way with his army and weapons. Both of our lives were in grave danger. After waiting at the bus stop for a good half hour, we caught a bus headed north. Unfortunately, the bus was packed. Only a few scattered seats remained. Kevin squeezed himself beside a little old lady and I had to walk all the way to the back of the bus and settle for the cramped space next to two young black dudes. After being in captivity, I didn't feel too comfortable in their company. For a while the ride was quiet. They ignored me and I ignored them.

I daydreamed about my old fair-weather friend, Nina, and how I suffered under her wings. *If I wouldn't have involved myself with her company, none of my misfortunes would have happened,* I reasoned. Tears of mixed emotions watered my eyes. I sighed. *Well, look at the bright side: I saved her baby from being sold. Would Nina have rewarded me for my defiance?* I asked myself. *It doesn't much matter now, does it?* I smiled contentedly. *I finally have my freedom. That's more than she would ever offer.*

The dudes looked over at me, noticing the luggage bag on the floor between my legs. "Vacationing?" the slim next to me asked.

"You could say that." I answered briefly, wishing he would mind his own business.

"Where ya headed?" he continued to flirt.

"Uh . . . to a resort," I fibbed.

"Ooh, which one?"

"Ah, one of the Rockies," I answered curtly. I had mastered the art of skillful lying.

"It must be nice to be able to travel a lot, ain't it?" he remarked, implying that I must be rich because I'm white.

"I . . . I only do it once a year." I wanted to convince him of my frugality.

"Shoo, on my job I can't take no time off for no reason, not even sick days," the kid griped.

The two dudes whispered back and forth to one another, then shook hands on agreement.

I felt uncomfortable. The large-framed muscular dude by the window seat tried to place me. "You look familiar." He paused. "I know I seen you somewheres before."

"Well, there are many look-a-likes," I rejected.

He insisted, "No, I seen you before." After placing me, he snapped his fingers, "Yeah, you used to work the block on Ripple Street. You a hustler?" he boldly asked.

My face turned red with chagrin. *Would it ever be possible to run away from that world?* I wanted to find another seat, but the bus was loaded with standing passengers. "Yes, I used to do that stuff but not anymore," I corrected.

"Yeah, you associated with that Latino kid, umm . . . Shawn, right?" he continued stirring up the issue. There was no hope in getting my point across. I again tried to ignore them. He whispered to me, lowering his head, "You still do weed, don't ya?"

His partner asked, chuckling, "You still fuck for a fee?"

I said indignantly, "Leave me alone. I'm not a part of any of that anymore, okay?"

The guy sitting by the window opened his leather jacket. I thought he was going to draw a gun when something more interesting caught my attention. A packet of weed stuck out from his inner pocket. The dudes now had my full, undivided attention. "Is it pure?" I gazed at it.

"Pure as the plant itself," Slim winked.

The window guy made an offer, "I'll sell it to ya for forty bucks. And it's worth every cent."

"No additives?" I wondered.

"I said pure as the plant, lady," Slim got impatient.

The window guy added passionately, "Makes ya so horny, you'll want'a fuck all night long."

"You got forty bucks on ya, right?" his partner asked skeptically. "Cuz the price is non- negotiable."

"I only have a twenty," I expressed regretfully.

"I'll cut a deal with ya. I'll sell ya half." It was a deal. I took the twenty out from my bra, right in front of them. The dude split the weed in half and stuffed the broken pieces into another plastic baggie. The exchange was made. I quickly stashed the little packet into my pocket.

The dealer teased, "A hard habit to break, huh?"

Fortunately, the bus made a stop, and the two dudes got off. Kevin and I were finally seated together. But after what I had just done with the money I stole from Kevin, I fell short for words. We sat in silence for some time, then Kevin placed his hand on mine and smiled. "We'll be there in about 20 minutes," he assured. I couldn't smile back for I felt so ashamed of myself. It was as if I had cheated on him. I guess I was starting to get attached to him whether I intended to or not. Silent tears of anger and confusion rolled down my cheek. I really needed to tell him about myself, but I just couldn't. I was too afraid he'd dump me. I felt a deep sense of relief when we passed the "Welcome to Philley County" sign. Funny how I ran away from this town hoping to find happiness elsewhere only to return homesick. I had hopes of making a new beginning for us as a couple. He saw me grin. "Think we'll be safe here?" he asked.

I nodded. "I'll never go to Fowlersville again," I assured him.

Philley County was very provincial compared to urban Fowlersville. For the first time in a long time, I saw greenery everywhere. Trees and valleys lined the bus trail. I inhaled the fresh spring aroma of pine and cut grass, walked the crime-free streets, and unwound from the commotion of the long, tedious trip.

For a few days, we slept at an inn not far from the bus line. It was a temporary stay so Kevin could search for a job and further establish himself in the new community. I would also have to find work to help him out, but for now Kevin felt I deserved a vacation. He wanted me to relax.

Reflecting back, I found it to be nearly incomprehensible how Kevin could make such a huge sacrifice for a young woman he had just met by saving her, then moving out of town on impulse. Though I tried to deny a fluttering heart, I was falling in love, again.

One week later, Kevin accepted an offer at a service station. Though he would have to work some nights and weekends, he was grateful to find a local job that did not require transportation to work. We settled in a terrace apartment near the metro line. Things were looking up.

At night I cuddled up beside Kevin under cozy satin sheets, resting my head on his warm hairy chest with his arms tucked under me. Since he'd come home exhausted from a hard day of work, I wanted to massage his back. While trying to please him, I gazed into his tired eyes, but something wasn't right. He didn't respond to me. I kissed him on the lips only to have him turn aside. "Would you just sit still and listen to me." He was annoyed by my distractions. He was trying to tell me everything that happened at the station that day. I thought he'd want me to comfort him. Any other guy would have yearned for it. Confused by his discontent, I backed off. After he had nothing more to say, I resumed, massaging him, wishing for feedback.

"That's enough, okay." He pushed me away.

"Why?"

"Why what?"

"Why aren't you interested in me?" I asked bluntly.

"I'm just not in the mood," he raised his voice as if irritated by my bringing up the issue.

"So, I'll put you in the mood." I tried his patience, rubbing my finger along the curve of his lips and tickling his ears with my tongue.

"You really know how to turn a man on, don't cha?" he sighed.

I was gratified that I was finally arousing his interest. After massaging him for some time, my fingers gently caressed his genitalia, "You bet," I said with finesse. I fondled his erection. He moaned as I applied pressure on his soft spots. Oddly, he restrained his male desire for some reason. He pushed me away again.

"What's wrong?" I demanded.

"I can't. Not now anyway."

"Why not?" I asked exasperatedly.

"Denise, you've been raped. God knows what kind of diseases those filthy dogs had," Kevin finally expressed his concern.

"What are you trying to say, that I'm diseased?" I was outraged.

"Well don't you think we should know?" he suggested.

"I thought you told me you had already taken me to the hospital and the doc checked me over."

"Yes, but they didn't take a blood test. You could be infected."

"I'll call the hospital first thing tomorrow morning. For now, we'll use a condom," I winked.

Kevin disagreed, "No Denise. Just in case something should go wrong, we best be on the safe side, don't you think?"

"No, nothing'll go wrong. I can't believe you're so . . . so neurotic over this. You're ridiculous." I shook my head in disbelief. "Why don't you just be forthcoming and tell me the truth, that you're not attracted to me."

"You know that's not true."

"I've known you for two weeks now and you haven't shown any desire for me at all."

"I assure you I'm very attracted to you. I just want to play it safe."

I tried to read his mind. "I know what you want. You want to play rough, don't you," I snickered. "You like S&M." I practically tore my nightgown open, flashing my chest. I grabbed his dick in a hurried fashion. He protested, pushing me off, again. I resisted. I tried to hold him down. We ended up wrestling. He got out of bed and left the bedroom without a word. I chased after him but once he shut the front door, he disappeared.

"Why are you treating me this way?" I cried, banged, and kicked at the innocent wall partition in angry frustration. He didn't mention where or what he was up to. I wasn't sure if he'd return at all. I understood that he wanted me to see a doctor, but why did it bother him so? None of my clients cared if I was safe or not. I mean, gee, I agreed to use a condom. I wouldn't give him anything communicable. He could be lying about being attracted. Why did he have to be so fuckin' safe all the time? Why couldn't he just live a little? I was so frustrated with this relationship I had the urge to hustle to find someone who desired me. Maybe, at heart, I really did belong in Fowlersville.

ADDICTED

High voltage acid rock pulsated through the walls and floor. The vibrations rattled the window blinds. Puckered lips slowly exhaled cannabis fumes. Thick smoke rose, formed in the musty air, then disappeared. In the darkness, rays of moonlight lit the contour around the nipples, against the curve of the thigh and across the knee. The nude legs spread wide open on the carpet. One hand inside the panties wildly stroked the clit while the other wedged a burnt cigarette butt between the fingers.

My imaginary lover mounted me, indulging in his own ecstasy. The moans were inaudible. I was stoned out of my mind, wasted from the weed I purchased on the bus. As pleasure released, the bedroom rocked back and forth in sync with the heavy jolting beat of the music. Vivid! Colors glowed in the darkness. Deep orange, passionate red, and metallic purple made me so horny, I rolled off the bed onto the floor, thrusting my imaginary lover. Oh God . . . I'm cumming . . .

The bedroom light flicked on! Kevin stormed in complaining about the noise. He turned off the stereo. Bad timing on my part, when I'm in the middle of an orgasm. He took his jacket off, babbling something about a receipt. Apparently, he just got back from the grocery store. He asked me a question, but I didn't respond. It came to his attention that I was masturbating on the floor, completely undressed. "Is something wrong, Denise?"

"Juss fine." I sluggishly smiled. "Oh baby, I want you bad." I gawked up at him with glazed-over eyes trying to focus in on the features of his blurry face.

It didn't take long before Kevin spotted the brownish-yellow particles scattered about the mattress and floor. He snatched the rolled cigarette from my locked fingers, sniffed the substance, then raised his voice. "Is this marijuana?" he suspected.

"Aw! C'mon babe, join me. I'm surfin' for ya."

"Where did you get this?" he insisted, standing over me. "Tell me. I didn't know you had a drug problem. Where did you get the money for this crap? From me? Because forty bucks have been missing for some time, but I thought I misplaced it. You had no cash on you when I rescued you. Good Jesus, I wish I had known this before!" He shook his head in disbelief then sat himself down on the mattress, watching me strung-out. He hid his face with his hands as if he was about to cry but pulled himself together.

"I wanna fuck ya," I whined.

Kevin insisted, "You need help—major help. I told you to see a doctor."

I rambled on, not hearing a word he spoke, "But I can suck your dick so hard I can make you want to cum all over me and I can eat you over and over and have you thrust in me . . ."

"Denise!" Kevin shouted, trying to get my attention.

I carried on, "I can kiss your willy till ya thrust them in my mouth and make me ooze . . ."

He shook me. "Denise, don't you hear me?"

But I continued on like a broken record, "And I'll make your dick thrust harder in my cunt and then up my ass and I'll swallow your cum and . . ."

Kevin left the room abruptly. When he returned, he splashed my face with a mug of ice water, shocking me out of my trance. I began to cry. "Well, c'mon, what are you waiting for? Beat me! Slap me across the face, kick me hard in the stomach, punch me in the stomach, bruise and bang me up, blacken my eyes, make me blue and bloody. You've got me cornered. I can't escape. Here's your chance," I provoked, surrendering my soul to him.

Kevin was utterly perplexed by my behavior. "Why should I?" he mumbled, unsure of what to say.

"Because I deserve it. You have to punish me. Don't you see, I'm bad. I'm a really bad person. I'm possessed by Satan. You must beat the evil out of me and teach me a lesson. You can't let me get away with this. You better hurt me before I get badder and hurt you," I babbled on in my psychotic episode.

Kevin sneered at me. "You're sick. You know that. You're really sick. You need some kinda therapy. I'm going to make an appointment with a clinical psychiatrist. You definitely need help."

"Why won't you hurt me?" I urged, "You don't love me." I couldn't understand why Kevin wanted to help me. It just didn't add up.

HEART TO HEART

Kevin was resting beside me when I awoke in the late morning with a pounding headache. He affixed an ice pack on my forehead. "I was really concerned about you last night." He paused. "I had no idea you were hooked on . . ." He sighed, "Dope. Are there any other secrets I should know about?" He fell silent, lowering his head in sadness. "This relationship isn't starting off on the right foot."

"You hate me, don't you?" I presumed. I knew he wanted to leave me and that was what he was leading up to. I screwed up majorly.

"I don't hate you," he comforted. "But I think you have a sickness, and you need help."

"I'm not sick. I just wanted to make love to you last night and you refused me, making me feel inferior. You're sick, not me. Are you impotent or something?"

"No." He laughed at the thought. "Like I said before, I'll feel more comfortable when you get the results from your checkup." His eyes bobbed over my drawn blood-shot eyes. "Tell me, how long have you had a drug problem?"

"It's not a problem," I defended. "Just because you don't use doesn't make it a problem. In fact, it's quite therapeutic, for your information."

"Denise, it's illegal and it's making you erratic." He sighed again, searching for the right words. "I'd understand if you're having a hard time coping with what happened to you, but is there some other problem you're not confronting me with? You need to open your heart to me. That's the only way I can help."

I attacked him. "What are you, some kinda shrink?"

"No, a shrink wouldn't care about you the way I do."

"You don't fool me. You don't even know me. And you don't care. In fact, I don't know why you ever bothered to rescue me in the first place. Did my nude body send off some kinda sweet aroma that drew your pheromones to me or are you my keeper? Because you act like you're not attracted to me, I'd say you're my keeper."

"Don't give me your flack. You desperately wanted me to save you. As I told you before, I asked you at the time if you were held against your will and you said 'yes.' Did you want to retract for spite because I caught you on dope?"

I lowered my head and mumbled, "Yes," admitting he was right.

"Well, I can't let you do that to yourself. But I can help you if you let me," he reasoned.

"I don't want help," I resisted in tears.

"Do you want to die? Because that's exactly where you're headed." He held my chin rigidly to hold my attention. "Talk to me Denise, don't bury your dark secrets."

"Can't you just leave me alone and find someone else more your type? You have no need for me. I'm just burning your fuel. Spare me the grief and dump me now, while it's still early," I mourned.

"You want me to leave you so you can turn back to your goddamn pimp?" he yelled.

I was flabbergasted. "So that's what this is all about? You knew about it all along, didn't you?"

He looked away as he just had a slip of the tongue, giving away his secret knowledge that kept us apart. "Mr. Ruxton told me at the bar. He bragged about capturing a hooker." He cleared his throat, changing the topic. "I just want to be safe. I mean, suppose I was sleeping with a different woman each night? Try to see it from my perspective. Look, I just want to get to know you first and you're not giving me the chance."

"So why did you bother to save me if you knew I was a hooker?" I reverted back to his earlier statement.

"I didn't see you as a hooker, I saw you as a . . . a victim."

"A victim? What are you, some kinda saint who comes out of nowhere and takes me away from my daily humiliation then sexually deprives me? What are you saving me from, pleasure? 'Cause pleasure is the only thing keeping me alive. I need it."

"Denise, you can't be serious."

"What do you want from me anyway?" I raised my voice to him in frustration.

"I want a genuine relationship with you. Not a fling or a casual affair. A true, caring, trusting closeness. I want us to be open with one another about everything," he described his ideals.

"I'm sorry, I don't think I can handle that," I expressed regretfully.

"You'll just have to learn to communicate. You're no coward, are you? And I think you like me as much as I like you and you want to make this work," he stated confidently.

"You don't fool me," I sneered him down. "I know your type all too well. You're all backstabbers. Cold-hearted backstabbers. I came miles to avoid Mr. Ruxton only to regret it. Okay, you want me to share my thoughts with you? I've had thoughts of starting my own call girl business."

I saw tears forming in Kevin's sad little-boy eyes. We both broke out in tears together. Kevin held my hand. "You really have been hurt, haven't you?" He cleared his throat, offering me a tissue. "You're too afraid to seek help, aren't you? You're afraid of the world."

I nodded. "You can tell?"

He drew closer to me, hugging me tight. "Sure, I can relate. I've had my disappointments and letdowns too. It's all in the eyes, ya know. I saw fear in your eyes at the first glance. Now it's just surfacing. It's time to heal." He kissed me.

"You don't hate me?" I asked, sniffling.

"Only if you hate me." A teardrop dribbled from his eye.

I sobbed, "I don't hate you. Just please promise me you won't ever leave me."

"I promise, not only will I never leave you, but I'll always be there for you if you promise me, you will never close yourself off from me or cheat on me. You must try to confide in me—be honest and open with me. Is it a deal?"

"Oh gosh that's hard. I don't think I have enough strength to do that. It's too painful. I'd rather wither away," I hyperventilated in tears.

Kevin rubbed my back as we swayed back and forth in our tight embrace. He lowered his voice to a whisper as he looked me in the eyes, "It takes courage. And I know you have courage. I can see it in your eyes. You have withstood the test of time. I think you're ready. You just don't know it yet."

"And what if I fall apart and lose everything?"

"I think you already lost everything. Now you have to claim it all back." We held each other so tight—wouldn't let go. "Let's just start with the present. You need to tell me everything, as far as you can remember, okay." He repeated, "But you must be honest."

I rested my head on his lap. He not only promised me that he would not judge me in any way or report me to the police but that anything I'd tell him would be confidential, only between him and me. He reassured me he would only send me to a shrink if I would willingly go. I confessed to him my experiences during prostitution. I explained the correlation behind Nina and her pimp and why Mr. Ruxton kidnapped me. I prided myself for making up a false story regarding the whereabouts of baby Tia and paid respects to Shirell for saving my life when I was forced into CHASE FUME. I also mentioned the nightmarish experiences I endured with Brad and my escape from the confines of the Bower's cellar.

"Wow!" he exclaimed at the remarkable stories.

"See. I'm a criminal, Kevin. I broke the law. I even murdered."

Kevin argued, "You didn't do it intentionally. You told me Brad drugged you. If it makes you feel any better, I probably would have done the same if I was in your shoes."

Looking back at it all, I insisted, "Everything just happened, as if it was an accident waiting to happen. I swear I didn't do anything to provoke any of it."

"Well now that we're together and safe in your hometown, you should try to patch things up. You can start with your parents, improve things at home," he suggested.

"No Kevin, they hate me. I never want to show my face there again."

"Don't worry, I'll be here for you. I promise I won't let you down, but you must promise to face your problems and deal with them, remember?"

I refused, "I can't. It's too scary." I wanted to avoid Kevin so that he wouldn't force me to relive that hell, but I knew he was right.

"Don't you think they're worried about you?"

"No. I don't think they even care. Mr. Bower was very abusive, Kevin. In fact, I don't even care to talk about this again," I struggled off his lap bolting away from him.

Kevin followed me into the bathroom. I saw his reflection in the mirror as I blew my nose on a tissue. He placed his arms around me, kissing me tenderly on the forehead. He said as he rested his chin on my shoulder, "Could you tell a doctor your deepest and darkest fears if I held your hand? Could you trust me to let it all go in my presence?"

My swollen red eyes met with his in the mirrored reflection. "You won't give up, will you?" I rubbed my worn cheeks against his firm embrace.

"Can't hurt to try," Kevin persuaded. "What have you got to lose?"

"I guess." I cleared my throat. My heart wanted Kevin, but my head only wanted sex and dope.

DR HAMILTON

Dr. Hamilton was an acclaimed and prominent hypnotist, psychotherapist, and psychiatrist with an excellent track record. Notice how they inserted the word "psychiatrist" at the end of the title. With the attitude I had toward shrinks, I was almost reluctant to cooperate.

I sat with my legs crossed and a cigarette dangling from my forefingers in the rather cozy doctor's office. Though I behaved like I didn't give a shit, I was just a bit nervous about seeing a shrink for the first time. Kevin sat beside me, holding my hand, as promised. Dr. Hamilton was of Middle Eastern descent. The little man with the bifocals resting on his nose and a receding hairline must have been in his late fifties. The soft-spoken man was perceptive and crudely to-the-point. He had his notepad ready to go under his thumb. "Ah, Denise Bower, right?" he began the session.

"Yeah," I answered with disinterest.

"And ah, Kevin O'Connor?" The doctor glanced over at him through his bifocals.

"Yes sir," Kevin confirmed.

Dr. Hamilton reclined against his right shoulder in his old squeaky armchair. "What seems to be the problem?"

Kevin began, "Dr. Hamilton, sir," he addressed, trying to present the issue at hand without offending me. "The story I'm about to tell you may seem hard to digest but about a week ago I rescued this lovely young lady who was kidnapped into bondage by a pimp. She was involved in a prostitution ring, as I explained to you over the phone. But last night I caught her using pot. She's hooked on dope. We're here because she needs to come to terms with her tragedy and her drug habit so that we can have a normal and healthy relationship. I was hoping you could help her," he asserted as if on a witness stand before jury.

The doctor briefed over the script. "Yes, you did explain everything I have noted here." He confirmed then turned his attention to me. He folded his hands, patiently smiling. "Denise, would you care to add . . .?"

"Not really," I grunted, interrupting him.

Dr. Hamilton, still smiling graciously, commented, "Ms. Bower, you don't take a liking to me, do you? If I'm correct, I cannot help you. But I do like you. I like all my patients. I believe in each, and every one of them, that they can heal and lead a happier life. I also have faith in you. I hope you will think it over and give me a chance to get to know you better," he simpered.

"I don't got no bad feelings about you," I assured him. "It ain't nothin' personal."

"Well, I'm glad to hear that. So then tell me what's on your mind." He sustained his grin.

"I just don't like shrinks." I glanced over at Kevin. "My boyfriend wants me to talk to my parents but there's no way," I made clear, shaking my head.

"I see." The doctor played with his pen, tapping it against the table, pondering. "Can we discuss your parents for a moment? What have you got against them?"

I whispered to Kevin, "I'm really not comfortable with this. Can we leave now?" He caressed my hand as if to say *hang in there.*

"Denise," Dr. Hamilton tried for my attention, "are you afraid of your parents?" He searched my eyes for answers. I did not reply. "Did they ever hurt you?" He paused. "What did they do that was so bad? Didn't they love you?" He restated and reiterated, prying for a response.

I snapped at the doctor, "I see you like to read minds, Doc. Very impressive. Then you know that I'm not worthy of anything to them. They're simply rotten parents."

"Did they abandon you? Were they abusive to you?" he continued to stir.

"Yes." The flashbacks surfaced.

"Physically or emotionally?"

"Both," I declared in a huff.

"Very good," the doctor praised. "Now tell me, is it true that you have a drug habit?"

I nodded almost proudly.

"Why did you turn to drugs? What are you suppressing, Denise?" Dr. Hamilton tried to probe into my psyche.

I didn't know why. I knew that there was once a reason, but I couldn't remember. "My friends told me it would make me feel better. And it does. It makes me feel . . . it just makes life more peaceful, the way it used to be."

"If it used to be a good life, when did it change for you?" Dr. Hamilton asked, itching his stubbly chin with undivided attention.

I was stumped by his question. I didn't know. I forgot. I closed my eyes, glimpsing into the far reaches of my inner soul, then I felt like trembling. "I think it happened when I got out of bed one morning. It was a really strange experience. I was just totally different." I paused, preoccupied in deep thought, trying to remember things so vague in the vast past. Once my eyes opened, I felt so naked and vulnerable.

After moments of silence, Dr. Hamilton cleared his throat. "Tell me Denise, do your parents approve of your friends?" The doctor didn't give much credence to my words. But I knew that what I just described was the heart of my problem. I couldn't relax after that. I didn't know what to do with my hands. I wanted to light another cigarette. Dr. Hamilton asked several more questions that went right over my head.

The doctor concluded after the hour was over that my peers had much to do with all this mess I was in. Hamilton reviewed his notes, "Apparently the relationship you had with your parents lowered your self-esteem and subjected you to negative peer influences. I'm going to prescribe a medication to help you relax and hopefully break your addiction to the substance abuse. With your permission, I'd like to have a consultation with your parents to discuss your situation with them. However, in no way will I coerce you to see your parents." He clapped his hands together. "First, I'm going to treat you for your addiction so you can think more clearly. Then, when you're ready, I'll arrange further sessions to discuss the issue regarding your dysfunctional family unit." The doctor jotted down the prescription then handed the slip to me. "Take this antidepressant, Tromitan, once a day. Ask the pharmacist only for the brand name—no generics, understand. And please remember: no alcohol. The two don't mix," he cautioned. "Good luck!" He winked.

I left Dr. Hamilton's office feeling a bit more at ease because he assured me that he wouldn't pressure me into doing anything I didn't feel comfortable with.

At the bus stop, Kevin asked me how I felt. I wasn't sure. He patted me on the back and said, "The doctor has faith in you, and I do too. You'll pull through. But I want you to cooperate with him, okay."

It all sounded good and well, but Kevin still refused to have sex with me until I consulted with the practitioner at the hospital I was discharged from. He was so set about it, too. I was earnestly afraid that the test results would show positive that I was pregnant with Mr. Ruxton's baby or with some weird disease such as an STD. But if I didn't follow up with the test results, it would be the next topic of discussion at Hamilton's office for sure. I shouldn't have had to tolerate Kevin's bullshit anymore. I'd get the virgin drunk if I had to.

3RD CONFRONTATION

My lazy ass was melted into the couch. For countless hours I watched soap operas while polluting the air with nicotine joints. Restlessly, I wobbled a can of Budweiser between my legs, shifting the fizz about. My mind drifted to Dr. Hamilton. Stumped by his question, "If it used be a good life, when did it change for you?" his voice echoed in my mind. "I think it happened when I got out of bed one morning. It was a really strange experience. I was just totally different." Why did I say that? Did I have a hangover or was I trashed? I remembered Mr. Bower found Ecstasy in my bedroom then beat me for being in possession. I never felt as lost and disoriented as I did that morning.

Dr. Hamilton wanted to make arrangements to meet with my folks to discuss my situation. Kevin and Hamilton suggested I try to work things out with Ray Bower. How could I explain that I'd had explicit sexual nightmares of Mr. Bower raping me in bed, not to mention the occasions he tried to drown me. Why shouldn't I look forward to the old folks? I chuckled.

The craving for dope hit me, but I had no spare cash on hand. I reached into my pocket for some goodies, but all that I came up with was that stupid prescription, Tromitan. Curiously, I opened the pill bottle. The tablets were tiny enough to be swallowed without a problem. I placed one tablet on my tongue. It tasted like candy. It slid down my throat with a sip of beer.

Easy. I waited for a reaction, but nothing happened. *Ah shit, just a fuckin' sugar pill.* I popped another in my mouth. Still nothing. *It's a placebo, man. Doc's a quack. A typical fuckin' shrink.* I continued to pop tablets in my mouth one after another as if it were a box of candy.

Antidepressant, I laughed. *Who's foolin' who.* After swallowing a few, I had satisfied my sweet tooth.

I felt woozy. *Uh-oh! Maybe it is . . . I just OD'd on Tromitan. Can it kill me?* Emergency! The moment I got up from the couch, my head felt like a brick.

I thought I heard someone call my name. I was sure Kevin wasn't home from work this soon. The voice was so faint I could have mistaken it for the television. To be sure, I tapped the tube off with the remote.

"Denise." I hear the distant call.

"Yes," I answer, searching in all directions.

"Jes . . ." the voice pronounces.

"Who's there?" I ask, surveying the room, looking inside closets and outside the windows. Is someone in the apartment with me? Where?

"Jes . . ." the voice echoes.

I can't make out the whisper. I'm getting paranoid. I'm convinced that someone is haunting me. Should I call the cops? I grab a butcher knife from the kitchen cupboard. "Where are you?" I threaten.

"Jessy," the voice pronounces a name.

I race from room to room with ammunition in my fist, ready to strike anything moving. I am the terminator.

"Jessica," the voice articulates.

I tremble, frozen in place, in a trance, remembering my long-forgotten self—my evil imposter. I surrender the knife to the floor, conceding that this voice I hear is, in fact, inside my head. Buried deep within my subconscious, lies the soft-spoken vocals of none other than Jessica Wheaton. Just as I shed a tear, a high-pitched noise pierces through my eardrums. "Don't you remember me?" the vexing voice screeches in a distorted echo chamber. Why? I ask myself. Why has she come back to haunt me? Why couldn't she just put it to rest?

It's as if a force sucked all the dreadful memories right out of my head only to zap it back when off guard. All the evils of my past flash before me at once: Father beats me then pushes me down the staircase, Richard restrains me on the mattress, forcing his way in me, falling through a bottomless pit, wrestling with Sugar over drugs, Mr. Ruxton attacks me with his cigarette butt . . . "NO!" I cry, trying to shut out the deafening echoes with hands over ears.

It worsens, penetrating the fiber of my every nerve. "Don't you remember me?" I'm possessed with the urge to mutilate myself. I want to rip the hair out of my head until I'm bald. My nails tear into my scalp to relieve the pressure. Oddly, there isn't one trace of blood on my fingers, only . . . soil? I examine the area around the mutilated scalp and—indeed, it's soil. My body has become nothing more than . . . earth?

Suddenly, my arms and legs become as stiff as wood! I'm afraid to move, that my fragile joints might snap like a branch. I'm scared—really scared. I don't know what's happening to me. One-by-one, my limbs turn to dirt and blow away! I'm returning to earth! I am dirt! I've become what I feel. The dirt crumbles. I collapse to the floor shapelessly.

Unveiled under the mass of dirt is my imposter!

My body reappears like a magician's trick, standing, facing her. She informs me she has returned to finish me off for good. If she truly wished to accomplish this, she'd be better off to stay in hiding, allowing me to believe that I'm my own worst enemy. But the question begs, why did she wait so long for this moment? She says she heard my death wish and is eager to assist me in my destruction. Most thoughtful of her. I had no clue she's been watching over me all along, waiting for me to overdose on medication. I guess I have a change of heart after seeing Jessica face to face. I won't give her the satisfaction of my destruction after all she's done to me. Now that she's come out of hiding, I have the opportunity to make her burn in hell!

We wrestle neck-at-neck, strangling, scratching and tearing at each other, endlessly. I can't defeat her for we are equal in strength and hatred. After much fighting, it becomes clear that neither of us can be destroyed. My only option is to run. I give her a swift punch to the eye, leaving her momentarily down. I lock myself in the bedroom, praying that Kevin will be home very soon to rescue me. I don't know how much longer I can hold out. As I turn around to catch my breath, I'm startled to find her standing in the bedroom with me. I slowly back away, carefully watching her every move.

"Leave me alone!" I demand with courage. She just stands there. Doesn't move an inch. Suddenly the lamp from the night table falls to the floor beside me! I dodge it! She telepathically caused the lamp to topple over. She transforms into Denise Bower. It's so eerie to be looking at my clone, and at the same time, a mirror image of my reflection as Denise.

"What's wrong?" she snickers with open arms, smiling innocently, standing pretty in a floral dress. Denise is now an eight-year-old child. I can't begin to fathom why she chose to disguise herself as a little girl. Though she is inherently evil, she seems so adorable. She

folds her hands behind her back. "Can I have a Tootsie Roll?" she asks politely, spoken like a little sister would, tilting her head from side to side, pleading, "Please." I'm aware that this is some sort of trap but don't know what she has in store for me.

"You don't fool me, Jessica," I affirm.

She giggles, "Don't be silly, you're Jessica. Jessica always has goodies in her pockets cause her mummy gives her whatever she wants. C'mon, gimme gimme. I'm hungry." She puts out her little hands, waiting.

I think to myself, so she's jealous. Is that what this is all about? The haves and have nots? You got—I want? I notice my reflection in the mirror. She is right. I'm switched back to Jessica. But I know this is only temporary—just a tease. We've been playing head games much too long. It's time to stop. "Switch me back!" I demand.

"What? I thought you wanted to be Jessica. Now make up your mind."

"What's it to you what I want? I hate you and you hate me. The rest is games— tricks on the mind, isn't it?"

The little girl pouts, "Jessica, why are you mad at me? I don't hate you."

"You don't fool me. What did you do to Stephanie? Did you play games on her too? And how long do you intend to play your little games? Look, I have parents who love me, you know. I feel like I've been kidnapped. I want to know what kind of satisfaction you get out of this?"

Denise switches back to a teenager. "I don't know what you're talking about. All I want is a Tootsie Roll and I won't bother you again. Deal's a deal." Again, she extends her palm.

"I know your father sexually abused you. Your secrets are now my secrets. Is that why you did this to me? So, you could pass the pain onto someone else and free yourself of it?"

She lowers her head. I hope I struck a nerve. "I guess I'm the one who's spoiled now, huh. Being you, I've had experiences I never would have dreamt of. Thank you. I live in a beautiful house in the country, sitting up on a hill, with a built-in swimming pool. I have a doggy, good friends, and super parents. It's most gracious of you," she snickers.

"You fuckin' devil. I don't know how you did this to me but you'll pay. You're not getting away with this. If I could, I'd rip you to pieces right now," I grunt in fury, grinding my teeth.

"Oh, stop complaining, you've got Kevin. He's a hunk of a guy," Denise points out, batting her thick eyelashes.

I frown. "Yeah, great. He ain't interested."

"Don't worry about that, you'll corrupt him real soon."

"What?"

"I believe the little girl wanted a Tootsie Roll," she reminds.

"I don't have . . ."

"It's in your pocket. Tootsie Roll and we'll call it a truce. I'll leave you alone."

"I don't believe you."

"Jessica, if we're ever going to reconcile, we're gonna to have to start trusting each other," she insists.

I search my pocket but all I find is a fifty-dollar bill. I look up at her. Another magic trick to fool me. So, what does the money represent? "This ain't no Tootsie Roll," I point out.

She gestures. "Oh, what a shame. I guess you'll have to sacrifice the money instead. That blows your chance to buy more dope," she scorns.

"That's not fair. It was your addiction, not mine," I argue.

"Why would you want to give me the fifty when you can use it to get high?" Denise ignores my accusation.

"Shut up!" I snap.

Denise tests, "How much is a truce worth to you? Can you hand it over or do you need a hit? It's that simple."

I got smart. "I don't think you know what a truce is. You're just like Nina."

"But how would you really know?" She cunningly winks.

The only thing I know for sure is that I'll do almost anything to get rid of her. Besides, what have I to lose? I search her eyes for clues at this vulnerable moment. As she reaches her hand out to mine, her fingers wiggle for the money. My hand shakes with skepticism as I attempt to hand over the bill. I have too much difficulty letting go of it.

Magically, the fifty becomes animated in my hand. Like a little cricket, it hops from hand to hand. Suddenly I hear wicked laughter. A shockwave of electricity zaps through me. I see stars.

THERAPY

He called my name several times but I couldn't respond. My body ached as if I got hit by a mad truck. "Denise?" His hand gently caressed mine. It took some time before I was able to look up at Kevin. He sat beside me on the edge of the bed. I saw the same tender sorrow in his eyes as when he freed me from captivity. I was clearly in a hospital. "How do you feel?" he asked softly. My eyes wandered around the room in quest for answers. "Relax, everything's okay," he assured.

In fear, I searched his eyes. "What am I doing here?"

Kevin's eyes were reddened with tears. "Don't you remember?" He sighed. "You tried to . . . kill yourself. I found you lying on the bedroom floor with a lamp cord wrapped around your neck. You left evidence, Denise. Empty pill bottle and empty beer can. You overdosed on Tromitan. Tried to electrocute yourself. Ya know, the doctor clearly instructed you not to mix alcohol with the medication. Please tell me, why did you do it? You didn't even consider me—that it would hurt me to see you this way. I thought we had agreed to be honest and open with each other. I thought you were smarter than this. What do I have to do to stop you from hurting yourself? Police you? Put you in a straitjacket?" Kevin went on and on.

I was appalled by his story. I didn't remember being in the bedroom, much less overdosing on Tromitan. So why did I hurt myself? Then the flashbacks came to me. I remembered standing face-to-face with her. We wrestled and bickered. The thought of her still haunted me. Oddly, none of it seemed real but it did indeed happen.

"Am I alright?" I asked.

"A few burns but you'll heal," he assured.

I was saddened by it all. "You weren't there for me."

"I wish I was," he expressed regretfully. "I can't be everywhere." There was a moment of silent sadness between us. We both wanted to cry, again, but held the tears back.

Kevin cleared his throat. "Did you have a breakdown?"

"I guess you can call it that," I surmised.

"Dr. Hamilton wants to have you put under hypnosis. He didn't realize how serious your condition is."

"Why?" I asked in outrage.

Kevin relayed, "He thinks you're repressing a lot of stuff. He's hunting for deeper clues to your problem. Look, he's very reputable. I have faith in him."

I didn't like the idea of being placed under psychiatric care but I knew I had no choice now. I also knew I would be compelled to speak the truth no matter how painful it would be.

I sat in Dr. Hamilton's pastel blue office, puffing away on my cigarette as if it were a pacifier. My attitude toward shrinks hadn't changed in the least. I was ready to blame the incident on the prescription.

"Why are you nervous?" Hamilton asked, sitting back in his noisy armchair.

"How do you know I'm nervous?" I was testy.

"You're smoking like it's going out of style."

I tapped the ashes into a tray. "Kevin told me you're going to put me under hypnosis."

"I don't have to. The only thing I need to understand is why you attempted suicide. "The doctor treated my concern respectfully, putting me at ease.

I hastily blew smoke with my eyes closed, slouching in my seat. "I know what happened, but I can't discuss it—it's too weird, okay?"

"Try me," said Hamilton.

"But you won't understand . . ."

The doctor saw fear in my eyes. He brushed his notes aside. "Look Denise," he interrupted, "I know you still don't trust me and there's no reason why you should with the experiences you've had with men. But let's make a deal, alright." He leaned forward, resting his elbows sturdily against the desk, folding his hands while piercing into my eyes. "If you catch me in breach of your confidence in any way, I want you to sue me for every penny I'm worth, deal?" Hamilton stated firmly. "I'm placing my entire career on the line to ensure you the strictest of confidence because I have a hunch that I can help you," Hamilton remarked optimistically. "I prescribed Tromitan for your condition because I knew it would give me the desired results. I didn't plan on you overdosing but that's exactly what you needed to do to release your repressions. The Tromitan, in effect, was your hypnotic."

I felt a sense of relief. "You're not going to put me in drug rehab?"

"Is that what you're afraid of? Dear, you are already in drug rehab. What you see is what you get. One nice cozy little office.

There is no voodoo, magical potions, or witchcraft here. We do things the conventional way," he humored me.

I semi-grinned for the first time in his presence. "Well doc, you're very convincing."

"If I were that good, you'd have no problem telling me what you experienced last night," Hamilton argued.

I thought about it for a while. I decided to test him. "I've been very frustrated with Kevin, lately. He's been denying me sex ever since I met him, ya know. I feel like he really isn't interested in me. I think he wants to change me into someone more his type. I'm just not the pretty schoolgirl he's trying to make me into. He won't give me any pleasure. I haven't had a good fuck in the longest time. Do you know what it's like to be horny and out of practice? My boyfriend says he loves me but he won't dare screw me." I loosened my shirt, showing some cleavage. I was trying to distract the doctor, whereby taking his mind off the issue at hand.

"Is that what bothers you?" the doctor asked with a straight face.

"Wouldn't it bother you, doc?" I asked. He didn't answer. "He thinks I've got some kinda fuckin' disease," I fretted like a little child.

"Would you like me to schedule an appointment with my secretary to have you examined? The results would be kept strictly confidential," the doctor reassured.

I was disappointed that the doctor sided with Kevin. "No doc, you know what I think? I think he's using it as an excuse because he's not attracted to me. I think he's gay." I nodded, blinking my thick mascara-waxed eyelashes wildly, sitting in an alluring posture.

"But don't you think it could be remotely possible that you might be a carrier of a sexually transmitted infection?" Dr. Hamilton wisely used the euphemism "carrier."

"What difference does that make? Men used to fuck me night after night and wouldn't reject me for nothing. If they didn't care and they were payin' for it, why should Kevin care when he'd be getting it for free?" I threw my hands in the air, infuriated.

"Did you use protection?" Dr. Hamilton continued to drill. "Sometimes." I fibbed.

"You could be pregnant."

"Not a chance. Besides, I'm regular."

"Well, I think Kevin is just a little concerned about your welfare."

"But why should he care?"

"I presume he loves you."

I sat back in the chair, contemplating. "That word 'love,' shit man, drives me crazy. I mean what is love anyway?"

Hamilton attempted to explain, "I think he cares deeply for you and wants to see you get better. Don't you have those sort of feelings for him?" the doctor asked. "Don't you care about him?"

"I don't know Doc, I mean I do like him a lot, but I just don't understand that caring part, ya know."

"Let me ask you, Denise, how do you feel about yourself?" Hamilton jotted down some notes, absorbing me thoroughly.

"Well, I'm really good in bed, I mean I got a great figure for that kinda stuff. Guys go for my big boobs and wet pussy, ya know. And I can really make good money doin' that shit . . ."

"But do you like yourself?" Hamilton interrupted to make a point.

"Well Kevin loves me so I must be worthy, I mean he saved my life."

"But do you like yourself?" Hamilton repeated almost rhetorically.

I drew silent, feeling very uncomfortable.

Hamilton changed the subject. "Do you have friends, Denise? I mean girlfriends."

"Yeah. I hadn't seen 'em in a while though." I cleared my throat, hoping that I wouldn't have to answer any more self-esteem questions.

"Have you ever been able to confide in them with a serious problem?"

"Yeah," I thought about Vicki Norris.

"Had they ever helped you?"

I chuckled, "I guess not. They got me hooked on dope in the first place."

"So, they made your problems worse, in other words."

"Yeah, I guess."

"Have you ever turned to Kevin for help?"

"No!" I snapped, "That's why I'm here in the first place. I really don't like the idea of going to a fuckin' shrink, you know."

THERAPY II

The doctor seemed a bit exasperated. He must have felt the conversation was going in circles. He wasn't getting anything concrete out of me. He tore up his notes and started from scratch. "I can understand that. But now that, I presume, you've accepted help, you must open up your darkest side and express yourself to the fullest to benefit from my services. I mean give me 100% of yourself," Hamilton required.

I remained silent. The hour was drawing near, and Hamilton was not getting anywhere.

"I can merely conclude from the little time we have spent together that you have low self-esteem. But that doesn't explain completely why you tried to kill yourself last night. So far you have only vented about being sexually frustrated. Is there anything else you can tell me?" Hamilton paused, tapping his ballpoint pen against a pad of blank paper. "I've got to find out more about you—your inner being," he restated.

My eyes wandered over to the framed painting on the wall behind Hamilton's desk. It was an impressionistic portrait of a young, scared child cradling a puppy in her arms, guarding it as if to fear that someone malicious would take it from her. I identified with her. As I gazed into the painting, I spoke softly, "I heard a voice."

"Voice?" Hamilton raised his eyebrows with intrigue. "Voice from where?"

"From within me. It was calling me by her name."

"Whose name?" Hamilton asked with increased enthusiasm.

"Jessica Wheaton."

"Who's she?"

My eyes followed the contour of the frame, not once looking over at Hamilton. "She's a dream-like phantom who's been haunting me for the longest time. She's possessed by the devil. She won't leave me alone. She's the root of all my problems. She stole my identity and tried to destroy me with hers. But I know who I really am, and I must never forget it."

"Who are you really?"

I looked Hamilton straight in the eyes. "I'm the real Jessica Wheaton trapped in Denise Bower's body."

The doctor had a lump in his throat. Maybe I'd said too much. I waited for a reaction. He cleared his throat then continued on, as if unsurprised. He must have thought I was a real head case. I hoped he believed me.

"This . . . devil, you named," he stuttered. "Wh . . . wh . . . why do you think she wants to hurt you?"

"Because she's jealous of me. She's from a dysfunctional family so she robbed me of my good fortune. She took everything I worked so hard for away from me," I asserted, teary eyed.

"And she is the reason why you tried to kill yourself?" the doctor wanted to clarify.

I nodded, "That's it in a nutshell. Like an anxiety attack. I need to escape from this body. My body needs to be switched back to

Jessica Wheaton. I don't like this new life I'm living. I need the stability Jessica had. I need the closeness of my peers and parents. The only thing I have going for me is Kevin. And what good is he if he won't give me pleasure? That's what keeps me alive. Pleasure. Kevin thinks caring about me is good enough. But I can't love in this state, I can only feel physical pleasure. I thrive for the physical, you see. I can't grasp LOVE anymore. I learned that love is a lie. I'm stuck with these feelings because they are now mine. They were hers. The truth is that I'm my enemy's self. So, I guess you're right, I hate myself. But if I were Jessica, I would love myself, not in vain, I assure you."

Hamilton nodded. "How can I help you find your old self?" The doctor acted as if he were complying with my nonsense.

"I have to make her want to repossess herself."

"Had you tried this approach?"

I nodded. "She denies the whole thing. She wants to humiliate me. She says she doesn't hate me but that's a lie. She knows what she's done, and she's having a field day being me so why bother. See, I'm at her mercy because I don't know how she got me this way."

"So let me get this straight. This . . . devil or enemy-self you call Jessica, in physical reality is Jessica but in spiritual reality she is Denise and you are Jessica," the doctor restated, still baffled.

I nodded, confirming what he just said. "Exactly doctor. She stole my identity."

"Interesting!" the doctor expressed with a raised eyebrow. "This is an incredible case."

He fell silent for a short time, biting his lip. I was unsure of what he was thinking. I wished, at a time like this, that I had the power of telepathy. "You don't know how this happened, huh?" The question popped into his head. He must have been loaded with questions but only a few did he ask.

"My hunch is that she drugged me because this all began when I awoke in someone else's bed feeling tipsy. Of course, it was in HER bedroom and HER father who accused me of taking pills that were hidden in HER bedroom."

"So, the real Denise is currently walking around in Jessica Wheaton's body?" Hamilton restated, trying to absorb it all.

I nodded. "It's eerie, isn't it, to think your girlfriend or daughter may not really be who you think she is. They make for good spies," I chuckled.

"How do you suppose she's gotten by with her new physical image all this time? I mean, isn't it kind of hard to know what the former one said to the same person the day before? Don't you mess up and get caught?" he wondered.

"Yeah, I stumbled a lot in the beginning, but I remembered important names and events that pertained to my new identity. Eventually, I gathered clues within her memory. Things such as child abuse and incest. It's like being in a scary movie." Tears came streaming down my cheeks.

Doctor Hamilton handed me a few tissues. "Fascinating! Could it be possible for me to trace your . . . your enemy, ah . . . Jessica, right?" I nodded. He explained his plan, "I'd like to arrange a group therapy session for the two of you—with your permission, of course."

"Won't do any good, I'm telling you. She's selfish. She'll refuse to admit to any of it."

"Admit to what, drugging you?"

"Yes Doctor, the whole conspiracy."

After pausing, the doctor asked curiously, "Had you ever tried to seek help sooner?"

I lowered my head in grief. "No, because I knew it would be too hard to prove something like this. And I didn't want to be locked up in a loony bin. I had to keep it to myself and eventually I convinced myself that I was her . . . that's until I saw her again."

A long reign of silence came over both of us. "Doctor Hamilton," I broke the silence.

"Yes."

"Will you still be able to help me?" I anxiously awaited an answer, skipping a heartbeat. "You do believe me, don't you? You did ask me to confide in you . . ."

"Yes Jessica," he affirmed by calling me my real name. "I believe your story. I'm just unsure of how to help you at the moment." He paused. "We'll need further sessions because our time today has run out. I'm going to keep you on Tromitan under heavy supervision for now.

"Unfortunately, I have to inform you that, because you're a minor under the law, I'm required to contact your parents regarding your whereabouts. Sorry, it's hospital policy. But I swear to you, our discussion will be kept absolutely confidential."

"Doctor, did you say you're unsure of how to help me? Cuz I think you're my last resort."

REUNION

I was quietly reading a magazine in the hospital bed when Dr. Hamilton entered the private room. He marched in holding my chart. I doubted he was carrying my discharge papers with that sort of entrance. I looked up at him smiling, but he didn't return with a smile. He stood at the foot of the bed with hands behind back. The magazine was tossed to the floor. Without expression, he asked, "How are you doing today?" as he had some more pressing issues at hand.

"Okay," I simpered. "Am I going home soon?"

"Soon," he assured.

I asked anxiously, "Did you talk to my folks?"

He raised his eyebrows. "As a matter of fact, I did, just this morning. Your folks heard the good news that you're doing well and are thankful that you're alive at all. They miss you very much and are eager to see you." He cleared his throat. "In fact, they're in my office right now making arrangements for you to come home."

"Over my dead body!" I protested. "The way they treated me, they . . ."

Hamilton intervened. "Quite the contrary, Denise. They showed me your report cards, deficiency notices, a stack of late-to-class slips, suspension letters, not to mention speeding tickets and bail receipts. Denise Bower was a major disciplinary problem. She's been truant for the last five years. Frankly, with this track record, I couldn't blame the Bowers for being tough on her."

I snapped, "Yeah, I know all about that shit, but I'm not her so I shouldn't have to take the punishment for it, ya know."

The doctor pointed out, "Jessica, until you resolve your conflict, you're still Denise. Remember that." he corrected.

"But I'm innocent, don't you understand? I'm the victim," I pointed to myself.

Hamilton scooted himself beside me on the mattress. "I understand how you feel but think of it sort of like getting the flu. You never chose to get sick, but the virus chose you as its host. When you catch the flu, you have no choice but to lie in bed and rest regardless of the demands on your life, in order to get better. Your condition is much like a virus so you must see it through. You must fight it. To pretend that it doesn't exist or it's not your problem is only to fool yourself. I don't care if you switched bodies with the President of the United States or a high-profile celebrity, you must take responsibility for the role you play."

Tears gathered in my eyes. "I understand what you're saying, Doc, but there are things you don't know about these people. They've done terrible things to me in the past, and in my mind's eye, I've seen horror movies."

"There are two sides to every story, aren't there?" Hamilton noted. "Look, all I'm saying is that you have to stop running away from your problems. You have to work things out," Hamilton repeated Kevin's adage. The doctor paused to smile. "You know, it's funny how you resemble your mother."

"Yeah, I remember," I smirked. "So now that you met them, do you take a liking to them?" I asked bitterly.

The doctor looked me in the eye. "Jessica, I'm not passing any kind of judgment, and I don't expect you to. I'm merely relaying a message to you. Try not to take it so personally.

Besides, you don't know how lucky you are. Wouldn't you rather your parents try to amend the relationship than abandon you? In so many of my cases, the parents or legal guardians go to great lengths to abandon or neglect their child. Some change the locks on the doors; others change to an unlisted phone number to eliminate any chance of their kid tracking them down."

I thought it over.

Hamilton added, "They're even willing to go for counseling."

I shook my head. "You're not serious. Did they really say that?"

Hamilton cleared his throat once again. "Well, there is a catch. They had me type up this contract." He handed over the papers. "There are certain conditions you must agree to in the terms of this contract." Hamilton walked me through the documents. "All that legal jargon means that you must agree to change your attitude and conduct. They expect you to return to school and attend each, and every class, steering clear from drugs and your old circle of friends. They added here that you are to do whatever it takes to turn your grades around to enable you to graduate, including extra credit assignments, spending each, and every evening studying, and completing homework assignments to be signed by your parents. And finally, the Bowers require that you report to them each time you leave the house."

I was outraged! "Gosh Doc, don't you think all that's a bit harsh? I don't think it's at all fair. I can't make up for truancy overnight, ya know. I feel they're making this into a business agreement. Why do we need a contract? Why can't you just supervise the whole thing?"

Doctor Hamilton explained, "Because you've made this into a legal situation. They're trying to keep your butt out of Juvenile Detention."

"But . . ."

"Jessica, you're a smart kid. You did exceptionally well in school—an honor student. You have nothing to fear. What are you afraid of?"

"They'll treat me awful," I pouted.

"Give them another chance."

I thought it over, studying Hamilton's eyes. "Will you be by my side?" I was asking for protection.

He nodded. "Of course I will. Had I disappointed you yet?" After Hamilton's long-winded sales pitch, we both contemplated more thoroughly whether the reunion was a good idea or not. Hamilton comforted, "I won't pressure you to sign the contract. You can think it over.

But I do think you should take this opportunity to have a reunion with your folks. I mean, you're in a hospital—a secure environment. They can't harm you here."

I sighed.

After a moment of silence, he asked, "Can I invite them in?"

I nodded half-heartedly.

Not a moment sooner, in flew the mosquitoes. I held onto the emergency button by my headboard. The couple hurried over to me, pretending to miss me. He was a tall husky guy. She had makeup plastered to her face and was drenched in perfume. Her dangling jewelry made for fine percussions. They greeted me with, "How are you, dear?" I received bear hugs and wet kisses. The nickname "Dini" was used once again.

Mr. Bower studied me. "Oh, how you've grown over the years; you've become a young lady, haven't you? Your mother and I have missed you so much. A day wouldn't go by without thinking of you. We left your bedroom just the way it was the day you disappeared, hoping you'd return." He smiled sentimentally.

My only reply was, "Fine."

Dr. Hamilton peeked into the room to check on things, as promised. He clapped his hands. "So how is everything going?"

Mrs. Bower turned to Hamilton. She smiled brightly, "Would it be possible if we could spend some time alone with Dini? We have to make up for lost time."

Hamilton waited for me to answer. My eyes said no. He saw me clutch the emergency button. "If you need me, just push the buzzer," he advised me with a grin stapled to his face, closing the door behind him. I was disappointed with him. I thought he agreed to supervise the meeting. He wasn't sitting right by me.

Mr. Bower slid two chairs over by the bed. Claudia handed me a dish of fudge brownies she prepared as a get-well gift. "It's your favorite recipe." She shrugged and giggled sheepishly. Ray placed a little gift box on my lap, insisting I open it. After thanking them both for the gold-plated earrings, they handed me two greeting cards. One was signed by Timothy and the other by John, both my brothers.

"They sent you their wishes for a speedy recovery." Noticing the confusion on my face, Claudia explained the cards, "Your brothers wish they could've made it into town to visit you, but you know how busy they are with their families and work."

I remembered the vision of Timothy holding me when I was a child. I begged him not to move. John was leaving for Penn State University. The brothers abandoned me, leaving me vulnerable to these damn parasites. I was very close to both of them. I tossed the cards aside in resentment. "They're too busy to see their little sister at a time like this?" I griped.

"Now Dini, don't be foolish," Claudia tried to appease my sore feelings.

"Did John graduate from Penn State yet?" I asked.

Claudia looked at her husband wondering just how bad off I was. "John graduated in 1969 when you were with us. He's a physical therapist now."

Silent uneasiness filled the room. The Bowers pretended to have grieved over the news of my attempted suicide. Claudia's eyes were reddening as if she was going to cry. She cleared her throat several times before she could speak. Ray's face turned a sick pale white. Great acting job. Claudia momentarily grinned. "We had a long discussion with Dr. Hamilton. He is one of the finest doctors around. I'm confident that he'll take good care of you," she said, followed by an uneasy disquiet. Neither parent really came prepared with words.

Ray took his turn. "Look Hun, I know we've had our differences." He chose his words carefully as he attempted to mend things between us. "But you didn't have to run away from home." He placed his arm around his wife. "We are family. We work out our problems together. We don't avoid each other. I thought all that was understood. Apparently not. We must have gone awry raising you. You're the youngest. We didn't know what kind of attention you needed. I wish I knew about this long ago."

Claudia picked up where he left off, as his voice was growing hoarse. "The doctor told us about your condition, and we want you to know that we are here for you. I know you've been through a lot, dear, but I hope you've learned your lesson. You should've turned to us instead," Claudia lamented.

Ray added, "And rest assured, you're still covered under our insurance for further treatment."

Unsure of exactly what they were talking about, I asked, "Just what did the doctor tell you?"

Ray looked over at Claudia for approval. She nodded. He disclosed, "Dr. Hamilton diagnosed your condition as a Multiple Personality Dissociative Disorder."

My mind went blank as if I was electrocuted once more. *Is that what my very trusted doctor told you?* Dr. Hamilton apparently didn't believe me after all. Kevin was clearly wrong about him. That psychiatrist was definitely a quack. And just how many personalities did they imagine I had? Did this mean they were now afraid of me, or they were going to drug me up from here on out? Now everyone would get wind of this, and I would surely end up in a mental institution, just as I feared all along. My impulse was to be discharged from the hospital immediately and never to hear from that quack again.

Saved by the door—Kevin popped in. "How ya doing, Mr. and Mrs. Bower?" he greeted them.

"You met?" I asked him.

"In the lobby," Kevin explained. He winked, informing me that he poked his nose in Hamilton's office, and Hamilton told him that I was approved for discharge if I was ready.

I grunted, "I'm homesick."

The Bowers smiled proudly. Claudia suggested, "It'll be nice if you'd stay with us, dear." I wished I could tell Claudia where to stick it, but I had to be on good behavior.

"Well, my stuff is with Kevin, but thanks anyway."

"Yes dear, but school is only blocks away from home. It would be more responsible and convenient for you to move back home. You did sign the agreement, didn't you?" She nodded her head in a cocked position. The couple waited anxiously for an answer.

"N . . . ot yet," I fumbled. "I . . . I . . . I can't focus on that just yet."

"Oh, I understand. Well, take all the time you need to get well, of course," she concurred, knowing full well my lack of interest in her offer.

TIME LAPSE

Sweetheart Kevin had big ideas about celebrating my homecoming from the hospital. He took me to Video Fusion, a local nightclub that just opened. I thought the place was really cool. Neon lights lit the revolving bar countertop and stools. Huge video screens displayed psychedelic patterns racing around to the beat of the music. Celebrities performed hit songs on the central screen. The joint definitely had that nightlife ambiance to it.

Initially, Kevin wanted to pop open a bottle of champagne to make a toast to our future together, but not such a good idea in hindsight. Instead, he bought me a soft drink.

He gazed into my eyes, and I melted. I fell into his arms, holding him tightly. My head rested against his shoulder. I pressed my eyes shut, apologizing from deep within my heart for all the trouble I caused.

"Forget it, I just want to see you well," he assured, kissing me passionately.

"Did I ever say thank you?"

"For what?" he asked.

I lowered my head and sighed, for the words didn't come easy. "Thank you for . . . for caring about me." I was not used to expressing gratitude toward a man. "Thank you for saving me from my stupidity and thank you for being so supportive—there, I said it."

Kevin glowed. "Wow! I can't tell you how happy I am to hear you say that, Denise."

"Dini," I corrected him.

"Who?"

"That's the nickname my parents used since I was little, ya know, short for Denise."

"Oh okay, I'll have to remember that. May I ask you a question, Dini?"

"Sure," I smiled brightly.

"I remember you not feeling too comfortable with Dr. Hamilton. Are you okay with him now?"

The smile on my face disappeared. "Why?" I questioned. "What did he say to you about me?"

"Nothing. He just wants me to keep a close eye on you. Make sure you don't do anything stupid. I don't have a problem watching you real closely, do you?"

"Not at all. In fact, he brought me to appreciate an important person in my life."

"And who may that be?"

"I'm gazing right into his eyes at this very moment." Our eyes locked.

"Would you care to dance?" Kevin offered.

"I thought you'd never ask. It would be my pleasure."

We slow danced through three lovely romantic melodies, swaying from side to side, arm- in-arm. For the first time, my urge to be with a man was because I loved him, not because I lusted for him. Behold the music of love and the fire of passion, if only it could burn forever.

He was mine, and I desired no other. He uttered, "You have such soft hair," as his fingers gently combed through.

"All the more for you," I winked, brushing the long full-bodied waves aside.

In the corner of my eye, I could've sworn my one-time friend, Vicki Norris, was on the dance floor. I had to do a double take. Of all people, what were the chances? She was dancing with a tall blonde dude. I could've been mistaken, there were lookalikes. Besides, this Vicki was a very young version. When I saw her face close up, I was a deer in the headlights!

I excused myself to the restroom to avoid her. As soon as I came out of the stall, I bumped right into Vicki as she entered the restroom. She instantly recognized me. I walked on, ignoring her, pretending to be oblivious.

"Dini!" Her eyes widened in surprise. "What are you doing here?"

She caught me! I thought she'd slap me across the face for what I'd done to her at Nina's apartment some time ago, but instead she got emotional and hugged me. "Where've you been all these years? I missed you so. How are you doing?" She came up for air. "Wow, I never thought I'd bump into you here of all places." Her eyes were filled with tears of joy. "It's been so long . . . Let's see—three years give or take?"

THREE YEARS! My mind went into a funk. I just saw her a few weeks ago. She's not even pregnant. Did she have an abortion? Who was that blonde she was dancing with? And why did she look so young? Skin supple, unmarked and ageless. I looked at myself in the mirror. I, too, looked much younger.

After zoning out for some time, I heard Vicki ask, "Tell me, what have you been up to?" Before I could say a word, she grabbed my hand and walked me over to her booth to meet her friends. There sat the old familiar Christina Bates with her date, an obvious mismatch. I waved to Christina before Vicki ever had the chance to introduce us. Christina seemed puzzled, as if she didn't recognize me.

"You remember me? Dini?" I felt uneasy, almost embarrassed. With a blank expression on her face, Christina couldn't place me. How could this be? How could I have met her, and she not recognize me? I knew I wasn't on anything.

Vicki distracted us, introducing me to her boyfriend. She whispered in my ear, "This is Bill. Isn't he a hunk? Whatcha think? Can I pick 'um or what?"

"What about Todd?" I slipped. Unfortunately, she heard me over the loud music. "Todd who?"

"Todd McKane," I clarified.

Vicki shook her head in disapproval. "Him? That clown from 7th grade?" She had a puzzled look on her face. "This is Bill from Mt. Stony High. He's been seeing me for the last six weeks." Bill kindly slid over a spare chair so that I could join the group. Vicki continued to pry, "So what have you been up to? John told me that you were suspended the last time I spoke with him. Fill in the gaps."

John? I remembered that name from flashbacks. He was my first lover, that is, besides Ray. I felt as if I had been somehow displaced in time. How could this happen? Four individuals waited for my tell-all story. How was I supposed to know what I did some three years ago after I broke up with John when I'm not even Denise? I tried to piece the events together in sequence. "I . . .

got pregnant, dropped out of school . . . uh, I had an abortion then .
. . then uh . .

Vicki interceded, "Who's that guy you were dancing with?" pointing to Kevin who was sitting by the bar patiently waiting for me.

"Kevin's my boyfriend," I grinned with delight.

"What happened to John, you broke up?" Vicki speculated.

I thought about it. Again, I wasn't sure of the sequence, but I made a logical deduction. "I left John because he didn't treat me right. He would drink then get real abusive."

Vicki shook her head in disappointment. "What a shame, I thought the both of you looked so good together."

Christina interrupted to inquire about my friendship with Vicki. "So how did the two of you meet?"

Vicki waited for me to tell the story that I knew nothing about. I shrugged my shoulders and said nothing. Vicki blurted to Christina, "I met Dini when I was about ten. Wheaton introduced us." She pierced into my eyes with resentment as I was supposed to do the dreadful storytelling.

I was in shock! Suddenly I recalled: at age ten Denise had just moved into town, the new kid in 4th grade. I was the tomboy, swinging along monkey bars and playing by the stream.

During recess the two best friends, Jessica Wheaton and Vicki Norris, played hopscotch, jump rope, and clap games together. I was restless so I wanted to stir up some trouble. I went out of my way to show who was boss, so I separated the two girls. I'd challenge all the girls to do daring things and if they would, they'd be my best friend. And all my best friends were to taunt the "others" who refused to do stupid or illegal things like pouring a bucket of sand into the school restroom sink or placing a cricket in someone's purse or a "kick-me" sign on someone's back. The "gang" soon formed, and each member would specialize in the art of bullying the weak or inadequate. The "others" became castaways. Wheaton was one of the first to go. She wasn't cool. Vicki became my best friend. She was a master risk-taker.

Abruptly I took off, without a word, to join Kevin. Kevin commented that I looked as if I'd seen a ghost.

"I bumped into an old friend," I explained briefly, looking away from him.

"Really? Here?" He was curious. I knew what he was about to say. I guess he had good intentions. He just wanted to share my world, but he didn't understand.

I had to distract him. "Yes, but we really should be going. It's getting late." I glanced at my watch.

"What's the hurry? We just got here." He knew something was up. "Introduce me to your friends."

"I really don't think that's a good idea. Let's just leave," I urged, tugging on his arm like a bashful child.

"What's wrong?" he questioned.

I promised, "I'll discuss it later." Kevin abided. He slid his jacket on.

Unfortunately, on the way out, Vicki and her friends stopped us in our tracks. "Where you guys going?" she wormed at me for avoiding her. She had me introduce Kevin to her. She whispered in my ear, "He's square, isn't he? BORING," she emphasized. I resented her comment. I had a good mind to slap her across the face but I restrained myself. I overheard Vicki whisper to Christina to stall with Kevin while she worked on me. "Listen here." Vicki pulled me aside. "Give me your number and I'll call you sometime. This time we must stay in touch," she insisted. I didn't want anything to do with her, but I knew it was inevitable as long as I was Denise. She jotted her number down on a napkin. Slick Vicki slipped something in that napkin, rolled it up, and inserted it into my pants pocket.

"What was that?" I suspected.

"What do you mean?" She feigned innocence.

I knew then what it was. "Look, take it back 'cause I'm going clean. I . . . I really . . ."

Vicki growled, still whispering with an evil eye and a superficial grin, demanding, "Just HOLD it for me . . . pal. I didn't say you had to use it, did I? Don't be so curt with me. We're friends, remember?" She ground her teeth, trying not to make a scene. "What's the prude done to you anyways?" she remarked.

I raised my voice in protest, "I don't have to hold your SHIT for you. You don't understand Vicki, I'm not into that . . ."

She placed her hand over my mouth. "Shut up, gee! Don't get so hysterical." I reached into my pocket grasping for the napkin.

Vicki muttered angrily, "Don't you dare!"

Just as I was about to pull the napkin out from my pocket, Kevin put his arm around me. I felt trapped. I wasn't about to risk getting caught. He'd have me back in Hamilton's office in no time. I had no choice but to leave it alone. I gave Vicki a dirty look as if to say, *I'll get you back for this.* Not a second too soon, I darted out of the club with Kevin following behind.

TIME WARP

"What was that?" Kevin exclaimed, referring to the little scuffle at Video Fusion. I tried to explain the unexplainable, "I told you; she was an old friend of mine."

"An old friend, my ass," Kevin got hot raising his voice. "She looks like a damn crack addict." He pointed his finger. "You stay away from them, hear me? And that Chris girl with the big boobs was flirting with me. You need to steer clear from that trash. I'm tellin' you. I know what trouble looks like. I used to have those biker types as customers at the Hilltop!"

"Yes Daddy," I folded my arms, annoyed by his overreaction. "Why do you think I wanted to leave? I didn't know they were there. And it wasn't a setup. Trust me."

He put his arm around me, falling silent. I knew he was thinking things through. "Denise, there is something that has been troubling me about you and I wish you could explain it to me. The moment I rescued you from Ruxton's hands I knew you were a prostitute but then the drugs, the suicide attempt, the overdosing on Tromitan, avoiding your parents, and then your mom tells me that you have Multiple Personality Dissociative Disorder but not to say anything.

What's going on? I'm afraid to go to work because you might hurt yourself again or I'll find you in some dark alley brutally murdered. Is there something I should know? I'm afraid that you haven't told me everything because I'm not seeing the whole picture."

I closed my eyes. He was asking for the truth. The truth that I foolishly shared with Vicki, that I always tried to suppress to function in the world I lived in and that Dr. Hamilton had documented. I'd been living a lie and survived quite well doing so. I couldn't disclose the truth for it would blow my cover. "No Kevin, you're not," I answered, staring off into the vast oblivion. "For one, I don't have multiple personalities. That's a lie that Hamilton made up. He isn't to be trusted," I corrected. "I'm sorry for all the trouble I caused. As you can tell, I'm a very messed up individual, and you've been very tolerant of me. I've been lost for a very long time, continually searching for myself. The circle I used to hang out with aren't my real friends. They're Den . . ." I must have slipped into a deep trance, babbling to myself as Kevin was listening attentively for answers. "They're younger. All of them, and Christina said she didn't recognize me."

"Younger than who?" Kevin didn't follow.

"I'm younger too. How could that be?" I was thinking out loud to myself.

"Compared to who?" Kevin tried to understand the cryptic language.

"And . . ." I paused. "When I met the girls, they were uncertain about my behavior and wondered if I slept with you the night before. I wouldn't have dreamt of . . ." My eyes went through his eyes as I had a revelation. I met Kevin when I was in captivity, but he was my boyfriend before I left Philley. How could that be? Not the same . . . He looked younger—dressed better. I was freaking out by this mere observation. All I heard was, "What do you mean, you wouldn't have dreamt of it?" I couldn't respond, for the puzzle pieces were being unraveled at this very moment. Vicki was pregnant in Fowlersville when she visited with Todd. She presently hadn't met Todd. I felt dizzy like a burst of energy from a bolt of lightning hit me. For the first time, I could see clearly. I had undergone a time warp. Perhaps many time warps. And the answer to my problem—to find the passage door—was woven in the time warp. The answer didn't lie within the bed in which I awoke. The answer certainly wasn't running away from myself. Something or someone was controlling the great leaps in time, and I needed to stop her. Yes, Denise had put me into this "story" and was toying with it.

Past midnight I cuddled beside Kevin, resting my head on his chest. I wished I could share with him what Vicki stuck in my pocket. But I couldn't. I led him to believe it was condoms. He didn't question me. I had a good mind to flush the dope down the toilet, but I didn't. Just in case, I held onto it for a time of desperation.

"Dini," he called out to me as we were dozing off, using my nickname.

"Yes Hun," I replied, half awake, afraid of his suspicion.

"What were you babbling about outside the night club? It didn't make any sense."

I had a sigh of relief. "Oh, nothing. I was just trying to tell you that there are a lot of issues that I need to sort out."

He cleared his throat. "Is it me, Dini? Am I part of the problem? Is it about us?" he asked with grave concern, looking sadly into my eyes.

I grinned. "No dear. You're for keeps." Smiles were posted on both our sleepy faces in the quiet. Though Kevin couldn't understand what was wrong with me, at least he was assured it had nothing to do with him. Again, we relaxed together with our eyes shut, cuddling. "Kevin," I called out to him.

"Yes Hun," he responded, massaging my hand under the sheets.

"You know what you said about building a relationship with my folks and going back to school?"

"Yes."

"Well, I've been giving it some thought, and I think it would be best for our future."

HIGH EXPECTATIONS

It appeared to be something out of a horror movie: an old wooden cottage with black shutters positioned on the top of a steep hill with the full moon shining above. You could smell the burnt coals of the witch's brew from the active chimney. The trees were stripped of leaves and color, revealing their skeletal remains. The only thing missing was a howling wolf and the stench of death. I thought to myself, *do I really want to go through with this? C'mon, the Bowers aren't devils or murderers. I'm making too much of this.* I hesitantly followed the path of shrub bushes leading to the porch. As I approached the front door my nerves rattled, but I had to do it. I only rang the doorbell once before it was attended.

Claudia Bower greeted me at the door, pretending to be delighted to see me. No hugs or kisses were exchanged. I walked along the dusty tile floor in the very spot Mr. Bower once dragged me across. I glanced over to the framed painting, which caused the first scar on my head. Standing in the living room, I could remember the faint scent of bacon and eggs, which I was not entitled to, awaiting me before school. Then, there was the staircase. I remembered all too vividly how I rattled and rolled down the steps only to have Mr. Bower beat me once I landed.

Claudia informed me that "Father" wanted to see me in his study. Why couldn't he have come to the door to greet me? Because everything the Bowers said in the hospital was bullshit. And I knew it. What was I expecting? A surprise party with my brothers jumping out of closets to hug me? These people didn't know how to love. I had to keep in mind that I wasn't home to work things out with the Bowers. I had an ulterior motive.

I stood in the doorway of Denise's bedroom in dismay. I knew now that there were no magical powers to her bed. I didn't suppose there was anything within her room that would've led me to a hidden passage of transformation. The dented Uncle Sam poster was still mounted on the wall in front of the bed. I recalled Mr. Bower finding Ecstasy pills somewhere hidden in this bedroom. I checked the bathroom cupboard to see if the Bowers had restocked aspirins since. A little bottle of generic aspirin smiled at me. I sat along Denise's bed, folding my hands in my lap, then sighed. The room was indeed left the same as I remembered. In fact, the rock star posters decorating the walls curled and yellowed with age.

I gasped at the framed picture on the center of her desk. It was a picture of me and Kevin together! But Kevin and I had never participated in a photoshoot. His hair was long, tied behind his back, clothes were torn, a bandana wrapped around his forehead. He hadn't shaved in days, forming a beard and mustache. And I . . . . I looked pretty pathetic myself. I was heavy, face covered in zits, wearing a low-cut tank top. Kevin would never permit such indecency, as I knew him. We looked like . . . . he emphatically insisted I stay away from "biker types." I was curious when the picture was taken. I took the photo out from the glass frame and examined the flip side for a date.

I felt a tap on the shoulder. I jumped. "Oh Father, you scared me!"

"Good morning," he said with his head held high. He didn't seem overjoyed to see me either. "I understand you decided to return to school. It was a wise decision. Tell me, did you sign the contract yet?"

He caught me off guard without an explanation. "Well . . . I 'ya . . . no. I really haven't gotten around to it yet." I felt myself shake. The husky man eyeballed me for the longest time. Was he going to beat me again? I took a deep breath, preparing for combat. My fist was ready to take him on. I was no longer afraid of him. In fact, I wouldn't mind smacking the crap out of him.

Instead, he extended his hand to me. "I want to be proud of you, Dini." He wanted a handshake. Was this a business relationship? "Can we at least shake on your promise to abide by the contract? I need an affirmation," he insisted. I saw nothing wrong with that. I shook his hand. "But . . ." He pointed his index finger immediately after the handshake. "Before we leave well enough alone, I'd like you to come into my office for a moment."

I knew then that I wasn't off the hook so easily. Ray had me sit down on his guest chair in his small reclusive office. The room was poorly lit, only by the window and a desk lamp. He brushed his mail aside to make room at the center of his desk. He pulled out two large manila packets from his desk drawer. Within one, he retrieved a yellowish paper. I could tell by the seal on the stationary that it was some sort of government document. I thought he was going to show me that he found more dope stashed away in hidden places, but instead he was just sharing his mail. What a relief.

He cleared his throat. "Denise, you've been missing for three years now. The County Police have been searching for you ever since. Your mother and I thought the worst happened to you until Dr. Hamilton called. But I didn't call you in here to ask for an explanation as to why you ran away. We can't change the past even if we'd like to."

He fixed his stony stare on me for quite some time then proceeded to open the second envelope. My fists were clenched in my lap ready for the unexpected. "Mother and I had to file a missing persons report when you disappeared. Needless to say, it was hard. Well, a few weeks ago, we received this official notice in the mail which indicates the many infractions of the law thus far reported." He paused. "Are you aware that the police are looking for you?" Ray shed his powerful eyes onto my face, once again. "Do you realize the gravity of this situation? They want to have you arrested and thrown behind bars." He noticed the blank look on my face as I didn't care. "The police are after you," he restated, raising his voice. "They already paid us a visit a few nights ago. In their investigation, they traced the drug therapy insurance forms and concluded that you were back in town. They questioned us on your whereabouts. Of course, being your parents, we covered for you due to your psychiatric condition. We told them we hadn't heard anything but assured them that we'd notify authorities as soon as we knew something. We lied for you," Mr. Bower stated bluntly, hoping to get a reaction out of me. "Because we want to give you a second chance. Dr. Hamilton thinks you deserve it before we make up our minds to admit you to rehab. Once you're there, there's no chance of clearing your record."

I had a good mind to ask for an attorney.

Ray continued as he read the document in the dim light. "Here's the list of charges . . ." He handed me the summons. He wanted me to see it with my own eyes. Charges listed included possession of and use of illegal substances, breaking and entering private property (robbery), assault and battery, vandalism, accessory to shoplifting, illegal solicitation and indecent exposure (prostitution), theft of car and wallet, evading the scene of an auto accident, and last, but not least, homicide. Below the violations, in big black bold smudged print, probably due to excessive copying, stated in almost outrage-shouting words, were the threatening orders: YOU ARE HEREBY SUMMONED TO A COURT HEARING FOR ALL ABOVE INDICATED INFRACTIONS OF THE LAW. FAILURE TO APPEAR IN COURT IS A SERIOUS OFFENSE AND IS SUBJECT TO A FINE AND/OR IMPRISONMENT.

I gazed at him in disbelief. "You think I did all this?" I swallowed. "Including the murder?"

He burned me with his angry eyes. "We will let the court decide that, but if you did . . ." He smirked at me accusingly. "There could be serious consequences, Denise. It could mean life in prison," he cautioned.

I cleared my throat. "So, you're trying to tell me that you're giving me another chance, and if I blow it, you'll report me," I reiterated.

"Your record will clear in a few years if you behave yourself. You're still young. The law is lenient on minors. But you must abide by the contract you read in the hospital. I want it signed. Any breach and your butt's in jail. Do you understand?" he stated firmly.

"Yes."

"Good," he nodded. "Now I expect you to go back to school in a drug-free environment. I mean it, Denise. I want to see a radical improvement in your behavior, and I don't think that it's expecting too much, as you stated to Dr. Hamilton."

That little bastard told the Bowers everything? I shook my head. "School is half over. Can I get some help? I mean, I'll try my darndest, but I may need a tutor . . ."

He interrupted abruptly, yelling at me, "No! What you need is discipline. I want to see you study your ass off. That means no phone calls and no parties. I want you to think, eat, and sleep your homework. You're not to go to bed until you have satisfied all the requirements. If you have a problem, you ask your teacher. It's your responsibility to be informed. I don't know how many times I've told you that." Ray banged his fist against the desk. He drew silent then sighed. "Alright, enough said, you're dismissed to your bedroom," as if I were in boot camp. Should I salute him?

All alone, I lay in Denise's bed. *Homicide?* I thought to myself. *I had a frickin' car accident.* I chuckled. My angry nerves soon calmed from the ridiculous charges. No Kevin to vent to, cuddle with, or hug. I listened to the air vents switch on and off and the annoying crickets chirping away outside. I could not sleep—too much anxiety filled my head. For some reason I felt less competent than Jessica. I'd been away from school too long and was mentally unprepared for the challenges ahead. School had become synonymous with failure: HOMEWORK! DEADLINES! PRESSURE! GRADES! PUNCTUALITY!

BACK TO SCHOOL

The knapsack strapped to my back was so heavy I nearly collapsed from its weight. How I ever managed to support four hefty textbooks, a loose-leaf binder, and two workbooks against my back was beyond me. I removed the knapsack from my aching back and dragged it along the floor. It sat in the middle of the busy corridor while I paused to catch my breath. I needed a set of wheels. Passing students called me a weakling. How could they expect me to travel from class to class, up and down the stairwells, hour after hour with a ton of bricks on my back? There were no bellboys or go-karts here. What was with the pushing and shoving? How was I supposed to remember my locker combination? Why didn't they have a refrigerator for lunch bags? Returning to school took some getting used to.

Halfway to class, students were chanting my return. "Bower's back!" I didn't realize how popular I was. That was definitely an asset. Someone blindfolded me from behind. "You mess with me and I'll put you in a headlock," the voice grunted. I broke free from the restraint. I thought that voice sounded familiar. Vicki, Marie, and Paula stood before me giggling. Marie slapped me on the back and winked. "Good to see you back."

"I'm tellin' you girls I saw her last night at the club with another guy," Vicki insisted.

"You have a new boyfriend? Tell me—tell me," Marie was determined to get some gossip out of me.

I rolled my eyes.

Paula inquired, "So why did you come back? Weren't you suspended?" One question after another, I was being interrogated by the paparazzi.

I corrected Paula, "I wasn't suspended."

Vicki clarified, "Yes you were. John told me."

Marie pried, "Tell me the latest poop."

I backed away. "I can't. I have some business to take care of," I remarked disdainfully, trotting away from the three gossip machines.

"Business? What kind of business?" Vicki asked as she pursued me down the hall. "Come back here, I want to talk to you."

"I can't be late for class," I muttered half-heartedly.

"What's up with you?" Vicki objected with a sour face.

I tried to blow her off. "Nothing."

"Why are you going to class? C'mon, join me in the lounge for a smoke."

"Some other time," I asserted.

Vicki folded her arms, annoyed. "This isn't the first time you've been suspended, you know."

"Is there something you want?" I was curt with her, stopping abruptly.

She eyeballed me for a while, without a word. She just stood there baffled.

Mrs. Higgins was in the process of passing out test results when I scurried into Biology class, screeching onto a chair in the last row. And deja-vu, my paper was slammed face down on the desk. "Good to have you back in class, Denise." The teacher grimaced. "If you stick around long enough, you might just learn something."

I turned the ditto over. Denise Bower's signature was at the bottom of the page. It was dated a week ago. How could that be when I just returned today? I shrugged my shoulders, blaming the circumstance on another time lapse.

I examined the test. It was in essay format. Denise's illegible handwriting scribbled over the answer box. I read the questions and was pretty confident that I knew most of the answers. If only I could take the test over to prove to Mr. Bower that I was capable of better. Yes, I was really Jessica and could utilize my brain more effectively than pot-head Denise.

Considering knowing how strict Mrs. Higgins was, I went up to her desk and stood before her ready to argue with righteous pride.

She simpered, "Ms. Bower, I gave the class ample time to study, and we had a review last Wednesday. I think you've used up just about all the opportunity I can offer."

"But I've been absent."

"You were suspended. No excuses, I'm sorry."

"I can do an extra credit assignment to prove myself."

"Denise, you haven't handed in a single homework assignment since the first day of class. Have you lost your mind? Do you really think that three-quarters through the school year you can make up for all the losses a week before report cards go out?"

I shut my eyes. I couldn't believe time was shifting again. Mrs. Higgins thought I'd been attending school since the first day.

"Please Mrs. Higgins. I know I can do better. Please give me just one last chance."

She was perplexed by my perseverance. "Just tell me why you haven't put any effort into your work all this time. I mean, what has caused you to have a such a change of mind?"

"It's hard to explain, Mrs. Higgins, but I lost a dear friend and I'm trying hard to cope with the loss, but I think I'm getting over it now."

Mrs. Higgins studied me for the longest time. She wasn't sure if I was telling the truth or making up some story. "I'm sorry to hear that. I wish you would have informed me sooner. You know that's what counselors are for. Maybe you should see one."

"Maybe I should but right now I just want to pass this class. I want a fair chance."

"I'll tell you what. You do an essay on botany, a really good job, and I'll consider giving you more extra credit assignments. I want you to explain plant function and how plants affect the environment and the ecological cycle," she instructed as she was jotting down the assignment. "You are to hand in this paper first thing on Friday. No less than two pages. And I mean comprehensive, well-researched material. Legible if not typed, okay?"

I agreed and thanked her. I figured it would be a breeze since I, as Jessica, had already passed the botany test. As I turned away from the teacher's desk, I noticed Jessica sitting in the middle of the third row, hiding her face and giggling. She must have overheard the entire conversation. My plan had worked! I was in the same science class with Jessica. I finally had the opportunity to stare her down. She sat with Ann Millian, of course, whispering back and forth. Ann glanced over at me and giggled. I felt like beating the crap out of her right in the middle of the class session, but instead I returned to my seat with my nails digging into my fist. The botany extra credit homework assignment would have to take a back seat. I tore out a piece of loose-leaf paper and jotted on it, *"You're fucked,"* with a black marker. I folded it up and asked classmates to pass it to Jessica. Ann Millian intercepted the note and read it. I was confident that she'd report the note to the teacher, but she simply trashed it. *The war has just begun,* I said to myself.

THE NOTES

I made myself comfortable at my bedroom desk. A blank piece of lined loose-leaf paper lay lifelessly before me. Rubbing my hands together psyching myself up. Alright, here I come, ready to make a killer on my botany presentation. Not a problem. My ink pen was ready to roll. I read the teacher's instructions carefully: In no less than two pages, explain plant function, how plants affect the environment, and the ecological cycle.

Not a thing came to mind upon reading the instructions for a fifth time. Was a sixth time necessary to obtain the genius buried deep within me? At this point I was merely memorizing the written instructions. "C'mon, focus!" I demanded of myself. I glanced at the hour. After much time passed, I acknowledged that I was poorly equipped for this report. To top it off, I left the textbook in the school locker thinking I didn't need it. It would've been too thick and boring to review anyway. As for my notebook, it contained mostly doodle and gossip chit-chat. To my dismay, not a single note was taken during class sessions. This information was supposed to be in my frickin' brain. Out of frustration, I threw the pen against the wall. "Damn it! That's why Jessica laughed at me in class. She knew I was making a fool of myself. The shit is in her memory, not mine. But not to worry, for I refuse to be defeated. Miss Smarty-pants will get trampled on and pay a high price for this. I will steal her notes during class then I will have the most comprehensive essay that ever crossed Mrs. Higgins' desk. Jessica will surely fail the finals with no notes to study from," I chuckled.

The following day I strolled into science class and sat my butt down in the row directly behind Jessica. Mrs. Higgins was curious as to why I chose to change seats. I told her I had trouble seeing the blackboard from the last row. She bought it. She raised her eyebrows as if pleasantly surprised that I appeared to be motivated. Motivated I was, but not in the class session. The entire period I spent mocking Jessica. I'd yank at her hair to annoy her. When she turned, I pretended to be taking notes intently. Although she knew I did it, she resumed her work in hopes that I would leave her alone. I didn't. Repeatedly I pulled on her hair, kicked and pushed at her chair. Each time she was unresponsive except to fidget in her seat or push her chair forward, away from me. She continued to ignore me, which irritated me further.

Hallelujah! She finally turned to me in distress. "Stop it!" she insisted.

"Stop what?" I acted oblivious and annoyed.

"Stop fooling with my hair and my chair. Leave me alone!" she demanded.

I sneered, "Why would I want to play with your dandruff?"

At the end of the class session Jessica cried that her notes were missing. She courageously accused me of swiping them. "What are you up to?" she asked desperately.

"What's your problem?" I jeered. "I didn't do nothin'. How could I take your notes if I'm sittin' behind you? Duh!" I defended myself.

Ann intervened. "I saw you reach over and snatch 'um when she got up from her desk. Thief," she accused valiantly.

I was pissed. My fist was clenched, ready to break a nose. I stood tall, raising my tone. "Who are you calling a thief?" I charged, "You're a fuckin' liar sittin' beside her cheatin' off her, fuckin' accusin' me, you fuckin' asshole. What, ya think I'm stupid or something?"

The two trembled as they watched me go off.

"Don't fuck with me, smart-ass." I warned Ann, lassoing my finger in the air. "I'll fuckin' whip your ass."

"Please just give me back my notes," Jessica asked mercifully.

I snapped, "You deaf or something? I said I don't have your fuckin' notes. You probably put them back in your notebook, you bonehead."

"Thief," Ann repeated under her breath.

I was fuming! I snatched Jessica's notebook from her grip, slammed it to the floor, and stomped on it, popping the binder.

"I'm tellin' the teacher," Jessica cried.

I growled, "I dare ya, you fuckin' sissy." I bullied her, "That's what you get for accusing me of stealing your notes. And if you cause any more trouble, I'll beat the shit out of you."

It didn't take long to figure out that I stole the wrong set of notes from Jessica. I didn't need the current notes of the day. The botany lecture was last week's lesson. Jessica had again made a fool of me. Again, I could feel her laughter in my gut. No! I would not be defeated! I wanted the notebook!

I knew to turn to Susan Henler for help. She was perfect for the job. She had a reputation for being mean-spirited. She wouldn't be messed with by anyone. Her boyfriend owned a Harley Davidson and she was a black belt. Since I was in a time warp, Susan hadn't yet witnessed my initial scuffle with Jessica, so she thought I was just taunting Jessica. I explained to Susan that Jessica reported me to the teacher, and I was going to teach her a lesson she'd never forget. I lied to Susan, and she bought it.

I knew about when Jessica would be at her locker. We approached Jess as she was turning her combination lock. I noticed the notebook at her side. "Hey." I stood before her. "You're in big trouble. I heard you reported me to the teacher."

Jessica's eyes widened with alarm as she opened her locker. "I did not."

"Liar!" I slammed the locker shut before she had a chance to toss her notebook in. I whispered to Susan, "First chance, grab her notebook." I glanced around to see that no faculty was nearby then pushed Jessica against the locker. She strapped the loose-leaf to her chest. She must have known what I was after. I hissed in her face, "Ya think you're smart, don't ya? What, you a teacher's pet or somethin'? Think you're special? Goody-two-shoes maybe? Gonna hafta teach you a lesson." I stomped on her foot. She recoiled, involuntarily loosening her grip on her notebook. Susan quickly snatched the loose-leaf from her.

"Give me back my . . ." she cried.

I grabbed Jessica into a headlock, forcing her mouth shut. Waving my finger in her face, I whispered in her ear, "Shouldn't be dishonest with me, Miss Prissy. I said no tattling. Let's see if your smart-ass brains will save you from me now." I pushed her to the floor then off I went with Susan and the notebook.

Susan asked curiously, "What do you want with her notebook?"

"I'm going to cheat off her notes," I explained.

Susan thought it was a brilliant idea. The two of us broke into a wild laugher as if we had gone mad. "Did she really report you to the teacher?" Susan straightened her face.

"I'm not gonna chance it, ya know what I mean."

"Yeah, but now I think she'll report the both of us to the principal," Susan cautioned. "That's a bit more serious."

I sneered at Susan. "Don't think like a coward. I know you're not a wuss. I need to teach her a lesson, and I will do whatever it takes. She doesn't scare me."

Susan nodded, complying with me. She was giving me the ammunition I needed—power.

THE STUDY TRAP

Iflipped through the pages of Jessica's notebook, scanning dates. Voila! My finger landed on last week's botany lesson: 5/12: Asexual Reproduction. Beside it she jotted, *see chapter 6*. That was it? No notes? Honor student Jessica Wheaton had no notes? Wait a minute . . . this wasn't my handwriting—this was Denise's scribble. I slammed the desk—damn it! Once again, I was deceived by the devil herself. To think the attack on Jessica would be a victory for me. Who was I kidding? What was I to do now? I promised Mrs. Higgins a complete paper by Friday morning, or I'd ultimately fail science class. Mr. Bower wouldn't have the last word with that. After all the clever preparation, I was stumped. Come again. I should have no trouble extracting pertinent information from the textbook because I was the real Jessica.

While the topic of sexual reproduction was exciting, asexual was questionable. Botany had nothing to do with intercourse, which made it boring. To top it off, no text in a 3"thick book could keep my eyes glued to the page. I sat at the bedroom desk laboring to stay awake over my extra credit report. Growing weary with time, I stared at meaningless words that virtually ran together. I wasn't absorbing a thing. What was happening to me? Instead of writing intelligent paragraphs on the structure and function of plant cells, I was drifting off on my anchored armrest. Did I no longer possess the cerebral functions for intelligent cognitive processes? Had I been reduced to a total imbecile? I felt hopeless.

"Dini!" Mr. Bower startled me awake, yelling at me. His fist hit the desk, rattling my nerves. "I dare you fall asleep again," he admonished then darted off. I glanced at the alarm clock. It was pushing 12:30 a.m. and I hadn't constructed one sentence on the blank sheet of lined paper. I gazed into the textbook: Mitosis and meiosis are two forms of cellular reproduction. Reproduction . . . I pondered . . . what, cells fuck?

I reached over to the wall phone. "Don't you touch that!" Mr. Bower snapped. The Gestapo must have been keeping an eye on my every move. I shut the door. Moments later, the door flung open with HIM hovering over me. "If I have to tie you down to your chair to make you do your homework, I'll do it!" He forbade me to close the bedroom door. I was to have no privacy yet ace this class. *What was wrong with this picture?*

I didn't know how to keep my shut eyes open and thoughts from scrambling. On top of it all, the urge hit me! "No! Go away!" I demanded. "Bad timing. I can't do that anymore." The longer I abstained from the urge, the more feeble-minded I grew. I knew it was just a pocket- reach away. I didn't want to do it again, but my body forced me. I had no choice. I was convinced that if I wouldn't pursue the Speed, I'd involuntarily fall asleep, and the Gestapo would surely beat the crap out of me. I retrieved the napkin Vicki slipped into my pants pocket. As I unfolded the napkin, the answer became as clear as day—Vicki's ink-blotted phone number wrapped the precious capsule.

I give the textbook one last spin. The words on the page shift in place as if microscopic spiders crawl about. Why bother? I sigh. I sit back in a reclining position. Oddly the door is closed. I turn the knob.

It's locked from the other side! I'm sure Ray wouldn't permit a closed door let alone a locked door. I repeatedly knock, yelling for him to unlock it. My call is unanswered. How could he be so cruel? Great, I'm captive in my own bedroom. Once more I lift the receiver to call Kevin but . . . the line is dead!

"Damn it!" In outrage, I throw the receiver into the mirror. Denise Bower's image shatters into millions of fragmented pieces. This should've alarmed Mr. Bower but no response. I proceed to escape through the window, but once I lift the blinds, there's no window! Disbelieving my eyes, I grope the wall.

Meanwhile, thunder rattles the room. I try the door again, wrestling the knob. I call out for someone to answer—anyone. Still no response. Is no one home? Have they abandoned me? I attempt to knock the door down with the weight of my body, but I injure myself doing so. I yell, "The contract mentioned nothing about incarcerating your own daughter in her goddamn bedroom!"

I sit on the bed sniffling and wiping tears off my cheeks, feeling hopeless. I snatch the last tissue in the box. A cold drop of water bounces off the back of my hand. This drop is no teardrop. I look up. The ceiling is cracked!

I bang at the door in urgency. "The fuckin' ceiling's leaking!" Instantly the entire ceiling collapses open! I shriek! Rainwater pours down on me in full force, splattering all over my head, soaking everything, including my clothes, notebook, and textbook.

I hammer at the door in panic, urging someone to rescue me. "It's flooding in here! Please help me, anyone—please!" For a fleeting moment it occurs to me that this is no accident. Mr. Bower has arranged this as a form of torture.

The Uncle Sam poster, rock and roll pin-ups, and male centerfolds that decorated the walls suddenly wilt in shreds as debris setting sail in the pool of rainwater. The bed begins to float. Furniture turns over. I climb onto the bed, balancing my weight on the mattress. The soaring water level rises above my shoulders. My clothes are drenched, clinging to my freezing body, and hair whips against my face. Shreds of paper and closet sports equipment surface over the water, meandering on their own course.

My head hits something hard. It's the ceiling! The ceiling sealed itself. No dents, cracks, or leaks. In fact, the ceiling fixture is intact. I swim over to the ceiling fixture in the pool of junk. But once I grasp for the fixture, it falls into the tank of water.

The only positive side to this hysteria is that it stopped raining. Water currents push me around. I set afloat on my back. There are only about three inches of air between the surface of the water and the ceiling. Within minutes, I will run out of oxygen and drown.

To add to the terror, I spot a . . . a giant tarantula within the depths of the water. This can't be possible, but it is moving. I gasp! The tarantula is way oversized—about the height of a grown man. It's damn near hard not to panic when a spider-looking creature crawls upside-down on the ceiling toward you. It stops, freezes, then darts forward. I swim for my life as it chases me around the tank. Its enormous tentacles wrap around my legs. I wrestle it, kicking and splashing it away while struggling to stay afloat. I swing the heel of my shoe into its black, monstrous eyeballs. I'm not certain what happened but I see sparks flying around and the four-eyed monster lights up like a Christmas tree. The critter is blown to pieces!

TATTLER

The flickering light bulb above awoke me. The light must have been left on all night. All along I had been resting on an open textbook. A photo of a tarantula stared at me. I gasped at the gross details then brushed the book off my desk.

It was Friday morning, and I hadn't done an iota of work. What was I to do after begging and promising Mrs. Higgins so? I hid my face in shame. *No! This isn't about proving that I'm smarter than Jessica. This is about disposing of Jessica. I must stay focused.*

Mrs. Floyd, the school principal, had me paged for a little chat before homeroom session. She seated me in her office. "Denise." She faced her paperwork with reading glasses hanging on the hook of her nose, but her eyeballs were on me. "The reason I called you into my office is because a parent contacted me to report that you stole a student's notebook. Is this so, Ms. Bower?" Mrs. Floyd leaned over in her chair, flicking her ballpoint pen with her right thumb as if it were some kind of annoying habit she developed to get her through the day.

"No." I shook my head in a matter-of-fact way.

"Denise." Mrs. Floyd grimaced. "Mrs. Higgins informed me about the extra credit assignment when I confronted her with the complaint. Level with me. What are you up to? You have been suspended a number of times and quite frankly, with a record like this, we're really thinking of transferring you. That means to another school system, understand? You're causing far too much trouble here."

I was silent.

She relaxed her elbows on the desk with her hands folded, rubbing her thumb against her chin. She took a deep breath. "I suggest you return the student's notebook promptly, or your parents will have to be notified. Though I realize notifying your folks will do little good since the office has already tried this approach countless times, this is our school policy short of removal." She paused. "Denise, I don't feel this school is the appropriate learning environment for your needs. I spoke with your counselor, and she can't reach you either. You have a serious disciplinary problem. You're disturbing other students and causing disruption for your teachers. We can no longer tolerate this behavior here at Eastwood." Mrs. Floyd pulled an expulsion form from her file cabinet. "Do you have anything else to say?"

"I want another chance," I insisted, grabbing onto the corners of her desk, accidentally knocking over her pencil container.

"We've given you all the chances . . ." she said as she reached to the floor for the container.

"Just one more chance," I demanded forcefully.

As she placed the pencil container back on the desk, a few papers went flying across the floor. She was annoyed that I messed up her desk. I hopped off my seat, retrieved the scattered papers, and returned them to her hand. She thanked me. "Why do you want another chance?" she questioned.

"I have to improve my grades, or my dad will slaughter me. I've been working all night on the extra credit assignment for Mrs. Higgins. I'm really trying."

"Is that why you stole the notebook, Denise?"

"It was a setup. I never stole anyone's notebook."

"A setup, ay?" Mrs. Floyd tapped her pen countless times, thinking things over. "What makes you think that?"

"Someone is causing lots of trouble for me as payback just because a long time ago I flirted with her boyfriend. It's about spite, Mrs. Floyd. Someone hates my guts."

"And who may this someone be?"

"I can't share that information or I'd be putting my life in great danger."

"Is she a part of the mafia?"

"You can call it that," I said with a blank expression, trying to keep a straight face.

"Okay. I'm going to investigate this 'setup.' I'm giving you one more chance. But one more is final." Mrs. Floyd waved her pen at me. "Now get out of here before I change my mind."

One more chance meant that I wouldn't be expelled today or tomorrow. It bought me time and time was all I had for ammunition. I was escorted out of Mrs. Floyd's office with a hall pass and warned that I was being closely watched.

LOCK HER

I remained focused, looking all over for Jessica. I had others scout her out. The word was that she was in Room 207 of the English department grading papers for a teacher. I should have guessed. I used to spend my homeroom mornings assisting Mrs. Tyler. I would volunteer to help her around midterms or on short notice. She'd prepare morning drills and tests while I graded papers. She'd lend me books to read over the weekend in exchange.

Having Susan Henler on my side was a big asset. I explained to her what happened and that I was prepared to retaliate. The resentment in my eyes spoke for itself and I knew Susan wasn't going to cop out. When we entered Mrs. Tyler's classroom, we had no trouble spotting Jessica silently hashing away at the papers on the teacher's desk. Conveniently, no teacher was present. Once Jessica noticed us, she raised her eyebrows in alarm then lowered her head, trying to remain calm. She said nothing. Regardless the number of times I saw her; I was just as amazed by my clone.

I casually strolled over to Jessica and leaned over her desk with my arms folded. After beaming my evil eye down at her for the longest moment, I blurted, "I understand you reported me to the principal."

Susan retrieved a pack of cigarettes as she shut the classroom door. She offered me one. "I have a feeling this is going to take a while." She lit mine.

I blew smoke into Jessica's face. "For someone who's such a smartass, such as yourself, you seem to have a hard time understanding *no tattling*, don't ya?" She coughed. I resumed, "What don't you understand about NO TATTLING?" Jessica refused to look up at me as her eyes dodged mine. "You can't avoid me. I'm like a thorn in your ass. I'll keep stinging ya till ya get it."

"She ain't talkin'," Susan pointed out.

"I'll make her talk," I assured. I snatched the red pen right out of Jessica's hand and tossed it. She quickly collected the test papers and shoved them into the teacher's drawer to keep them out of my reach. Still not a word out of her mouth. There were no buttons or alarms to activate for help, but she did look around the desk area for such.

Susan noticed Jessica's purse lying on a desk. Susan opened the purse, and the contents were dumped onto the desk with total disregard. "Ooh, look what I found—money!" Susan sniffed and wiggled the bills.

"Stop!" Jessica cried.

Susan exclaimed, "Ah, she does speak. And ma 'God it's in English. Go figure, we're in an English classroom." Susan dangled a set of keys in front of me. "I wonder what this goes to?"

"Just give me back my notebook, okay?" Jessica urged.

I banged on her desk, "I don't have your fuckin' notebook, you squealer," I yelled at her. "And I'm gonna fuckin' beat the crap out of you because you fuckin' reported me to the principal when I fuckin' didn't do nothin'!"

Jessica's eyes were streaming with tears. "Susan took my notebook, and you put her up to it," she asserted in a huff.

"You listen here—she didn't take your fuckin' notebook. If you weren't such an asshole about it you would have figured it out that it was in your locker the whole time," I hinted.

Jessica immediately got up off her cushy teacher's chair and darted out of the classroom heading straight for her locker. Susan and I followed. Jessica worked her locker combination then lifted the metal latch to open the locker when she heard our presence behind her. Jessica stood as still as a bug.

"Whatcha fuckin' 'fraida, huh? I ain't gonna touch ya inside the school halls, you pussy," I bellowed.

The locker was opened and Jessica's notebook, with everything just the way she left it, sat on the ledge.

"What the fuck's your problem? I couldn't have stolen it if it's in your locker," I argued. I slammed the locker on her, nearly slicing her fingers off. "Now I want you to go back to your parents and set them straight and clear things with the principal. Tell them how much of a ditz you really are and that you falsely accused US and you apologize."

Jessica quickly figured, "You put it back. The locker combination is in my notebook." Again, she worked the combination. Once opened, again I slammed the door on her. "I said I never took your notebook. Are you deaf or something? I didn't hear you apologize." I stared her down. "You're really being a smartass with me, and I don't like it. Now I said that I never took it. You left it in your locker, and I don't want to hear another peep out of you."

She said nothing.

I stooped to her level, drawing my face close. I wanted her to look me in the eyes so I could read into her thoughts. "You can't run away anymore," I said insidiously. "It's over." My eyebrows rose as I whispered, "The game's over." I smiled at her maliciously.

Her eyes widened with fear. "If you touch me, I'm gonna scream!"

"I see, well I can play that game too. Keep it up, Jessy. You're calling the shots." I pushed her into the lockers, ready to pop her.

"Let me go!" Jessica muttered.

"Let me go," Susan mimicked her. "Are you going to tell the principal on us again?" Susan spoke condescendingly. "Are we being really MEAN to you? Did we HURT your feelings?" she mocked her. Susan and I snickered.

I saw a teacher approach from the corner of my eye. "We gotta split," I cautioned Susan. I released Jessica. "I'll catch up with you later." I threatened her, "And if you want to live, I suggest you not say a word to anyone about this."

TEACH HER A LESSON

Susan and I caught up with Jessica in the cafeteria during the lunch hour. Jessica was sitting with her buddies Ann and Stephanie. I plopped myself down right across from Jessica.

Susan stood on surveillance behind her. Stephanie and Ann rolled their eyes—*not again.* Jessica had just unwrapped her chicken salad sandwich that her mother went out of her way to prepare. I remembered how Mom used to throw all kinds of herbs and spices into my lunchmeat. She was a good cook. It deeply disturbed me that my imposter was being treated to the same delicacies.

"What do you want now?" Jessica asked exasperatedly.

I leaned over to her. "I'm keeping an eye on you to make sure you learn your lesson."

"What lesson?" Jessica half-heartedly asked.

"I don't like tattlers," I reminded her.

"Well, I don't like thieves," Jessica spoke up for herself. Her friends were proud of her.

I poured her can of soda all over her fresh breaded chicken sandwich, making for one soggy second thought. "Ooh," her friends whined.

Jessica got up off the bench and muttered, "I'm getting the. . ."

Susan tripped her, making her fall flat on her face. Susan's foot pressed against Jessica's ear on the cold hard surface. With sadistic delight I rubbed the soggy dripping loose bread all over Jessica's face. "What did I tell you about tattling, or did you forget so quickly?"

Jessica slowly got up off the floor and sat back down on the bench in search of a napkin to wipe her face. She looked nervously at her friends as if to say, *"Do something!"*

"I think you should leave now," Stephanie hinted, standing up to me.

I grabbed the table salt and shook it in Stephanie's hair. "Would you like some pepper with that?" I teased. Susan couldn't stop giggling. Directing my anger toward Jessica: "Are you going to tattle on me? I'd like to see you do it," I challenged her.

My good buddy, Stephanie, did it again, took up for Jessica. "Any idiot can cheat in class and get away with it. Only morons steal NOTEBOOKS. Are you like retarded or something? What's your problem? You didn't get laid lately?" She put her hand to her mouth. "Oops! Sorry, I guess you're gonna have to beat me up for saying that 'cause I just had to get that off my chest." She smiled silly at me, blinking wildly as salt particles bounced off her eyelashes.

Though I was pissed at her, she was not the object of my abuse. I spit on Stephanie's half-eaten sandwich and walked off without a word.

"Ooh!" the girls were again sickened.

My partner in crime and I hurried into the restroom lounge. Susan was definitely ready for another smoke. "You gotta vendetta with Wheaton, don't cha?" she surmised.

"How did you figure?" I said sarcastically, puffing away like there was no tomorrow.

"What's the deal? She's a smartass or something?"

"It's spite. I'm getting her back for tattling." I used the same lame excuse.

"She got you suspended, didn't she?"

"Yeah, close to expelled."

"You're gonna beat her up for real, right? You can't let her get away with that."

"Yup. Sure will. It's all in the timing, ya know what I mean?"

"Sure. You just let me know when. I'll help you finish her off. She's easy. But that hard-nosed Stephanie is a challenge. She thinks she's Jessica's bodyguard or something. When I finish with her, she won't bother you again. I'll scare the shit out of her." Susan nodded dramatically, tapping her ashes. She slowly exhaled smoke fumes. "When you thinking of?"

"*When* isn't important to me. *How* is the question. It must be done methodically. I want to finish her off for good."

"Denise, you're not talking about . . ."

"Yes I am."

VICKI'S NEW DATE

Vicki darted into the lounge, interrupting our discussion. "There you are. I've been looking all over for you. Dini, I gotta talk to you."

"What—what?" She had me worried.

Vicki asked Susan to excuse us as she pulled me aside. As Susan trashed her cigarette and left the lounge, she said she'd catch up with me later.

"It's been really awful for me," Vicki said with a sad face. "Bill and I had a fight last night. He accused me of sleeping around with another guy. But honestly, I didn't. He didn't believe me. Then this morning in homeroom, Janie Parker threatened me to stay away from Bill. Ya see, he's the one sleeping around, not me. So, it's all over between us," she lamented.

I caressed her. "I'm so sorry, Vicki. I bet you've really been upset over him."

She overcame her sorrow instantly as she raised her eyebrows. "Yeah, but there's good news. Christina has been wanting to fix me up with this guy, Todd McKane, for some time now. I don't know, I don't want to rebound on anyone. It's an emotional time, ya know. But it's funny, she never thought Bill and I would work out in the first place 'cause we're always fightin'."

I was in shock. "Did you say Todd McKane?"

"Yeah, do you know him?" Vicki asked innocently.

"Well, he . . . he definitely sounds familiar. It . . . it sounds like a really good idea." I reminded myself that I was presently in the past, knowing full well that in the future I will have destroyed their relationship.

"You really think so?" Vicki so eagerly wanted to trust my opinion.

"Well, I . . . I hope he will be faithful to you—I mean I hope he will be better than . . . than ummm . . ."

"Bill?" Vicki reminded me. She studied me for some time. She made me feel rather uncomfortable. "Is something bothering you?" she asked subtly. "Are you and that dude Kevin getting along?"

"Yeah, why?" I felt butterflies in my stomach thinking that she heard he'd been running around too. My heart fluttered.

"You just don't look too happy. I don't mean to stick my nose in your business though."

"Kevin is very faithful to me. That's not my problem." I lowered my head, frowning.

"He's just not active in bed."

"He bores you?"

"No. I mean he's not active at all. We haven't done IT yet."

"No sex?" She was stunned.

"He thinks I've got some kinda sex disease so he insists I see a doc first."

"Ridiculous! He sounds like a momma's boy. You gotta break him of that. Ya gotta loosen him up. Ya know I have the perfect fix for that." Vicki opened her purse. And, as usual, the solution was some sort of pill.

"No Vicki—no more pills. The last one was a nightmare I'll never forget."

"This one's different. This is called Ecstasy. Slip a pill in his drink and I guarantee he'll be as horny as hell."

"Well, I . . ." I backed away hesitantly, thinking of all the trouble she'd already caused.

"Trust me with this one. Have I ever disappointed you?"

No Vicki, the flooded bedroom was just what I needed to soothe my nerves. And the tarantula added a very special touch. Instead of being nasty, which I had a good mind to do, the only words that flew out of my mouth were, "What if I get caught?"

"He won't know what you did to him. He won't feel a thing, promise."

"Thanks, but I really shouldn't . . ."

"Thank me later. I should charge you for this stuff since it's so hard to find but being that you're a special friend of mine, consider it a gift. I have to go now. I'll let you know how the date with Todd turns out, bye!" Vicki hurried out the door before I could stop her.

I reluctantly shoved the packet into my pocket. I thought it over. *Well, I sure could use some wild sex.*

ECSTASY

I surprise visited Kevin. Instead of appearing overjoyed to see me, he was hesitant—uncertain. "What are you doing here? You're supposed to be home studying."

I rolled my eyes. "Yes, but I miss you. I'm not used to being alone at night without you beside me in bed, you know." I wrapped my arms around his hot firm body, kissing him hard in the mouth. My tongue melted in his. We stood locked in a long-winded embrace.

"Wow!" he exclaimed from the loaded kiss. "I miss you too, honey, but . . . what about your schoolwork? I don't want to interfere with that."

At that moment my intolerance appreciated Vicki's little gift which was about to save my relationship. "Is that all that matters to you? Doesn't the time I spend with you mean something?"

"Of course, it does but this is a weeknight. We agreed to spend time together on weekends, remember?"

"I don't care. I want you now!" I grabbed for him, but he pushed me away. He was getting annoyed.

"Is there something you're not telling me, Denise? How are things at home?"

"Everything is fine. I just came over to see YOU," I emphasized. "What's wrong with that?" The Ecstasy in my pocket was calling for me.

"Nothing. I . . . just thought you'd have . . . trouble . . . adjusting," Kevin continued to badger.

"I take it one day at a time, okay?" I snapped at him. Once more I lunged for him with the intent of loosening his shirt.

He distanced himself. "Did you get yourself checked? You need to be examined, Denise. Please understand."

I had to snap him out of his train of thought. "I came here to make a toast."

"A toast—toast to what?"

I was curt with him for not having guessed. "Toast to my success in school, dummy." "That's a great idea but why didn't you call me first?"

"You don't like surprises?"

"It's not that. I mean, how would you know if I was home or not? I do work odd hours, ya know. Besides, if we're going to celebrate, we should include your folks. I'm sure they'd love to join us for such an occasion."

"This is only between us, Kevin."

"Alright, I'll get the champagne," he finally surrendered.

"No—no dear. This one's on me. Let me handle it," I stopped him midstream. "You can set the dining room table with a candlelight."

"If you insist." He paused with open hands and a raised eyebrow. "I've never seen you so enthusiastic about anything before. You sure everything's alright . . . grades, classes?" He wouldn't let me off the hook.

"Are you kidding? Grades couldn't be better. I'm happier than ever since you came into my life." I pointed, backing away into the bar nook. Watching Kevin's every move, I quickly popped the cork off a champagne bottle, poured into two champagne glasses, then impatiently waited for the fizz to settle while Kevin set the dining room table with a scented candle. The lights were turned off. My hands shook wildly as I fumbled around my pockets for the packet. The contents of the capsules were poured into his drink. The powders dissolved instantly. I reminded myself that his drink was in my left hand. *Don't screw up*, I warned myself as I took a deep breath. Here it goes . . .

His champagne glass was served promptly before I plopped myself down beside him. As he spoke to me, he glanced into his drink but didn't seem to notice anything odd. I held my breath. We made a toast to success in the coming school year, tapping glasses together. He sipped at his drink little by little while chatting with me. Kevin asked me the same questions over, and over, about my teachers and classes, likes and dislikes, the relationship with my folks, and health concerns.

I felt a bit uneasy for I didn't know what would happen to him beyond what Vicki described to me. He questioned me as to why I was so quiet, if something was wrong. I told him I was getting tired, and I didn't handle alcohol well.

He held my hand. "Listen baby. You can come over anytime you want. I just don't want to interfere with your schoolwork, okay." I nodded, watching him sip away. I wondered how long it would take for the drug to kick in. I was concerned that he wouldn't want to drink the full amount.

His behavior gradually changed. His hand squeezed and caressed mine gently. "You know you are special to me," he whispered in the wine-apple scented ambiance of his dining room. With eyes locking into each other's soul, we sat in silence holding and hugging in the darkness over flickering flames. It was the most romantic moment I'd ever had. "There's something I want to tell you." He placed his glass on the table with the few remaining drops. "I don't care what you did in your past as a hooker. I want you to understand that I don't see you that way. You are truly dear to me. You're my best friend. I want you to know that. And whatever you want to do is okay. If you're just going back to school for me, I don't want you to do that. I want whatever makes you happy, okay. Now, I know you have a drug problem but I'm here for you. You're a strong soul. I know you're going to be okay."

I smiled.

He placed his hand over his stomach. "I feel a little queasy, what's in that drink?" he joked.

I laughed with him, but my stomach flopped.

"I think I'm getting lovesick," he chuckled. His dilated eyes zoned into mine. Passion overcame him. The kiss seemed eternal. I melted like the dripping hot wax on the candlestick. I longed for this moment. After he withdrew from the deep kiss he uttered, "I haven't been fair to you. Fuck your checkup. There ain't nothin' wrong with you. Even if there was, I accept you no matter what."

Like a magnet he clung right back onto me, kissing me hard in the mouth. Eventually we slid to the floor as the passion grew intense. He was sucking and nibbling all over my neck and chest. Our clothes were hastily removed. In the candlelit darkness I could see the vague contour of his male physique. If only a glimpse, I finally satisfied my aching curiosity. Oh, how I had yearned for this moment.

Though he hurried his thrust, I thirsted for it, guiding his entry as we bobbed back and forth, in the heat of animal passion. I was uncertain which of us breathed heavier, moaned loudest, hungered for more, or cried of joy first. Perhaps it was I who was out of control, not a care in the world about pleasing or performing anymore. Gone was the hassle of arguing or pleading a trick to pay for my services. I couldn't focus on his expressions for I was in my own world with him in it. My body seized with orgasms for the first time. I wished the intense, warm, jolting volts could last forever but it quickly subsided. I promised myself to never forget what the heavenly flame feels like.

After resting with him for some time, the consequences of conquering Kevin became more apparent. He was soaked with perspiration as we cuddled in exhaustion. His dilated eyes were glazed over. He got off the floor and staggered his way over to the trashcan and, like a drunk, peed into it.

"Kevin, what are you doing?"

"Pissin'," he slurred.

"In the trashcan?"

To amuse himself, he squirted the wall then giggled, pointing to his misfire, behaving childishly.

Once he finished, he laid down beside me, gently caressing my body. For the longest time he rambled on and on with a slurred tongue about himself as if we had just met. He mentioned his life experiences and his future with me. He revealed a story about a serious relationship he had in high school which failed because he didn't accept her completely, but he insisted he learned from his mistakes and accepted me unconditionally. He commented on how beautiful my eyes were and how soft and silky my hair felt to comb his fingers through.

With a sudden burst of energy, he got off the floor, turned the stereo on, and began to dance. He tugged on me to join him. We were swing dancing nude, in the darkness. He dipped me a few times and swirled me around. It was like a fantasy. He paused to refill the champagne glasses. Kevin was having the time of his life. I'd never seen him so happy. I wished the evening would last forever.

We grew tired as the dwindling flame on the candlestick burned away silently. In the darkness, Kevin could see the path to the bedroom. Not an utterance about school, parents, or doctors from his mouth. I couldn't have asked for more. I only wished I was on what he was on.

KEVIN CORRUPTED

I reached for his hairy chest, but Kevin was not in bed beside me. At three in the morning, I heard rattling of bottles, rapid breathing, and clicking of cabinet doors. Why would Kevin be up at the crack of dawn when he was due at work in five hours?

Kevin was slouched over the bar with his hair uncombed, face pale, unshaven, and red-eyed. I'd never seen him so disheveled. Empty bottles and corkscrews lay along the carpet as he already ransacked the supply, drinking himself silly. My mouth fell open. "What in God's name?" Witnessing his erratic behavior, I was dumbfounded. His entire demeanor changed overnight.

He slammed his bottle down. "The feelin' . . ." he muttered. "Sometin' ga'me that incred'ble feelin'. And I," he burped, "been through every bottle and ain't got a hit from it yet." He stumbled toward me, at least in my direction. ". . . You help me find it? I need mur of it, whatever it is. Ain't nothin' here gave me that buzz."

His face lit with anger. Flashbacks of Brad mistreating me washed over me like a premonition: *Brad throws me off the barn bed onto the floorboards then accuses me of stealing his stash. He slugs me repeatedly then pulls me off the floor by the hair and shakes me.*

I took a few steps back as Kevin approached with his drunken breath. I covered my mouth in shame. *My God,* I said to myself, *I only wanted Kevin to make love to me. I didn't mean any harm to him. What had I done to my Kevin? Had I planted the seed to make him one of me? Well, wasn't that what I wanted all along with Mr. Square-to-the-T? No, I guess not. I respected him because he stood for justice. And now, shame on me, the man who saved me from bondage, I have just enslaved to drugs. I created a monster!*

Kevin shook me.

I cried, "Let me go!" I looked away from his angry eyes.

He forced my chin to his face. He asked if I put something in his drink. "Answer me!" he insisted, enraged.

I began to cry. "Please Kevin, it's three in the morning. Let's go back to bed and talk about it in the morn . . ."

He shouted into my guilty face, "I said answer me, damn it!"

I slowly sank down toward his belly, pleading, "I'm sorry, so sorry."

Kevin lashed out, "Why?" He pinned me to the floor.

"Let me go," I demanded. Flashbacks of Richard forcing me down on the bed raced through my mind. I was a hooker. I was a sex slave. Why now did I feel so threatened? Perhaps it was not the physical abuse I was so fearful of, but the emotional battery of someone so close.

"What you put my drink?" he muttered.

Should I lie or tell the truth? I was torn between two opposing realities. If I was truly Denise, I would lie just to shut him up. But if I was Jessica, I would let the truth be known to him because I loved him and wanted to save him from unnecessary evils.

'Don't tell him, Dini, he's just like all the others,' my inner voice protested.

'Tell him the truth to save him. He could be in grave danger. You don't know what that drug will do to him. After all, he saved your life!'

'No. It doesn't matter. All that matters is your survival. Run!'

'Run? To where? When will this vicious cycle of running away ever end? That's all you've been doing all along. Learn your lesson and tell the truth. Besides, he'll eventually find out anyway.'

I blurted, "It's Ecstasy. That's all I know," I cried.

His swollen red eyes filled with resentment. "What it do?"

"It made you want it," I wept, clearing my throat.

"Where you get it?"

"A friend lent it to me," I sobbed under his wrath.

"So that's where you been in school yesterday, playin' hooky witcher dope pushers. You lied to me. Why you lie to me? I ain't done nothin' but good. What I do wrong?"

"Nothing," I admitted sadly.

You think I'm stupid or somethin', slipping me a mickey with . . . what dat shit called again?"

"Ecstasy."

Kevin released me, feeling drained and very emotional. "Why you hate me?" He got off me, lost his balance, and fell klutzily to the floor. He cried like an infant. I didn't know what to say or do, watching him behave so pathetically.

"I don't hate you," I tried to pacify him, but he continued his childish whining for some time, swearing that he tried his darned best and failed as a boyfriend and felt burned. ". . . Ain't done nothing bad to ya, why you hurt me?"

So suddenly he came out of his stupor and uttered, "I need 'nother hit, ya hear. I ain't like feelin' like this. It felt so good—real good." He wiped his sniffle on his shirt. "Gimme more."

I heard him motion to me with his own lips that he wanted more but I was uncertain that it was really Kevin talking. He was giving me permission to do whatever it took to get him fixed on Ecstasy. A sadistic wave of pleasure consumed me as I had finally corrupted Kevin.

TROMITAN

I could feel the pulsating rock music blocks away. Fido was not outside leashed to a tree, so I peered through the basement window. Flashing colored lights bounced around in the darkness of Vicki's club basement. I heard giggles. Eavesdropping wouldn't pay in this case, so I knocked at the door. No one answered. I was sure they couldn't hear me over the high volume, so I rang the doorbell several times.

Finally, Vicki answered. Todd McKane stood behind her. I reminded myself that I was woven in a time warp. Vicki had just met Todd. She looked a mess. Her face was pale, drawn, and devoid of expression. Long matted bangs hid the disgrace of her pathetic eyes. She was strung-out. She did not look at me but through me. She didn't bother to ask why I was visiting. I guess it didn't matter.

With sluggish speech she introduced Todd, "I want ya ta meet ma boyfriend."

Young Todd nodded as he shook his long black hair aside. I had to dismiss flashbacks of him attacking me in Fowlersville. He, too, looked quite hammered. The joint held loosely between his fingers was his quick fix. "She here get wasted or what?" he asked her.

Vicki waved me in. "Come in . . . show ya what I got." She had me follow her to a glass end-table. White powders, scattered across the centerpiece, appeared to glow in the dark, creating a magical presence. "Don't just look at it, snort it." She handed me a straw. "Go ahead."

I backed off. "I . . . I didn't come here to get high. I need you to give me some more Ecstasy for Kevin."

"Never mind Kevin. Try some. It's the coolest shit." Her head wobbled as if her neck was about to detach.

She whispered something in Todd's ear. "You don't say?" Todd remarked. He turned to me with a look of surprise. "So how was it? Heard you tried it."

"No," Vicki corrected him. "Her boyfriend."

"Oh, your boyfriend tried Ecstasy." Todd grinned.

"Yes, and he needs more. I think he's hooked."

"She thinks he's hooked." Todd laughed with Vicki as if it was a real cool gag I pulled on Kevin. She giggled, whispering more silly things in his ear. Todd grabbed himself at the crotch making sexual gestures. "Was he a good fuck?"

I ignored his crude provocation. "I need more Ecstasy," I directed to Vicki.

"Well," Vicki's eyebrows rose.

"Well, what?" I demanded, agitated.

"Dini, you ain't stupid. You fuckin' steal for it. You know what I mean?"

"No, what do you mean?"

Todd kissed Vicki passionately on the mouth and around the neck. He put his hand in her pants whereby distracting her from me.

"Vicki, what do you mean?" I insisted.

The petting and necking continued uninterrupted. I was determined to get her attention.

I turned the lights on and stereo off, nearly blinding the two lovers.

"What the fuck's her problem? Her pussy ain't exercised enough? She need a 24-hour pump?" Todd fussed because the light irritated his sensitive eyes.

Vicki wanted the low down. "Did ya sneak it to 'um? Did ya enjoy it? Was he good in bed?" She shielded her eyes with her hands.

"Yes, it was great. Why are you asking?"

Todd slid his shades on then drew his face close to mine, blowing stale pot breath on my face. "'Cause your pussy's gonna have ta make some cold hard cash cuz it costs."

My eyes bounced over to Vicki's with uncertainty. "But you gave it to me for free," I argued.

"Girlfriend, that was a gift. Don't you see, I lose money when I give you stash. Stash costs MONEY. I was doin' you a favor." She squinted, trying to give me eye contact. "I'll give ya all the Ecstasy your heart desires, but it costs." Vicki rubbed her fingertips together. "I need some green, sister."

"I don't have any money," I confessed.

She pointed out, "But boyfriend does. He works, doesn't he? Take his money."

"I can't do that."

"You want Ecstasy, don'cha?"

She pissed me off, so I lost my temper. "Damn you, Vicki!" I pushed her.

Todd held me back. "Hey, hey, hey. Unless you gonna do her, you ain't touchin' my girl." Vicki threw a punch at me so I retaliated despite Todd's refereeing. He joked, "Why don't the two of you mud wrestle? Shit I'd like to see some action."

"She's all fucked up," Vicki demanded to Todd, still trying to reach over to fight me, "She needs a fuckin' tranquilizer."

I was outraged! "A tranquilizer? You're the fuckin' pothead snorting and shootin' up. Just look at yourself. You're a mess." I justified myself.

Like a mental slug to the head, Vicki informed me that she spoke to Susan yesterday and Susan mentioned that I was planning to finish Wheaton off. "Strange. Real strange. Says Wheaton's been tattling on ya. What the fuck you doin' stealin' her notebook?" Vicki questioned, "Why you actin' so strange if you ain't gettin' high yourself? You need to take a chill." And, as usual, Miss Rx reached into her pocket to hand me another type of pill. "Here, take this and you'll feel better."

I grew very intolerant of her ways. I knocked the pill right out of her hand. "No Vicki, no more fuckin' pills," I raised my voice. "So that you can make me pay for them once I get hooked? No, no more shitty trips and no more frickin' addictions. I'm tired of it all. I'm tired of getting wasted. Don't you see those fuckin' chemicals are messin' us all up? Can you not see that we're all turning into bloodthirsty monsters? It's taking over our minds and destroying our ability to reason. Don't you see that? You're fuckin' killin' us all," I shouted, trying to get my point across.

Todd suggested, "What we need is an orgy. I don't think the dude gave her a good enough fuck."

Vicki clenched her teeth at me, angrily pointing to the door. "Get the fuck out of my house. You ain't here to get dusted. Get the fuck out, NOW!" she opened the door and pushed me out, slamming the door behind me.

I gathered my composure on her patio. The lights were turned off, music on. I shut my eyes. Tears came streaming down my cheeks. I took a deep breath. FOCUS, I demanded of myself. Forget about Kevin. Forget about schoolwork. They were all just distractions—wasting time. I needed to focus on Jessica. I had to reach her somehow. It was urgent. Think, think.

Vicki mentioned tranquilizers. I remembered Dr. Hamilton prescribed a tranquilizer for me. It was designed to release repressed material, and it did just that. That's it! It's the only way I knew to reach her.

I rapped on Vicki's door, again. I heard her voice on the other side, "You're only comin' in if you snort. I don't want no fuckin' fights," she made clear. I accepted.

She sat me down on the sofa with a straw. "You're right, Vicki, I need a tranquilizer." I paused. "I have one in mind but it's only by prescription and I'm not seeing the doctor anymore. It's called Tromitan."

Vicki rolled her eyes. "I thought you ain't gonna do no shit no more. You gave me such a hard time about it. You're fucked up, girlfriend."

"Can you do me this one last favor?" I bargained. "I'll snort if you forge a prescription."

"Deal," Vicki agreed. "Cinch, I do it all the time. Just tell me the name of your doctor and show me what his signature looks like."

The straw rushed the granules right up my nose, in warp speed, through my sinuses and smack into my brain. My eyeballs bulged as everything raced around me. I gasped for air. It was all too foreign to grasp. Time stood still yet my entire life flew past me within a single minute! Everything was in slow motion yet racing at warp speed, so that my brain couldn't process it all!

"Gettin' a head rush, huh?" Vicki observed, winking at me. "Ooh!" I moaned.

Cuddling with Todd on the carpet, she commented as she kissed him, "Ya gotta good idea there, Love Bug, we should have an orgy. We could have a fuckin' drug fest. It would be sooo cool," Vicki envisioned, staring off into space.

For me, time was spinning out of control in a furious twister. My head rolled about as I was experiencing the weirdest delusions. Music became more than music. It was pure solid energy—a stream of consciousness. It stirred around in my blood.

The lovers were talking to me in different frequencies. It seemed as if my ears were channeling into various radio stations through static. I could not make any sense of it. Letters of the alphabet rolled off their tongues, danced in the air, spun around my head before entering my ears. Once I understood their garbled thoughts, I chimed in, laughing.

Next thing I knew I was holding a joint between my fingers lying face up on the carpet. Vicki knelt over me waving a piece of paper in slow motion. Once she freed it, the paper danced downward to my chest, landing like a feather. I held it. I could see ink blots but the rest was all a blur to me. "How do-do-do you-you-you like-like it-t-t-?" Her speech echoed.

"Huh?" I stared at her.

"Speed-d-d-d," she snickered. "Ain't it-it-it cool-l-l-l, ya know-know-know, the way-the way it messes-es with time-time-time and voices-es?" She handed me a magnifying glass. "Vision's little blurry-blurry-blurry, ay?" she remarked.

I held the magnifier over the paper. Instantly, I felt a jolt of electricity circumvent my brain. It was a prescription for Tromitan! I couldn't believe it. Vicki forged her signature on a pad of prescription paper. Was this just another hallucination or the real stuff? I asked her, "Are you sure about this? Suppose I get caught?"

Vicki exhaled from her cig. "Denise, that's not like you. You never used to worry about getting caught or getting trashed. What's gotten into you? You know the system's fucked up. We do this all the time. What's with you?" she questioned my behavior.

The most gratifying smile sealed my face as I shrugged my shoulders. Vicki's voice was no longer in an echo chamber and things weren't moving in slowing motion then jumping ahead in a New York minute. This was real! No need to explain anything anymore to Vicki. Nina would soon be attending the wild sex party. But I was about to put an end to this vicious chain of events.

HELLO ONCE AGAIN

Two Tromitan tablets lay in the palm of my hand. I took a deep breath. This was the moment I'd been waiting for. This time I used discretion and didn't overdose. I had to know if Tromitan could really help me. I swallowed.

Standing before the bedroom mirror, I observed myself while waiting anxiously for something to happen. Denise Bower stared at me back, not that I was ever anyone else. Who was I fooling anyway? The delusion of my existence as Jessica Wheaton was just that. A delusion. The lesson here was to learn to love myself the way I was, and I never achieved that.

What did I have to show for it all? Certainly not my relationship with Kevin that I alone destroyed. Not my academic achievements, for I could not commit to doing a single homework assignment that I alone initiated and pledged full responsibility for. I hadn't appeased any bad feelings between my parents or, for that manner, anyone else I met along my journey. I pretty much ran away from every hurdle like a coward. So, I guess all that I learned was self- pity.

My eyes deceive me as I see his reflection in the mirror. He stands behind me with his arms folded. I notice the expression on the father's face that he is displeased. Always displeased. Always telling me that I can't do anything right. And it manifested.

All at once the storm hits . . .

I lie in bed totally bare. My wrists and ankles are bound to the bedpost. Father is naked on top of me. He tries to make an entry but has trouble penetrating. I feel something razor sharp cutting away at my genitals, slashing the swollen baby skin. "You're too goddamn small. It's gotta go in," Father insists. I cry out for Mother though she'd never come to my rescue on any account. I yell at the top of my lungs, panting madly, gasping for air, nearly losing consciousness. My insides burn like a hot iron against skin. My cheeks are wet with tears, genitals ooze. I'm inflamed!

"No!" I screamed.

I'm playing outside when . . . I'm attacked by a hose. I'm drenched and shivering. "I promise I won't do it anymore, please Daddy," I beg, shielding myself with my elbows. I'm held down over his knees. I feel the lashing burn—the cold—the pressure inside my genitals. What's lashing at me? "Please stop Daddy, put the hose down!" I cry. It's forced into my mouth. Globs of freezing water. He's trying to drown me with a running hose!

"Stop!" I squeezed my head as if it was about to burst.

I hear Father call for me. I know better than to lock the bathroom door. Father would beat me if I lock any door in the house. He never trusted me behind a closed door. Hurry—what can I do? I panic! I have Mother's lipstick and blush all over my face.

Father will be angry if he catches me this way. I quickly sweep all Mommy's cosmetics back into her vanity drawer. Father pokes his head into the bathroom, noticing my reflection in the mirror. I can tell he's upset. "No Daddy," I toss my head in denial. "I wasn't playing with Mommy's makeup; it's my own."

Deservingly, Father accuses me of lying. "You had better wash every bit of your mother's makeup off, you hear me!" He scorns, "I never want to catch you wearing makeup again, little one. I told you before, makeup is only for pretty women like your mother." He fills the sink with hot water before immersing my head into it! Once he frees me, my face is inflamed. I cry.

"Ahhh!" I shouted, staggering about, on the brink of fainting, trying to avoid a third round.

Father drives me home from church. I'm seven. It's stormy outside. I turn the car radio on to break the icy silence. Father instructs me to turn the radio off. I don't listen. Father always drives in silence. I'm in the mood for some cheerful music. Again, he demands that I turn the radio off, or I will be punished. I don't want Father to think I'm a coward, so I ignore him. He pulls the vehicle over to the curb, coming to a screeching halt. Father raises his voice, ordering me to get out of the car and shut the door behind me. I'm all choked up, in tears. I obey, unsure of his intention. The rain sprinkles in. I never meant to get him that upset. I apologize. Father takes off with the car, leaving me stranded in the rain. I've little doubt that he won't return to pick me up. I shiver. I remind myself that I'm a bad girl, that I had just come from the Holy Sanctuary to atone and here I go again, sinning. I ask for forgiveness. Would Jesus forgive me for being bad?

I laid in a fetal position on the floor, crying like a baby.

My eyes catch something moving. A transparent pair of walking tennis shoes ascends the wall. The shoes stop a foot in front of me. Knees appear, followed by a set of hands. I never believed in ghosts but I'm about to be convinced. The bodiless image faces me.

Tennis shoes spread apart with legs at an angle toward me. The ghost reaches over to help me off the floor. I'm distrusting of the hospitable hand.

"Please," a voice insists, extending its hand.

"Who are you?"

"What difference does that make now? You've accepted yourself just the way you are, haven't you? You're a very troubled little soul, aren't you?"

"What?" She confuses me. "What are you talking about?"

"Oh, I heard what you just said but did you hear what I said?" "What did I just say?"

"Well, you've certainly impressed me," the voice rambles on without answering. "I never expected you to adjust."

"Adjust to what?" I ask as I get myself off the floor.

"Adjust to being you," the voice answers as the image forms a face. Standing in the sunlit bedroom, beside myself and the vanity mirror, is a transparent Denise Bower.

"This isn't really happening," I refuse to believe.

"So, do you REALLY like yourself?"

"Why are you asking? Are you some kind of demon?"

"No, not quite. I just want to say thank you for making my wishes come true."

"What wishes?"

"For allowing me to be you as long as I please." The transparent face smiles.

I'm enraged. "Are you crazy?" I throw my fist in the air, swinging random punches through the transparent image. "Get the *hell out of my life, you creep." Once I realize I'm wrestling with nothingness, I know I'm going crazy.*

"Alright, I'll leave you alone this time, but please, never again have an evil thought about me, okay? I'd really like it that way. Let's just be soul mates and go on with life just the way it is. Can we call it a truce? You not bother me, and I let you live peacefully?" The transparent figure gestures a handshake.

"Now you listen to me, Denise. You don't fool me. I know all about you and your games and I will win this. Do you hear me? Win! I'll destroy every morsel of your spirit. Just watch me," I threaten the ghost.

"Who are you kidding? My spirit is already destroyed. How many times do I have to tell you, I couldn't satisfy my father in bed or be it any other man. You see, I'm a born sinner. Nothing I did would make me deserving of love. My body wasn't attractive enough, brains never smart enough, and faith never strong enough. Each, and every man I screwed was a struggle to prove that I was worthy to be in bed with and maybe then I would earn Daddy's love. Well, that prophecy remains unfulfilled.

How would you like it if your daddy chased you around the yard with a hose at full force? Once he caught you, he'd flatten you over his knee, strip down your panties, and plug a pressurized hose into your genitals. Oh, you could hear him laugh so hard, his lap would shake. Ya see, I was his rag doll he could tear apart and destroy, and no one would ever find out. Not even after he tried to drown me with the hose inserted in my mouth. Yes, I was his little secret he could shred to pieces because I had no feelings. I was punished for showing feelings. Feelings were evil because they were mine.

Mother is beautiful and sacred. Trying to imitate Mother's beauty was a terrible sin I committed for I should know I am evil, and evil is ugly. Father knew I was bad when he caught me with Mother's makeup on my face. He should have drowned me in the sink and left me alone in everlasting peace, but no, I had to return to this hell.

But the worst punishment of all was the dead silence. That's the true face of the devil. I merely turned the car radio on but that's resisting the devil. I shivered that day, walking home in the pouring rain, wishing for lightning to strike.

Yes, my friend, being strung-out on dope is the way I envision heaven to be.

Regardless of what he says, regardless of what he does, however many times he beats me, however many times I dread being awoken by Father in the middle of the night with his nude weight on top of me, and no matter how painful it is to keep the secret between him and I, the sin of getting stoned is nirvana — total bliss.

Therefore, I'm ever so grateful that you have fully accepted yourself as Denise Bower. And I pray that you let me live in peace as Jessica Wheaton."

Appalled by the horrifying reality of all the flashback episodes, I place my hand over my mouth. "I'm sorry," I utter, "I'm so sorry." Momentarily grieving, as if someone had just passed away. I'm at a loss for words. My eyes fill with sadness, but at the same, I'm full of anger. I'm saddened by the details of her personal experiences, but angry with her for victimizing me to endure her nightmares. "I'm sorry to hear you had a rotten childhood, but you had no right to involve me in your ugly world. And how did you . . ."

"Jus' what the fuck are you on?" Kevin barged through the door at that very moment. I was on the cusp of persuading my imposter to disclose the ultimate secret to switching me back. I was outraged!

"I's lookin' all over for ya. Did you get me more? Cuz I need more." Kevin apparently didn't see the ghost. Neither did he see the reflection of Mr. Bower in the mirror. Because they were all delusions.

Kevin took me into his arms. I wanted to cry on his shoulder and tell him what happened but just as Denise had always kept every secret to herself, so did I. For I was now Denise.

"Ya freakin' out, babe?" He touched my wet cheeks with his fingertips. He knew I'd been crying but had more important issues to discuss. He kissed me tenderly. "Somethin' happened today at work and uh . . . well uh . . . I sort of lost my job."

"You what!" I shook my head, zapping back into the present moment. "You can't lose your job. We need the dough," I insisted.

"That's why I need a hit," he explained sadly.

SEDUCTION

The only source of light within Mr. Bower's office came from a tall desk lamp. The yellowish light casted a shadow onto his legal papers. His bifocals sat on the base of his nose. In his solitude, he studied his briefs while listening to soft classical music in the background. He would reposition himself in his chair, periodically, to adjust his comfort level. He uttered to himself now and then. He was so absorbed in his work that he didn't notice another shadow enter his office. This shadow approached him, stood behind his chair, then placed her hands over his eyes.

He grunted, "Claudia, I don't have time for games. Can't you see I'm busy?" No reply.

The hands uncovered his eyes then lowered to his shoulders to massage him. A soft young voice whispered into his ear. "It's me, Daddy. I thought you could use a back rub," I said. Startled by my presence, he jumped, got off his chair, then stood back. He appeared disconcerted and confused, studying me. In the darkness, he could barely discern that I was wearing any clothes at all. I had on a white tank top and a black leather mini skirt thigh high.

"What are you doing here?" he questioned.

My finger pressed his lips shut. "Sh . . ." I whispered. I put my arms around him and kissed him on the lips. I whispered, "Like we used to."

Father pushed me off him. "What are you doing? What's gotten into you? I'm your father."

I resisted his protest. "I'm horny for you, Daddy." I brushed up against him, riding his leg with mine.

He raised his voice. "What's with you? Are you on drugs?"

No, it must be my dissociative state, I felt like saying as I grabbed him, ramming my tongue into his mouth. I quickly worked his crotch with my hand before I'd lose any chance of seducing him at all. I knew full well that if I couldn't arouse him immediately, he would beat the crap out of me. And he was boldly resisting. He broke the embrace, pushing me off.

Fortunately, his breathing softened. He began to relax. This time when I approached, I blew softly into his ear, totally calming him. I whispered, "Like we used to." I was patient and non-pressuring. I felt him rise. He reached for my chest. I helped him remove my tank top. He saw that I was braless. My tits dangled in the man's face. "Suck 'um hard, like we used to," I whimpered. Hurriedly, Ray undid his belt. He had me on the couch in seconds. He suckled my nipples and kissed me about my neck.

"Aren't I good," I boasted.

"Aw, yeah," Mr. Bower moaned, slobbering all over me.

"And you said I wasn't good at it when I was young," I giggled. "So, I practiced just for you . . . to make you proud," I added.

He stopped in the middle of our passion. "What . . . what am I doing?" He froze in place, totally confused.

I spread my legs open. He noticed I wasn't wearing panties either, as I had come prepared for the act. I moaned, "C'mon Daddy, stick it in, I'm wet for you."

Mr. Bower turned his head away in disgust. "Why are you doing this to me? This is unlike you. What's gotten into you?" he scolded.

"Why Daddy? Why did you do it to me?" I tossed the question back at him.

"I don't know. God, I don't know." Sadness overcame him.

"Don't you get enough from Mom?" I asked.

"Shut up, you little slut, just shut up." He smacked me across the face.

"Oh, Daddy stop it—it hurts," I reminded him of the way I used to whine during the nightmarish sexual exploitations.

"Dini, I'm warning you. I said to stop it! Did you hear me?" he continued to scold. "What's gotten into you?"

Nevertheless, I continued ranting on, recalling the experiences despite his opposition. "Daddy, please don't do that anymore. Daddy, I'll be good, I'll behave, promise."

Ray turned red then struck me. He tried to strangle me. Fortunately, nothing he had done to me I hadn't experienced before with all the encounters of rape and torture. If only he knew what became of his weak and shallow little girl. She was now an unrelenting fighter. I dug into his backside and bled him up with my nails. He retreated. He was sobbing. The old, rigid, unemotional man was sobbing for the first time. I was pleased.

"Oh Denise, I'm sorry. I'm a sick man. I'm not a good daddy. It's all my fault. I confess, it's all my fault. Please forgive me." Mr. Bower reached for a tissue. He blew his nose then cleared his throat. A few moments of silence. The tears and sadness cleared instantly. His temperament had changed. His tone altered. "You set me up, didn't you? Where are the police? You're going to report me, aren't you?" He peered out the window.

"No, Daddy. Why would I set up my own father? I just wanted an apology. And I got what I wanted."

"How could you do this to me? I'm your father. You should be ashamed of yourself. Have you no decency? Have you no conscience?"

"Dad, I've been a prostitute. I learned the art of seducing men," I explained. Ray's eyes widened with disapproval. I snapped at him, "Don't look at me that way. You're just as guilty. I want to know why you humiliated me right in front of Mother and made her watch it all. And you accuse ME of having no decency?"

Father yelled, "What? How dare you involve your mother in this. You're a worthless piece of shit." He smacked me across the face, again. "Don't you ever blame me for your obscenities. I never raised you to cheapen yourself."

I gathered my clothes and dressed exasperatedly, acknowledging that Mr. Bower was a hopeless case. "At least sleeping around is not violating anyone. Incest is. Don't you dare ever touch me again or I WILL report you," I made clear, pointing my finger in his face.

"Don't you ever accuse me of incest. I'm your father." He was outraged, charging over to me.

"No, you're not. You never were, you filthy shit. My father would never abuse me." I slammed the door in his face.

EXTERMINATION

Fortunately no one witnessed my insanity as I made ominous faces at the restroom mirror. I knew my hours were numbered. It was just a matter of time before the principal would have my ass permanently kicked.

HER eyes met mine. The eyes spoke the language of deceit and hatred. Ironically, I resented everything that Denise stood for, only to turn into her. SHE opened her duffle bag beside the sink, searching hastily through it. It wasn't makeup or cigarettes she was after. Once she retrieved the prescription bottle, she examined the Rx sticker. She pointed out to me the authorizing doctor's name, which Vicki so readily forged. "Dr. Jules Hamilton." She giggled, thinking back at all the silly therapy sessions she had to endure. The stupid child safety cap was quite a challenge to open.

She showed me a baggy—the magical Ecstasy pleasure dust she purchased with Kevin's last paycheck. Not an ounce of shame in her eyes. I shook my head in disbelief as she revealed to me her intention. She was clearly obsessed to the point of madness.

The restroom door swung open and in came Susan and Christina, right on time, as promised. Hurriedly, I shoved my secrets back into the duffle bag, concerned that disclosing the information too soon might scare my buddies away.

I whispered, "Guys, bear with me, okay?"

"We're all ears," the girls gathered around me.

"Okay, ya ready to beat the crap out of Wheaton?" I paused, observing the girls for a reaction. I could tell they knew I meant business. They also knew I had gone mad. To them this was about proving how cool they were. It was all about status and social acceptance. If they creamed Wheaton, they'd be *totally cool*, beating up the underdog of the class. I glanced at my watch. "No time to explain. Susan, wait by the door and let me know when Wheaton arrives. She'll be coming through that door any second now."

"How do you know?" Susan wondered.

"Cuz Jessica comes in here to take a leak after lunch then goes off to her next class."

"How do you know that?" Susan asked, baffled. "Have you been following her around or what?"

"No. I just know. She does it every day like clockwork. I guess she has a weak bladder or somethin'."

Susan joked, "How do you know she ain't takin' a dump instead?"

"It don't matter, I ain't givin' her a chance to get that far." I reached into my purse. "Here, hold this." I handed Christina the bottle of Tromitan and a syringe.

Christina's eyes widened as she asked uneasily, "What's this?"

"I'm gonna poison Jessica for good with this serum." I opened the baggie of Ecstasy powders.

"What serum? What are you going to do to her?" Christina had that worried look sealed to her face as if she was about to be an accomplice to a murder. "We're not in chemistry lab, ya know," she tried to figure.

"I don't really know how the two drugs will react when mixed together but it will be very interesting, doncha think," I commented with enthusiasm. I merged the Ecstasy particles into the Tromitan bottle over the sink countertop, undermining her concern.

"I don't know, Dini. This sounds serious. I mean, I thought we were just going to beat Wheaton up. I didn't know about all this drug stuff." Christina backed away.

"Don't be a wuss," I challenged her. "All you have to do is hold her down. Easy."

"But . . ." she argued.

Susan alerted us. "Guys, she's coming!" she whispered excitedly as she peeked through the crack in the door. Christina and I hid behind the partition.

With difficulty, Jessica pushed the restroom door open, carrying a heavyweight knapsack against her back. *What a geek.* I shook my head. Once Jessica came halfway around the partition, she recognized our reflection in the mirror then raced right back to that overbearing door. Fortunately, Susan stood by the door blocking Jessica from an escape. Christina closed in on Jessica, cornering her. The knapsack dropped to the floor while the girls wrestled Jessica into submission. Susan's hand firmly sealed Jessica's fussy mouth and restrained her arms. "You're a frisky little booger, aren't you?" Susan snarled at her, trying to keep her under control.

I stood tall before Jessica. For the first time, I was all-powerful. "Did ya need to go to the potty?" I teased with a smirk on my face. Jessica stood as still as a doorknob. I folded my arms in a haughty manner. "Oh well, I guess the toilets are off limits today. Bad timing, huh? Where are your friends when you really need them to protect you from monsters like us, huh?" I joked. "Guess you'll have to have them walk you to the potty from now on."

Jessica, of course, did not think I was in the least funny. She had the fear of death in her eyes.

"I know what you're thinking. I owe you an apology for the way I've been treating you this school year. I've made your year a living hell." I noticed her notebook slid from the knapsack. A loose pencil rolled away from the notebook toward me. I picked the pencil up and examined it. "This point is much too sharp and dangerous for you. You could stick yourself, ya know." I let go of the pencil as it bounced to the floor then stomped on it, crushing into the lead, smudging the remnants along the tile surface. This action didn't faze Jessica much since she could obtain another pencil with little trouble. "I apologize for breaking your pencil point," I added.

My shoe then stomped over her notebook, popping the pages within, as I had done before, but this time I yanked the pages out. Jessica squirmed. She broke loose from Susan's grip long enough to yell, "Stop it!"

"What's wrong Jessica, did you study too hard for those precious grades?" I teased.

Jessica gave one last revolt. She twisted, shoved, and kicked herself free from Susan's captivity in pursuit of saving her school papers, only to witness the ultimate destruction of her labored work. The pages were tossed into a sink of hot running water, soaked instantly to shreds. Wheaton threw wild punches in the air as Susan regained control over her.

"And I'm deeply sorry for destroying your precious notes . . . we just can't seem to leave you alone, can we? Say, when's the last time you took a shower? I mean a good one. I think you're overdue for one. You smell," I plugged my nose.

The girls cackled.

"Let me go!" Jessica squirmed.

Susan warned, "I can't hold her much longer."

I stood a foot away from Jessica, studying her for a moment. She saw the devil in my eyes. I punched her in the stomach. "There, that should do it." I gestured to Susan.

Jessica knelt over in pain.

"Say, what kind of shampoo would you like? Head & Shoulders?" I teased. I had my buddies rolling with laughter. With all my restless anger, I grabbed Jessica from Susan, twisted her arms and dragged her into a stall. I dunked Wheaton's head into a toilet bowl. Naturally, she resisted me, squirming, and kicking. I wanted to drown her. I let my murderous hands take charge, forcing her head deeper into the bowl of dark water. The girls laughed and cheered me on in the background. It would seem as if I had taken a plunger to a stuffed-up toilet bowl.

Suddenly, flashbacks of dark water came into focus, breaking me into a cold sweat! They must have been a premonition of this very moment to come. I was in a state of shock!

Involuntarily, I released Jessica. Her head jolted me back, throwing me against the stall before I slid to the floor. Jessica pulled her soaking wet head of hair out of the toilet bowl, coughing, gagging, choking, spitting up water, and crying. We were both huffing away from utter exhaustion. She seized the chance to escape, crawling over me, darting out of the stall, only to be recaptured by Susan. Christina blocked the exit door.

Jessica cried, "No!"

Susan pulled Wheaton by her soaking hair. "Finish her off Dini," Susan insisted as she had Jessica in a cradle-lock. "She ain't worth all this trouble."

"Knock her out," Christina encouraged, "or she'll report us all."

I got off the floor, short of breath, in sort of a daze. I wanted to make the connection between the flashbacks and what just happened but there was no time to spare to think about it. I shook my head and retrieved the serum I devised. "That's what I plan to do," I reassured my buddies. When I approached Jessica this time, blood was oozing out of her nose and upper lip. Her right eye was bruised. Susan egged me on, "Punch her out." It appeared that Susan had already taken the liberty to slug Jessica multiple times.

Jessica stood weary and listless. She had lost her capacity to fight. She looked faint. But I had no remorse for what I had done. Rather a sense of victory. This time I would not be made a fool of. "I hate your guts." I ground my teeth in her face. "You're such a fuckin' loser. I hate you!" I repeated, nearly spitting at her. I truly wanted to maul her to death but just one push and she was flat on the floor helplessly moaning and weeping. I felt as if I had already triumphed the long-awaited battle with the raging bull. I lifted her sleeve. She followed the syringe with her blackened eye as I lowered the tip of the needle to her arm. I had no mercy, and I didn't care about the consequences of my actions. In fact, I didn't even care if I'd be suspended or expelled from school since I had nothing to lose. This would be a shot in the dark, but I had to do it.

Revenge is an animal-level emotion, I know. That was precisely what I'd been reduced to.

Christina advised, "I think we should go now before we get caught."

Susan suggested, "It'll appear as if she overdosed."

Though the girls were talking to me, they faded away. They could have been background music for all I knew. My mind was focused on injecting Jessica. Nothing else mattered. Somehow, I felt as if I was experiencing . . . deja-vu. The last I heard from the girls was Susan's impatient whining for me to hurry the injection, "C'mon Dini, we ain't got all day."

My inexperienced hand was quivering out of control.

EXTERMINATION II

Funny how I felt the aches of bruises and battery. Was I feeling Jessica's pain?

"Denise . . . Denise . . . I hear your thoughts. It's okay to think to me, it's only you and I talking."

"Who are you?" I thought.

"Who do you think I am?" I heard her say.

"You're Denise Bower," I confirmed.

"And you're Jessica Wheaton. Don't you love mental telepathy? No one in the whole world can hear us. We are soul mates."

"Soul mates, huh? No, not really. In fact, I don't like any part of this game. I don't know how you did this to me, but I want my body returned to me and I want it done NOW," I yelled.

"It's one vicious cycle, Jessica."

"What is?"

"You're in another dimension of time and space and you're stuck in it."

"I don't know what you're talking about."

"Sure, you do. Had you any experiences with lapses in time?"

"I . . ."

"Had your original thoughts and memories slowly vanished, invaded by the mindset of another?" she reminded.

"Well, yes . . ."

"That's what happens when you exist outside yourself. You lose touch with your former consciousness. Isn't sex wild that way? Wasn't it exciting offering your body to so many sexually deprived studs? Weren't drugs so stimulating? It's really a unique experience, wouldn't you say?"

"How do you kn . . ."

"I know the effects of Tromacy—Tromitan solution combined with Ecstasy, and the composition of your serum. Very potent. It switches you into a time warp with your victim. I've experienced much the same with your past. It's really psychedelic. Your mind becomes like a tape player. It rewinds back into another person's experiences and plays the drama with you as the main character. But the tape has a few bugs in it. It skips parts of the story, forwards then rewinds. When the tape comes to an end, it repeats itself over, and over. Ya see, none of what's happened to you ever really happened. It's all in your mind. Even the physical stuff never really happened to you. It's kind of like virtual reality but you're stuck in it. If you inject me with that serum, the tape will repeat itself exactly as you experienced, and there's nothing you can do to stop it. You will have forgotten all that you learned throughout your journey and awaken in my bedroom, again!" Denise emphasized.

"What?"

"Don't misunderstand me, the story is all very true. It's a splice of my life you've endured. Running away from a dysfunctional home, prostituting, drugs, car accident, jail—it's all on tape. A very sad story, though.

"Tromacy was designed to destroy your consciousness and identity by transforming your very being into mine. I was confident it would be a success, but it failed. I had hoped to escape from my problems in this way and live in your glorious world. But you got ahead of my game plan. I overlooked that the secret formula to the serum is on the tape as well."

"How do you know all this?" I was indeed intrigued.

"It's been tested in correctional and institutional facilities as mind-altering therapy. Dr. Hamilton knows all about this. I've played around with this drug before. I just love the control it gives me."

"You know you're sick. I don't believe any of this," I argued.

"Well then, let's recall history in the making . . . the guy who rescued you from the kidnapper is the same guy you avoided in the school cafeteria—Kevin O'Connor. Nina, the guest at Vicki's wild sex party, was also Richard's mistress. The house you and Vicki raided just happened to have been your own home. You caught me off guard that time. You see, I know everything that has happened to you because it was all part of my past you were living out. The serum I injected into you when I beat you in the restroom induced the body switch. You're about to do the same to me that I had done to you," Denise pointed out.

"You knew all along what you had done to me? Why did you . . .?"

"I think you know why. I don't want to be Denise anymore. I hate her. She's wasted. Jessica is much more sophisticated, and her folks are so wonderful. They took me to Disney, bought me a new car, remembered my birthday, played with me, even helped me with my homework. They're the warmest, most loving people I ever met. They care about my feelings. They want me to be happy. That's the difference. I could never have dreamt of a life like this. For once in my life, I feel loved and wanted. I just can't let you take all that away from me. I'm having too much joy being you. You see where I'm coming from?"

I ignored her. "You mean this serum is THE antidote I've been searching for all along?"

"Penicillin was also discovered by accident."

"This is not a joke, Denise, you've kidnapped my whole life from me. You've tormented me long enough. It's time to set me free!" I insisted.

"Please don't complicate things."

"Why are you so reluctant?"

"Don't ask such stupid questions. Why are you so anxious to leave my body? I don't think it's because you don't like my boobs."

"What's your problem? Your parents are rich. Besides, you have a hunk of a boyfriend."

"You tell me," Denise snapped.

"Well, I know your father abused you physically, emotionally and sexually. You aborted a fetus you conceived from your first boyfriend, John. Let's see, your father tried to drown you with a hose to your mouth and once in a sink . . . I know you were one of three kids."

"Not bad. Alright, let me put the story in sequence for you, shall I? I got wasted so my grades were fucked up. Dad kicked me out, so I stayed with my boyfriend, John. John treated me like shit, so I searched around for another dick. At the tavern, I met Richard. He invited me over to rape me, as you experienced, so I dumped his sorry ass and took off with his car. That's when Brad came into the picture. Well, after the car accident, I was so grateful Nina offered to help me out until she turned me into a hooker. What a fuckin' nightmare that was! I wish I never got involved with her. I mean, how could she have fallen for an asshole like Mr. Ruxton? But that's when I met my sweet hero, Kevin O'Connor. He's a saint in five letters. I knew he was sent from heaven at a time of desperation. Unfortunately, I wasn't emotionally stable enough at the time to have a solid relationship. Kevin was the only guy who cared enough about me to seek help for my addiction. He wanted to make things better for me so, on a trial basis, he had me move back home. As you know, the reconciliation with my folks was a total flop. That's when I got hooked on Tromitan, and that's when I wanted to put an end to you. Using that potent mind-bending drug, I wanted to victimize anyone who pissed me off. I stayed with Vicki during therapy and tested the drug on her, as well. Yes, I spent some time inside Vicki's little mind.

Vicki and I had a good time breaking the law. That's when we had the orgy, and that's when I awoke with a hangover. Dad found the pills and beat the shit out of me.

Eventually Kevin and Todd will get busted. Dr. Hamilton will place me in drug rehab for six months at juvenile detention, then for another six months at a halfway. I will reunite with Kevin at drug rehab. He and I will eventually marry."

"How do you know what'll happen in the future?" I wondered.

"I fast-forwarded the tape."

"Then why are you so reluctant to return to yourself?" I questioned.

"It's my parents I can't live with. They hate me. I wish I could make them love me like yours do, but when your own parents hate you, man, it tears through your heart. I've always loved them. They want me to hate myself, you see," she cried.

I advised, "I know, they over-expect. Your dad's nasty arrogant but you can't change that. Why not work at getting yourself together and forget about trying to please parents you will never be able to satisfy? You've come this far, I know you have the courage make things better."

"Shit, that's Hamilton talkin'. He told you to say those things, didn't he?"

"No, Denise. I refused his therapy, remember. This is coming from my own heart.

Look, if you had the brains to figure out how to forward the mind tape into the future, what are you afraid of? You'll be married to Kevin and . . ."

". . . and happily ever after. This ain't no fairy tale, Jessica. I have a criminal record. I've been in jail and in and out of rehab for several years. I can't get a legal job with all that and I have no money. I'm screwed. This is not a pretty picture. I need help. I can't do it alone. Don't you understand?"

"I'll help you." I offered.

"You?"

"Who would know you better than I? You may have intended to destroy my every fiber, but I have learned a great deal about you from being you. I became your kindred spirit, if you will. I'm your friend now. No one can help you more than I," I stated with resolve.

"That's very sweet but . . ."

"Just tell me how to turn things back to normal."

"Yeah right, once you become yourself and I, myself, you'll forget all about this experience. I mean, we'll still be at each other's throats. Nothing will have changed. You'll have erased the entire experience. No tape, no memories," she concluded.

"Well, I have a hunch things will work out. It's an intuition."

"You're just saying that to make me submit to your wishes," Denise figured.

"No, I really believe that . . . I can't hear your thoughts, are you still there?"

"Yes. I'm upset. I'd hoped that Tromacy would dissolve every molecule of your original identity, but it failed to work," Denise expressed.

"It would've if I didn't have reoccurring visions of you, which eliminated any doubt I might have had about who I really am."

"I wasn't trying to keep your spirit alive, Jessica. I was trying to torment your soul to death. I had no idea the terror I inflicted on you would turn on me. I guess it didn't work because we're in this together."

"What do you mean?" I asked.

"It's kinda of unclear to me as well, but if one of us tried to kill ourselves, the other would feel the hurt too and therefore try to stop the anguish through telepathy. You see, I felt your pain numerous times, but I wanted you to suffer, so after hassling your thoughts, the pain subsided."

"You mean you read my thoughts the entire time?" I was flabbergasted.

"Only when you were in anguish. It was just a feeling," she assured.

"But why couldn't I feel yours?"

"I was never in pain. Well, only the one time you cut my throat with a knife when you robbed the Wheaton residence. But don't you see, you could never kill me because it would be like killing yourself, wouldn't it?"

"I guess I had an apathy toward you, but now it almost appears like we are both the same person in a way," I expressed.

"Your mind tape memories were so beautiful. You're a pretty sharp cookie, ya know, how you demonstrated magnetic fields without batteries and won a trophy in 7th grade," she recalled.

"Yeah, yeah, yeah." I sighed.

"I mean it. I now appreciate your way of thinking," Denise admitted.

"Good, then maybe you can incorporate my problem-solving skills into your reality," I suggested.

"I guess. It's a nice thought. Would require a lot of hard work and sacrifice."

"Yup, there's no free lunch. But hard work can eventually reap positive results. Tell me how to stop the cycle already!" I demanded.

"'Alright pal, you win. Stick me, you fool!" Denise instructed.
"But you said that would repeat the cycle." I feared.

"I lied . . . OUCH!"

"Denise?"
"Yeah."

"Are you alright?"

"I feel kinda funny, you?"

"Well, when you said 'ouch' I felt a prick too."

"Isn't it cool?"

"I feel as if I'm floating away."

"Yeah, it's kind of like floating in a whirlpool of warm water. Sensational!"

"Are you afraid?"

"Sort of."

"I think it's working! I want to thank you for allowing me to return back to my reality. I really mean it," I insisted.

"I'm getting really scared, Jessica. Please stay with me."

"What was that you thought to me?"

"Jessica, I'm losing you!" "Denise? Are you there?"

"Jess . . . Jess . . ."

"Denise, please talk to me. Where did you go? Don't leave me yet!" I shouted to her. My body spun around, and around, faster, and faster within the warm liquid-like atmosphere.

FREE

I hear switching sounds for quite some time. I'm afraid to open my eyes, dreading that I'll wake up *again* in Denise's bed. But I really do want to trust Denise's word. With courage, I take a peek. I'm in *a* bed. Not Denise's bed. A hospital bed. I refuse to endure anymore hospital routines. Hell no! Which problem is it now: drugs, abortion, suicide, battery, or domestic violence? Fuck it all— just one big nightmare. I don't care anymore. Close eyes— play dead.

Wait! I think I hear a familiar voice. It can't be! Is she talking on the phone? Mom? My real mom? I'm in denial. This has to be another hallucination. My heart fills with curiosity—burns with it. Okay, I'll open my eyes.

When I do, I'm overcome with intense emotion as I experience the most blissful reality for the first time! A sweet angel sits beside my bed. "Mom?" I call out with a groggy voice, the soft-spoken mutters of Jessica Wheaton. My new voice empowers me. No dream could be more glorious. No drug could lift me higher. No other soul could offer more joy at this very moment. Still, with all the proof of this enchanted reality, disbelief hazes over me—this is too good to be true.

"Dear?" She anxiously draws near to me. "You're awake!" She rejoices in tears, "My baby is awake!" She dances around the private room, informing the nurses and staff members on duty, "My baby has come out of her coma." With outstretched arms, she looks up. "I have the Lord to thank," she cries. "It's been two horrible weeks." She can't announce my awakening to enough people, can't lay enough kisses on my forehead, and can't utter enough sentiments to describe how much she misses me. "Your daddy and I have . . ." she attempts.

"Momma, did you say coma?"

"Yes dear, but you have nothing to worry about. Everything will be alright. A wonderful doctor is on your case. His name is Dr. Hamilton, and he has everything under control."

"Dr. Hamilton!" I repeat with trepidation.

"It's a long story that doesn't matter right now. But this is a true miracle, darling." The same soft hands that nurtured me in my former life hold me once again.

"I missed you too, Momma."

Momma's eyes gleam with joy. "I prayed each and every day to see you wake." She can no longer hold back so many angry tears. She swallows. "They found you in the school restroom. They had no right to do what they did. But don't you worry, honey. I filed a suit against the school. Do you know who did this to you?"

I shake my head, dodging her questions intentionally. "Momma, I want to see myself in a mirror," I request.

Momma opens her pocketbook and hands me her compact cosmetic mirror. "Don't worry dear, you look fine," she assures.

I open the compact and immediately recognize myself—Jessica Wheaton, in the flesh, smiling back! I say to myself, *"Thank you, Denise. This is all that I ever wanted."*

Momma intervenes, "The police said that there were witnesses who saw a few girls in the restroom with you. Do you remember them by name?"

I shake my head, again.

Next thing I know, I'm seated in Dr. Hamilton's office for a private consultation. I feel uneasy about this reunion. He is, as I remember, a little old man with a salt and pepper receding hairline, still wearing bifocals but now with a pudgy belly. I never forgot this pastel blue office framed with certificates side by side on his wall. But, most of all, I recall the painting beyond Hamilton's desk of a young child in distress holding a puppy in her arms. Back then, I was deeply moved by it. I've a lump in my throat from all the sad memories. Here I am, surrendered back into Hamilton's custody after avoiding him due to a grudge. I clear my throat. "I saw you a couple times, didn't I?" I look away from him, offended by his past actions.

"Yes, and once in recovery." He reviews my chart. "The Tromitan," he gets to the heart of the matter, sensing my discomfort, "helped, huh?"

"You knew all along, didn't you?" I establish, "And you allowed it to happen anyway." I look him in the eyes.

"Correction. I didn't know that Denise was going to attack you by mixing this potent drug with Ecstasy. I may be a hypnotist but I'm sure not a telepathist. If I were, I'd make a killing and I wouldn't have to work anymore," he joked. "The devastation Denise inflicted upon you was entirely her own idea and intention. I would never set out to harm any of my patients. Why, they'd take away my license and have me locked up."

"Then how did you know?"

"It's on the tape, Jessica. I recorded brain wave transmissions from Denise." He explains that everything in Denise's young life passed through to my mind. In effect, it is simply a dream virtually played out in my head. He knows, though, that Denise has an animosity towards him.

Hamilton also points out that there are no clinical diagnostic codes for such a unique condition. Therefore, he reported my diagnosis as *multiple personality dissociative disorder* to be used for insurance billing purposes only. Unfortunately, this confidential information was disclosed to the Bowers to provide them with something to go on.

I think about Hamilton's explanation, and it makes reasonable sense. How else could he convince insurance to cover such an unusual case? I feel so foolish to have jumped to conclusions about his character, betraying him. I should've investigated the diagnostic claim further. Instead, I allowed resentment to get the better of me. I lower my head, laughing at myself over the misunderstanding.

The doctor repositions himself in his chair, lunging forward for emphasis. He folds his hands, rubbing his thumbs together. "Now that you finally awoke in good health, and you have been completely informed of the circumstance, the more pressing question is: how will you respond to this situation?"

"I'm sad for her," I simply state.

"But will you take revenge?" the doctor insists.

"No. I promised her I'd be her friend if she switched me back, and I intend to keep my promise."

"Good. That's what I was betting on." The doctor rises from his desk and stands before me. "I have something I want you to see." He extends his hand, asking me to trust him.

Hamilton and I take a long stroll down to the psychiatric wing of the hospital. He points to the window of Suite #166. And there she is, Denise Bower, lying in a bed wrapped in a straitjacket. Kevin sits beside her, his back to us. Kevin's long hair is tied back in a ponytail. He's wearing a black leather jacket with chains dangling down the side, the biker I made of him.

Hamilton says she's been having violent fits of paranoia and schizophrenia, so he must keep her from harming herself and others. She overdosed on the very stuff she poisoned me with. He isn't sure how long it will take for her to come around from the damage done.

Tears roll down my cheeks. Mixed emotions of relief and sorrow. Now that we are finally separated, her self-destruction continues. *She got what she deserves,* I say to myself. I have flashbacks of the ordeal she put me through, and it's as if I had lived her life. I mean, I've become her. I'm not the same Jessica I once was. I'm now Jessica Wheaton with a double-life experience that will always be a part of me. For better or worse these common experiences bind us. I wouldn't wish the suffering I endured on my worst enemy. I take a deep breath then open the door with Dr. Hamilton by my side. I stand before my virtual enemy, not with fear in my eyes, or hostility in my blood, but with a heart of compassion knowing that another soul is desperate. Yes, she tried to terminate me countless times because she wanted to destroy herself. But I know she will have a bright future because I'm now a part of her.

Kevin turns his saddened face toward me, unsure of who I am or why I'm standing by his girlfriend's side or, for that manner, why I even care. The biggest moment that fills my heart is when Denise turns her head toward me. Her bloodshot eyes focus on me, and it's not long before her drawn pale cheeks crack a smile. Tears come streaming down her weary eyes. I'm crying too. The tears are real as day is to night, and they speak of forgiveness. Her helpless hand, bound by the straitjacket, quivers as I touch her cold, numb fingers. She locks her fingers with mine.

AFTERWORD

My Personal Experience Being Bullied

The concept behind Enemy Self was actually founded in a dream I remembered which took place soon after college graduation in 1986. Though the plot is indirectly related to bullying, I was an outcast throughout grade school. What I'm about to express here is very uncomfortable for me and embarrassing, even thirty-six years later.

I graduated in the Class of 1983 in Baltimore County, Maryland, reluctantly on stage. There was barely any mention of me in the yearbook as I was unpopular. I was never notified or invited to any class reunions thereafter. Sadly, my period of social isolation extended from 4th grade to 12th grade. I was branded for nine years of grade school. Those days I stood at 5'1" and only weighed about 80 to 90 lbs.—very tiny and skinny boned with lots of chronic health concerns. My parents raised me with traditional values, including behaving like a lady and respecting others. They advised that I ignore the bullies and be an example for everyone, which made matters worse. I wasn't witty with the comeback lines and too tiny to take on a fight. The emotional pain, scars, and loneliness which I endured during those years are a permanent part of who I am today.

Being the non-conformist that I am, I was different and different was unacceptable and not tolerated in grade school mentality. I was a team player, not a competitor. I came to school to learn, not to fight to "fit in." I never went through a teenage rebellion phase. In fact, I was very close to my parents. Though I seldom laid my pen to rest since I learned to write, I could never bring myself to write about my high school woes. The most challenging aspect of being an outcast was not having friends. I was no one. The outcome was low self-esteem, suicidal thoughts, and hopelessness.

I endured daily emotional abuse. I was considered "dumb" by my classmates. Kids would whisper and cackle about me behind my back. Among the many names I was called, stupid, bulimic, anorexic, French-fry, and toothpick were the few I remember. I was afraid to raise my hand in class, that someone might snicker at me or challenge me. I was literally alienated by my entire class—not to be spoken to or sat next to. For years I had to face the feeling of emptiness throughout the day. I sat by myself, alone in a cafeteria full of students in groups, sharing, inviting, laughing, and celebrating without me, year after year.

Spitballs were scraps of paper chewed on to form a ball then crumbled and shoved into a straw to be spat at me during English class. Afterwards, the teacher asked me to clean the mess of wet paper balls piled beside my desk. For reporting the incident to the teacher, I was pushed, shoved and threatened in the girl's restroom after school hours. Fortunately, a social studies teacher overheard and spotted the scuffle as she was passing by and stopped the bully in her progress.

I would dread getting up in the morning to face my nasty neighbors at the bus stop. Locker doors were shut in my face. My notebook was popped because I refused to wear blue jeans in class. The back of my chair in class would be kicked or pushed. A *'kick me'* sign would be posted on my butt without my knowledge. I was the brunt of jokes. I was once cornered near a building and a tree, kicked by several girls at summer day camp. Needless to say, I never went to sleep-over camp. I would dread getting up in the morning to face my nasty neighbors at the bus stop.

Isolation came at a cost, however. To this day I have trouble standing up to haughty, arrogant individuals and am not much of a risk taker. I formed a singles group in my mid-twenties which benefited me greatly. I learned social skills, confidence, and became more outgoing. It took many more years to build my self-esteem, which most young adults acquire by their early twenties. I have never experimented with illegal (street) drugs or alcohol as most baby boomers have in my generation. I never had a sweet sixteen birthday party. My mother insisted that I attend my prom and had arranged a date who I considered repulsive. Looking back at that experience, I was grateful that I went to my prom in 1983.

"Kids will be kids," they used to say. Our society thinks it's acceptable for kids to be cruel to other kids because that's what kids do. Kids are not emotionally matured enough to understand differences. It would be a pipe dream to eradicate bullying behavior altogether, unfortunately, due to human nature.

My message is to raise children to accept differences in other people. Children need to be taught to respect and embrace differences. Children need to learn team-building skills from preschool years and on because they don't understand that what they say or do may hurt another and how that feels. After all, our differences are what make us unique. There is not one of us that is better than the other. We each have strengths and weakness, possess gifts and curses in life.

I'm trying to emphasize here that any form of humiliation should not be acceptable behavior among children and should not be tolerated. When the damage is done and these "bullies" become adults, many of them genuinely don't remember the pain they inflicted upon their victim. Most don't even remember that they bullied the underdog in grade school to fit in or don't know why they did it. They permanently traumatized their victims who DO remember precisely what happened thirty years later. Unfortunately, some of those childhood bullies grew into adults who continued to berate and taunt the "underdog," in relationships or throughout their career.

Through God's prayer, I finally made lifelong friends. God gave me the strength to complete my first novel, Enemy Self, a place I've never really experienced but a self-created world I escape to. A world apart in imagination yet so eerily close to home.

ABOUT THE AUTHOR

Suzanne Kovitz grew up in Baltimore County, Maryland. Now married, she resides in Cecil County, Maryland. Me, Myself & I was her first short story. Enemy Self is her debut novel for new adults, crossing over to adult themes.

Suzanne enjoys reading, philosophy, graphic design, her Pomeranians, brisk walks, science-fiction movies, kayaking, and travel.

However, more passionately, she loves interacting with her fans.

If you enjoyed the read, please let others know by completing a review on Amazon, B&N, and Goodreads. Thanks.

Website: enemyself.wixsite.com/website

Email: enemyself@gmail.com

Instagram: authorsuzannekovitz

Facebook: Facebook.com/Suzanne.kovitz

Follow on Amazon: amazon.com/author/suzannekovitz

Follow on Twitter: Twitter@suzannekovitz

Follow on Pinterest: Pinterest.com/blackbottom

www.ingramcontent.com/pod-product-compliance
Lightning Source LLC
Chambersburg PA
CBHW071917150726
47999CB00001B/19